A JOUR

OUT OF INDIA

A JOURNEY OUT OF INDIA

Anna K. Chacko

Rupa & Co

Copyright © Anna K. Chacko 2007

Published 2007 by

Rupa . Co

7/16, Ansari Road, Daryaganj,
New Delhi 110 002

Sales Centres:

Allahabad Bangalore Chandigarh Chennai
Hyderabad Jaipur Kathmandu
Kolkata Mumbai Pune

All rights reserved.
No part of this publication may be reproduced, stored
in a retrieval system, or transmitted, in any form or
by any means, electronic, mechanical, photocopying, recording
or otherwise, without the prior permission of the publishers.

The author asserts the moral right to be identified
as the author of this work

Typeset in SimonciniGaramond by
Nikita Overseas Pvt. Ltd.
1410 Chiranjiv Tower
43 Nehru Place
New Delhi 110 019

Printed in India by
Gopsons Papers Ltd.
A-14 Sector 60
Noida 201 301

My granddaughter Ayden Maya,
My mother Mary
My sister Elizabeth
And my daughters-in-law Mariko and Elishba

Contents

Acknowledgements

I would like to acknowledge the contributions of those in my life who have kept me sustained and engaged: my friend Robert Maietta whose perseverance and belief in the literary value of the story fueled my endeavours; my husband Bill Lollar whose constancy and tenderness have provided me with the fortitude to stay with the effort: my sons Andrew and Josef who have provided joy and meaning to my existence: my editor whose encouragement and faith have been vital to me.

1

An Inauspicious Beginning

I WAS THE FIRSTBORN. MY MOTHER, MARY, BECAME PREGNANT with me in the second week of her marriage. There were circumstances surrounding the pregnancy that fuelled Mummy's love for me. This love, while vast and unbounded, was fed by serious guilt and remorse.

Mummy was almost in the third month of her pregnancy when Papa hired a maidservant named Sayamma from the adjoining neighbourhood to help her with the running of the household. Sayamma was a wizened toothless creature, aged well past her actual years, given to dire mutterings and warnings to which my mother paid little heed. Rushing around the house dusting and cleaning tirelessly like a roadrunner, Sayamma punctuated her frenzied activity with an entire gallery of superstitions. As the occasion demanded, she paraded them out in every flavour.

Superstitions governed every aspect of Sayamma's life – some applied to the churning of butter, others dictated how one was to bathe after sex, and yet others were about how to comb your hair. There were irrational and terrifying superstitions like those that forbade saying 'Aiyyo' too often, since this was the name of the Devil's mother. Those who uttered her name could summon up this demoness from *Pathalum*, the nether regions of Hell. If this was done inadvertently or without cause, the consequences could be quite dire to those who had summoned her. The last was difficult to avoid since 'Aiyyo' is the equivalent of 'Damn', often used when one dropped things, like cups or plates. However, no superstition of Sayamma's was greater than the one surrounding the lunar eclipse. So on this one particular day of the lunar eclipse, Sayamma planted her little bird feet firmly in my mother's path refusing to let her out of the house.

"Going out on the day of the lunar eclipse is expressly forbidden by the Lord Ganesha. To do so while pregnant, is to invite disaster," she warned.

Sayamma could see by the look on Mummy's face that she was ill inclined to pay heed to yet another superstition, so she dragged Mummy over to the sofa and sat on the floor to tell her the story behind the warning:

"The Lord Shiva – the third and the most formidable of the Trinity of the Hindu godhead, had found a suitable wife in Parvati. Parvati, Uma, Kali, or Devi as they called her was more fearsome than her consort. Their first child was born while Shiva was away. When Shiva returned, he found an engaging young boy outside his wife's chambers. When Shiva insisted on entering the chambers, as was his right, the boy stood in his path and refused him entry. In a fit of rage, Lord Shiva decapitated the boy. His wife Parvati emerged from her chambers to find her headless son lying at her doorstep. She was inconsolable and insisted that her husband bring him back to life. In order to do this, Shiva had to find a head to replace the one he had severed, as it was not clear where the boy's original head had fallen. Shiva located the head of an elephant, which he placed on the torso and breathed life back into the boy. This elephant-headed being came to be known as Ganesha, a God who is revered by any God-fearing Hindu.

"He is the God of auspicious beginnings," she said wagging her bony finger at Mummy. "To thwart him would be inauspicious."

"We don't believe in Ganesha," Mummy replied.

"Why not?"

"We are Christian, that's why not. So for us, Ganesha doesn't exist," came Mummy's increasingly impatient rejoinder.

"I am a Hindu. But *Yesu Kristu* – Jesus Christ is still God's son isn't he?"

This drew a puzzled 'yes' from Mummy.

"*Yesu Kristu* exists whether I believe in him or not," Sayamma reasoned.

"We-e-ell ye-e-es," the logic had completely escaped my mother.

"Clearly then, even though you are Christian," she said with irrefutable simplicity. "Ganesha is still the God of auspicious beginnings whether you believe in him or not."

And then she went on with her tale:

"On his birthday, his doting parents threw a huge party in honour of their son Ganesha. Every one who was anyone was invited to the celebration. The moon, Chandra, was invited along with a large assortment of other Gods and demi-Gods. He was an irreverent one, this Chandra; and when he spied Ganesha, he convulsed with laughter and could scarcely control himself. When Ganesha asked him why he laughed, Chandra said that it was Ganesha's ugly head that was the source of the mirth. This raised Ganesha's ire and he cursed the offender saying that Chandra, the moon, would have to hide his face forever. Several of the guests intervened and averted a complete disaster. Ganesha relented and finally agreed that Chandra would only have to hide his face one day out of the year. It then came to be that this was the day of the lunar eclipse. All creatures in the universe were forbidden from looking at the moon on that day and those who disobeyed this injunction were to suffer severe consequences.

"It is especially bad for pregnant women to gaze on the moon on the day of the eclipse," Sayamma warned Mummy again.

"It may be best if you did not venture out at all," volunteered the little *chokra* boy – the house errand boy, who was listening with rapt attention.

My mother had been invited to a soiree with some of her more interesting friends on that day. She was irritated with Sayamma's nonsense and impatient to be on her way. She flung Sayamma's restraining arms away, almost toppling the old woman over. As she walked out the door, she looked up at the darkening sky and spied the eclipsed moon.

She turned triumphantly around to Sayamma and proclaimed, "See, I did not lose the baby and I did not die."

Six months later, I was born with a large omphalocele – a belly wall that had failed to close such that my guts spilled out of the gaping maw that was my abdomen. Of course my mother has steadfastly blamed herself for visiting this affliction on me by disregarding Sayamma's warning and disobeying Lord Ganesha's injunction. She was beside herself with sorrow and remorse, my father was grief-stricken and the reaction from our extended family did not help matters

"A first-born child, a daughter and defective, the poor thing", was the refrain I was to hear throughout my childhood, both from well-meaning relatives and those not-so-well-intentioned.

Daughters were a burden to parents causing them to have to prepare for the years ahead. Alliances had to be forged with the right families, weddings had to be prepared for, dowries and trousseaux had to be arranged. Finally, the daughter had to reach her destination – the husband's home while being safe, chaste, virginal and, God-willing, fecund. My parents had the added curse of a child who was born with an unsightly belly.

"Thank God, it can be kept hidden under the sari", was the consensus.

I was baptised on the day I was born, just before the surgery to correct my birth defect. This was done in case I did not survive and needed to be buried on consecrated ground. In the last century, successful repair of this birth defect was unheard of. However, my mother's sister – my aunt Anna, successfully repaired it, once again validating her reputation as a skilled and intrepid surgeon.

I was named Anna after my aunt who so skillfully saved my life. By Syrian Christian orthodox tradition, I should have been named after my paternal grandmother. Fortuitously, my paternal grandmother's name was also Anna – so all the Syrian traditions were fulfilled and everyone concerned was adequately propitiated and appeased.

My mother's tenacity pulled me through the difficulties of my birth defect and its subsequent repair. I survived the surgery and its complications but I was left with an unsightly set of scars marching across the length and breadth of my belly. As a result of my inauspicious beginnings, I was the object of sorrow for my father and a great challenge for my mother.

Casting a practiced glance at my scarred little newborn belly, which looked like an angry overripe tomato, Mummy's mother, Ammachy advanced a practical suggestion. "Let the child die," she said. Ever the eternal pragmatist, she warned, "Who will marry a girl without a perfectly formed belly button? The dowry will have to be huge."

When my mother pointed out that no future husband would ever have the chance to come within ten feet of her daughter's belly before marriage, Ammachy muttered darkly, "They will know. These things get out. Servants talk."

Ammachy was an unusually tall, elegantly regal woman of immense beauty. She was the most beautiful woman in our household. As the story goes, when she was brought into my grandfather's home, she was so beautiful that my grandfather's brother, in a fit of pique, had the entire state combed to find a woman more beautiful than Ammachy for his oldest son. He even waived the dowry. He eventually did find a very beautiful woman to be his daughter-in-law, but she could not hold a candle to Ammachy's beauty. In my universe, she was the epitome of loveliness and an authority on the subject. She saw in me an awesome burden to my parents who would have the unenviable task of gathering a large dowry and finding a willing family that would deign me acceptable as a daughter-in-law.

I was surrounded by many glorious creatures like my mother, my aunts, my grandmother and my sister who were all so beautiful it took my breath away just to look at them. In comparison, I felt ugly, flawed and unacceptable. They looked at me with their immense, knowing, brown doe-eyes filled with infinite compassion – or was it pity? Their compassion did little to ease my discomfort and my feelings of inadequacy.

Catching me weeping in front of the mirror Mummy would say, "Your soul is beautiful; beauty is only skin-deep."

Increasingly despondent, I would retort "Mummy, it is not important to me that my soul is beautiful or that beauty is only skin-deep. What matters is that I am not beautiful like all the others around me."

"It doesn't matter what the others find, in my heart you are the most beautiful of all," she said in attempts to mollify me.

"You would love me anyway, after all, I am your daughter."

My redoubtable mother tamed the *bête-noir* of my physical attributes or lack thereof. The dark beast became a powerful teacher. Early in life, I learned fortitude – obstacles and roadblocks served only to strengthen my resolve. However, it fostered fears – some of them real, others unfounded, but fears nevertheless. My mother blamed herself unjustly for my physical flaws. She strove valiantly and often successfully to bolster my flagging spirits with periodic pep talks, offering unwavering confidence in my abilities and unconditional love and support.

My father did not grieve at any of my shortcomings save one – I was not the son he needed, wanted and felt that he deserved. His sorrow was an unrelenting patina of grayness clouding my existence, leaving me with a feeling of inadequacy, discontent and dissatisfaction. I found it significant that he always referred to me as *Ponnu Mon* – golden son – the son he would never have. One of the earliest poems he ever read to me was one named '*If*' by Rudyard Kipling, the significant portion being:

Yours is the earth and everything that's in it
And – which is more – you'll be a Man, my son!

The poem was lovely, but all I chose to remember was that in my father's eyes, only a son could inherit the Earth – not a mere daughter.

The words 'If only' was the writing behind the palimpsest of my life – if only I had been beautiful, if only I had been a son.

By the time my sister Rachel was born two years after me, my father had resigned himself to not having any sons who would carry his name and his legacy.

As female offspring, we were a short-term proposition. We were to be given away in marriage to other families who would reap the fruits of his years of effort and travail. This was the price the fates exacted from him for having daughters – the cost that would be levied to educate us, raise us with rectitude and deliver us to someone else's household with sizeable dowries and innocence intact.

The days of our early childhood were halcyon days for my father marred only by the fact that he had no sons. Immensely successful in his business, he was surrounded by sycophants, hangers-on, and those who genuinely sought his advice. Along with Papa's growing wealth came the trappings and declarations of prosperity. The women in the household had to be outfitted with the accoutrements of wealth. The family had to move from a middle-class neighbourhood to one where the nobility lived. This was all designed to announce to the world that this man was prosperous.

This is how we came to move into the grand house-with-the-garden.

❖

The house-with-the-garden with its dreams and realities was to become an inextricable part of the fabric of our existence, looming large in our lives, overpowering and invasive, finally becoming the solar system in which we lived.

The house-with-the-garden belonged to a Muslim nobleman – Gore Nawaab – who had fallen on hard times. My father loaned Gore Nawaab a large sum of money, and he then allowed my family to live in the house in exchange. It was typical of my father's impulsive generosity that he didn't charge Gore Nawaab any interest for the money that he had loaned him, nor did he secure the title to the house. The terms of the repayment were incredibly generous. Gore Nawaab would pay the loan back at any time he was able.

"What if he pays us back tomorrow? Would we have to move out of the house the day-after?" my mother asked.

"He won't pay the money back tomorrow. That is a childish and irrational fear, Mary," Papa replied.

"That money would have earned interest in a bank. Now it will be paid back in dribs and drabs and there will be nothing to show for it. At the end of this deal, we will have neither the money nor the house."

When Papa knew Mummy was right, he would resort to the age-old device of – "A wife should not have to worry about these things. These are my responsibility," he said expansively. "I will take care of you."

"I can take care of myself. We have daughters. You should be worrying about taking care of our daughters," was her acerbic rejoinder.

"One must take care of people who have fallen on bad times," Papa countered. "God will visit blessings on our children and our children's children as a result."

"Aha!! I know what this is about. You fancy yourself as being munificent and generous. You think your fame for charity will be broadcast all over the town and people will respect you more. The truth is that people will laugh at you for being the dupe of all time." Mummy knew she had struck home with her customary anopheline precision.

She continued her parry and thrust. "No one will respect a man who cannot provide for his daughters. More importantly, society will pity your daughters and they will remain unmarried forever."

When there was no reply, she prodded further. "Charity begins at home. We should stay where we are. You should either get the title to the house or get your money back now." By the set of his jaw, she knew that he would not be swayed. She turned on her heel and stormed out of the room.

Nevertheless, we moved into the house-with-the-garden, over Mummy's objections and trepidations. My sister Rachel was an infant and I was three years old when we decamped.

The house was in one of the wealthiest quarters of the city of Hyderabad. It sat on the outskirts of the city, far from the noise and pollution, removed from the squalour and the mind-numbing poverty that permeated India. The street we lived on was wide and long, with splendid houses on either side. Most of the houses sat behind walled and gated enclosures.

Our house sat atop a knoll, surrounded by the garden. We had to climb at least a dozen steps on two sides of the house to reach the verandahs. The third set was in the back of the house and used solely by the servants. The verandahs led to the formal drawing room in the front, and in the back, to the bedrooms where my mother, Rachel and I slept. It was a grand old house, unusually large and of stately proportions. As a child, I remember the house being enormous and stretching for miles.

My father was determined to override Mummy's doubts about the move and the house by indulging her every desire for decoration

– she got anything she wanted. He, however, got neither her approval nor her sanction in exchange. In her eyes, it was, and remained, a foolish decision that imperiled all of our futures.

As with all Hyderabadi homes, the house sported a flat roof. But, this roof was special – Mummy had it framed with a gadrooned parapet on all sides. She had the house painted a faint salmon pink wash which contrasted nicely with the white of the parapet, windows and door frames. The windows were real French windows with individual windowpanes.

The glass for the panes had been poured over a century before. The glass in each pane had settled and was thicker on the bottom than it was on the top, and there were little air bubbles in some of the panes. Rachel and I knew that these bubbles held little fairies and elves which could be summoned up if we were ever in need of help and they would come bursting out of their glass bubble houses to our aid. Of course, we never thought to call on them, so we never actually saw them come out.

Hariprasad, Mummy's personal tailor, made soft and voluminous white voile curtains for all the windows. While the curtains everywhere else were pristine and white, the curtains in our bedroom were peppered with jammy fingerprints and smudges, evidence of our play in make-believe worlds. As children, we sat on the wide window ledges in our bedroom, ensconced behind the curtains. When they billowed into the rooms with the warm breezes of summer, we would pretend that we were important sheikhs and princesses living in tents in the Arabian Desert. I was always a sheikh wielding scimitars and sabers from my trusty steed and Rachel was always a *shahzadi*, a princess. My taking on the role of a sheikh had to do with the fact that I was not as pretty as a princess needed to be and also because I could pretend to be the son my father so desperately wished his first born to be.

The floors of the house were changed because Mummy said so. She decreed they be made of cement. The mason, Ramu, followed her bidding, pouring the cement to a glass-smooth surface and painting it a deep, deep red – the colour of congealing blood.

Then came the rugs; lying on a background of deep red cement, their colours and artistry came to life. So it was that early in life, I came to learn about rugs. Serendipitously, I also got a hint of what my mother was preparing me for.

My father paraded a whole host of merchants through the house. The rug merchants were the most fascinating of them all. There were beaky Jews and corpulent Iraqis, fair-skinned laughing Turks and tall, mysterious looking Baluchis who came tripping through the house bringing samples of their wares. I would sit on the floor and watch in wide-eyed wonder as Mummy and Papa examined carpet after carpet from regions afar.

"Look at the tight asymmetric knots," one would say, flipping the rugs over.

"These are vegetable dyes," while another pointed out the indigo, turmeric, vermilion and azure.

"Nothing can destroy these carpets," said the Baluchi. Seeing the disbelief on my face, he went on. "After the carpet is completed, it is set out on the desert sands. Camels trample it, babies soil it, the sun beats down on it – but nothing destroys it. It is washed in the morning dew and then sent to the merchants who travel to far away lands to find homes for them."

I was captivated by the stories and never sought to question them.

By the time I was six, there were area rugs on every floor. Papa's study had a delicate turquoise and gray Aubusson. His bedroom and parlour had the only fine Nains or Qashqais in our home. Mummy, on the other hand, had a penchant for nomadic Persian rugs. As a result, we had Baluchis, Gabbehs, Afghani kilims, and hosts of other unnamed similar tribal rugs on the floors of every room, other than my father's rooms. Mummy had no use for prissy fixings. Every one of her rugs was bold and bright, providing wild and provocative splashes of colour across the dark floors.

"Bibi," said one of carpet merchants, "I have a special one for you." He was tall and lean, with a head of tight curls coming into view as he removed his burnoose. Standing behind him was a shy copper skinned woman, her lovely face decorated with intricate indigo tattoos.

I stared at her until Mummy nudged me painfully in the ribs. "It is very rude to stare."

Spread before me was an unusual primitive-looking flat-weave rug – a kilim. Several of the motifs were those of tents and camels – these were rendered in tufts which stood up in a sort of bas-relief from the flatness of the rest of the rug.

"It is a special kilim, Bibi. This woman is the weaver. She comes from the Tawariq tribe," he said referring to the tattooed beauty behind him. "The Tawariq weave combination rugs mostly flat but with tufting here and there. She wove this rug as part of her dowry."

"If it is her dowry," I asked, "how can you give it away?"

"She is my woman and what she has is mine," he explained. "I can do anything I want with her property, or even with her," he said chucking her under the chin with a proprietorial fondness. She smiled shyly at him as he raised her face up, her eyes continuing to be downcast.

Mummy purchased the Tawariq kilim for our bedroom. After the merchant and his Tawariq woman left, Mummy came into the bedroom and told us, "No woman should allow a man to dictate her life, or to own her. No man should be allowed to bankrupt a woman's future."

"What does that mean, Mummy?"

"*Insha-allah* – God willing – you will not need anyone to sustain you but yourself."

My father, like most Indians I knew, was superstitious about the houses one moved into. Houses possessed a life and a spirit of their own, and could make or break the occupants. A house could be benevolent and visit great good. Then again, if one moved into the wrong house or did something to desecrate the grounds, vengeance could be swift and exacted without mercy. He knew that this house would be good for him and his family as long as we treated it with respect and did nothing to disregard the spirit of the house. In contrast, my mother simply viewed the house as a place to shelter us from the surrounding environment and not much more. Her garden, on the other hand, was altogether different.

❖

Life in the house-with-the-garden offered one common passion for my parents, a keen love of gardening. In those days it was unthinkable that anyone with any social standing would ever be caught actually working with the soil, the compost and the plants. One assigned these tasks to the gardener. Our gardener was quite happy to supervise while each of my parents tended their apportioned plots. It helped that high walls surrounded the property so they could pursue their gardening in relative seclusion behind the private enclosure, away from the eyes of society. My parents' passion for the feel of wet earth between their fingers and the comfort of watching young green things thrive was probably some atavistic reflection of their inadmissible peasant origins.

Even in their common hobby, they went their separate ways. Their gardens were independent and distinctive. Initially they shared this garden with a quiet and uneasy truce. They would often venture opinions, albeit unsolicited, on each other's handiwork. Over the years and for a variety of reasons, my parents grew apart and distanced themselves from one another. "Roses need phosphorous, not nitrogen," Papa would say, casting a scathing glance at my mother's rose bushes which looked absolutely perfect to me. "Anybody would know that."

"Planting fig trees next to bananas is utterly idiotic," Mummy would mutter, watching him bring saplings in from the nursery.

They rarely shared any of their expertise, joys, sorrows or disappointments in gardening with each other.

Mummy's garden was restricted to the area immediately surrounding the house. A low enclosure separated it from the circular drive and the *port cochere*. Papa's preserve was around the perimeter, immediately inside the garden wall. Their respective gardens were as different as they were from each other in character and ambience. Just like the rugs in the house, each of their gardens was diametrically opposed to what one would have expected from their personalities. It was as if their rugs and their gardens allowed each one of them to become what they did not allow themselves to be in their everyday lives. In a strange way, this seemed to somehow balance them.

Mummy has always been precise, stern, authoritarian and demanding. Her garden, by contrast, was an unruly and undisciplined display of riotous exuberance with plants of every variety, form and fragrance, growing in unchecked freedom in any direction they chose to take.

Papa, on the other hand, was a dreamer – impractical enough to drive those who surrounded him to distraction. He was consistently full of grandiose schemes and implausible plans. His garden was laid out in precise patterns, rigidly following some formal order demanded by an inner implacable deity.

"Your father is imprudent and foolhardy in all things," Mummy said as she took over and ran the household with its finances. His improvidence had become a persistent source of consternation for her.

"We have two daughters to educate and provide dowries for," she said in desperation. This appeared to have little or no effect on Papa.

Mummy was cautious and resourceful; this translated into some version of the Midas touch. Anything she touched turned into a financial success, much to my father's chagrin. This, of course, deepened the rift between them.

The rift grew deeper still when he brought home a champak sapling for his garden, which is called "Paak Laan" by the Chinese in Hawaii. This was the only tree we ever thought of as having a real personality and a gender, probably prompted by my father's attachment and devotion to the tree. In our minds, the champak was female. It was strictly a flowering tree. The sapling was temperamental and we often worried that she would die. However, she flourished and started bearing flowers in less than a year. She grew ultimately to a height of forty feet and bloomed profusely. Her flowers had pale ivory petals were long and slender, looking for all the world like graceful fingers. The perfume from these flowers was extraordinarily heady. The tree herself was tall and willowy. When the wind rustled through her branches, her leaves produced a sibilance all their own. Early in the morning, my father would walk around the garden examining every plant, shrub and tree. When he came to the champak, which he left for the very end, he would gaze at her for a very long time as if he could not get enough of her. This would irk Mummy no end. We could never quite fathom Papa's attachment to the champak tree until several years later.

In the far southern corner of the house-with-the-garden, an area was set aside for my mother and father to experiment with different plants. As always, their choices were as different as they were.

Mummy began her experimentation with orchids. While foraging up in the mountain fastnesses of the tea estates of Travancore, she discovered and fell in love with these exotic flowers. They grew wild in the crotches and forks of the large jackfruit trees around the plantation. We were familiar with the large, showy Cattleyas that were used as corsages for the English women, but the others were a mystery to us. Mummy, with her unerring instinct, found many other fascinating species: oncidium, dendrobium, Vanda, pahiopedilum and cymbidium. Her favourites were the Phaelenopsis, or "butterfly" orchids, as she called them. These grew very well in the moist climate of Travancore; but they wilted in the dry heat of Hyderabad. However, Mummy was not one to give up so easily. She had the *maali* rig a contraption with water pipes traversing over a covered area. Small showerheads were fitted in at regular intervals along these pipes. When the water was turned on, these contraptions would spray a mist of water down on the delicate plants that required tropical environments. She grew pansy orchids, which had oxblood blooms and bright gold trim. Then there were the spider orchids, with long pale lemon coloured arachnid petals showing clusters of violet spots. The Phaelenopsis orchids, her favourites, were the most demanding of Mummy's plants. How she managed to make them grow in her garden was nothing short of a miracle. The blooms were much smaller than the ones on the plants that she had originally found. The petals were flat and fan shaped. The sepals were thick, of a pale opaque white, and had a tracery of fine green veins. These veins gave the flower a watered down chartreuse tinge instead of the more usual unrelieved white. Finally, the central petal was forked with its tips ending in a brilliant, fiery orange.

Papa became extremely successful in his experimentations with grafting the most delicious but finicky of mangoes on the hardy village stock. The mangoes would start to flower and fruit in the year after their grafting. He lavished his mango trees with great love and attention, although not as much as on his champak tree.

Among our favourites was the nameless small mango which yielded a mouthful of the most delicious juice. They were the *chausa* mangoes. When they were ripe enough for consumption, they turned a deep scarlet at one end and graded through a fiery red - bright orange - golden yellow – to a pale green at the stalk. The servants would bring them into the house by the dozens in large reed baskets. The mangoes were then packed in straw to prevent them from becoming over-ripe and rotten. Rachel and I would hold them in the palm of one hand, pull off the stalk with the other, and suck out the refreshing juice. By the time we were done with it, the mango would go from being firm and turgid with juice, to a shrivelled shadow of its former self. We would then proceed to tear off its skin and suck the flesh dry, taking immense pleasure in having the golden juice drip between our fingers, down our chins, and over our bibs.

Papa got a new variety of mango called the *Pedda Rasaal*, which translated into "large and juicy". They were an ugly hybrid from the south. In the summer, however, the unprepossessing fruit ripened to perfection. The mangoes were plucked early in the morning before the birds awakened so they could not get to them first. The servants washed and placed them safely in the refrigerator until evening. Following our afternoon naps, we were served mango juice laced with clotted cream – all swirled gold and white in little Coalport parfait cups.

The most remarkable of the mangoes was a special variety called the *Baynishaan*. It was a perfect Persian name for that royal fruit, translated as "without flaw, without blemish". When we first moved into the house-with-the-garden my father tried his utmost to get one of these for his garden. They were rare and hard to acquire. It was rumoured that they grew only in the Nizam's gardens. Some years later he did get a Baynishaan sapling, which completed his collection of mangoes.

It was the garden of that house where we lived that molded us and gave us metaphor after metaphor for life. It shielded us like a womb, surrounding us with warmth and comfort, sights, sounds and smells that we would remember well into our old age.

❖

Our house-with-the-garden sat on the banks of a stream formed by the runoff from Hussain Saagar, an artificial lake built by the

Nizam some miles away. During the monsoons when the sluice gates of the lake were opened, the stream would fill up and breach its banks, swirling out of control and washing the land on its way to the River Musa. We could not see the stream from the garden because the walls around it were very high. The high walls were designed to keep the snakes out. The snakes did not know this, however, and they frequently found their way into the garden anyway. Most, but not all of them, were harmless.

The stream on the other side of the garden wall meandered through scrub, underbrush and Deccan mesquite. Most of these mesquite trees were home to subterranean termites and ants. They built large anthills, which stood four to five feet tall with their delicately fenestrated towers. They looked like miniature watchtowers standing guard over a wild and woolly landscape. According to the servants, when the summer was at its peak, the ants or termites vacated the premises and the anthills were taken over by snakes – usually cobras or hamadryads.

And then there were the *kewra*, screwpine clusters that dotted the landscape. These were grasses which probably belonged to the pandanus family. They were far more fragrant than the pandanus leaves themselves. The leaves of the grasses, which were long and stiff, could be folded into ornate bows and spun into the braids worn by the women in the area. The younger leaves were white and were those favoured by the local women to decorate and perfume their hair. According to the servants, cobras also loved the smell of the kewra and could be found among these grasses.

Papa planted tall Moringa-moringa trees near the garden wall. They bore long fruit with hard green exteriors and soft fleshy interiors. The fruit of this tree carried several seeds in every pod and each seed resembled Napoleon Bonaparte's tricorn. When the fruit was young, the seeds were tender and crunchy, and were often included in shrimp or lentil dishes giving them an unusual nutty flavour. Eating Moringa-moringa dishes was definitely an acquired taste and as children, we were not particularly fond of them.

The moringas were a nuisance on multiple scores. They grew to a height of fifty to sixty feet, had firm enough branches such that they could hold the weight of a large well-fed snake that had just successfully raided the hencoop. Since the branches were so high off the ground, it was difficult to get to the snakes. Another reason for detesting the Moringa-moringa was that every spring their trunks would be completely infested with hairy caterpillars, which would fall from the trees and find their way into the house. When one stepped on one of these caterpillars, it oozed an odious green, slimy liquid, which the servants refused to clean due to some recently concocted superstition of theirs.

When Mummy planted Chinese bamboo near the hencoop, snakes took up residence there. It turned out to be a mistake to have planted the bamboo; it took off with the enthusiasm of Jack's beanstalk. Before the year was out, the bamboo thicket became extremely dense. Snakes constantly hid out in the thicket so they could snag the stray chicken or the unattended egg. We were told specifically to stay away from the bamboo. Knowing that tales of snakes might not deter me, the servants reported that tigers actually lived there, since I was very afraid of them. The thicket was scarcely large enough to hide a tiger's tail, but the threat was enough to encourage me to stay away.

The Moringa-moringa trees and the bamboo thickets were yet another source of disagreement for Mummy and Papa. She wanted the moringas gone and he wanted them to remain. He wanted the bamboo thicket razed to the ground and she would have none of it. Between Papa's Moringa-moringa trees, Mummy's bamboo thicket, the kewra grasses on the other side of the wall, and the hencoop in back of the house, the snakes found life safe and satisfying in our home. Of course, neither Mummy nor Papa would admit that there were snakes around the house and in our garden.

The-house-with-the-garden had several verandahs which provided means of entrance into the house. The one on the southern side was used by the artisans who came to make things for our family and the vendors who would come to sell their many wares.

There was Pandarinath, the goldsmith, who would come to the house with his little blowtorch and minute hammer, sitting cross-legged on the floor for hours on end making exquisite jewellery fit for a queen. One always had to be watchful just in case Pandarinath's hand slipped and he put more copper in the solder than gold. He did not mean to cheat any one; it was just that the heat from the blow torch frequently caused his palms to sweat and his hands to slip into the stash of copper, rather than the gold.

Rajanna, the *dhobi*, washer-man, came every week with wonderfully clean, pressed, fresh-smelling cotton saris, underclothes and bed linens. Miraculously, every article of clothing or linen, no matter how large, was folded and pressed into rectangles of exactly the same size. Mummy would sit in her chair with a little book in hand and tally the list of the clothes he had laundered and brought back against a list of those he had left with the last week. The servants would parade back into the house with this stash of clothes and put them away in large camphor wood armoires. After all the lists had been tallied and every item of clothing was accounted for, the Chokra boy was sent to fetch the soiled clothes from the *mailedaan,* the hamper for dirty laundry, which Rajanna took back with him.

In the evenings, Sayanna, the *gowli,* the cowherd, arrived with his water buffalo and cows. The tinkling of the cowbells at the other end of the lane alerted us that he was coming. His was an elaborate ritual. Squatting by the side of the buffalo, he would pat her belly affectionately. With great flourish, he would take the vessel into which he was to collect the milk and tip it over. This was done to make a show of demonstrating that the vessel into which he would milk the animal was empty of water. It was not an uncommon practice, if one was not watchful, for the cowherds to collect the milk in a container which was half-filled with water. The customer was none the wiser for it. If they were not vigilant, they paid the price of undiluted milk and received a watered-down version instead. The explanation for watery milk given by the gowli grew more fantastic with each instance of discovery:

"The moon is full."

"Last year's monsoons have watered down the blood of the buffalo."

"The calf drinks up all the cream and only the water is left behind. What can one do?"

"It is the Kalyug, evil times signifying the end of the world. This is why the milk is watery. We are lucky that the animals don't give blood or bile instead of milk".

Under the supervision of the servants, Sayanna milked his buffaloes and poured their rich, frothy milk into the waiting copper pots that were then taken into the kitchen to be boiled several times in order to kill the bacteria that might have contaminated the milk.

There was Hariprasad, the tailor who made the Singer sewing machine sing while he fashioned anything from a *choli* – blouse or a quilt, to a slipcover for Mummy's sofa. Hariprasad was the most interesting of the entire parade of vendors who came to the southern verandah of the -house-with-the -garden. He habitually chewed tobacco and drank *shendi*, a fermented drink made from the areca palm. By the time we got back from school he was always in a very good mood. He developed what seemed to be an additional mouth in his left cheek. It was so curious that he could blow spittle and tobacco out of this second mouth, almost as well he could out of his first. Hariprasad's "second mouth" turned out not to be a mouth at all; it was actually a cancerous ulcer that had resulted from the tobacco that he had chewed most of his life.

It was always great fun to watch these vendors interact with Mummy and the senior servants.

One memorable summer in mid-March, upon our arrival back home we piled out of the motorcar and ran up the verandah steps to avoid the blast furnace of the noonday sun. Hariprasad was waiting. He was not his usual jovial, drunk self. His eyes were bulging from terror, more so now that his face had become progressively emaciated from the cancer.

"*Sahib*, I saw several cobras in the *munge ki phalli*, the Moringa-moringa trees near the hencoop." When Hariprasad reported that he had seen snakes in the trees, my father decided that he would track them down and kill them. He instructed us all to go inside. He intended to take a long bamboo pole and strike the snake with it, flinging it off the tree branch and on to the ground. As my father spotted the snake in the tree, my mother was on her way up the steps leading from the garden into the house.

Hariprasad set up a hue and cried, jumping up and down excitedly, "*Naag ara re* – the cobra is coming."

My father raised the forty-foot bamboo pole into the first of the Moringa-moringas, maneuvering its tip between the snake and the branch on which it lay coiled. This was no ordinary snake. It was not a mere cobra; rather, it was the deadlier hamadryad. Hissing ominously, the snake raised its hood. Because hamadryads are extremely aggressive, we thought it would come rushing down the tree and lunge at its aggressor. Instead, it whipped from one Moringa-moringa tree to the next, in one lengthy bound after another. By this time, my normally pacifist father had turned into a killer. Papa went after the snake in hot pursuit with his pole, which by virtue of its weight and length was extremely unwieldy. He finally succeeded in obtaining some purchase with the pole. Levering its mid-section against one of the lower branches, he managed to insinuate the pole's tip under the snake's belly. With a sawing motion, he pushed the pole up even higher. Now, using the branch holding the snake as a fulcrum, with a powerful flick of his wrist, he flipped the snake out of the Moringa-moringa tree.

We were at the window watching in amazement as the hamadryad came sailing out of the tree and into the air. Our amazement soon turned to horror. Mummy had not heeded Papa's warning to retreat inside the house and she was still standing on the verandah watching the proceedings. Amazingly the snake flew through the air and landed directly across her left shoulder. Without turning a hair, she grasped the tail of the great hamadryad and whipped its head several times against the floor of the verandah. The snake was probably merely stunned when it went sailing out of the tree, but by the time Mummy was done with it, it was clearly dead.

Carved into my consciousness, for one indelible moment, there stood my mother with the hamadryad coiled around her forearm, its head dripping blood on the verandah floor – a veritable female Perseus with the bloodied head of Medusa the Gorgon. Mummy had slain the beast that had been hiding in Papa's Moringa-moringa trees.

❖

I can remember back far enough to when my father and mother were gentle and even cordial to one another. Then, all of a sudden, things changed. Although harsh words were rarely ever exchanged in our presence, or any acrimony witnessed, as children we sensed a palpable and increasingly impenetrable wall between them. This was occasionally sprinkled with wistful nostalgia from my father and an aloof and supercilious disapproval from my mother. It was shortly after we moved into the house-with-the-garden that my parents' marriage was over, but I never really knew why until several decades later.

Papa had the most remarkable collection of fountain pens which he had collected since he was sixteen – there were Mont

Blancs, Parkers of every model and in every colour imaginable. There were Schaeffers, Pelikans, Watermans, Viscontis, and so on. He kept them clean and gleaming, each in their own leather case and nestled in satin which had yellowed and started to powder with age. He started a new journal on each of his birthdays, such that he had a diary for every year of his life. His chronicling was factual and detailed, written down in his lovely script in beautiful leather-bound journals.

We gathered around his table watching him as he took the pens out to arrange them like little soldiers on his rosewood desk. He would touch each one of them fondly with a slight smile on his face as if they were familiar and beloved children. He filled their barrels with carefully strained Parker ink of different colors writing in his ledgers in his tight, beautiful script. His diaries were always written with India ink. Since this ink clotted rapidly, he would carefully wash the pens that he had filled with it with warm water that he sluiced in with an old hypodermic syringe always boiling the syringe before and after use.

"Why do you boil the syringe, Papa? Do you have to?" I would ask.

"Ah, but I do. You never know what fungus will do when it reacts with the ink. It might coat the barrel and make the ink congeal even faster."

His lovely pens always provided us with a strong association to Papa.

Many years later, as I leafed through his journals, it became clear to me who he had been as a young man – a man with great aspirations and high hopes. He saw himself as a successful entrepreneur. He *was* very successful indeed, until the age of thirty-seven.

On his birthday, Papa would have the family astrologer-cum-palmist-cum-soothsayer, Kishan, summoned to cast his horoscope. Kishan was spare and nearly toothless; he wore thick soda bottle glasses. He would come with a little cloth satchel filled with little pieces of paper, a well-thumbed book on astrology and a soft pencil with an eraser. We watched as Papa held out his palms while Kishan pored over them, smoothing the creases out as if they would go away and reset into new lines. He squeezed Papa's fingers together to see if there were crevices between the fingers.

"You have large spaces between your fingers. Money will flow through like water. You have no discipline in spending."

He flipped his hand over and peered at the lines on the side. "You are going to have a son who will carry your dreams into the future; he will rescue you from your own foolishness."

Papa's face lit up. He knew then that his future was assured. I could see the faraway look in his eyes.

"What is he saying, Papa?" I asked.

He did not answer but rather patted my head absently as he continued to dream.

Kishan left and Papa sat down to write in his journal. He opened up a roll of thick white paper and reached for his pens and pencils. We watched as he started drawing. His dreams swiftly translated into fanciful extensions for the house – a separate bedroom for his son, a common study for the two of them. He panned a gazebo in the garden for my mother, where she could laze about and read during her pregnancy.

Almost a month later, my mother discovered that she was pregnant for the third time. She was furious with herself, angry with my father, and caught in the toils of an impotent rage directed at God. My father, on the other hand, developed an air of smugness overnight when he learned the news. He strutted around the house like our prize bantam rooster.

Mummy, practical as always, feared that my father's spendthrift propensities would spell an end to our affluence. She would then have no one to depend on other than herself. She knew that if we were to become poor, another mouth to feed would tax her resources beyond her capacity. She already had two daughters to be raised and the family had to have enough money saved to afford the dowries. The daughters also had to be virtuous and virginal. In addition, Mummy had her own agenda – she was going to raise us to be independent, which meant that there would be expensive educations to be paid for. Another child would restrict the possibilities for the two she already had. In her mind, there was only one solution to this unwanted situation.

I found myself often waking up at night, partly because of the unfamiliarity of the surroundings of the new house, but more because of the muffled arguments emanating from my father's bedroom. The house-with-the-garden quickly became a battleground for them – the scene of their almost silent skirmishes and what I feared would be the dissolution of their consortium.

One Sunday morning, the even tenor of our breakfast was replaced with a tension in the air. It was a grander spread than the usual Sunday fare and the servants set a fifth place at the table.

"Who is coming to breakfast?" I asked.

"The great lady herself," one of the less deferential servants retorted. She was referring to my aunt Anna who was a very important person in our world. Her company was not to be sought lightly.

"Like God descending from Heaven to assist ordinary mortals," added the servant.

"You are not to loiter and lollygag after breakfast," the cook warned us. And indeed, we did not. We were given permission to excuse ourselves even before we asked for it. We were not privy to what subsequently transpired at the breakfast table. My aunt left an hour later. We watched from the bedroom window as she descended the steps to the driveway. My father was at her car holding the door open for her. She turned back to look at Mummy, who looked like the wrath of God.

"I will not do this for you, Mary," my aunt called to my mother.

"Very well then, I will have to rely on myself," my mother replied.

A week later, Rachel and I came home from preschool to find the house unusually quiet. The servants were walking around with stricken looks and speaking in unaccustomedly hushed tones. My mother was gone. My father was beside himself with worry. He waited every evening thereafter at the top of the steps leading up to the house. When it was clear that Mummy was not coming home, he would retire to his room. During those weeks our servants looked after us. They were a great deal more lenient than Mummy would ever have been.

My mother returned a month later with a lighter step and a strange resolute smile on her face. No words were exchanged between her and my father. The chasm had opened up between them and it was never to close again. Mummy, not finding any support from her sister found herself a family friend, a gynaecologist, named Dr. Sheshadri. He performed the abortion she had insisted on.

My father's spirit faded visibly – life seeping through the crevices between his fingers. The script in his journals, which though still beautiful, developed a fine quiver and lost its boldness and resolve. About a month into the diary was the last entry for that thirty-seventh year:

"I lost my son, my future, and all my dreams. I will go to my grave with no one to whom I can pass my legacy."

My mother had gotten an abortion and my father stopped writing in his journals.

In doing the unthinkable, my mother had deprived my father of a son and his family of an heir. My father also knew that the spirit of the house had been offended and that a price would be exacted for this desecration. He was certain that lurking out there in the wings was the unnamed dread of imminent failure. He knew little of what awaited, but when it struck, he was convinced that it would be swift and remorseless, inexorable and irrevocable.

2

Papa's Family

MUMMY HAD OTHER DEMANDS PLACED ON HER BESIDES JUST Rachel and me.

While my father had been considered a great catch in the marriage arena, the alliance did not come without its own shackles. Mummy had to assume the role of becoming a mother to my father's three young brothers: John the oldest, Matthew the second, and Joey the youngest. In her mind, this placed her in metaphorical leg irons.

My uncles were much younger than my father and had been raised by him after his own mother's death in childbirth. My father was sixteen at the time of my grandmother's death.

My paternal grandfather worked as a manager in one of the largest trading and shipping firms in Travancore. His work often took him away to Allepey, a port town that was north of where his family lived. My paternal grandmother was fourteen years old when she married my grandfather. He seemingly only came home long enough every year to get her pregnant again and again. From the age of sixteen until thirty-two, my grandmother had a baby every year. Several of the children died in childbirth or shortly thereafter. All but one of the sixteen offspring was male. This was of course considered somewhat of a feat and made my grandfather quite a legendary figure in the community. However, only four males survived into adulthood.

As the tale goes, my father was at home when his mother went into labour for the sixteenth time. He often recounted that as she lay there bleeding to death, she enjoined him to look after her three boys who ranged in ages from one to three, and the baby girl that she had just given birth to. The girl child was sickly and required constant attention. Mercifully, some childhood ailment claimed her life shortly after her birth. She was laid to rest in a small grave at the foot of her mother's burial plot.

My father left Travancore sometime after his mother died in childbirth. His father had remarried soon after his wife died. My father and his three brothers, John, Matthew and Joey, who were the scions of the first family, came to be of dwindling consequence to their father. He was determined to strike out, making a life for himself and for his infant brothers. Travelling north to Hyderabad to make his fortune, he brought his three young brothers with him. He succeeded in accumulating great wealth in various business ventures, starting with virtually nothing. It was into this stronghold that my mother later came when she married my father. She had to contend with my father's unconditional love for his brothers and his unquestioning acceptance of their version of the truth, particularly that of the youngest, Joey.

My father did not become the young financial empire builder that he hoped to be. Rather, he was a gentle dreamer with an artist's sensibility who made money with one hand and gave it away with the other. His fierce determination to save his three brothers from becoming homeless and farmed out to distant relatives had driven him to amass his first fortune, but it would have required him having sons in order to motivate him to build another.

John was the oldest of my father's wards. He was smart and erudite, thoughtful and considerate. He managed my father's businesses and shops. He had an air of seriousness about him that intimidated everyone around him, so much so that his business associates would rarely try to deceive him. John came to be my favourite uncle and I loved him dearly.

Matthew was the middle brother. As an uncle, he was affectionate but he lacked the quick wit of my father and his other brothers due to his epilepsy which he developed at a very young age. His convulsions significantly disrupted his education and his life with frightening regularity. As a young child, I was shocked to witness his uncontrolled convulsions, with frothing at the mouth and biting of his tongue followed by a period of loss of consciousness while lying in a pool of his own excrement. When medications later became available, Matthew's convulsions were eventually controlled. But by that time the damage had been done. As a result, he was slower than the others and consequently was labeled as such. He completed his studies at home with a series of tutors hired by my father and eventually took up a trade rather than going to college like the others in the family.

Joey was the youngest of my father's brothers. He looked exactly like my uncle John, with the same face, the same hair, and the same athletic body with the exception that his skin was very dark, almost blue–black. It was as if God had taken two paintbrushes, one dipped in gold and the other dipped in Lampblack to paint John and Joey with a single stroke of the hand. Joey attended grade school in a different town which was two days away by train. He was a boarder with several other boys who came from affluent homes that could also afford the private schooling. He would come home for summers, Michaelmas and Christmas.

❖

My earliest memories of my uncle John were of him rescuing me from my father's wrath.

One Friday when I was very little, our old cook Sebastian who was Catholic prepared fish for dinner. As a young boy, Sebastian had served with an old Burgher family in Travancore where he had learned to cook, and he did so fabulously. He had the sweetest smile ever, a thick dark beard, and brown eyes rimmed with the milky arcus one sees in elderly people. He seemed older than anybody I knew.

That day Sebastian had cooked pomfret, *karimeen* – a flat fish, which when laid on the fish plate stared up at you with one eye while the other eye was buried in sauce. While the dinner was being prepared, I sat on the *korandi*, a small low stool in the kitchen and watched him with great concentration.

"I can gut the fish and remove the central bones as easily as you can extricate a rupee coin from your Mummy's silk-lined velvet purse," he boasted gently, watching my eyes become as large as saucers.

He seared the fish in drawn butter with fenugreek leaves and shallots. The skillet in which this whole process was done was "very, very old". Sebastian said it belonged to *Avrachen* – Abraham, the father of the Jews.

"Did you know Avrachen, Bastian cha?" I asked.

"Of course, why else would he give me the skillet? His wife Sara was my very own aunt," he said emphasizing "very own" with that strange little nodding of the head that is characteristic to Indians. "Yes, yes," he added with some more nodding.

Annu, the servant who assisted Sebastian, had prepared the sauce with cream of coconut and kosher salt, mixing in a hint of ginger and garlic paste. She set it to simmer in a seasoned terracotta pot, which Sebastian reserved only for cooking seafood. The reserving of pots for certain food and the use of kosher salt was probably some leftover ritual from the days when everyone who was anyone was a Jew and others did not matter. It made eminent sense, though, since meats cooked in a fish utensil would not taste right.

"When the sauce starts to dance like Annu on the festival of Shivaratri, that's when you slide the fish in." This was a sly reference to the fact that on the festival of the great dancing God Shiva, Annu had imbibed enough *shendi*, an alcoholic drink and *bhang*, marijuana that she felt no pain. Apparently she danced and danced through the night only to be severely hung over the next day.

Then, as a final touch on the dish, Sebastian sliced the Serrano chilies into thin slivers of green and fanned them out on the fish. This was done in one swift movement like a croupier, dealing a deck of cards. In a separate saucepan, he heated walnut oil until it started to smoke, throwing in a pinch of mustard seeds and nigella. When the whole blend started to splutter, he added it to the fish in the pot, covering it and letting it cook just a bit more.

Annu was busying herself preparing "string hoppers" for dunking into the fish gravy. Traditionally, hoppers are a breakfast food. Sebastian, however, defied all tradition and served them with the fish. They were made with rice that was soaked overnight then finely ground and mixed into a paste with hot water. The paste was then put through a press similar to a pasta maker and squeezed into coils. These coils of rice paste were then covered with sweet grated coconut and steamed until they were soft "like your hands," according to Sebastian.

Just then there was a knock at the door and the Chokra boy opened it, letting my uncle John in. He announced that he was staying for dinner as he and Papa had to go over the week's accounts. I was sitting at the dining table in a high chair when my father came back from a tour of his shops and businesses. Mummy had returned from the school where she was teaching Math. The servants scurried around setting the table for dinner. I sat at my father's right hand, my mother sat at his left, and my uncle John sat on the other side of me.

I had a habit of rocking my high chair which annoyed the adults. The rocking became even more agitated when I wanted something, be it water, more fish, or hoppers.

Papa looked at me with growing irritation. "I have told you several times to stop that rocking," he commanded.

I continued to rock the chair, unheeding. I did not notice the gathering annoyance on Papa's face as he stretched out his leg and used his foot to tip my chair backward. In an attempt to bring the chair back into balance, I leaned forward and fell to the floor. The plates went careening over the table as I fell and sliced my chin. It was only a small gash but I set up a caterwauling that could have awakened the dead.

Uncle John leapt to his feet, scooped me into his arms and ran with me into the bathroom. There, he gently bathed my face, washing the blood away. He sent Sebastian to tear up one of Mummy's old, clean voile saris and fashion a bandage. He wrapped the voile bandage over the wound and tied it neatly in a bow under my chin. If I had a straw hat, a shepherd's crook and some sheep, I would have looked like Little Bo-Peep.

Sitting in my father's rocking chair with me in his lap, my uncle patiently fed me my fish. Of course I milked the situation for all it was worth, grimacing with pain while I chewed the food. As a special treat, he had Sebastian make custard for me. He then released me to the Chokra boy who helped me brush my teeth and Annu who helped me change into my nightclothes. I came back into the parlour to find my uncle, who was normally always deferential to my father with his voice raised in unprecedented anger for what had happened earlier, wagging his finger in my father's face. This was all the more shocking as it is very uncommon for a younger brother to raise his voice to an older one.

"*Accha*," which was the honorific for "older brother", "that child is the jewel in our crown. She will bring honour and glory to our household. You could have killed her."

"You are making too much of a minor incident," my father said retreating before the onslaught.

"God saved her at birth. She is destined for great things. She was chosen for us, remember that."

This interchange took the whole household by surprise. Everyone waited in stunned silence for the apocalypse which never came. I stood at the door between the kitchen and the dining room, wide-eyed and drinking in the whole scene. I had forgotten that the gash in my chin was supposed to hurt and smiled widely at the fact that I was "the chosen one".

Uncle John noticed from the corner of his eye that I had returned. He stopped his tirade in mid-sentence and held his arms out to me. He sat down in the rocking chair and I climbed into his lap. My uncle John sang me to sleep that night and when I awoke the next morning rubbing the sleep out of my eyes I was still in the rocking chair curled up in his lap. He had just rescued me from great peril; he had become my saviour.

Uncle John was known to be extremely frugal and was teased unmercifully by his brothers for it. However, for Rachel and me, his gifts, even if small, were more precious than fine gold. Nothing given to us by anyone else ever measured up to what was bestowed upon us by Uncle John. His major gifts to us were a love of literature, poetry and song; but the greatest gift of all was one referred to by us as "The Royal Enfield Ritual". I was just a young child when this great ritual began.

His British motorbike, a Royal Enfield, was his pride and joy. It was a considerable black motorcycle with its wheels, handlebars and all other shiny chrome parts polished to a high gleam. To this modern steed, he affixed a leather sidesaddle bag in which he could carry his books.

Every Sunday after Matins and Holy Communion, Rachel and I would wait for him outside the garden gate. Presently, the motorcycle would appear in the distance a low and throaty roar heralding its appearance. We would crane our necks to see him riding toward us. The sheer joy and excitement of having our uncle come home was almost unbearable. Anyone looking down Himayat Nagar Lane would see a couple of crazed children jumping up and down shouting with joy. Our unhinged excitement would continue until he drew near enough for us to see his indulgent smile. Doing cartwheels, we would follow his motorcycle into the garden. He would park the bike and alighting slowly climb the stairs with each of us hanging on to his arm; he in his Sunday best and we in our clean white frocks which had become soiled now from the cartwheeling and carrying on. When he had reached the top of the steps, he would hand us his solar *topi*. Then there was the inevitable competition as to which one of us would get to hang his solar topi on the hat stand.

We would follow him into the living room while he settled into the planter's chair near the window. Being the older of the two, I was the one designated to fetch his briefcase from the saddlebag on his motorbike and set it by the chair. This started the Royal Enfield ritual which was followed religiously almost every week for the next several years.

I can still see the whole thing today, more than a half century later. I close my eyes and the entire scene comes back, painted in my brain and on the back of my eyelids, filling me with the same sense of anticipation as it did when I was five.

Uncle John clears his throat and pushes his glasses down to the tip of his nose while he regarded us gravely.

"Have you been good little girls this last week?" he asks with a small smile forming and playing on the corners of his mouth as he crinkled his eyes.

"Oh Yes! Yes indeed! Really, really good!" we sing out in unison.

His smile broadens as he reaches into the pocket of his coat. A gasp of joy follows our silence of anticipation. With slow and deliberate movements, he withdraws a single bar of Cadbury's chocolate. . He now removes the purple wrapper with its long and flowing, loopy Cadbury script. He puts the purple wrapper aside and then proceeds to deliver the chocolate bar from its silver foil encasement. Out comes his shiny Swiss Army penknife and with precise spare movements he cuts the bar into three equal sections. One piece each is placed in our outstretched cupped hands with the same degree of gravity and reverence as a priest delivering the host. Finally, taking the third piece, he pops it into his mouth. His eyes are closed in ecstasy as he savours the chocolate. We imitate him doing the same.

When this is done, he reaches into his breast pocket and withdraws a freshly laundered handkerchief. With great delicacy, he inserts his index finger into the center of the kerchief and delicately wipes our lips free of any invisible chocolate remnants that might have carelessly lingered. Then, with great care, the kerchief makes its way back into his pocket. The purple wrapper is folded and fashioned into an arrow, and given to one of us for use as a bookmark. The foil wrapper becomes a chalice or a swan, which we store carefully among the things that were precious to us.

Then follows the next step of the ritual. He places a hymnal, a book of verse, and a book of literature on the cross bar of the arms of the planter's chair. He invariably taught us a new hymn every fortnight. We were expected to have learned the *contralto* or the *descant* during the week so that we could sing in harmony when he opened up the hymnal. He would read to us from Somerset Maugham, Charles Dickens, Victor Hugo and so on. Finishing one section then starting another, he stops in the middle and puts the book away until the following week. This ruse was designed to keep us engaged. What he didn't seem to realise was that he did not have to resort to any such ruse; we loved our uncle so very much that we would have stayed keenly interested had he even opted to read us the grocery list.

We then run down the front steps to his Enfield. Rachel would climb up on the front with me behind him sidesaddle. Roaring out of the gate and through the neighbourhood on the motorbike, we would head to a Brahmin vegetarian restaurant that had just opened for business.

It was uncommon in the nineteen fifties for people with any social standing to eat in restaurants. The restaurants that were open were mainly Iranian, usually frequented by truck drivers, rickshaw pullers and the like, not by "decent people". A Brahmin restaurant was not only unusual; it was also acceptable to the higher strata of society. In India of a half-century ago when caste-based segregation was the order of the day, it would have been unthinkable to accept food from someone of a lower caste. However, it was fine to accept food from a person of higher caste. Anyone could order food in a Brahmin restaurant, since only men of the highest caste prepared it. It naturally followed that the Brahmin restaurant became a thundering success.

Shown to a table with great pomp and circumstance, we would order from the menu. We had to choose from the three items that were served for breakfast: *masala dosa* – a large paper thin rice and lentil crepe served stuffed with curried potatoes; *idli* – steamed fermented rice and lentil flour cakes which were served with yogurt and green chili pepper sauce or lentil soup; or *dahi vada* – deep fried split pea dumplings seasoned with crisp bits of onion, poblano peppers and ground ginger smothered in slightly sour yogurt. After all of this, we were treated to *lassi* – buttermilk mixed with creamy yogurt, whipped and frothed, then sweetened to excess with sugarcane crystals. During the summer months, we ordered lassi flavoured with mango. By the time we were done, we were stuffed to the point of discomfort.

Clambering back onto the Enfield we would head home.

The last part of our ritual was the poetry. My uncle's love of poetry was infectious. He read from an assortment of poems. Sometimes there would be sad ballads, occasionally there would be limericks, and sometimes, nonsensical nursery rhymes. Once in a while, he would spring a surprise on us and read from "*The Song of Solomon*" or from the Psalms. Had it been read in church, we would have found it terminally boring. Yet when Uncle John read it, it took on a new dimension and a cadence that was vibrant and hypnotic.

The ritual remained unchanged even though the venue eventually shifted. It never lost its fascination or sweetness, despite years of repetition. Of course as we grew older, we were more dignified in expressing our delight at his arrival. As we grew taller, we merited separate rides on his Enfield, riding pillion on the back seat as one or the other of his little sons rode on the front.

❖

Much of my childhood has faded into the murky past save for routines which have traced indelible tracks in my memory. One such practice was waiting for Papa to return home from work. At the age of three, this was the biggest event of my day. This predictable and comforting routine was always the same – one that my father, the Chokra boy and I performed everyday for what seemed to be an age. These were precious moments that my father and I shared – times when he belonged neither to my mother nor to the baby sister who had just arrived; my father was all mine.

It was at the end of the southwest monsoon season in the year nineteen forty-seven when all the adults were celebrating India's independence that our routine was abruptly shattered. Exploding on to the scene and into all of our lives came Joey – the youngest of my uncles, my father's favourite brother.

That particular day I waited for my father's Vauxhall to pull up into the port cochere as I had done every evening as long as I could remember. I counted the brace of squeaks followed by the heavy thunks of the car doors as they opened and closed.

Squeak-thunk, squeak-thunk.

Squeak-thunk one – the driver opens his door and closes it.

Squeak-thunk two – the driver let my father out of the car and closed the door after him.

I listened for their footsteps as they came up the gravel path and onto the stairs. It was always the same number of steps. I counted them on my pudgy little fingers using both hands, and again on those on the left the second time around – fifteen footsteps in all. The Chokra boy opened the door tentatively for fear that the heat would invade the home if he were not watchful.

I stood expectantly in the cool gray shadows beside the stairwell and, as always, watched my father with profound absorption. He sat down on the well-oiled rosewood bench by the door as he untied his shoelaces and looked up at me with a conspiratorial half-smile. As if on cue, I ran to his bedroom and fetched him his sandals. He waited for me to help him out of his shoes and socks and slip into the comfortably worn sandals.

The Chokra boy sidled in sideways like a giant brown crab and proffered the newspaper and a heavy glass tumbler filled to the second ridge from the top with a pale yellow-green opalescent liquid – Papa's customary nimbupani. In the winter, the nimbupani would be replaced by tea with cardamons floating to the top of the wrinkled membrane of tea stained cream, which was served in my father's favourite chipped white cup from his college days. I relished his smile and that softly expelled sigh of relief as the hot soles of his feet slapped against the cool leather of the sandals.

This day started out different from the others and I remember it with pristine clarity. It was unbearably stifling, humid and miserable. Everyone had been waiting for the southwest monsoons to be replaced by the northeast rains which would bring some relief from the heat and humidity.

"This year the northeast monsoons are unusually late," Sayamma, declared, but that is exactly what she had said every year. "Late monsoons bring plagues and ill-humors," she warned. Little did she know that cholera and typhoid actually came with great regularity every year with the monsoons whether or not they were late.

The gravid leaden clouds hung low over the city as they had for the past week. Nothing stirred, not even the houseflies which lay inert in the torpid heat. The shades were drawn and the doors shuttered to keep the summer blast resolutely out. The Poinciana which the servants had arranged artlessly in a vase on the hall tree in the entryway was listless and wilting wearily in the heat.

I remember awaiting my father's return from the factories that he owned. I hoped that there would be some surcease from the monotony of the day. Papa's car pulled up and I heard the familiar squeak – thunks, and then counted the steps as I always did, until he entered the house.

The Chokra boy handed my father an envelope in addition to his usual nimbupani and the newspaper. The nimbupani frosted the outside of the heavy glass tumbler. My father's eyes had not yet adjusted to the darkness of the shuttered house. He should have seen the characteristic yellow colour of the envelope with its Indian telegraph seal, but he did not. He gave the envelope a cursory glance and cast it aside almost thoughtlessly by the shelf on the hall tree.

He was headed to the parlour with his juice in hand and his newspaper tucked under his arm when he stopped in mid-step, swivelled around, and picked up the envelope. I could see his fingers trembling with feverish haste as he tried to open it with one hand. Young as I was, I felt a nameless cold fear clutch at me while watching my father's body crumble as he scanned the telegram. The glass with the nimbupani slipped out of his grasp splashing its contents and splintering as it smashed against the edge of the hall tree mirror, breaking its corner into fine long slivers.

I was captivated by the showers of light as the mirrored shards came crashing down at my feet. I squatted down to look at them, gingerly picking one up and slicing my thumb in the process. I observed in fascination as my bright red blood beaded on the silver glass, forgetting to cry out at the pain. It was only when the Chokra boy shouted in alarm at the blood that I joined in the pandemonium. My father stared at my bloodied hand with seemingly sightless eyes.

Hearing the noise, my mother came rushing out of the parlor. The Chokra boy, who was not a boy at all, lifted my father's buckling form on to the hall bench. Papa's body was wracked with sobs as my mother snatched the telegram from him.

"Your brother Joey has run away again," Mummy commented with ill-concealed annoyance. "Your daughter is bleeding to death, and you are obsessed with that scoundrel."

Since I had no desire to die, her comment served to alarm and frighten me even more. I set up a wailing which brought all the servants rushing into the hallway. My father looked at me and then down at the blood which had started to clot like patches of carmine bubble gum.

"What am I to do?" he asked abjectly.

In that moment, right before my eyes, my father was transformed instantly from a shining hero to a helpless victim. In my mother's household, little quarter is given to victims. As a result, my father receded into a meaningless state for her – nice to have around, but inessential for survival.

With her customary resolve, Mummy summoned the appropriate functionaries and my older uncles. With her habitual dispatch, she sent them all scrambling to the four corners of the earth in search of my errant uncle Joey.

A week, or maybe it was a fortnight later, my uncle John found Joey hiding out in Madras – holed up in a seedy restaurant cleaning dishes to pay for room and board. Uncle John then brought him home against Joey's wishes. Joey cut a sorry sullen young figure in his torn clothes with unkempt hair as he stood in the foyer silently glaring at us. The only sign of resignation was in the way that he held his head on his skinny little neck, as if awaiting a blow from a machete to sever its tenuous hold on life.

While Uncle John probably wanted to teach him a lesson by not allowing him to change or clean up before bringing him home, it only served to congeal the sorrow in my father's soul. My father's keening cry as he reached out to gather him into his embrace was followed by solemn promises of never letting Joey out of his sight.

True to his word, my father had Joey move in with us. This was to be the heaviest of Mummy's shackles. Her chafing under their restraint insured, in a perverse sort of way, that we would somehow inherit the burden.

Joey was fifteen years old at the time. There was more than enough room for him in the big house-with-the-garden but he stayed sullen and distant, barely communicating with the rest of the family. I tried to draw him out with offers of my mangled half-eaten sweets. I even tried to engage him with one of my prized possessions – a severely beaten up and dog-eared deck of playing cards. The two jokers in the deck were my favourite cards – smiley characters in gaudy *Pierrot* costumes. Knowing that Joey loved to paint, I thought he might especially like these cards. Instead, he snatched them out of my grasp. Walking deliberately and wordlessly out into the yard with me trailing after him, he held them aloft, tore them into shreds, and flung them with a flourish into the drainage ditch on the far, far side of the garden. I watched in agonised silence as the coloured bits of my earthly treasures floated away to the end of the garden drains where they were trapped in the ooze and detritus of the flowerbeds.

Over the ensuing weeks, it seemed that Joey had relented some. It was as if I had made the ultimate sacrifice, and therefore, his final cut. I could now be graced with his favour and he even occasionally smiled at me. This modest trust, however, was to be forever shattered when one day he beckoned to me and I followed him into his room. What followed was strange, painful and unpleasant.

My uncle Joey sexually molested me. Without penetrating me, he fondled me and touched my body in places I dared not speak of. He seemed to derive great pleasure from this act. I didn't know what to make of all of it but I knew that it did not seem quite right. At the age of four I had no words in my repertoire to describe what was happening to me but I recall appealing to my father and my older uncles to intervene. All I could think to say in my childish vocabulary was that Joey was "bothering me". That did not seem to generate the reaction that I was looking for so then I struggled with another set of words.

"He is tickling me, Papa, and it hurts."

My father looked up from his accounting ledger with resignation and annoyance at the many interruptions.

"Joey, don't tickle the child, she might quit breathing from laughing too much. Her belly hurts more from laughing because she has that repaired birth defect, you know."

"Now, there," he said ruffling my hair fondly. "Come back to me if he tickles you again and we will both give him a dose of his own medicine. We will tickle him around his belly and in his armpits and on the soles of his feet until he screams for us to stop."

I knew then that my father would never understand, and I dared not tell my mother for fear of unleashing her fury. Heaven only knew what would happen to Joey if my mother came to know my bitter secret. In my childish imagination, my mother was the female reincarnation of Shiva, the Destroyer. It is said that when provoked he would open his third eye and rain destruction all around. Where Shiva's wrath was myth, the reality was that my mother's third eye was to be avoided at all costs. Her rages were famed; they were cold, all enveloping, fierce, and lasted for an eternity. If I were to summon up enough courage to tell her, the landscape of my life as I knew it would evaporate. It had the potential to become the spiritual version of a nuclear wasteland – bleak and joyless. My father and his brothers would be banished forever to some infernal hell and I would live with the constant sorrow of never seeing my saintly father and my beloved uncle John again. So it came to pass that I remained quiet for a very long time.

❖

A parade of servants came in and out of our lives – coming and going through our household with fair regularity. My mother was a demanding employer, and as a result, was unable to retain servants for any significant length of time. She had little tolerance for inefficiency and even less patience for fools. My father, by contrast, was a lenient employer and would impose no discipline on his servants at all. They could actually steal him blind and even if he knew of it, he would do nothing, insisting that they were lazy or dishonest because they simply could not help themselves. His servants would stay only until they eventually ran into the buzz-saw that was my mother.

When I was about four years old, a young woman came to the gate of the house-with-the-garden looking for employment as a maidservant. She said her name was Lakshmi. She had adopted that name for herself; it was the name of the goddess of prosperity. Later, I learned that her real name Pochamma was one that she despised. The name Pochamma was one that would have identified her as an "untouchable". Untouchables were an entire group of people in India who were considered beneath the four major castes: the Brahmins, the Kshatriyas, the Vaisyas and the Sudras. They carried out tasks shunned by the other groups such as the cleaning of privies, the tanning and curing of animal skins, the disposing of animal and human remains, and a multitude of other necessary but undesirable functions.

Although "untouchability" was generally considered an issue only among the Hindus, Christians who had been converted from the higher castes continued to safeguard their privileged status. Despite the fact that our families had been Christian for two millennia, for those who worked in our homes or gardens and groves, the stigma of untouchability remained a reality. The untouchables who served us could not stand in front of us lest their shadows fell across us. They ate separately, they did not touch us, and we were not to touch them.

Lower than the untouchables were the truly destitute of India – women who had been abandoned by their husbands, widows and orphans. These luckless creatures were even more vulnerable to the depredations of the rest of society.

By virtue of her untouchability and by the fact that her husband had left her, Lakshmi was doubly cursed. She had not only lost all means of support, but she had been relegated to an even lower rung of society. She decided to take her life into her own hands, gave herself a new name and went off to seek employment. She believed that her original name of Pochamma was an announcement to the world at large of her inability to battle circumstances of birth, station in life and fate. So she became Lakshmi – the goddess of wealth and prosperity.

Our Lakshmi could not have been more than eighteen or nineteen years old. She was a diminutive, very dark skinned woman whose face was covered with the scars of small pox in childhood. She was quite homely – short, dark, pockmarked, and had the whitest teeth I had ever seen. Her teeth appeared whiter than most, partly because they protruded a little, and partly because they sharply contrasted with her extremely dark skin. With her small beady eyes, she looked remarkably like a little dark rodent.

She was always extremely neat and very well groomed. Her sari was clean and carefully draped around her rather shapeless form. Her hair was pulled back severely and tightly wrapped into an unadorned bun; not one strand of hair would dare escape. She wore a perfect, big red dot in the middle of her forehead and a small collection of jewellery to signify she was married. She wore small silver stud earrings and her marriage chain, which was no more than silk threads entwined in a cord that held the *lingam*. As a small child, I loved the smell of Lakshmi – basil and jasmine with overtones of the dish she had prepared for us that afternoon. There was something immensely comforting about the smell that accompanied her.

When Lakshmi arrived at the front gate, she was very forthright in saying that she desperately needed a job as she had no husband and three children to support. She appealed to Mummy's pragmatic nature with her matter-of-fact view of her own plight.

"I will love and care for your children even better than my own," she promised. She was, in fact, true to her promise.

"What will you do with your own children?" my mother asked with alarming visions of Lakshmi's three little ragamuffins running rampant over her orderly household.

Lakshmi was quick to respond with, "They will go to school during the day and my mother will look after them in the evenings."

Untouchable children or even children of servants attending school, was still a new concept in India at the time. Mahatma Gandhi had initiated the movement in an effort to lift the poor, who were mostly untouchable, out of their extreme poverty. Educational programmes and incentives were being provided for the economically depressed classes. So, Lakshmi's children went to school and were looked after by their grandmother while Lakshmi looked after us. She was certainly not the prettiest servant in the neighbourhood, but she was definitely the most dependable and could be relied on to ably look after the household in Mummy's absence.

In short order, Lakshmi gained enough status in the household to insist that my mother allow her to plant a large variety of jasmine, mogra and chameli, in the garden. Mogra and chameli actually belong to very different phyla and look very different but are generally classified together in the local vernacular as jasmine. Both intensely fragrant, they put out white flowers that opened up in the late hours of the evening. By dawn, the buds unfurl their petals completely and diffuse their fragrance into the early morning air.

Lakshmi planted mogra and chameli in the garden. With help from us, she planted mogra bushes on either side of the steps leading to the house and the chameli on the pillars that framed the front verandah. The maali had told her time and again that she would have to strip the leaves off the plant in the spring in order for it to put out its blooms in summer. She ignored his advice until it became abundantly clear that no amount of coaxing would wheedle flowers out of the stubborn little bushes. Lakshmi finally relented and we helped her pluck out the leaves. Miraculously, a fortnight later, there they were, at every leafy junction to the mother stalk, triads of tiny little mogra buds.

"Shiva's *trishul*, (trident) little mother," the maali said matter-of-factly, as if it were the most reasonable explanation in the world. "If you sacrifice the young leaves to Shiva, he accepts your sacrifice and sends you the sign of his trident."

The mogra were ugly little shrubs proliferating unrestrainedly on the steps leading into the garden. In the summer, all the effort they had been expending throughout the year in putting out their gnarled branches and leaves came to a halt. Then they burst into bloom covering the shrubs with an exuberance of fragrant globular flowers. At every leafy junction to the mother stalk, there were triads of tiny little mogra buds – fat little white globes, incandescent in the deepening dusk of summer. The chameli, on the other hand, were delicate vines that had deep, dark green leaves. The chameli flowers grew in clusters on deep pink stalks and had long delicate white petals with faint pink tips, like the fingers of a Siamese dancer.

Every evening, Lakshmi wove the mogra and chameli into long garlands with sacred basil and adorned her pictures of the gods she worshipped. Most of the prayers that she offered were for the safe return of her errant husband. He was much older than she, and physically unprepossessing. He was, however, blessed with a roving eye and the attention span of a monkey. By the time she was eighteen, she had borne him three children, accumulated a multitude of pawn tickets for her meager stash of jewellery, and developed a fervent desire to support herself and her children irrespective of his wanderings in and out of her life.

Her last attempt to find him came one summer when the mogra and chameli were in full bloom. She seemed to think of this as a sign that she would locate him and succeed in convincing him of the error of his ways. There was a hurt look in her eyes as tears flowed unchecked over her pockmarked face when she bade us farewell to look for her vagrant husband.

"I will be back, I promise," she said in response to my tearful entreaties asking her to stay. I had found myself already becoming very attached to her.

The chameli and mogra seemed to know that Lakshmi had left. They withered soon after and had to be replaced by batch after fresh batch from the nursery. Their reluctance to flourish remained this way until she returned some months later.

When Lakshmi left to look for her husband, Mummy found Narsa to take her place. Narsa was Hindu, but had served in many Muslim households where the meals prepared were the most delicious in all of India. This explained the mystery of the marvellous mouthwatering dishes she cooked for us every day.

Narsa was tall and enticingly pretty with dancing eyes and a swing to her hips that kept us amused and the menservants distracted. She kept her hair coiled in a wonderfully intricate chignon – hair twist, at the nape of her neck. Occasionally it would come undone and sweep down to the upswing curve of her buttocks. She would cluck in annoyance when it fell and then retrieve it back into a secure knot again. Every gesture of hers was exaggeratedly graceful; her walk, her talk, her glance over her shoulder at others around her. All the while she would sing under her breath and when she thought no one was within earshot, she would give way to a full volume rendition. For all her prettiness and grace, her singing voice left much to be desired as it was always a strange falsetto.

Her most intriguing feature were her hands, they were enormous in size, but shapely and beautiful. She always decorated them with the intricate henna patterns commonly sported by Muslim women. In addition, her nails were always painted a bright red, which was an uncommon luxury for servants since foreign toiletries were expensive. In the web between the thumb and index finger of her left hand was an unusual tattoo. It was intricate and inscribed within a circle the size of a dime. Narsa told us that it was a calligraphic representation of her name.

As little children, we were intrigued by her song – promises of beauty deliverable by sunrise. She was full of many secrets as to how the Muslim women managed to consistently look so incredibly delectable and would share these mysteries with us. After washing my hair, she would have me lie down on a soft silken pillow, which was propped up on a basket turned upside down. Under the basket was an incense burner filled with smoldering *lobaan* and *ood*, frankincense and myrrh. The heat and smoke from the frankincense would dry and perfume my hair as it diffused through the holes in the basket weave.

In summer, before bedtime, she would help us string mogra and chameli into garlands. She then wove it into our braids so that our hair would be fragrant in the morning as the flowers bloomed overnight. She would rub sandalwood paste into our freshly bathed faces and a special paste on the secret parts of our bodies.

In winter, she would fashion young kewra leaves into elaborate hair ornaments and adorn our braids with them. She would use rosemary and thyme to tone down the heady and overpowering smell of the kewra.

Every afternoon, she ventured off for hours on end, ostensibly to buy herbs for us, returning just before Mummy and Papa got home. She said she was going into the "dark" parts of the city to secure these herbs that she was going to grind up into her special pastes.

"The secret ingredient," she said, "is *aami haldi*." This was a variant of *Haldi,* turmeric. The common turmeric is bright yellow in colour and is the powdered dried root of the turmeric plant.

"Aami Haldi smells like heaven," she would say, holding up a dab for us to smell. It had the expected pungent bite of turmeric, but underneath it all was the unexpected fragrance of vanilla and ripe mango.

"What does this do, Narsa?" I would ask.

"When you rub it on your legs, forearms, underarms and private parts, hair will not grow there. You skin will become as smooth as *sang-e-murmur*" – the highest quality of marble. When a man touches your skin, he will be driven insane by its smoothness. Kohl in your eyes, jasmine and kewra in your hair, sandalwood paste on your face, aami haldi on your skin – you will be more beautiful than the Mumtaz Mahal," she would say.

I could picture whole lines of handsome men swooning as they looked into my eyes, touched my skin, and smelled my hair.

"When will this happen, Narsa?"

"By tomorrow at sunrise," she'd reply.

At sunrise, I would rush to the mirror to see if any change had been affected. I would find Narsa standing behind me. She would bend down from her great height and whisper in my ear.

"Look," she would say, "look, your skin is becoming translucent like alabaster. Some king will marry you and you will have the Taj Mahal built in your honor, just like the Empress."

With Narsa standing behind me, I could see the alabaster in my skin. However, the instant she left the room it turned back to looking like putty.

Mummy had learned that Narsa left the house for several hours every afternoon. She said nothing about it for a while. One day she discovered that Narsa had been pilfering from the pantry. She again held her peace until she lost a valuable piece of heirloom jewellery, a jewelled hairpiece. Convinced that Narsa had taken it, she sent the Chokra boy to follow Narsa on one of her afternoon disappearances.

"*Amma*," he reported on his return, "Narsa goes to the Purani Haveli section of the old town."

"Are you sure?" my mother asked in disbelief. That was the section of town where dancing girls, prostitutes and courtesans lived.

"Yes, Amma," he said nodding vigorously.

"Is there anything else?" she asked, watching him hop from one foot to the other as if he had something else to say.

"She is a *hijra*, Amma; she is a eunuch."

In Hyderabad, and in many of the cities of India, there are communities where the *hijras* or eunuchs live. They lived in enclaves and communes where they looked after one another. They learned to sing and dance; many of them composed exquisite poetry and music. Several of them were accomplished cooks. In the old days of the Nizams and their nobility, their main occupation was dancing and amusing a variety of clientele – male of course. There were many of them who ventured into prostitution.

"Did Narsa see you?" Mummy asked.

"Yes Amma, she was very angry and slapped me very hard," he replied rubbing his cheek as if it still hurt. "She has very big hands, you know."

Narsa never came back to work for us after Mummy confronted her with what she had discovered. We later learned that Narsa had simply been going back to visit with her commune. The meager amount of food she had pilfered was for some of her kind who were too infirm to work.

Mummy found her hair ornament two days later. It had fallen behind the dressing table with a mirror; and was later retrieved when one of the servants was sweeping for cobwebs. I was saddened by the fact that Narsa and her promises of beauty had come to leave us over the accidental loss of a hair ornament and my mother's subsequent suspicions.

Lakshmi returned to us some weeks later without her husband, but with a resolute look in her eye. She became utterly devoted to my mother and me. Our goals became hers; anything that we would set our hearts on, she would eagerly facilitate. She soon became the steady mainstay of our existence. The mogra and chameli, seemingly grateful for her return, dutifully started back where they had left off, blooming once again.

3

Mummy's Family

BOTH MY PARENTS' RESPECTIVE FAMILIES MOVED FROM THEIR ancestral homes in the Hindu kingdoms of Travancore-Cochin and Malabar. They left the lush, green coasts of southern India to come to live in the Muslim city of Hyderabad on the arid plains of the Deccan plateau. The basic reasons that impelled these two families to move were different, but their ultimate goals were the same. They both had moved in search of opportunity and materially richer lives, and in Hyderabad, they found them.

Hyderabad was ruled by the *Nizam-ul-mulk*, Osman Ali Khan, who was reputed to be the wealthiest man in the world. It was the richest kingdom in British India and held great promise for the entrepreneurial and intrepid.

It was my aunt Anna who was responsible for my mother's family moving to Hyderabad. Anna completed her medical studies in Madras (now known as Chennai), in southern India just before the second Great War. She received a commission as a surgeon in the Nizam's army in Hyderabad, an unusual position for a woman at the time. As she embarked upon her commission, Anna took the entire family with her – her parents, a sister

Lizzie, her only brother Benjamin, and her youngest sister Mary.

Mary was my mother.

Samuel, Anna's father was a brilliant but ultimately irresponsible man who was incapable of holding down a job. He possessed an immutable sense of self-righteousness which aggravated successive employers and cost him several positions. Consequently, his family never knew where he was going to land, or whether or not he could support them. Samuel squandered both his inheritance and the dowry brought in by Anna's mother Elizabeth, our grandmother, whom we called Ammachy.

In landing the position in the Nizam's army, my aunt Anna had brought the ship home. This meant that Ammachy could now depend on her oldest daughter as a means of financial support, never having to rely on her husband Samuel again.

However, despite the newly found security of Anna's job, my maternal grandparents still had the unenviable burden of three unmarried daughters on their hands. Marriages were not about a man and a woman or a husband and a wife; they were about one household becoming joined to another for generations to come and producing suitable offspring who would ensure the family's place in "history". In order to marry a daughter off, parents had to provide sizeable dowries with the value of the dower dictating the desirability of the bridegroom.

Dowries were the bane of existence for Indian families irrespective of religion. Hindu, Muslim or Christian parents with daughters knew they had to slave all their lives to insure the future of their daughters as the alternatives were unpalatable. Without dowries, they would be condemned to marrying unsuitable men – unsuitable based on age, status or communal affiliation; or they would remain unmarried leading lives of unfulfilled desperation. An unmarried daughter was a potential source of difficulty which might invite ignominy on the household. Parents, therefore, worked to one end – to have their daughters married into suitable households.

With Samuel flitting from one job to the next, no money had been set aside to pay the dowries for his three daughters. These young women desperately needed to find husbands and homes. The lack of a dowry in Anna's case was not much of an obstacle to her being able to secure a suitable husband. She was quite attractive and to add to this, she was a doctor. At the behest of the Nizam, she left for Edinburgh where she earned her Fellowship with the Royal College of Obstetricians and Gynecologists. With the wives and concubines of the Hyderabadi nobility for patients and her skill as a gynaecologist and obstetrician, she became inordinately wealthy. Men were constantly vying for her attention.

Lizzie, the second daughter, was loveliness personified. All of creation worshipped at Lizzie's altar. This meant that men would view her as a trophy and ask for her hand in marriage, dowry or not. She was a tall, wispy, golden-skinned thing with flyaway curly hair, a lovely laugh and a mole just outside the upper right corner of her mouth. When she turned fifteen, she wanted nothing to do with studying or school. And, at her insistence on being married, her parents arranged her marriage with a much older man. Lizzie and her new husband left shortly thereafter for Africa where he amassed considerable wealth and returned to Travancore several years and four children later.

My uncle Benjamin was the only son and the most adored in my mother's family. My earliest recollection of him was as a captain in the First Lancer regiment of the Nizam's army. He was a handsome, extremely good-natured young fellow with winning ways and a wide flashing smile. He followed his sister Anna into the Nizam's army.

The third daughter, Mary, was my mother. Providence intervened for her. Her dowry was waived due to totally unexpected circumstances – my father Isaac fell madly in love with her. He had known my mother and both of her sisters in the "old country", Travancore, when they were all young children converging on the same school from a series of different little townships, villages and hamlets. By the time my father renewed his acquaintance with my mother's family in Hyderabad at the age of thirty-one, he was a wealthy man owning several successful businesses: movie houses, biscuit factories and an assortment of retail shops. He was handsome and showed great promise. He was the perfect catch. When they met again, Mummy had matured into an accomplished and handsome woman of twenty-four. However, at twenty-four she was decidedly past marriageable age, and given her father Samuel's improvidence, there were no great marriage prospects on the horizon. Falling in love had never been a priority in Indian marriages before, but in this case it was a necessity, since Samuel was incapable of paying any dowry.

Papa married Mummy with great pomp and circumstance. Breaking from convention and tradition, Isaac funded his own wedding, which was reported to be spectacular. My mother, by all accounts, made a beautiful bride. A sepia tinted photograph of her taken at her wedding occupies pride of place now on my night table, her eyes wide and inquiring, and her mouth generous and sweet. The most striking feature of the photograph is that my mother has her arms resolutely crossed across her chest, almost as if in defiance of what fate was to hand to her. Knowing Mummy's prescience, she must have had some premonition of what life had in store for her.

❖

The relationship between my mother and her sister Anna had always been a rocky one. Anna was the apple of my grandmother's eye leading to envy on my mother's part and guilt on the part of my aunt. Ammachy lived with Anna in her grand household which only served to fuel the fire. From Mummy's point of view, there was the feeling of compulsory gratitude toward Anna who had rescued the family from penury and moved them to Hyderabad. Then there was also the feeling of inadequacy, because Anna had become a doctor while Mummy was only a teacher, despite

Mummy being much smarter. From Anna's position, there was guilt at having hoarded the lion's share of Ammachy's affection.

Being quite pleasant-looking *and* a doctor, Anna could have had her choice of husbands, but she felt unworthy. This feeling of unworthiness came solely from the tiresome Indian societal condemnation of not having a dowry. At the time of her marriage, her family was still struggling to get out of the stranglehold of their straitened circumstances. All of Anna's accomplishments – her education, her enterprise, her rescuing her family from poverty, and her boundless potential for wealth – none of these factors in her mind or in the eyes of Indian society could erase the shame she bore of not having a dowry.

Anna's husband had been a widower with two children when he married her. His machismo and superciliousness must have been attractive to her in some primal sort of way. She consented to marry this second-hand person and live a life of submission and obedience at home, while experiencing honour and wealth in her work.

Her married life was one marked by abuse from her husband and constant nagging from her mother. Her husband, who had an insignificant job as an insurance salesman, wielded a stranglehold on her pocketbook, spending her money like a drunken sailor on pay day while she had to beg for spending money for herself. Like all victims wallowing in their own victimhood, she chained herself to this subjugation in silence. Ammachy hated her son-in-law, but could say or do little to assuage the situation.

In her professional life as a surgeon and obstetrician Anna was excellent at her craft. She was highly respected by both her peers and by the inhabitants of the city. Women arrived from the farthest reaches of the kingdom to have her care for them. There was many a time that she would deliver a male infant in aristocratic households and receive gifts of gold coins and diamonds in an amount equal to the weight of the newborn as payment for her medical services. Likewise, the female babies were weighed against emeralds and pearls.

Anna would often contribute an ornament or two that she had received to our dower chests – jewellery which would go with us to our future husbands' homes. It would be unthinkable to send a daughter into another household inadequately bejewelled and adorned. On occasion, Mummy would show me the jewellery Anna had given. One of the most cherished possessions was a black pearl pendant that had come to us through my Aunt Anna's reputation and prowess as a gynecologic surgeon and obstetrician.

She was once consulted by one of the Nawabs – Muslim aristocrats, to attend the labour or "lying-in" as they called it of his fourth and most favourite wife – Ayesha Begum. Most of the royalty and nobility of the state were Muslims of Persian and Turkish descent. They were distinctly Aryan – tall and pale skinned, in contrast to the commoners who were mostly Dravidian or Semitic – darker and more swarthy and stocky.

Ayesha Begum was a Hindu woman, and in her youth, the wife of one of the minor rajas in the kingdom. The Nawab was on one of his hunting trips when he stopped for a midmorning repast at the home of the raja. Most Hindu women did not veil themselves as the Muslim women did. This was how he first saw her.

She was a red-haired, green-eyed, vivacious and tempting little morsel and the Nawaab simply had to have her. The raja was, in all likelihood, handsomely recompensed for his loss. The Nawab returned without any of the game he had set out to retrieve, but instead, with a far greater prize. Ayesha Begum became his fourth wife.

The Nawab doted on her, indulging her every whim. She was not just relegated to the position of concubine, which was the common lot for many a young woman who tickled the old man's fancy. Most of the young concubines would occupy his attention for a fleeting moment and then be condemned to live out their days in one of his many palaces like exotic pets – fed, clothed and cared for, but rarely summoned for royal favors.

On this occasion, my aunt was gone much longer than usual. Ayesha Begum must have had a long and protracted labour. Aunt Anna appeared exhausted when she finally returned home.

"Well, is it a boy?" I wanted to know.

"Yes," she replied.

"Is he healthy?"

"I'm afraid so."

The Nawab was out of the country at the time and was expected to return within a few weeks. We knew that the usual jollity and celebrations had to wait until he returned. We asked if we could see the baby because we knew that if we went to visit Ayesha Begum on this auspicious and happy occasion we would be privy to all kinds of wonderful treats: delicious chocolates from Switzerland, fine pastries from Paris, cakes and comfits from England, and above all, the wonderful sweetmeats from the Nawab's own kitchens. My aunt, however, seemed reluctant to give us permission to visit. She finally relented though and took us to the private ward set aside for the aristocracy.

It was oppressively hot as we walked onto the ward. The curtains had been drawn and the room was dark. When we entered, a wan and haggard looking Ayesha Begum greeted us. We were taken aback by her transformation. We had remembered her as being full of life and laughter, and now she seemed a mere shadow of herself. I detected a stark terror in those young green eyes of hers, like those of a cornered and frightened animal.

Presently the nurse brought the baby in to be fed. She drew the curtains aside to let the sunshine and fresh air in. After removing the clothes that were wrapped around the baby, she put the child to Ayesha Begum's breast. There was a uniform gasp from those who were gathered around. There, nestling against that perfect alabaster breast, was the blackest little baby in the whole kingdom. He was perfectly formed from the top of his nappy little head to his bottom of his little black toes.

Then there was a noise outside the ward and the door suddenly opened. There stood the Nawab, weary from his travels. He ran forward to greet his beloved wife, stopping dead in his tracks as he caught sight of the child. One could have heard a pin drop in the silence of the room. We waited with bated breath for the thunderclap expected to follow.

"Here is your son, Excellency," said Ayesha Begum with an assumed gaiety, holding the baby out to the Nawab.

"I am so sorry, my dear," he said as he handed the baby over to the nurse. He embraced his wife saying, "It is indeed as I have been informed."

He turned to explain to my aunt as if it was the most natural thing in the world. "We believe, Doctor, that one must be very careful with what one looks at throughout pregnancy. As everyone knows, the baby will closely resemble what the mother has been seeing through the term of the pregnancy."

He had given specific orders to remove all the crippled and homely people from his wife's sight. However, her chambers were protected by Nubian guards. Since they were constantly in Ayesha Begum's view throughout her pregnancy, this obviously accounted for the fact that the young princeling was born in their likeness.

Each one of us children received our very own gold coin set in black South Sea pearls to celebrate the birth of the "Black Princeling".

Early in life, I painfully came to realise that I would never be classically beautiful like Ammachy or curvaceously pleasing like Mummy. Nor would I ever radiate the beauty possessed by my aunts. While my second aunt Lizzie who lived in Africa was far and away the most stunning of her sisters, my aunt Anna was in a class all by herself.

Anna was not fine featured like Lizzie, but there was a certain dignity and bearing that she exuded which far out-weighed her lack of noble features. She was tall and light-skinned – a trait that Indians prefer in their women. She had a well-proportioned body, a mellifluous voice with a hint of firmness beneath, and above all, an imposing presence. She had a feline grace about her that defied imitation.

Although not beautiful by conventional standards, her attractiveness elicited worshipful admiration wherever she went. The awe she commanded and the charisma she projected were qualities that I had not witnessed before and have not since.

Every birthday I would receive a bauble or two from Anna which went to my dower chest. For my seventh birthday, she gave me a necklace made up of a dozen finely matched cabochon emeralds about the size of large almonds which hung from a very fine chain of gold.

Ammachy said that emeralds would not look "too bad" against my dark skin.

She went on to qualify, "Now rubies, diamonds or sapphires are a different matter. Your skin has to be like the August moon – pale like the cream from buffalo milk to set those off."

"I will never get to wear diamonds or rubies or sapphires," I cried to Lakshmi, showing her the emerald necklace.

"You can have anything you want; you just have to have money enough to buy it," she replied.

"Oh, I know that," I explained, "but I won't be buying them because they will not complement my skin."

With realisation dawning she asked, "Has that crazy old woman been giving you advice on fashion again?"

When I answered tearfully in the affirmative, she somewhat despondently said, "If you were a retarded child, you could be forgiven for not learning anything of true value." Looking at me pityingly she continued, "If your skin were the colour of buffalo milk, you would have to be either very sick or very dead. You have skin the colour of sandalwood and you will drive men insane with that tone. Pale skinned women are boring. Look at those poor Angrez, they are stuck with women who look dead and act dead."

"Lakshmi, I want to be beautiful, not smart," I replied. "Anyone can be smart, not everyone can be beautiful."

"When you are smart and accomplished, your beauty will shine through. You will be so gifted that you will be prized for your intellect more than your skin color. Now get back to your books," she commanded.

Sometime in early childhood, I abandoned my dreams of eternal good looks to something more practical. I knew that I had to do something that would make me different, marriageable, acceptable and rich.

"If I am never going to be pretty, I am going to be respected and rich," I proclaimed.

I decided I was going to aspire to be like my aunt Anna; I too would become a respected doctor. This was a goal that did not require the intervention of an indifferent or capricious Maker. *I* was going to do it. I resolved that I would observe my aunt very closely to imbibe the star quality that she possessed. In the end, I too would set my sights on going to medical college and become a doctor.

❖

Soon after the family moved to Hyderabad, my maternal grandfather Samuel caught pneumonia and died. Ammachy then moved in permanently with Anna, her husband and their two sons. Although the house in theory belonged to Anna, no one ever thought of it as being hers; it was tacitly acknowledged that it was Ammachy's house. Ammachy had become the materfamilias of this grand household which was palatial with its own magnificent garden and numerous servants.

Trades people with the finest of wares from far away places would come to the house at the beginning of every month. Since Anna was extremely wealthy, they knew that they had a ready

and willing customer for their merchandise. Ammachy was the
other half of the equation. All the furnishings for my aunt's home
and articles for my aunt's wardrobe such as saris, negligees,
jewellery, hair ornaments and such, were procured by Ammachy.
Having been raised in a wealthy household as a child, Ammachy's
tastes were quite refined and exclusive. The articles she acquired
were exquisite, precious, and invariably expensive. The single
exception to this formula was Anna's shoes, which Anna chose
for herself.

It was always a great day filled with anticipation for us when
Mummy packed us into the car to go to Ammachy's house to
watch all the haggling and carryings-on with the merchants. It
was even more enjoyable to see, touch and smell the multitude
of offerings.

Anna had a dressing room which was larger than the living
rooms of most houses. The walls were lined with rosewood, ebony,
cedar and teak armoires which contained the purchases made for
her by Ammachy. There were armoires for saris worn to ordinary
occasions, armoires for saris worn to special occasions; and then
there were armoires for nightwear, armoires for soaps, toiletries
and perfumes, and so on. Some made of steel were always kept
locked and reportedly contained her vast collection of jewellery,
gold and precious stones which she was rumoured to have received
as payment for delivering babies for the aristocracy.

The widest of the armoires housed row upon row of shoes
in every colour imaginable. Anna's shoes were made by a Chinese
immigrant who called himself Mr. Ching – Mr. Yehuda Ching.
Remarkably, the shoes he made for my aunt were incredibly ugly.
They were clumsy looking things, but this was not Yehuda Ching's
fault. My aunt insisted on wearing shoes that looked like
clodhoppers, for what reason I did not know. The workmanship,
however, was impeccable.

The children in the household found Mr. Ching endlessly
fascinating because he was so different in his appearance. Tall

and spare, he looked like one of those well preserved mummies in *National Geographic*. His sallow face was framed with high cheekbones and a square jaw. His remarkable face was crowned with a thatch of spiky, coarse, thick black hair that looked like the horse hair stuffing in our sofas. He always had his hair combed back and tied with an unobtrusive small black ribbon. When he smiled, his eyes which were small and shaped like waterlily petals turned into little slits that slanted upwards. His even, white teeth were so big that they looked like the cattleguards on the front of a railway engine. When he smiled, it seemed as if his smile were painful with his skin stretching over his outsized teeth. Lakshmi named him "Mr. Horse-teeth". His hands were enormous like ham hocks with incongruously long and graceful fingers. The rest of him stayed hidden behind the strange clothes he wore. His syntax was atrocious and his pronunciation even worse, particularly with his "Ls" and "Rs". He said he was a Chinese Jew which was why his given name was Yehuda. Up until that point, I had thought that all Jews looked like the Jesus Christ on the Catholic calendars of our old cook Sebastian – blond hair and blue eyes with a docile expression holding a bleeding heart in hand. But after seeing Mr. Ching, my idea of what Jews looked like was radically altered and totally confused.

One fine summer Saturday, Mr. Ching arrived with his cousin, Yehuda Chang. Mr. Ching said that his cousin was from Khirgizstan.

"Many of my cousins there, running Silk Road." As usual, his English left a lot to be desired.

Yehuda Chang looked nothing like his cousin Yehuda Ching. He was even taller and bigger-boned than his cousin. He was so handsome that most of the women along the lane leading to Anna's house would stop in their tracks just to get an eyeful of him. His green eyes were the colour of the finest emeralds fringed with eyelashes that were strangely thick and very dark for a man with hair as blond as his. His nose was high-arched giving him the look of a regal bird of prey. His skin was like the shoe leather Mr. Ching used for my aunt's shoes – ruddy, dark, and criss-crossed with fine lines from years of exposure to the sun of the northern deserts. He dressed in voluminous djellabas, "like *Lawrence of Arabia*," I thought. He strode rather than walked with his strange flowing robes adding to the majesty of his stride. His voice was deep and resonated from some distant belfry in my soul.

"He does not look like he is your cousin, Mr. Ching," I remarked.

"He Jew, me Jew and we cousin," said Mr. Ching with finality and ill-concealed annoyance.

"Imagine being so rude," Mummy said, mortified with my forward behaviour. "Now we will have to make it up to the man for your abominable antics and buy something we don't even want." After all, these were trades people and one was supposed to treat them with utmost respect, particularly since they came from far-off lands.

I developed an instant and enormous crush on the green-eyed Yehuda Chang adoring him with all the fervour and intensity of a six-year old novice entering a convent. His djellabahs ballooned into my dreams, his green eyes pierced my every conscious moment and his sonorous voice echoed down the corridors of my prepubescent mind. Finally, not being able to contain my obsession with him any longer, I announced to my family that as soon as I was grown up I would marry Yehuda Chang. When Mr. Chang heard of this, he laughed clapping his hands with delight and said that he had brides in every country and was looking for one in India. He went on to say that I would be perfect for him because I was young and nubile enough to look after him in his old age.

Getting down to business, Messrs. Ching and Chang unpacked their wares for the family to view. There were leather pouches of strange looking roots which looked like wizened old men. "Will give old men rots of strength," Mr. Ching explained.

There were amulets and beads in turquoise, coral and carnelian from Tibet. There were huge chunks of lapis lazuli from Afghanistan. There were prayer wheels from Lhasa and nomadic rugs from Baluchistan. While they were fascinating to me, Ammachy considered this to be gypsy trash and dismissed it as such.

Mr. Chang finally unwrapped a package which was fastened in several sheets of tissue paper. Lying there, glistening on gaudy pink paper, was a dressing gown made of black charmeuse. Embroidered all across the front were gleaming phoenixes and chrysanthemums. The collar folded over like a shawl and was made of pale pink silk to match the chrysanthemums. I could see my aunt's eyes devour it. Her face thickened and coarsened with a strange intense lust. She bought it instantly to wear at night, just before retiring.

I was heartbroken that Mr. Chang had nothing similar for me. Sensing my disappointment, he came back the next day with a gift for me. It was a small pot of chrysanthemum, pale pink like the embroidered ones on my aunt's robe. Mr. Yehuda Chang left the next day and we never heard from him again. I planted the chrysanthemum in the garden, but it did not last more than a week. It was dead within the seven days. In yet another week I forgot all about Mr. Yehuda Chang and his emerald green eyes.

Yehuda's chrysanthemum embroidered gown was the only colourful garment Anna ever wore. In public, being a widow, she could only wear white. But in the privacy of her dressing room she was answerable to no one. My consciousness of my nascent sexuality came there in her dressing room as I would hide behind her cheval mirror and watch as she stepped out of the bathroom clad in her long cotton chemise. Pirouetting in front of the mirror, she would slip into her dressing gown and reaching into the shoulders of the gown, she would slide the straps of her chemise off her shoulders and press her freshly washed perfumed cheek to the gown's pink shawl collar. The chemise would fall gently to her feet with a soft rustle. Holding my breath I would watch Anna dance silently with her reflection in the long mirror. Her long prehensile fingers would smooth the lustrous black folds of the thick silk over her breasts and down her belly, lingering on their way down. There were some evenings when she would take even longer in the dressing room, her hands hesitating and resting every so often as they wandered down, moving back and forth across herself with increasing frenzy and finally coming to rest with a long quiet sigh.

❖

I knew Yehuda Ching was in love with Mummy, although she never gave him any encouragement whatsoever. Mummy was young and lovely when Mr. Ching first came into our lives. Her relationship with my father was almost non-existent by that time and she certainly was young enough to have enjoyed the attentions of a man who clearly adored her.

He would bring little gifts for her every time he dropped by – a little jade charm, an embroidered silk purse, Chinese incense sticks, and the like. One day, he came to the house in a lorry and unloaded a large Chinese glazed pot.

The pot was larger than both Rachel and me. We had to stand on a set of bricks to peer in over its edge and it was wider than it was tall. It was an unprepossessing ugly brown and the rampant tigers in bas-relief on the outside of the pot were an even more unappealing yellow.

The idea, Yehuda Ching explained, was to make a lily pond in the pot. The only place to buy water lilies was at *Bagh-e-Aam*, the Public Garden – a botanical garden and zoo commissioned by the Nizam for his subjects. Yehuda Ching was the first to take us to the Bagh-e-Aam.

Once we entered the Bagh-e-Aam, we entered a world far different from the city. There were beautifully laid out gardens and fine lawns enclosed by tall crenellated gates. There was a meandering stream in the garden with well-manicured banks. The stream fed several ponds on the premises. Several black swans made their homes around the ponds and the stream.

The Nizam's gardeners raised a variety of water lilies and lotuses for the ponds and the stream. The water lilies had slender petals and were much smaller than the lotuses. They came in many brilliant colours – purple, lilac, yellow, fuchsia and white. The lilies floated on the water without an apparent stalk. The lotuses were in a different class altogether. They had large petals, large enough to drink water out of and their blossoms grew on a long stalk. When the blooms had not yet opened up, the stalks would stand right up out of the water. But, by eventide when the flowers eventually bloomed, the stalks would droop with their heavy load. They flowers came only in one colour – a faint dusky pink that faded to purple at the tips. While the water lilies were without fragrance, the lotuses had a heavy musky scent.

If we went to the garden during the day, the lotus buds would be tightly closed and wrapped around the center. But by evening, when the lotuses unfurled their petals, they released their fragrance on the city. This was the time when the bustle of the city would reach its most feverish pitch. There would be the noises of the buses and motorcars, horns honking, vendors hawking their wares, rickshaws and cycles with their bells clanging as people would be wending their way home. The heat and the dust would rise and stay suspended in the air until all of a sudden, as if the Great Conductor of the Great Orchestra had raised His baton and then suddenly dropped it to usher in the grand finale, the sounds of the city would die down. The heat of the day would sink back into the earth like some retreating demon only to rise up again the next day.

We brought the water-lilies home wrapped in newsprint, dripping ink-stained water all over our clean white frocks. We didn't care – this was a great new adventure. Mr. Ching filled the pot with water and floated the lilies on the surface.

Mr. Ching's devotion to Mummy continued for several years in the form of small gifts. Mummy neither acknowledged his feelings nor did she reciprocate them. Her attitude of *noblesse oblige* managed to keep Mr. Ching's unrequited passion at bay.

Yehuda Ching eventually decided to leave India. He came by the house to bid us farewell. He was no longer dressed like a Chinese man. Even his shuffling gait had been replaced with a firm footedness that surprised us all. He wore regular Western clothes and a small cloth saucer on his head.

"I am going to Israel," he announced. Surprisingly, he had lost his Chinese accent.

"What is that?" I asked pointing to the funny looking cap on his head.

"It is called a Yarmulke," he responded.

He had his hands poised behind his back. His eyes were twinkling with mirth as he presented me with an elaborately wrapped parcel. It was a red packet of specially made Chinese paper that looked like oilskin. He unwrapped it for me. Inside was a fine gold pendant in a design seemingly made up of several swastikas. The pendant was suspended from a leather thong. He fastened the thong behind my neck and the pendant danced enticingly on my chest.

"That is the Nazi cross," I said fingering it with curiosity.

"Indeed it is not," he replied. "It is an ancient religious symbol for well-being. *Su* – good; *asti* – being. It represents Shiva in his dancing form: Lord of the Dance. When Shiva dances, his limbs are positioned liked the swastika. Only he can do this dance."

"Oh thank you, Mr. Ching!" I said wrapping my arms around his neck.

"Oh, by the way, my real name is Yehuda Haleevie," he said extricating himself from my skinny brown arms.

"So why did you call yourself Ching?" I wanted to know.

"I didn't, Indian government did. Easier to give Chinaman Chinese name than name of Jew," he said lapsing back into his

Chinese speech – dropping the last consonants, again mixing the Ls and the Rs, and delivering an entire sentence in his familiar singsong fashion.

He took tearful leave of all of us. He gave my mother a beautiful jade bangle – a perfect circle of bright vibrant green. He said it was Imperial jade. As he slipped it on Mummy's wrist she was visibly embarrassed that a stranger would touch her hand. Since this was his last day in Hyderabad, nobody said anything. On any other day, he would have been rewarded with a stinging slap for the undue and unwelcome familiarity in touching a married woman. It would have been impolite and ungracious to remove the bangle in his presence, but as soon as he left the house, Mummy removed the bracelet and put it away.

We were never to see Mr. Ching again.

Had she succumbed to Yehuda Ching's advances, our prospects of marrying into families of worth would have vanished. But my mother stayed on course, totally focused on us and our futures. She was determined to deliver us blameless and chaste into the households of our future husbands, no matter what the personal cost to her.

❖

As a captain in the First Lancers of the Nizam's army, Mummy's brother, my uncle Benjamin, cut a striking figure in his uniform. He was a handsome man with a deep and lovely laugh. During the Great War, Benjamin fell madly in love with a vivacious and showy woman named Gracie. Gracie was in the WAACs (Women's Army Auxiliary Corps) when my uncle Benjamin met her. Gracie was so completely different from anyone we knew. She was always laughing and flirting outrageously with everyone and everything.

One of the most sensuous acts that I have ever seen was Gracie smelling Mummy's roses. Mummy had grown roses close to the drawing room window so that their perfume would waft in through the open windows in the summer. An endless variety bloomed all through the winter until the southwest monsoons hit. The most exotic of these were the King Edward roses. They were an ancient variety that she had acquired from gardens in the Muslim quarter of the old city. They roses were like huge pink goblets of heady musky perfume. On her very first visit to meet us I watched Gracie, from the dining room window. She stopped at the foot of the steps leading up to the house to look at Mummy's rose garden. The King Edward roses were in bloom at the time. She reached over to draw one of the flowers to her and proceeded to bury her face in the middle of one of the gigantic blossom. Then she raised her head, closed her eyes, and looking up at my Uncle, she smiled in ecstasy.

Gracie was tiny, extremely curvaceous, and wore her clothes such that no one was ever left in any doubt as to her endowments. Her hair was a mass of unruly curls instead of being bound in the tight and severe chignon like all the other women in the family. She also painted her nails, used lipstick, and smoked cigarettes with a long, fancy cigarette holder. "Anyone who would paint herself up like that is just a strumpet," Ammachy commented when she first set eyes on Gracie. "Look how all the men hover around her. A Jezebel, that's what she is." This of course made us all the more fascinated with her. There was little love lost between Ammachy and Gracie, whom she clearly saw as not being good enough for her only son.

In his lovesick state, Benjamin announced over everyone's objections that he intended to marry Gracie. To the distress and consternation of the family, he even deviated from the dowry routine by refusing to demand any. Ammachy claimed that her heart was irretrievably and deliberately broken in the process.

Fidelity was a silliness that Gracie had little time or patience for throughout the course of their marriage. As a result, Benjamin was frequently heartbroken. But, Gracie would always make up with him in the most charming manner and all would soon be forgiven and forgotten. Peace and happiness would again reign in their little kingdom until her next escapade. She gave him three young sons and an interesting life. Gracie's hold on Benjamin caused him to stay madly in love with her until the end of his short life.

Among the adults in the family, Gracie had only one ally, my mother. God gave my parsimonious mother two stashes of love, a very fixed and finite quota of unconditional love and second one of the conditional variety. She has been frugal with the first lot apportioning of it out to different people in her life. It was almost as if she would run out of her store of unconditional love if she was profligate and injudicious in her use of it. There were very few people that I knew of who were the beneficiaries of her largesse; I received the lion's share, next was her brother Benjamin.

However, Mummy did have that second cache, a larger amount of conditional love to go around. She doled this out with a little less thrift since it could always be revoked. Those who received it were usually the people who were associated with the beneficiaries of the first kind of love – the unconditional variety. Therefore, by virtue of the strength of the bond with her brother, his wife Gracie became the recipient of my mother's love and protection. This served to protect Gracie from my grandmother, who could be an absolute harridan if she so chose, which she did often enough. If nagging could have been refined and elevated to an absolute fine art form, Ammachy would have been a master at it.

When my sixth birthday was approaching my uncle Benjamin asked me, "What would you like as a gift?"

"I would like to be as beautiful as her," I said shyly pointing to his wife Gracie.

"She is the most beautiful woman in the world," he laughed. "But you can be the second most beautiful."

"How?"

"It is the smell of your aunt Gracie that gives her that air of beauty and refinement."

I did not associate refinement with my aunt Gracie's brand of beauty – it was more of a seduction, primal, elemental and earthy. As a child I could not describe or define any of these things, but knew them instinctively. In any case, I preferred Gracie's kind of magnetism to Ammachy's Ice Queen elegance.

On my birthday, Uncle Benjamin brought me a present of a honeysuckle vine. He showed me how to pull the flowers off their sepals and suck the bottom of the little trumpet-like flower for the reward of a minuscule drop of sweetness. He laughed with delight to see our amazed faces when we accomplished this.

"That smell and taste of sweetness is my Gracie," he proclaimed with the pride of possession showing in his handsome face. "It will thrive well outside your bedroom window. If you smell the honeysuckle every morning, you will become almost as beautiful as she."

I played a deliberate role in the permanent rift that developed between Ammachy and my aunt Gracie. Ammachy discovered that I had planted the honeysuckle vine outside my bedroom window in the hopes that I would be as lovely as Gracie.

"Her brand of looks is not something to aspire to," she said within earshot of my uncle.

Benjamin looked up, his face reddening. "My wife is the most beautiful woman in all of creation."

I added to the imminent explosion. "She is as beautiful as a cinema actress and you are not." This elicited another of Gracie's lovely tinkling laughs.

"Cinema actresses are women of dubious character," Ammachy said with enough venom so that everyone knew that she had obliquely referred to Gracie's cuckolding of her husband.

Inevitably, my poor uncle was forced to take sides because of my unreasonable worship of beauty.

To avoid the immutable discord and disharmony between his wife and his mother, he requested a transfer to one of the outer provinces of the Nizam's dominions.

It was early in summer when I watched Uncle Benjamin pack his convertible motorcar with his suitcases. His children were in the back seat and aunt Gracie sat in the front with him. Mummy stood crying in the driveway begging him not to leave.

He backed his car out toward the gate when the most extraordinary thing happened that I would scarcely believe had I not seen it with my own eyes. On my father's side of the garden was a custard apple tree. One moment it stood perfectly still, and the next, it leaned over so that its branches got caught around the car. It was almost as if the tree had embraced the car and was loath to let it go. All of the servants were standing respectfully in the driveway. Suddenly a high keening sound emanated from the tree setting off an unbelievable wailing from those who stood there witness to the event. My sister Rachel was too young to understand what was happening. I, myself, was trying to make some sense of all the crying and carrying on.

The maali's wife said it portended evil. Moving rapidly for an old woman, she flew to the side of the car and begged Uncle Benjamin not to leave. He smiled at her indulgently and reassured her that all would be well.

Later that year he contracted typhoid and was forced to return to the city for hospitalisation and treatment. Uncle Benjamin died shortly after returning home at the age of only thirty-three. Ammachy consoled herself with the fact that since both her son and Jesus Christ had died at the age of thirty-three, Benjamin had gone straight to Heaven and all was forgiven of those who had remained behind.

Even in death, the women who said they loved Benjamin the most – Ammachy and Gracie, quarrelled over the most trivial things, what he should be dressed in, whether it was to be a military funeral and whether the coffin should be teak or rosewood.

In utter disgust, my mother took charge and brought Uncle Benjamin's body from the hospital morgue to our home rather than my grandmother's. In India in those days, there were no funeral homes; bodies were brought home for viewing and final services. We watched as the pallbearers stumbled up the steps and into the living room. The coffin was placed on a temporary bed-like platform that had been constructed for the viewing.

Mummy's "King Edward" roses were plucked and woven into garlands with scatterings of tinsel, jasmine and rosemary. Large pink mounds of the King Edward roses covered his lifeless body, his hearse and his coffin. King Edward roses had been among my favourite flowers. They now came to be a reminder of death, permanent loss, and broken promises. Their scent, once exotic, now seemed cloyingly oppressive and revolting. The rose garlands and flowers swathed the coffin and the platform. Enormous blocks of ice were placed in tubs under the bed as it was said to delay the decay of mortal remains in the oppressive heat. Fans whirred listlessly overhead to circulate the air, which had become stifling and heavy. The women were crying and the men spoke in hushed tones while the unattended children rented the air with mindless chatter and laughter. The Syrian Orthodox priests added to this cacophony with their falsetto, chanting *"Kyrie Eleison"* in Aramaic and endlessly swirling censers filled with *sambraani* – the special blend of frankincense around the coffin. The cloying fragrance of the frankincense and the musk roses hung in the lifeless air over the lifeless body. The old woman who had looked after my uncle when he was a child set up a high pitched wail. Soon thereafter, others joined in. The children looked at each other with a desire to escape this strange and apparently meaningless activity.

Next it was the turn of the Anglican priests. Mercifully, they completed their rituals with efficiency and dispatch. It was completed with that staple Anglican funeral hymn –

"*Life is real,*
Life is earnest,
And the grave is not its goal.
Dust thou art to dust returnest,
Was not spoken of the soul."

I peered under the sheet at the foot end of the bed surprised to find my uncle's feet still there. I had fully expected that he would have started turning into dust beginning with the feet and moving toward his head until his whole body disintegrated like Ozymandias, the King of Egypt. My uncle had died of typhoid at four in the morning and here it was well after four on the following evening and he still had not turned to dust.

❖

My parents and their families had friends of all faiths. Our house became a gathering place for a wide variety of people who loved discourses on literature, art, music, world affairs and other topics of common interest. Even as young children, we found their Muslim and Parsi friends to be particularly engaging. While Benjamin was alive, he had often been accompanied by his closest friend from the Army – Major Mustapha. We thought of Major Mustapha as Benjamin's brother, and started calling him "Uncle" Mustapha as a result.

Uncle Mustapha was a Muslim aristocrat. He was the most gloriously swashbuckling of any of the men to ever visit our home. He was as tall as a bulrush with fine chiselled features and a flawless face, and cut a swashbuckling figure in his uniform. He had the loveliest and slowest of smiles – a smile which could twist my heart into the tightest of knots. It was not his smile though which held me in thrall; I was fascinated by his nose. It was fine and high arched – like a scimitar I thought. Uncle Mustapha had a pimply little son Farrookh and a lissome daughter Aaliya who was a smaller copy of his wife Fareeda – a supremely beautiful and refined woman.

It was a couple of years after my uncle Benjamin died that we first came face to face with religious riots in Hyderabad – "Curry pogroms" as we were to refer to them later. Religious and racial strife in our fair city taught us several lessons early in life.

In the late nineteen forties through the early fifties, the Hindus and Muslims were embroiled in a raging conflict. Since we were neither Hindu nor Muslim, we were left alone for the most part.

One day during the riots, there was a huge commotion at the gates of the house-with-the-garden. We looked out and there was Uncle Mustapha rattling the gates, begging for them to be opened. He was wild-eyed with fear and terror. Blood streamed down his face. His beautiful nose was crushed and in its place was a mangled mess of flesh, blood and bone. He had his dog Bowzer with him. Our Hindu servants looked on without moving. Mummy and Papa went racing down the steps. They opened the gates and dragged him in. They hid him in the storeroom behind the large gunnysacks of rice and wheat.

By nightfall, there was a huge crowd outside the gates with staves and sticks demanding that we give up any Muslim we might be harbouring. Mummy walked to the gates with a bravado which I am sure she did not feel. Bowzer followed her while she addressed the crowd, telling them that no Muslim was being hidden on the premises. They seemed convinced that she was telling the truth and began to leave. However, Ram, one of the youngest of the hooligans in the crowd whom we recognised as the boy who once worked in Uncle Mustapha's garden, looked intently at the dog for a moment.

"Come here, Bowzer," he said as he knelt down to pet the dog. There stood Bowzer, wagging his tail happily at the one friendly face in the rabble. Ram looked up at Mummy with a triumphant look in his eye having caught her in a lie.

"He left the dog with me before going away to Pakistan," was her explanation. The crowd then immediately fell on the poor dog and mercilessly beat him to death seemingly satisfied with Uncle Mustapha's proxy. Finally they turned, as if on one heel, and left as abruptly as they had come. That is the only instance that I have ever heard of an animal dying the death of a religious martyr.

We did not see Uncle Mustapha again until one chilly winter evening some years later. I was sitting on the verandah, doing my homework with Mummy, when he drove up through the gate in his gray Vauxhall motor car. The car had suitcases tied to the top and loaded in the trunk. His wife and his son Farrookh were in the car with him. His daughter Aaliya had died the year before in one of another Hindu-Muslim skirmishes.

Uncle Mustapha looked very different from what I remembered of him when my Uncle Benjamin was alive – he was now aged and defeated. It was not the same handsome man who came limping up the steps. His scimitar nose was replaced by a broken, misshapen one. He looked drawn and haggard, soul-weary and beaten. His arms were loaded down with three packages. Two of the packages were wrapped in brightly coloured foil and the other was wrapped in burlap.

Papa came out of the house to greet him and they embraced each other. Nothing much was said. Uncle Mustapha handed Papa the burlap package which contained a rare Baynishaan mango sapling, the one that Papa had yearned for to complete his collection. Both of them wept unrestrainedly for a long while as Mummy looked on in sorrow. She reached out and touched the white scar which ran down his forehead to his nose and spilled on to his left cheek which was caved in. Extricating himself from the embrace, Uncle Mustapha ran hurriedly down the steps, got in his car and was gone – gone from the religious strife of Hyderabad and gone from our lives.

We immediately tore open the remaining foil-wrapped packages. The smaller one was significantly heavier than the other; it was a cast iron statue of Bowzer, Uncle Mustapha's dog. The other package contained a porcelain plaque of Field Marshal Montgomery with a personal statement from the Field Marshal himself to the then Subaltern Mustapha commending him for his extraordinary valour in war. The plaque has long since disappeared, but the statue of Bowzer still sits on a bookshelf in our home, propped up on a hymnal after its leg was broken off somewhere in time.

At sundown that very day, my father and mother, in their only joint effort in the garden, dug a deep pit, filled it with compost and gently set the Baynishaan sapling into the ground. The tree flowered profusely the following year and the very first fruit was eaten on Aaliya's birthday. We named the tree Aaliya Baynishaan in honor of "Uncle" Mustpha's deceased daughter.

4

Adornment, Artifice and Awakening

I WAS ONLY A YOUNG CHILD WHEN MUMMY DECIDED TO SEND me to an evening school to learn Indian classical dancing in an attempt to coax some inner beauty and grace out of me.

"Classical Indian dances come in several flavours," the principal of the dance school explained. "The choreography, the accompanying music, and the costumes differ wildly based on their ethnic and geographic origins."

Mummy selected bharatanatyam for me. I might have done better at one of the more delicate northern dances that were pretty and not quite as rigorous and disciplined. But this was not to be. Mummy was adamant about her selection as she felt that dance had to be strong, with purpose and to convey meaning – such as the essence of India. Pointless light cavorting on a stage accompanied by northern music was a personal affront to her sensibilities.

Personally, I had no interest in learning this or any form of dance. I merely went along with it to humour Mummy, who believed she had a virtuoso on her hands. So, I was packed off to dance school every evening after regular school to learn to become the most skilled dancer in India and make my mother proud.

I was initially seduced by the jewellery that one wore for the official debut – long garlands of flowers fashioned from fine gold; heavy earrings chased with diamonds, pearls, emeralds and rubies in elaborately coiffed hair; sapphire and moonstone chokers, rings, bangles and bracelets of gold that glinted alluringly with every pirouette. However, there was one item I had not counted on – the anklets.

Unlike the elaborate gold jewellery which was only worn on the days of public performances, the dancers always wore tight heavy silver anklets with myriad small bells on them weighing about two pounds apiece. The idea was that the bells would tinkle prettily in tune with the dancer's steps. More importantly, they would weigh the dancer down so that the steps would be well considered and ponderous.

I became increasingly disillusioned when I discovered that much of the jewellery was fake – made out of base metal, tinsel and brightly coloured glass. In some long forgotten age, the jewellery had likely been real and was probably the bequest of kings and princes to their favourite temple dancers.

I chafed at the discipline, the extreme athletic prowess that was required, and the pointlessness of it all. I could see neither grace nor beauty in any of my movements. I was convinced that "elephantine grace" was a phrase coined especially for me. Furthermore, I detested the man who taught us dancing. I was also clearly his least favourite pupil because I was ill-disciplined, rebellious, contentious and sulky. I found that all my missteps were detected by him as he paid close attention to the rhythm and the cadence of the anklets against the drummer's beat. I protested to him that the anklets hurt and I wanted them removed.

"Without them, you can hurt yourself," he warned sternly. "The anklets will make your legs powerful and muscular. They will center you and keep you captive to the dance."

"Without those anklets," the drummer added, "the steps and movements can become wanton, abandoned and without discipline."

I complained long and bitterly about the anklets and how they shackled me. Mummy was unmoved by my protests or my tears.

"Shackles have their uses," she said. "To learn when to don shackles and when to shed them is the beginning of wisdom."

Many Indians believe that God's representatives on earth are one's parents, teachers and lovers. Teachers who introduce the student to the art of dance are the object of great veneration and adulation. It is that first teacher who opens the fledgling dancer to the possibilities of the dance and the potential within that is awarded all the praise and accolades, not the dancer. Radha – the star pupil in our dance class, was my first true teacher of the art of the dance.

Radha could not have been more than twelve when I first met her. She was short and squat; her skin was pockmarked from smallpox. Her teeth were uneven and splotchy and her facial features were unremarkable – ugly even. It mystified me that she was the dance instructor's favourite pupil until one day I was allowed to observe her.

When Radha started to dance, those who watched would lose themselves in her grace and her style. Once the dance started, that homely face would be transformed in a flash to show pain or sorrow, anger and humiliation. Her most intriguing dance was the "Dance of Awakening". The ecstasy on her face coupled with the sinuous grace of her body released us from our earthly preoccupation with our perceived limitations – we forgot the squat body, the hopelessly ugly face and the dreadfully flawed skin. All we could see was this heavenly creature who transported us into another world. I was very young when I met her. I waited shyly in the wings of the dance stage to talk to her.

"How do you do it?'" I asked. "Change into a goddess, I mean."

"You have to be awakened by a god," she replied. "The Dance of Awakening is important. When a god touches you into wakefulness, you can never be ordinary or ugly ever again, no matter what the mirror tells you."

With that, Radha changed my perspective and instilled in me an appreciation for the art of the dance and the adornments that accompanied it. I wanted to dance like her and be awakened in the process.

❖

"Decent god-fearing Christian women don't need to learn to dance. Only heathens condone the manners and lifestyles of common *nautch* girls." This was a barb from Ammachy to my mother.

"I like learning to dance, Ammachy. I get to wear coloured silks and jewels," I said in a vain attempt to defend my mother who rarely needed someone else to do so. "Besides, I will become awakened when I dance."

"Decent god-fearing Syrian Orthodox women only wear white," Ammachy continued disapproving of my inclination for bright heathen colours. "Colours are only for seduction. Your Uncle Benjamin's wife Gracie was a case in point. Good Christian women don't need to seduce."

"That's all very well for you to say," I retorted. "Beauty is effortless for you. I have to devise camouflage to distract from my defects."

"One has to be grateful for what God gives one. He gave you life and that ought to suffice." Clearly she did not want to continue the discussion any further.

Ammachy and my aunt Lizzie always dressed traditionally in white *chatta-mundu-kavanis* looking like a pair of splendid albino peacocks. Even their walk resembled the strut of the peafowl. Their ivory coloured clothes never seemed to get soiled. The *Mundu* was a sarong type garment that was draped and tied to fit snugly across the waist. After the length of cloth had been wrapped across the lower part of the body, the excess would be folded into fine pleats which hung out over the buttocks in a fantail. The *chatta* was a shapeless blouse that looked like a loose fitting T-shirt and the *kavani* was a length of fine voile to cover the breasts, which was worn only when going out. The most adornment that Syrian Orthodox women would allow themselves was a tiny rim of gold on the kavani.

"Part of the preparation of raising girls in a strict Orthodox Syrian Christian household is to insure that they will be adorned only by their God-given beauty and not by a lot of flashy jewellery," Ammachy would say.

"It must have been the Sabbath when it came time to hand out beauty to me. Almighty God took a rest that day and then He forgot me," I would retort.

"The idea is that you should develop your inward beauty which will shine through and compensate for any other troubles," my mother would say mildly trying to forestall the storm of tears and impotent rage boiling at my ugliness.

"No coloured adornment should ever be used – no glass bangles, no make-up, no red dots on the forehead," Ammachy went on.

"What about the gold jewellery, huh?" I asked eyeing her gold bracelets and not so insubstantial necklace.

"This is not adornment, it is a sign of how God has blessed me," she rationalised.

Beautiful women like Ammachy, my mother, my aunts or my sister looked beautiful without artifice, and the homely women like me stayed the way God intended them to, propped up by sizeable dowries.

Nail polish, lipstick, other artifice and adornment were strictly forbidden in our home. I had very little recourse to compensate for my lack of outward beauty but to resort to secret little tricks out of sight of my parents and known only to us and our servants.

All through childhood, I could depend on a very active imagination and resourcefulness to help overcome the curse of being plain in a household of beautiful women.

The gates opening into the garden were large and made of wrought iron. Rachel and I would frequently open one of them and I would climb halfway up, swinging back and forth on it. Mummy grew Rangoon creepers along the gateposts. Less than half the summer had passed after the creepers were planted when it seemed that they grew and flowered in wild abandon. Soon the gates were festooned with cascades of salmon and scarlet flowers.

Rachel and I would pull the petals off the Rangoon creeper flowers and stick them on our fingernails with spit, pretending that we were grown-up and had long painted nails like Gayatri Devi – the Maharani of Jaipur. These petals were a safe substitute and offered the same flight from reality. I could always simply pull them off without having to incur my father's wrath or displeasure and we would not have to hear of any of the tales of women who put on nail polish. I had a pretty good idea of what my otherwise gentle father thought of nail polish. We had heard veiled tones of warning, of course, that Lot's wife had turned into a pillar of salt because she tried to get back to Sodom and Gomorrah to put on her nail polish.

I was six years old when a neighbour – Mrs. Khader gave me a bottle of Cutex. Mrs. Khader was an Englishwoman married to a Muslim Nawab. She was always full of laughter and generous to a fault. She was a wonderful cook, except for steak and kidney pie, which she served up on special occasions. The dish smelled strongly of goat urine and looked equally unappetising but we loved her dearly and did not have the heart to tell her that we abhorred the concoction. Her husband's failure in business did not seem to take the joy out of her existence. Life for her was always at best a matter of laughter and joy, and at worst a matter of reflection and inward prayer.

I came home one day with the bottle of nail polish, my newly acquired treasure that had come all the way from England. My father took one horrified look at it and before I could fathom what was happening, he had snatched it from my hand and flung it in a wide swinging arc over the garden wall and into the stream which meandered behind the house. The lid had come undone in the process and I could see the cyclamen pink droplets showering their way down from the arc. For many days afterward I would squat on the driveway in dumb grief looking at the drops that had found their way on to the asphalt, over the manhole cover and into my father's side of the garden.

The drops of nail polish were like the fabled blood of Abel, crying to Jehovah from the stones demanding revenge. And Jehovah dutifully delivered as I had expected He would.

For some unfathomable reason, Papa decided to remove the manhole cover with its drops of Cutex. Rachel and I stopped our hopscotch game to watch him, and before our horrified eyes, he dropped the heavy disc on his foot. From where we stood, we could hear the crunch of his bones and the cry of his pain. Mummy came rushing out of the house and helped him to the steps. She washed his foot in cold water with far more solicitousness than I had ever seen, and for that matter, was ever to see again for the rest of his life. I felt an overwhelming sense of remorse wash over me as I asked for absolution for having petitioned the Almighty to avenge Papa over a bottle of Mrs. Khader's Cutex.

It was not uncommon for us to start dreaming at a very early age of a securing a good husband. Of course there were several things we could do to help with the selection and ease the process along such as hoping, praying, and indulging in the odd superstition or two, particularly when I felt that I would have to rely upon more than my "inner beauty" to accomplish the task. We could even hope that there was the odd prince that may not yet have come to light. I inwardly hoped that a little supernatural nudging might uncover some royalty among the Syrian Orthodox Christians in the potential pool of candidates.

A whole host of superstitions and stories were invented to escape from the stuffy propriety and orthodox rigidity of home life. One of these superstitions had to do with securing the unsecurable – a prince for a husband. This was the Legend of the Kiss Curls.

As all proper young Indian girls did, we wore our long hair braided in pigtails which hung far down our backs. For those who were fortunate enough to have curly hair, stray wisps which escaped the confines of the braid would coil into tight little curls on the nape of the neck. These were given the fanciful name of "kiss curls".

As the legend went, a prince would come along and kiss the curls. The more curls you had, the more kisses you received. I decided to experiment with the kiss curls.

Delicate wild pink and white *antignon* grew with mad abandon along the east wall of the garden. This was not a favoured planting among our crowd but it was typical of Mummy that she would defy all convention and grow things that others would consider unseemly. Yet when the task was finished and the result was as she had envisioned, she would extract grudging admiration from her detractors with a smug self-satisfied smile. Rachel and I loved the antignon.

"Amazing," I said as I snapped off the tendrils of the antignon vine and fixed them on the back of my neck with spit to form the much desired kiss curls. "It's amazing how you can change your life with spit. I'm going to make hundreds of kiss curls and get hundreds of kisses from a prince."

"What will the prince do after he gives you the kisses?" Rachel asked. She always had the irritating habit of looking past the immediate joy to an irrelevant beyond.

"It doesn't matter," I replied. "I would probably swoon from delight. He will most likely marry me after he has kissed me."

"You will probably have a baby," Lakshmi said from her perch on the verandah where she was cleaning the rice for dinner. The connection between the kiss curls and the babies escaped us, but the promise of having a real live baby to play with was far more inviting than playing with some celluloid doll. Even more importantly, getting princes to marry us was a supremely alluring prospect.

We frantically pulled off more of the antignon tendrils and stuck them on our necks in an ever-increasing frenzy in the hopes of conjuring up babies and princes.

Then the quiet summer air was suddenly split with a heaven-rending scream. There, crawling in my hair was a *cumbly boochie*, a hairy caterpillar. Princes, kisses and babies paled into insignificance relative to the prospect of cumbly boochies in my hair. I jumped up and down trying to dislodge the tenacious little tendrils with little success.

"Maybe, just maybe," Rachel offered, "the cumbly boochie is like the frog that is waiting to be kissed and will turn into a prince that will kiss you back."

There seemed to be some logic to this order of thought so I decided to test Rachel's theory. I figured that since Rachel came up with the idea in the first place, she would make the perfect guinea pig for the testing. I picked the caterpillar up gingerly on the end of a stick and offered it out to Rachel to kiss. Being the great sport that she was, she obliged. It wasn't long after the kiss of the cumbly boochie that her lip swelled up. Mummy had to slather it with lacto-calamine lotion to tame down the itching.

He must have been the wrong cumbly boochie, as he did not turn into a prince. Lakshmi killed him shortly thereafter so he didn't even have the opportunity to transform on the off chance that he might have really been genuine royalty.

"Princes inherit wealth; they don't have to work for it. You want a man who will work for his fortune," Lakshmi said.

"How about a hard-working prince?" I reasoned.

"No such thing," she said with a great finality.

With that she ended the fantasies of the kiss curls and the princes, and with it went my hopes of ever marrying royalty.

❖

Mummy had a friend who once gave her some rose cuttings. They were cut at the correct angle by the maali and planted in the earth. They were very exacting in the care that they needed. After much anticipation and waiting, they put out fresh green shoots. I was soon to discover that this was no assurance that they had "taken". The majority of them eventually died. There were three, however, that grew to "adulthood".

That summer, the cuttings put out their first buds. Rachel and I would wake up every morning and race down to see if they had made any progress. After what seemed to be an eternity, they blossomed into the most beautiful roses in Mummy's garden. They were a perfect golden yellow which shaded into a pale lime green where the petals joined the sepals. The buds were long and tightly curled. The petals swirled around each other in a tight little vortex while the sepals opened up like long graceful fingers reaching for the sky. They smelled of a strange and tangy tea, which was not altogether unpleasant, quite different from the *Rose de Mai* which grew under the window of my father's bedroom.

We named them "The Yellow Drummond Roses" because the man who had given the cuttings to Mummy was an old friend of my uncle Benjamin – a tall Englishman by the name of Drummond, Cedric St. John Drummond, with the St. John pronounced "Sin Jin" as he often reminded us. To us he was "Major Drummond", formerly of the First Lancers. However, Lakshmi informed us he was no longer a major.

"He was asked to leave the First Lancers because he did unspeakable things," she said.

"Like what?" I asked, "To whom? Who asked him to leave?"

Lakshmi had a uniquely well-honed talent. She could drop a salacious statement into the afternoon silence like poking a stick in to a wasp's nest. Then she'd listen to the clamour it generated with a masterfully feigned surprise. I stared at her intently seeking to have my enormous curiosity satisfied.

"It was the Maharani Victoria that asked him to leave, who else?" she replied.

"But the Maharani has been dead for many years."

"Well, she did," Lakshmi said with an exasperated finality which clearly would not tolerate any more silly questions. She finally relented and went on, "It was to Major Mustapha's daughter, Aaliya, that Major Drummond did all those unspeakable things. She died from the disgrace of it." And here we thought that Aaliya had been killed during a religious riot. Since there was no more explanation forthcoming, we subsided into silence thinking of poor sixteen-year-old Aaliya. She was tall, lissome and lovely. She had long, thick, dark hair which reached down to her ankles. Her skin was a golden olive with nary a blemish.

Major Drummond came by one day on his bicycle to check up on his roses when I was around six years of age. I was sitting on the steps with my head resting on my hands, my elbows on my knees, and my eyes closed soaking up the late afternoon sun. Papa was at work and Mummy and Rachel were asleep. The servants were in the back of the house probably also taking their afternoon naps.

"Why are you sitting in the sun?" he asked of me. "Your skin will turn black."

"Oh, I am already ugly," I replied, quite matter-of-factly.

Ammachy had told me over and over again that I was "ugly" and I had accepted this as a fact because she was the ultimate authority on the subject. When she remarked on my ugliness, it was not done with any malice; it was simply a statement of fact, as if she might have been discussing the weather. She did it merely to alert my parents that there might be tough days ahead with large dowries and such to compensate for my obvious homeliness.

"I might as well enjoy the sun," I said opening my eyes. "I will become a doctor so I shan't have any difficulty finding a husband. I am very clever, you know."

"But there are no ugly women, my dear," he replied. "They are all like rosebuds. They just need to be opened up, very gently of course."

He was silhouetted against the sun and appeared in the form of a tall black cutout that blocked the sunlight. A minute later, as my eyes adjusted, I could see him. He was tall and very pink. He wore a white *kurta* – tunic, and drawstring pants. When he removed his *solar topi*, I noticed that he had very little hair, and what he did have was white. He had a moustache which was very full and waxed to fine upturned points on either side. What caught my attention were his eyes; they were green. They were dull green like pond scum, green like the marbles that my cousins hoarded as if they were treasure. The green irises had small flecks of brown on the outer rim, like little sentinels guarding a circular patch of green grass. He placed his *pince nez* over his right eye and surveyed me, moving his head up and down like a mynah bird eyeing an earthworm. His long legs loped easily off his bicycle, which he parked by the steps.

"Come, let me show you," he offered, holding his hand out to me. We walked off toward the yellow roses hand in hand, this very tall very pink Englishman and a very small very dark Indian girl. I noticed his fingertips were stained from tobacco. His fingers were long and his nails were impeccably manicured. With my fist closed tightly around his finger, there was still enough of his finger left over to protrude beyond my fist. He released my grasp and bent over to select the prettiest bud among the yellows and with a swift snapping motion, he broke its stalk and held it out for me to see. I could not see where I looked like this rosebud. My incomprehension must have shown on my face.

"Come, let me show you," he said again. We walked up the steps to my father's side of the house and into his den. It was a bright, minimally furnished room. We rarely entered it except by invitation. There was a daybed along the window, which overlooked the eastern side of the garden. There were two doors leading into the room, one that came off the verandah, and the other that led to the interior walkways of the house. Major Drummond seemed to know where things were. He opened the top drawer of my father's highboy and pulled out a large hand mirror, which I realised was my father's shaving mirror. He took out the shaving brush and held the mirror and the rosebud together. He settled himself comfortably on the bed.

"Come, let me show you," he said for the third time, this time in a husky conspiratorial whisper. I stood there expectantly. He pulled my dress and chemise up and drew my panties down, ensconcing me between his thighs. He opened my legs and set the mirror between them. I had to hold the mirror with both hands, as it was too large for me to support otherwise. I looked into the mirror in wonderment as he gently spread me apart and stroked me with the shaving brush. It was then that I saw what he meant. Down there, I was like a rosebud, tightly curled smooth petals leading into a central vortex. He kept up the slow gentle movements with the brush until I began to feel as if I had eaten a surfeit of marzipan and chocolate.

Suddenly, the back door burst open and my mother came swooping in like the Archangel Gabriel with the flaming sword, followed by the servants. I don't remember what she held in her hand, but I saw it coming in a wide swipe like the scythe of the Grim Reaper. Then there was blood, Major Drummond's blood, all over my chemise and my father's bedsheets.

There was utter pandemonium all around. Mummy was screaming like a banshee. Major Drummond beat a hasty retreat out the door, leapt onto his bicycle and sped down the driveway through the wrought iron gates. My father's shaving mirror shattered into multiple shards and slivers of silver as it fell from my hands. I walked in slow motion to the verandah wanting to thank the major for what he had shown me and return his solar topi and pince nez which he had left behind in the confusion. He didn't seem to care about them any longer.

Lakshmi descended upon me, gathered me into her arms and swept me into the bathroom. She quickly pulled off all my clothes and discarded them into a small heap outside the bathroom door with the blood stained sheets. I stood there naked and shivering while the servants heated water in the boiler, stoking it with charcoal and firewood. Lakshmi kept holding me and stroking my head as if something dreadful had happened to me. When the water was sufficiently hot, she bathed me with far more gentleness than she had ever done before. I even got to use Mummy's special sandalwood soap from Mysore.

"Tell me a story, Lakshmi," I said, pressing my advantage as the victim the adults perceived me to be. I loved Lakshmi's many stories and always found them interesting.

I did not hear the usual impatient, "I have other work to do, Bibi." It must not have been a memorable story because I do not recall it. It was, however, a memorable day.

The servants gathered all the clothes, sheets, the topi and the pince nez in a heap, and under Mummy's supervision, hurriedly burned the pile in the inner courtyard under the tamarind and mango trees.

Rachel, who must have awakened from all the noise, was at the bathroom door as Lakshmi dressed me in clean white clothes. The three of us stood there on the inner verandah looking silently over the balustrade at the fire and smoke until it dwindled into a pile of ashes. The pince nez remained unchanged and lay there glinting in the late afternoon sun.

"What happened?" asked Rachel, still half asleep and dazed.

"I found out that I am not really ugly, even if Ammachy thinks so. I saw so in the mirror. I am like a rosebud, the yellow one."

"Of course you are not ugly," Lakshmi said, turning and looking at me with infinite tenderness.

The rest of the afternoon buzzed with a flurry of activity before Papa came home. New linens were put on the bed and the room was scrubbed clean to remove any traces of blood. There were no telltale signs of the skirmish that had ensued earlier in the afternoon. By evening, the maali had pulled up the yellow rose bushes and replaced them with full grown white ones from the nursery. There was not a hint that the Drummond yellows had ever even been there.

I quickly came to the tacit realisation that I was never to speak of this again to anyone, least of all to my father.

5

Life At School

MY MOTHER SENT US TO ST. GEORGE'S SCHOOL, A "VEDDY PROPAH" school run by the British which was initially intended strictly for Muslim aristocracy. Our admission to the august institution had been secured by my Aunt Anna's exalted position and our regular attendance at the Anglican Cathedral.

Every morning at the beginning of the day we sang the school song:

"Thy daughters O School join together in greeting,
Our home of the present,
Our home till the last.
...School of our joyous days,
St. George's accept our praise,
Loyal and true .... Dum-de-dum, dum-de-dum from Miss Greg's piano...
Is the tri-i-i-i-i-bute we bring." Ta-dum, ta-dum – piano simulation of drum roll.

The founders of the school had commissioned a large painting for the assembly hall. It was a painting of St. George the patron saint of England, the caped fellow who slew the Dragon. St. George loomed above us in the great assembly hall suited up in full armour, mounted on a huge stallion, pinning down a writhing fire-breathing dragon with his trusty lance. He was probably painted by one of the pre-Raphaelites. He looked like a girl from a Rosetti painting – beautiful green eyes, auburn hair and full lips. The only hints that St. George was a man were his muscular arms and the cleft in his chin. Way in the background, there was the requisite distressed blond maiden standing helplessly near a gazebo or mausoleum wearing the medieval equivalent of a wet T-shirt. She could easily have been St. George's twin with a different hair dye and costume. Emblazoned below the painting in gold lettering was our School motto: *Perseverantia Omnia Vincit* – Perseverance Conquers All.

Every morning the entire student body would assemble in the school hall to sing hymns from "*The Book of Common Praise*" and have the school principal start our day off with the Lord's Prayer and the Collect for the Day. The principal always wore her heavy black cap and gown to the morning assembly. When she was so inclined, which was fairly often, the principal prayed a long and lengthy prayer for the Nizam, for the prime minister of India and for the head of the Commonwealth. Then there were prayers for the benighted races of the world who were without the light of God in their lives. The prayers never seemed to end.

And to make matters worse, our principal had a serious stuttering problem. This invariably gave rise to occasions when she would get stuck at some place in the prayer, like a needle caught in the groove of a phonograph record. Her sizeable body would convulse and twitch and the black cap and gown would heave in unison with her erratic motion. The student body would start fidgeting and murmuring. The teachers who stood in single file behind the principal would look on in resignation at this show – *tamasha* as they called it. However, they were hawkeyed and watchful. If they caught anyone one of us giggling, we were verbally reprimanded and sent home with notes to our parents describing our "lack of social restraint and distressing proclivity for common and vulgar behaviour."

To assiduously avoid being labelled as "common", I taught myself a ploy. I would concentrate on St. George and his Dragon. It was during one of these thoughtful moments that I learned to contemplate the school motto and what it could possibly have to do with St. George. Then, one fine day, it dawned on me – it had to do with the horse.

That poor creature had a limpid-eyed chap on his back wearing heavy steel plated armour while fighting a fire-breathing dragon. It must have been tough on the animal, with trying to avoid the heat from the dragon, dodge the creature's evil looking talons, attempt to keep this armour-wearing man seated while the armour got hotter from the dragon's fire, striving all the while not to be distracted by the wailing from the maiden who should have had the common sense to simply run away.

An involuntary "Aha" which accompanied this revelation escaped from my lips. I found myself in the principal's office trying to explain that I was in fact not laughing or fidgeting. I even went to the extent of comparing myself to St. John the Divine who had some startling revelations in his time. Not only did I get sent home with a note, but Mummy was summoned to Sister Kathleen Culshaw's, the principal's office.

"Anner (which is how the British thought "Anna" ought to be pronounced) has great potential if she would just not let her imagination run wild," said Sister Kathleen Culshaw. Mummy was mortified and as punishment, refused to speak to me for a whole day.

Lakshmi, of course, had a different view of things. She was always ready with an opinion regarding the English and was quick to protect us from their influences.

"Those English are lacking in simple gifts; thank God you are not. Imagination makes life bearable," she proclaimed.

At St. George's, the girls' school was separated from that of the boys by an ancient old English graveyard and the Cathedral. We would sometimes scramble over the crumbling mossy walls into the graveyard to look at the plaster or marble cherubs and seraphs that stood guard over their dead charges. While curious about the people who lay buried there, we had little interest in the boys on the other side of the graveyard. We knew that our parents would arrange our marriages. Early in life we instinctively realised that there was no point in letting our hormones rage and push us into situations from which there was no retreat. Instead, we let our imaginations run riot, making up stories about the poor English who lay there dead in a foreign land, far from their own in the service of a vassal country.

This was where the foundations of our educational lives were laid – Rachel's and mine – a Christian family and a Christian school, in a Muslim environment, with Lakshmi, my Hindu guardian.

❖

In the early spring, when the wild *cleome* bloomed on the far side of the garden, the butterflies arrived in hordes. There were hundreds of them all over the garden, fluttering away as we chased them, taking flight into the pale spring sun. I fancied I saw Titania the Queen of the Fairies among those lovely little creatures.

I was in the second grade at the time and Mrs. DaCosta was our class teacher. She was a little Eurasian woman with buckteeth, beady eyes, and a faint moustache above a pinched little mouth which gave her an uncanny resemblance to a rodent. Her loathing of me was only surpassed by my hatred for her. Nothing I ever did was good enough for her; I was always second best. First place in my class always went to Shireen, the daughter of the richest dentist in town. She was a pretty little thing with soft wavy brown hair and a dimpled smile who grew up to be every bit as lovely a woman as she was a child.

Our science project for spring was to draw or paint a picture of butterflies in our gardens and bring one in for a "show and tell" project. Shireen had her father do her drawing for her and the result was beautiful indeed. There were butterflies all over the page. There were wonderful yellow and orange butterflies, others in resplendent purple and turquoise, and more in pink and green. I had never seen any butterflies quite like those, and I am sure, neither had anyone else. It was indisputable that the painting was raucously beautiful. Mrs. DaCosta held it high above her head for the whole class to see. There was no mention that Shireen had not taken part in the execution of her homework. She got all the credit and was graded highly on her father's work.

Not to be outdone, I went home crying to my father and asked him to do the same for me. My father loved to paint and was extremely talented. He smiled at me and set to work.

Any painting that my father did was done with meticulous attention to every detail – from the assembly of the drafting table on which he painted, to setting out the pots of water colour, to his careful choosing of the brushes, to the sharpening of the lead pencils, and then finally, to the painting.

One of the parts of this operation I enjoyed the most was the selection of the colours he was to use. The paints were stored very carefully in beautiful little jars inside a large teakwood trunk. The trunk served as a seat for my sister Rachel and me when it was shut. It was kept locked at all times with a huge brass lock made by a smithy in Liverpool, England, which read "Royal Lock Makers to H.M. the Queen" on the back. The trunk had all sorts of fancy drawers where the paints were stored in some mysterious order known only to my father.

Papa would bring the jars of coloured paint out one by one, holding them up to the light and twirling them so he could read the labels aloud. We loved to hear the strange and lovely names: "ultramarine, alizarine crimson, caerulean blue, azure, burnt sienna, ochre and vermilion", watching all the while with wide-eyed wonder as the paint swirled lazily round and round in the jars.

Papa's brushes were carefully stored in bags made of chamois leather, which he painstakingly unwrapped to choose which ones he would use for the task at hand.

The cleaning rags were not really rags at all; they were old cotton voile leftovers from our summer chemises which were carefully hand-hemmed by the darzi into rectangles. After using them, Papa would have them washed and dried in the sun and then folded to be stored back in the box.

Way at the bottom of the trunk was a long necked pot made of hammered bronze which he filled with water for his paintbrushes. He had yet another bronze pot for pouring water into the first. It had a long sinuous spout and was even more graceful than the first. The duty of filling it with water belonged to Rachel and me. We always jostled with each other to be the first to fetch the water in the pot.

It was a Saturday afternoon in March, as I recall, when he sat down to paint the butterflies in a large art book with blank pages. Rachel had taken advantage of the fact that I had pushed her out of the way to get the water for the paints. She found herself a comfortable place on the teakwood trunk so that the only way I could see the painting in progress was to stand on the other side of the drafting table. Watching my father paint was a fascinating pastime. We watched him for hours on end with rapt attention, Rachel from her perch on the trunk, and I from my stance, pelican-like on one foot at a time at my father's right hand. As the afternoon sun faded into the purple and indigo twilight, the servants drifted noiselessly in to light the lamps in the room.

By suppertime it was done. The palest of yellow fairy creatures filled the page. I gasped in amazement at the spidery little legs and the green veined powdery wings. With deft and delicate strokes, he had painted the flirtatious dancing cleome in the background. And way, way off in the distance, he had painted me in, chasing a butterfly.

I could hardly wait until Monday morning arrived. When it did, I went up to Mrs. DaCosta's table and showed off my painting. She looked at it for a very long time. I could see the smile starting at the corner of her mouth. I could hardly contain my delight. At last, at long last, I had beaten Shireen at the game. My father was far more artistic and talented than Shireen's father, which proved unequivocally that I was smarter than Shireen.

"Go back to your desk," Mrs. DaCosta ordered.

I stood at my desk knowing that Mrs. DaCosta would now announce to the class that I had scored the highest grade on this project. She raised the book up high above her head, just as she had done with Shireen's. The whole class gave an audible gasp at the sheer beauty of the painting. She swiveled around to display it to everyone.

Another gasp then followed as she proceeded to rip the page to shreds.

"No one is to have their homework done by their parents," she exclaimed.

As the rage came boiling up into my throat and the hot scalding tears flowed freely down my face, I reached into the inkwell on my desk and flung the inkpot at her.

"You are a half-breed slut.(seems rather young to be using this language!!) You have little breeding and even less honesty," I screamed as I flounced out of the class. I have yet to know where that came from. My parents had never mentioned the unmentionable "half-breeds" within earshot of us.

My parents' reactions to the entire episode were as predictable as they were different. My father seemed to shrink into himself as if he had been whipped. My mother, on the other hand, drew herself up tall and proud and marched off to school. I can still hear the drum roll and the trumpets in my head as I saw her ascend the steps to the principal's office like an avenging *Boadicea* to the rescue.

The rest of the term was a blur and my classmates and I were never to see Mrs. DaCosta in our school again. My mother would always be there to save me.

❖

Missionaries from different parts of the British Commonwealth ran our school, the school for boys, and the Church. Several of them came from Australia, some from Canada, and the most important of them, from England. There was a definite pecking order among the missionaries based on their country of origin. This translated into the kinds of positions they held; the Australians and the Canadians were assigned to teaching the younger students or teaching geography or history, while the British taught English language and literature to the high school students. The principals of the schools and deans of the Church were always British.

One of the features that was peculiar to the school curriculum was that it included instruction on gardening. The British were passionate about their world-famous gardens and tried to impose their style of gardening on us. Each class was given small plots of school grounds where we could plant anything we desired – as long as it was British. During lunch breaks and after school, we were encouraged to tend to our little gardens.

It followed that we would learn more about the British flowers and plantings that we had only heard of and read about, rather than learning about those indigenous to India. We were encouraged to grow daisies, hollyhocks, dahlias, gerberas, violets and other typical English flowers in our little school gardens. They often mutated to straggly scabrous looking things in the inhospitable climates of the Indian plains and plateau. The only places where these plants would grow as they might have done in Surrey or Kent were in the hill stations of India – where the air was cool and wet – not parched and arid like that in Hyderabad.

The maalis who often helped the students tend their gardens predicted that the British flowers would not do well. The teachers and the students chose to ignore their advice. We found, much to our chagrin, that the gardens were indeed the disaster the maalis had predicted. The worst of these disasters were the hollyhocks. They were pale, dowdy and powdery, with ugly glabrous leaves and unprepossessing stalks. They added very little colour to the garden with their prissy, insipid flowers and made a general nuisance of themselves, shedding their pollen on our clean cotton frocks.

The teachers served to supervise and judge our efforts at gardening. Some of the more junior Australian teachers were awarded the task of offering us advice on what, where and how to plant. One of these teachers was Miss Blakeslee.

Miss Blakeslee was a big-boned, lovely young woman. She had thick brown hair that had a verve and bounce to it, which owed nothing to the hairdresser's talents. Her clear gray eyes would frequently cloud over if she were disappointed with my performance at school. She had broad, high cheekbones and a very straight, unremarkable nose. She sat across from me in Church. I loved watching her mouth, which was unexpectedly wide, smiling in repose and puckering up in disapproval when she caught me staring at her. Somehow, her teeth were not the usual dingy white you saw with the contingent of teachers from Australia.

In her valiant fight against the heat of the Indian summer, Miss Blakeslee wore sleeveless, flowered frocks made of cotton voile. Her necklines were a predictable V, which plunged as much as her churchy character would permit. It was natural for our curious eyes to start at her shoulders and stop at her breasts; they were large and paradoxically pert for their size. "Please God, if you give me nothing else; just give me breasts like Miss Blakeslee." During the silent session at every evensong I attended, this was my one constant prayer. She had the flattest stomach I had ever seen and was quite well put together. My scarred belly would never be flat, but I could certainly hope and pray for great breasts like Miss Blakeslee's to distract potential suitors from my physical shortcomings.

The only physical attribute out of sorts, however, was that Miss Blakeslee had extraordinarily fat and misshapen ankles. Lakshmi had a ready explanation for this.

"The Old Queen, Victoria Regina," she volunteered, "possessed stout ankles." Clearly, since she was the mother of all Britons, they were all the proud owners of this one distinguishing feature – stout ankles.

On a few other memorable occasions, I saw Miss Blakeslee outside of school and outside of Church.

Our study at home faced the road that ran in front of the house. We could peer out from behind the curtains through the mullioned windows to watch what might be happening in the street, this being far more interesting than having our noses buried in our textbooks. One day, shortly before the monsoons burst, being thoroughly bored with the day, I climbed on to the ledge by the windowsill. Outside the window on the other side of the road was a rickshaw. The front of the rickshaw was covered with a *purdah*. It was common for Muslim women to travel in rickshaws with a purdah to preserve their modesty and to insure that they would be hidden from inquisitive eyes.

The rickshaw puller was a young man with skin the colour of roasted coffee and a smile as bright as the sun. It was clear that he had been pulling a rickshaw for some years; he was well muscled and sinewy. He seemed deeply engaged in a conversation with the passenger inside. He laughed often and loudly. This seemed odd to us, since it was not acceptable to engage in idle conversation and chit-chat with rickshaw men – least of all for Muslim women of good families and social standing. Rachel, seeing me absorbed in watching the scene unfold, climbed up on the ledge with me.

We watched in fascination as he presently climbed into the rickshaw which then proceeded to rock gently at first, and then in heaving spasms, drunkenly back and forth for what seemed like an eternity. There was strange squealing noise and then, who should come tumbling out from behind the curtain, but Miss Blakeslee – her dress askew and her hair dishevelled. The next day, the same scene was repeated as if choreographed.

Finally, Lakshmi caught us in our voyeurism and with the stealth of a tiger, she pounced up behind us. The rickshaw had started its mad rocking and I watched Lakshmi's jaw clench. She hurried out the room and on to the road, screaming like a banshee, tearing open the purdah and revealing the rickshaw man and Ms. Blakeslee with their clothes and limbs in wild abandon and disarray in the cramped little rickshaw. We watched from the window in wide-eyed amazement as Ms. Blakeslee and her wondrous breasts came spilling out of the rickshaw. The rickshaw man seemed to shrink into the shadows and blend with nothingness. Lakshmi tore the purdah off the rickshaw and flung it at Ms. Blakeslee.

"Cover yourself and get home," she commanded.

Ms. Blakeslee stumbled backward under the assault and stepped on her voile dress, rending it quite beyond repair. She looked tragic and so like the figure of King Cophetua's beggar maid in my poetry book, it broke our hearts to watch her ignominious retreat. We craned our necks as far as we could to watch her hurry down our street into the churchyard and out of sight.

"There are decent people living here. Why don't you find one of your own kind?" Lakshmi screamed at the retreating figure of Ms. Blakeslee.

"And you," she said turning on the hapless rickshaw man, "be gone! And take your business elsewhere."

"What were they doing in the rickshaw Lakshmi?" we wanted to know.

"Missy came to get her dress repaired."

"Why would the rickshaw man know how to repair her dress? He is not a darzi."

"Rickshaw men are very talented. Now get back to your studying."

Lakshmi subsequently had Mummy install heavy shades on all the windows that faced the street so that we would not be witness to the multiple talents of other rickshaw men.

Shortly thereafter, Miss Blakeslee and her stout ankles fell in love with, and married a fellow Australian, the Reverend Stanley McFarland. Everyone in the parish heaved a collective sigh of relief. God in His Heaven seemed to have quelled the roiling boil of the tropics and our prudish churchy world had subsided back into its customary sangfroid and tepid insipidity.

Reverend Stanley McFarland sang tenor in the church choir with the most nasal voice in the parish. He had a large posterior and a strange waddling gait. This concoction of characteristics, along with his name, earned him the name of "Donald McDuck" from the most irreverent of our crowd. Donald McDuck's only salvation were his incandescent blue eyes. However, Lakshmi quickly put an end to any adolescent crush I might develop for incandescent blue eyes.

"Men with blue eyes," so she claimed, "cannot make successes of their lives." Presumably because they had precious little wherewithal to do anything successfully, she went on to explain.

"The blue-eyed have very little in their heads, Bibi," she said. "The blue is the sky showing through."

After she became Mrs. McDuck, the most astounding transformation in Miss Blakeslee took place. She became pregnant soon after her marriage. When the baby was born, he proved to be an enormously fat little fellow who always seemed ravenously hungry. Most women of substance did not breast-feed their babies – newborns were ordinarily fed a diet of watered down cow's milk. Mrs. McDuck flew in the face of convention and good taste and she doggedly breast-fed the baby like the untouchable women did. This would have been fine, except for the fact that she did it quite openly and in public, which shocked most of us who were not used to displays of this nature from women of class. I figured that this was her nominal rebellion against expected propriety and correctness.

Her change was as swift as it was astounding. Her "ankle stout", rapidly took over. It waged an inexorable march over that magnificent body of hers. Everything became stout. Her pleasing boniness vanished into a blanket of stout.

It was at the same time that the hollyhocks took over the daisy bed in our little school garden.

◇

Schools and offices closed at mid-day during the summer months in India. This was a tradition first started by the British who were known to wilt in the oppressive Indian summer heat. The sizzle would begin in the middle of March as temperatures would start their climb heavenward. The sky would become a large bronze wok up-ended over a blistered flatbread earth during those months. It was so hot by noon that the air danced in a constant shimmer above the asphalt on the road. The days were windless and dry. Even the usually pesky houseflies lay torpid from the heat in the luscious summer lethargy. Relief was not granted until June when the southwest monsoons would come hurtling out of the Persian Gulf and the Arabian Sea and deluge the parched earth with a merciful and torrential rain. We loved the summer when our days were short, hot and full of excitement. Make believe and play lasted all afternoon. Evenings were punctuated with treats from the kitchen, cool mango drinks laced with cold, thick milk and fairy tales read to us by our parents well into the blanketing night.

By mid-summer, schools closed altogether for a six week vacation. It was then that we would travel as a family back to my father's ancestral home in Travancore, at the southern tip of the Indian peninsula. After my father had successfully established himself in business, he actually bought the home in Travancore from my grandfather where we would journey every summer.

It was a pilgrimage of sorts. In addition to the immediate family, the party travelling home invariably consisted of a wide assortment of cousins, aunts, and uncles who were all journeying to their own ancestral homes. My grandmother, my aunt and her sons, my mother, Rachel and I went home every summer, accompanied by our Malayalee servants.

In preparation for the trip, the servants would start packing suitcase after suitcase to tide us through the months of summer. On the day before the journey, the preparations for the cooking would begin. My aunt's Muslim chauffeur would slaughter the fowl according to the strict dictates of the holy Quran, since he could not eat anything that was not *halaal* – the Muslim equivalent of "kosher". The Hindu servants would not eat anything prepared by one of another caste, and since one could not be certain of who might have prepared the food sold at the train stations, it was advisable to prepare one's own food. Special dishes were cooked so that they would last for the three-day long journey to the south. They were packed into tiffin carriers and the containers were stacked one on top of another, held in place by an elaborate system of interlocking handles. Water was boiled to fill *suraahis*. There was a constant supply of sweets and savouries of every kind stuffed into picnic baskets.

There would be books for us to read, games for us to play, and a hundred other things for us to do on the train. The family would reserve a whole compartment which meant that we could spread special mattresses and comforters out on the seats to make ourselves as relaxed as possible. Between the children, there were the usual fights over which of us would get to sleep on the upper berth.

We lost ourselves in the rocking motion of the trains as they went clickety-clack over the rails. We pretended that the wheels sang to the cadence of "Connecticut-Connecticut-Connecticut" while travelling fast over the Deccan plain and slowing down to "Massachusetts-Massachusetts-Massachusetts" while labouring over the Western mountain range. We loved listening to the Anglo-Indian train conductors with their singsong voices, the strident calls of the food vendors and the chai-sellers, the lonely whistle of the train as it wound its way through the hot Indian summer nights, and the hissing of the steam engine as it neared station after station. The terrain changed each day. The first day we steamed through the dry, scrubby vastness of the Deccan Plateau. The second day displayed the brackish salinity of the Madras coast. Finally, by the third day, we were enveloped by the tropical lushness of Travancore. There, the climate, the people, the flora and fauna, the general ambience, every conceivable thing, was different from that in Hyderabad. It was as if we had stepped onto a movie set for Stanley and Livingstone with its dense vegetation, torpid heat and heavy humidity. It was almost as if we were in another world.

For us, the journey was one long picnic. For the adults, it was a different matter. They had to worry about whether there was going to be enough water to drink and bathe. They would worry about the soot from the locomotives and whether the children and their clothes would ever be cleaned of the grime. They worried whether there would be any undue delays on the journey home and whether they would have to wire ahead to inform the servants on the other side of the delay.

Delays along the tracks were infrequent, but when they occurred, it was occasion for great excitement. While my mother and aunt remained in the compartment and worried as to whether or not they would make the connection in Madras, we would disembark with all the others. We would walk up to the front of the train and watch the huge black engine snort steam as it waited impatiently to start again on its long journey. The engineers and young men who stoked the boilers were usually Anglo-Indian. Their hands and faces were blackened with soot thereby accentuating their incongruously bright blue eyes. They watched us as we stared back at them in utter fascination, as if they were a species separate from the rest of the human race. They were not Indians like us, nor were they English like the teachers at school. They lie somewhere in between, all with varying positions on the Anglo-Indian spectrum.

One summer, we were still on the Deccan Plateau and had not yet crossed the Eastern Ghats into the Madras Presidency when the train unexpectedly came to a screeching, grinding and groaning halt. The servants were the first to disembark and came back with the exciting news that a young woman from a nearby village had thrown herself on the track in front of the moving train. Railway officials were being summoned from a major town somewhere along the track to investigate what had happened. This meant that we would be delayed for quite a while.

We walked all the way to the front of the train with the servants holding firmly on to our hands so that we would not be lost in the throngs that surged forward to watch the spectacle. Once at the front of the train, it was advantageous to be a very small child – one could ease one's way in between the milling and jostling adults to get a front row seat for the happenings, which was what Rachel and I did until we found ourselves right next to the engine. There, right beside us, was the young forlorn Anglo-Indian engineer sitting on the platform next to the track crying as if his heart would break.

"Oh God," he sobbed between great gusts of weeping. "I didn't even see her; I couldn't stop in time."

Rachel put her little hand on his shoulder. "If you stop crying, I will give you my chocolate," she told him.

He looked up at us, somewhat startled, and began to smile unevenly through his tears. He put his hand out for the chocolate. We were surprised to see his face. The tears had washed away much of the soot, and there was his face – as pink as any Englishman's.

On the far side of the track, on a makeshift stretcher, was a form covered with a sheet marked "Property of the Indian

Railways". A severed young arm lay across the side of the stretcher which was all we could see before the servants whisked us away.

In the early days of our childhood there were no trains that went directly into my father's village. Instead, we had to disembark at a coastal town which seemed far away from the village. Then, we would take a boat up the backwaters through the estuary upwards into the Pamba River which flowed past the town closest to my father's ancestral home. Servants met us at the moorings there and we then took a taxi to the edge of my father's property. There still remained an interminable trek along the edge of rice paddies by the side of rubber plantations and through coconut groves to get to my father's house.

Every square millimeter of the land was planted or grew something green on its own. There was the bright young green of the rice plants, the deep green of the ferns that grew on the banks, the dull emerald green of the lemon grass, the chartreuse of the amaranthus plants, and the pale yellow green of the nutmeg and mace plants by the well. Curiously, this climate sported very few flowers. One never found any roses or jasmine, no dahlias or columbine; only gardenias, amaranthus, tuberoses and an occasional remarkably plebeian hibiscus.

It was always evening by the time we reached the banks of the Pamba River. Nightfall was imminent by the time we arrived in my father's village. George, who was the major-domo of sorts, led the entourage to the house with a lighted torch. The servants who followed in single file cautioned us to avoid stepping into the rice paddies for fear of disturbing the cobras and kraits that made their homes along the shallow slopes. The remainder of the servants awaited our arrival on the front verandah where they could see the procession of lighted torches weaving its way for over a mile toward the house. We walked past the little rivulets, across a crude plank bridge over a creek, along the mud paths, and finally up the steps into the compound surrounding the home where my father had lived as a child when his mother was alive.

None of the modern conveniences such as running water and electricity, which were available in the cities, existed in the village. The houses had their own wells and septic tanks; kerosene lamps provided light. Summer for us was like a supreme adventure. We bathed from cauldrons filled by the servants rather than from the faucet, and read by lamplight.

The food was also very different from the fare that we were used to during the rest of the year. There was fish aplenty in Travancore and it was prepared in a multitude of different ways served with tangy hot red sauces, or rich yellow sauces redolent with coconut milk. Rachel and I loved mackerel deep-fried in sizzling hot coconut oil after marinating for hours in a pungent paste of fresh ginger and ground Telicherry pepper. There were tiger prawns and shrimp, pompano and butterfish. Vegetables of all kinds abounded in the garden and as such, a wide assortment graced our table at every meal – lightly sautéed, steamed, or stewed. We loved all the variety.

Evening prayer was a big daily household event and a lovely time for gathering. Dinner would be over, the family and all the servants having been fed. Everyone would gather around on the front verandah. My father would seat himself comfortably on the planter's chair where no one else would dare sit without his permission. George would bring out the old family Bible and light the lamp by my father's chair. There would be a reading from the Old Testament and one from the Gospel. A reading of one of the epistles of St. Paul would follow.

There were two large sepia coloured photographs of my grandfather and grandmother mounted on the wall above the door leading into the house. They stared directly down at the Bible in my father's hands, so we knew that my grandparents had selected the readings. The only thing that prevented me from falling asleep or protesting the inclusion of St. Paul and his tedium was the fact that I was convinced that my father was acting on direct guidance from his long-departed parents to do so.

Our favourite part of the whole evening was when the servants brought out the hymnals, which were Anglican. My father's brothers were blessed with beautiful voices and we filled the night with the heart-rending harmonies of the lovely old hymns from the well-worn leather books.

Summer vacation was always too short, lasting only about a month and a half. We had to return before the rains set in. The monsoon season was a dangerous time to travel as flash floods could wash away entire sections of the railroad track and there was always the potential for severe outbreaks of typhoid and cholera. More importantly, school was to begin again.

6

Papa's Exile

A MAN WITH ONLY DAUGHTERS HAD TO BE CIRCUMSPECT ABOUT his life and careful of his surroundings. No taint of dishonour or improvidence could be associated with such an unfortunate person. Furthermore, he could not afford to have his family associate with unseemly people such as those of a lower caste, or Eurasians – those of mixed Indian and English descent. More simply put, he and his family could not associate with people of a background different from his. Our family, like all other Indians, viewed foreigners with suspicion. People of mixed descent were looked upon with distrust and even some degree of contempt for cohabiting with the English.

"What kind of Indian would marry *Angrez?*" we would hear.

To the British, Eurasians were an uncomfortable reminder of their lapses. "We were sent here to govern and improve their lot, not consort with them," was the common sentiment. There were trusts set aside for the support of the Eurasians, but socially they were in a class by themselves. The Eurasians probably felt that it was politically expedient to ignore the Indian part of their background. They wore English dresses, ate bland English food, and deluded themselves into referring to England when they talked about "going back home". This attitude earned them equal contempt from both the English and the Indians.

Across the street from our house-with-the-garden was a rambling house with its own wild sprawling garden. The house belonged to a rowdy, loud Eurasian family named the Cotters. How Eurasians came to live in this neighbourhood was always a mystery and a matter of speculation for all those around.

The Cotter father – Ian, was a handsome man with curly blond hair, blue eyes, and a ready laugh. His wife Irene was as black as the ace of spades with a red gash of a mouth and dark smiling eyes. They had an assortment of children: Ivan who looked like his father, Ivy, Ida, Imogene and India who were all made from the same mold as their mother. They called themselves the Seven Eyes for the first letter of their Christian names and had it inscribed on a plaque, which they had installed on one of the gateposts.

Despite the fact that these Eurasians were the most gregarious and generous of the people who lived in the neighbourhood, the Indian families remained distant and cool toward them.

"They drink beer," said one of our adults accusatorily.

"Her father was a common fisherman or an untouchable," said another.

"The men and women dance with each other and she smokes." These comments were endless.

The Cotters, for the most part, ignored these unkindnesses from our adults.

However, the children from all the houses around loved the Cotters with their ready laughter and their willingness to share their largesse, if they had any. Mr. Cotter was a very good marksman and often bagged interesting game which Mrs. Cotter fixed with imagination and verve. It was at their house that I learned of the taste venison and peacock, of *ghurial*, crocodile and *neelgai*, moose.

One day, Mrs. Cotter made me a small garland of fragrant blooms from some that grew on a Puukenikeni vine near the gate to their house. The flowers were small and shaped like trumpets with an unremarkable yellowish green colouring. It was their fragrance which was so unusual and beguiling – citrus-like with overtones of vanilla and spearmint. My mother loved the flower instantly and wanted a plant for her side of the garden. She decided to give up the usual reserve which she ordinarily kept for the Cotters and ask for a sapling or seeds.

"Mary, I would not do this if I were you," warned Mrs. Cotter. "There is a superstition attached to the vine. Once you plant it in your garden, your husband's affections will be deflected elsewhere."

Mrs. Cotter adamantly refused to give Mummy the vine. This stopped all communication between them and we were expressly forbidden from playing with the Cotter children thereafter. The Cotters must have finally had enough of the cold-shouldering from all the Indians in the neighbourhood and they eventually left for Australia.

After their departure, a young woman who worked with an American company moved into their house. Her name was Linda Beauregard. She was from Louisiana – "Loosiana". Ordinarily, American accents were difficult to understand. We had an even greater difficulty keeping up with Linda Beauregard. Although we understood little of what she said, we loved listening to the long drawl and the slight sing-song quality of her conversation. She was the object of a great deal of curiosity and speculation for the children as well as the adults in the neighborhood.

"I am Cajun," she announced in explanation.

We thought she had said, "I am kitchen."

"How strange! They are named after rooms in their houses," the adults commented.

"Her mother probably gave birth to her in the kitchen."

We were soon to learn that Linda Beauregard's full name was Belinda Beauregard, but she refused to let anyone call her Belinda.

We called her "BB", which was fine with her. Since BB was kind of Indian sounding, like our "Bibi", that made it fine with us too. We readily made friends with her.

My mother, still not to be deterred by Mrs. Cotter's previous warning, urged us to ask BB for a sapling of the fragrant and beguiling vine that she still wanted – the one that Mrs. Cotter had refused to give her.

"Whatever are they called in these here parts dawlin'?" BB asked.

We shrugged our shoulders in unison.

"It is called Puukenikeni in Hawaii, which is where I once saw it. Y'all can have as many as y'all want." Much to Mummy's delight, we went home with a handful of saplings which we planted right away. The maali brought in a large rattan pole to provide the vine with support. In less than a couple of months the vine took off and grew to the top of the pole.

We did not learn until years later that it was the same time that my father had acquired a mistress. Of course we ascribed this dalliance of my father's to nothing other than the planting of the forbidden Puukenikeni vine in Mummy's garden.

❖

When I was not quite nine years of age, my father's businesses crumbled; disaster set in for him and all his ventures. As a very young man, Papa had been eminently successful at running several businesses – he owned several movie theatres, Oriental rug shops, an automobile spare parts concern, a biscuit factory, rubber and coffee plantations, and tea estates. But all this wealth vanished, along with his drive and talent for accumulating it. He had been virtually unstoppable until it happened. It seemed like a row of tumbling dominoes – everything came crashing down. We went from being extremely prosperous to decidedly middle class.

What happened to that drive and that talent and why it disappeared has always remained somewhat of a mystery to me.

I have theorised that he lost his spirit, or more poignantly, that his spirit had been broken – by my mother and the loss of his unborn son. In his mind, my mother and her actions were the causal agent for his failure.

My father lost his sense of identity with the loss of his wealth. Had it been Mummy, she would have picked up the pieces and crafted another life. He, on the other hand, chose to ascribe all blame to my mother. My father's enthusiasm and skill was replaced with recklessness and desperation. He was always going to make that final redeeming kill in business; he would be established in perpetuity and for posterity as the great, wise and intrepid entrepreneur. He progressively ventured out into more and more risky, high yield endeavours. He was determined to show my mother that he could, and would, succeed. But, he no longer retained the confidence in himself nor the support at home to stay the course. He continually failed, badly and repeatedly.

At the first sign of major failure, my mother zeroed in on him. With her uncanny ability to hit her target directly and without error, she would go for the jugular and draw blood with a vengeance. My father was easy prey for her; like the soft underbelly of fish, he was defenseless, without aid or protection.

One evening, my father and my uncle John were poring over their ledgers and accounts discussing yet another unforeseen loss. They heard a soft rustle of a sari behind them when they looked up to see my mother at the door. Rachel and I were playing hopscotch out in the yard. We heard the familiar tone of my mother's voice raised in anger; my father said something softly in return. We couldn't decipher what he had said; I only know that he sounded beaten. I heard my uncle attempting to placate her. Rachel and I both dropped our hopscotch stones and moved as one to the door of his study to listen more closely.

"Nothing you touch will prosper, ever!" I heard her say to him.

Shocked and pained, my father remained silent.

My usually soft-spoken uncle looked at my mother with his wide brown eyes full of unshed tears and said, "*Kaali Zabaan* (This term seems more in use in north India) – black tongue. You will surely visit misfortune on this family."

My mother has a small irregular pigmented area on the underside of the tip of her tongue. Superstitious Indians, and even those who were non-superstitious, avoid conflict with women that have black marks on their tongues. They seem to have the ability to make pronouncements, particularly dire ones, come true.

"Don't trifle with me," my mother turned on my uncle with the aggression of a roused hamadryad – a king cobra. Hamadryads are easily aroused and swift as lightning. They can race with unbelievable speed and strike with unerring ability. My mother could out-distance and out-strike any hamadryad in India.

"It is not my black tongue, you stupid boy!" she hissed at my uncle. "It is your brother's foolhardiness and his pretense to be smarter than he really is that's to blame." She continued her strike, jabbing at my uncle repeatedly with her finger, "You, you support him unquestioningly in all his recklessness, even when you know better."

She dashed away her scalding tears of anger with the edge of her sari and spread her hands in a gesture of supplication to God. "The inheritance of my children is gone like the wind. What will I do now?"

From that time on, it was self-fulfilling prophecy. My father subsequently failed at every venture he undertook. Since she had no great expectations in his abilities to redeem himself or his family, my mother set about to restore our standing with a vengeance. The first order of business was to get the offending cause out of her sight.

Mummy sent my father to work in Arabia and she became the mainstay of our little family.

In the early nineteen fifties, hordes of expatriates from Travancore left for Arabia, always referring to the Middle East as Persia.

"Why Persia?" I asked.

"Because the Peacock Throne is there and we are going to bring it back," Papa replied.

"It was taken as spoils of war by Nadir Shah and now it belongs to them, Papa."

"There are many ways to get back your property other than with the sword, my child."

This sounded like a significant pronouncement and succeeded in silencing me. I later learned that this was a typical trick that adults used to confuse us children into silence.

The Syrian Christians from Travancore were among the first of the Indians to go the Middle East to work in the British Petroleum Company as clerks, accountants or engineers. The unskilled labour pool came from elsewhere in the Indian subcontinent, as well as the Philippines, Korea and so on. The fact that the Christians from Travancore came from old Yehudi stock and were ready to pick up their belongings and leave their families behind to go pitch their tents in the remotest corners of the earth in search of a few more rupees, rupiahs, ringits or dinars, had earned them the appellation of "Wandering Jews".

My father was possibly in the first wave of that diaspora. The odd thing about this exodus was that their families stayed at home in India. This may have been due to the fact that neither the Saudis nor the British wanted the bother of accommodating the families of the workers. Families were not allowed, nor was extramarital cohabitation. There were no Indian women available in Arabia. Arab women were rarely ever seen, and if they were, they were off limits to Indian men and any attempt toward a liaison would bring swift and barbaric punishment. To Indians from a newly liberated India, consorting with white women would have been unthinkable and this forced celibacy ensured a fidelity of sorts.

These men sent money back home while they themselves lived in Spartan facilities in Arabia. Homes, large and ostentatious ones, sprouted up all over Travancore within the decade. Lanes and alleys, which had been lined with very poor dwellings for several years, were becoming well-paved roads sporting large houses with electricity and running water. Wives grew more prosperous looking – sporting elaborately coiffed hair, sumptuous silks, gold and several rolls of *avoirdupois* (fat). They sported mundu, chatta and kavanis of the most refined of cottons. They wore gold ornaments and there was the occasional diamond. Daughters were married off with sizeable dowries supplemented with even more gold. Sons were sent off to study in England so that they in turn could demand, and often get, large dowries and even more gold for themselves.

But before saving money for dowries was even to be considered, all debts that the family had accumulated would have to be paid in full and my father's debts were onerous and many. My mother took an immutable stance; she insisted that none of the wages she earned as a teacher were to be used in order to pay off his debts. She also would not condone his remaining in India to try his hand at any other business ventures. So, my father was banished to Arabia to remake his fortune, pay his debts, and make provision to pay our dowries.

Papa did return home to India practically every summer though. Initially, we would all go to fetch him at the station. He invariably came home early in the morning on the train that arrived from Bombay to Hyderabad. He would be followed by several porters who would unload his steamer trunks and suitcases into the waiting cars.

On one summer arrival, I noticed that some of the trunks were much heavier than the others and required more people to carry them into the house. There was one memorable occasion when one of the *coolies* stumbled and unwittingly jarred open one of the heavier trunks. I rushed over to peer in, and there they were, bar after bar of *Rowntree* milk chocolate sitting on top of yet another layer of box after box of *Black Magic* chocolate.

"Aha! That is why they are so heavy. It is all that chocolate!" I said to Rachel, having solved the mystery of the heavier trunks.

The porters unburdened themselves of the trunks in the drawing room. My uncles hurried to pay the porters and the cab drivers. Then, in painful slow motion, they drew down the blinds and bolted the doors. Sitting down cross-legged in front each of the trunks, my father and his two brothers carefully laid out the boxes of Her Majesty's very own chocolate. Presently, on the carpet on the drawing room floor, there sat numerous neat piles of chocolate.

Mummy and I were known for our weakness for chocolate. We sat down on the floor and delighted at the thought of eating our way through the bars and the boxes. We did not even get to finish one box before something else caught my attention.

My uncle Matthew dusted his hands off after unloading the chocolate and said to me, "Now you go on, run back and play with your sister."

"Why?"

"Because all the chocolate is out; there is no more chocolate left."

"What are all those things left in there?" I asked, pointing to row after row of cotton sacks spread out across the bottom of the trunks, their mouths closed with flimsy drawstrings.

"Just rubbish," he said, "we will have to throw the rubbish away."

"I want to see what kind of rubbish is in those sacks," I persisted.

My poor uncle Matthew, not known for being particularly swift on his feet, was cornered. "Just Arab kind of rubbish," he said.

"Why wouldn't Papa throw Arab rubbish away in Arabia?" I wanted to know. "What is Arab rubbish anyway? Is it very different from Indian rubbish?"

"Let them see the fruits of the servitude," my uncle John finally said with resignation.

With a heavy sigh, my father sat down and opened one of the little "rubbish" sacks. He drew out a heavy bar of gold with the words "Credit Bank Suisse" stamped across the front. I reached out to pick it up, but it was unexpectedly heavy and I almost dropped it.

"How did you get this past customs?" demanded my mother, in a quiet and angry voice. Obviously, she had known nothing of this.

The Government of India strictly forbade the importing of gold. Where gold was about thirty-five dollars an ounce in the "real world", it was worth ten to twenty times as much in India. If one got caught bringing it into the country, the fines levied and imprisonment sentenced would have been devastating.

"I had to bribe them," my father said shortly.

"What's it for?" Rachel asked.

"It's for your dowry, so you can marry the Maharajah of Baroda," said my uncle Matthew with a laugh.

"Who would marry your daughters if you went to prison?" asked my mother in a great rush of anger. "You and your brothers always have to take the easy way to riches and to freedom. You will never learn."

"I intend to start a business again with this gold, Mary," my father replied.

"No, you won't," my mother commanded with great finality. "You will pay off your debts with this gold and you will go back to Persia and make money like all other disciplined God-fearing people."

Finally, my father's debts were paid off. Then, in the eyes of society, we were no longer of questionable value. Paradoxically, it was then that we saw our life of outward affluence melt away. I was to find out later that it was not a slow disappearance of our wealth that crept up on us while we were unaware. Rather, it was a deliberate, planned and remorselessly draconian act.

My mother forced my father to leave the house-with-the-garden. My father then returned to Arabia and Mummy moved us into a smaller house. The leaving of the garden broke my mother's spirit. I remember her walking around the garden at the end of our stay in the big house, gazing at all the plantings she had so lovingly cultivated as if she were about to take leave of dear, old friends. This was the only time in my entire life that I had ever seen my mother sob inconsolably and shed copious amounts of tears.

Leaving the house-with-the-garden was an action that my mother had initiated in order to reduce our expenses to a more manageable amount, an amount that she herself could handle solely on her income as a teacher in the government, without ever again having to depend on my father. If he had squandered his fortune before, he would do it again, as far as she was concerned. Nevertheless, she felt betrayed and put upon by him.

"Your father did not keep his end of the bargain," she was to say many years later.

"What bargain was that, Mummy?"

"To provide for your dowries, while I raised you blameless for suitable boys."

My mother's forcing my father to leave the house-with-the-garden was her way of cutting off all avenues of retreat. Nothing Mummy ever did was by fluke or happenstance; hers was always a deliberate and carefully orchestrated action.

"My heart-light is always trained on you," she would say. "There is nothing else of value."

"Then why do we have to leave the house, Mummy?" I asked, whining.

She sat down with a great sigh to explain. "Hernan Cortez, when he landed on the shores of the Americas, scuttled all the ships that had accompanied him. This ensured that none of his captains would go back to Spain, thereby forcing their commitment to the New World." My mother had done the same for us with her actions, although at that age I failed to see the connection between Hernan Cortez and our circumstances.

We moved into a small home with a tiny strip of a garden. Rachel and I enjoyed planting the odd jasmine or rose bush. We planted a bush here and a plant there as well as a vine around the dining room window. Mummy, however, resolutely refused to have anything to do with the garden in our new home. After leaving her garden at the old house, she had obliterated all her yearnings for the smell of wet earth and the touch of young green things.

There was yet another member of our reduced coven – Lakshmi. After my father had lost his businesses, all the servants were let go except for Lakshmi who was the only one retained. She was efficient, thrifty and completely committed to us. By the time we moved out of the house-with-the-garden, she had become proficient at the duties of every kind of servant: cooking and cleaning, shopping for provisions and produce, even supervising our studies, despite the fact that she was completely illiterate. I loved her dearly and was shown abundant love in return. She was my guardian angel. She looked after me, fretting over me and my endeavours, chastening me with a look which was far more eloquent than words and praising me for minor victories. Any confidence that I was to develop in my own abilities was in no small way related to her constant bolstering of my self-worth. She imparted me with lasting gifts of wisdom that were to guide me in the years to come. She was my shadow until I was married and finally left India.

Papa continued to come back to India every summer from the Persian Gulf. But, he was an alien, distanced and isolated in a household inhabited and ruled by multi-dimensional females who had little patience and understanding for the foibles of men.

❖

Mummy had had to sell a lot of the furniture from the house-with-the-garden since the small house would not accommodate most of it. She made a game of allowing us to select what we would keep and what we would not. We picked the things that were essential and then got to pick the things we loved.

Mummy picked my father's teakwood chest which was used for storing my father's art supplies. His highboys, her dressing table, and the larger sofa sets were all sent away to auction houses where they fetched very little of their value. Rachel picked the planter's chair. Even Lakshmi got to choose – she picked a meat-safe with perforated wire fronts and an elaborately curlicued *Art Nouveau* pediment. I picked a Victorian wingback chair for the living room which was covered with fancy scarlet chintz from Manchester. The covering of the arms was worn and re-upholstering would have been prohibitively expensive, so, Mummy crocheted snowy white antimacassars to cover the arms. She even crocheted spares so that every week we could get one set laundered and place fresh ones on the arms.

Our small house and our newly straitened circumstances could no longer accommodate anyone beside Mummy, Rachel, me and Lakshmi – at least initially that is. After we moved into the small house, the four of us became inseparable, protecting each other with an uncommon fierceness which would continue into our adult lives.

Our uncles visited us regularly from their home in Secunderabad: John on Sundays and Matthew mid-week. Joey would come to visit every Saturday evening. Saturday was the day that preparations were generally made for the upcoming week. Sunday was a day of relative rest for all, including servants in middle class homes.

Saturday evenings involved Lakshmi in the pantry preoccupied with cleaning the rice for the upcoming week. Rice was purchased by the pound, or *seer*. Mummy, in her usual suspicious fashion, thought the grocer added small pebbles to the rice to get paid more. Since rice was the major staple, cleaning out the pebbles was by no means a small task. Even on Saturday, Mummy was often late at the office catching up with the week's work. Rachel would be out playing in the yard.

When he visited, Joey would sit in the living room in my chosen Victorian chair. He would pick up a book under the pretense that he was going to read to me. I remember keeping my eyes tightly closed through the entire process that followed so I could see no part of him or his actions. I could only feel him fondling me, and initially, it hurt. At the same time, he would stimulate himself. The antimacassars were invariably soiled by the time he left. It played out perfectly because Saturday evening was the time to change the linens in the house and give them to Rajanna, the *dhobi*.

On those Saturday evenings after Joey was done with taking his pleasure, I would be crying, partly from fear and partly from shame. Even as a little child, I must have sensed there was something terribly wrong about this.

"If you tell your mother or anyone else about this," he warned, "no one will believe you. Everyone will know you are a bad girl and they will give you away to an orphanage." He was very cruel with his warning, undoubtedly knowing that it would achieve its desired effect.

It was not uncommon to hear stories of children who were kidnapped or abandoned and ended up in orphanages. Some were maimed intentionally and sent out to beg for alms and many were sold into servitude. I had seen many children of my age on the streets begging for alms, some whole, some crippled and I was deathly afraid of becoming like one of them. There was no one I could go to who would assure me that this would never be my lot in life. So, I remained quiet.

On one occasion, when it hurt a great deal, I remember crying. He looked at me with a cold anger in his eyes.

"Stop it now!" he demanded, delivering a stinging slap across my face. "If you don't stop crying, I will do this to your mother and to your sister too."

Hearing the slap and the crying that followed, Lakshmi came running in. "Is something the matter?" she asked.

"I have read this to her so often and she doesn't seem to remember it," Joey feigned, pointing to a passage in the book that he had picked up earlier. Since Lakshmi was illiterate, he could have said anything or picked up any book, it would not have held any significance for her.

It is not uncommon in India for immediate relatives to participate in the rearing of children. An uncle or aunt disciplining a child is accepted and one does not think to question it. I am certain that the concept of my uncle sexually molesting me must never have crossed Lakshmi's mind.

The sexual abuse continued until I reached the age of eleven when it stopped suddenly. I believe it ended because I was no longer a child and therefore for him, I must no longer have held his interest.

It would be unfair to say that I continued to feel victimised by Joey through all those years. As I grew older, I did acquire the words to express what was happening and could have exposed him, but I did not. As I grew into pre-pubescence, I transformed from becoming a helpless victim into a willing participant. Like with Major Drummond, I began to enjoy the sensations of orgasm from clitoral manipulation. I started to savour the salacious sensations of anticipation and climax and surfeit, followed by self-loathing and disgust, until the next time. While I was afraid of him, I looked forward to his next arrival, tacitly and instinctively complying with assignations and leaving surreptitiously, not looking back and not attaching any significance to what was happening. It was the guilt that I felt with the enjoyment of these feelings stirring in my growing body that further ensured my silence.

By the time I reached puberty, a widening rift had developed in my mind. Sex was furtive, and while enjoyable on a very carnal level, it had little to do with true love. I could not reconcile the intense feelings of pleasure with fear, shame and sense of violation.

I reasoned that with true love, one took a vow of fidelity before God and all His holy angels and ecstasy was confined to the prayer book and the kneeler. By the time I was eleven, Joey no longer came around and I thought that chapter in my life was closed.

❖

Fetes and fairs were held regularly by our school to raise money for all kinds of worthy causes. These funds were earmarked for saving the Hottentots of Africa, the Gonds of Orissa, or the Aborigines of Australia. Students, or rather their parents, donated abundantly in kind or in cash to put food and craft stalls together and there would be myriad amusements.

The students paid admission for entrance into the fair grounds which were set up in the school's sports arena. In addition, there was money levied for admission to each of the amusement stalls. Students spent unconscionable sums of money to purchase food and knick-knacks. The *ayahs* who accompanied the children to school would give their charges money to spend. The money came in rolls of rupee notes bundled and tied together with string in an ingenious fashion such that you could pull a single rupee bill out from the inside of the roll, with the roll remaining intact. Most of the children brought hundreds of rupees to spend at the fair. Lakshmi, on the other hand, would give Rachel and me one rupee note each on the day of the fete. We could easily go through this meager sum in less than half an hour.

I would often whine to Lakshmi when she was in the mood to listen. "I only have enough to buy a plate of *kachori* and *bhel* and one or maybe two *gulab jamuns*." These were types of savouries and deserts that were not common fare in our budget-constrained household.

"Stop that carrying on, think of all the starving Chinese," she would argue. "You are a lucky Indian child, you could be one of them."

To make matters worse, unlike the other students, Rachel and I had to go home for lunch due to our financial restraints. Most of our classmates came from wealthy families; their fathers were noblemen, senior officers in the Indian Army or highly placed officers of the Indian Administrative Service. A whole entourage of servants attended each child, even while at school. They would sit under the large tamarind trees in the schoolyard. These were trees that grew to heights of over fifty to sixty feet and spread out like huge umbrellas and each servant-entourage would stake out turf under the shade of one of the tamarinds.

During the lunch interval the children would spill out of the classes and head straight for the tamarind trees. Dhurries, would be spread out at the base of the trees; *tiffin* and food laden picnic baskets would be brought in from the waiting motorcars. There would be the *ayah*, whose duty it was to supervise the feeding of the child, the driver who chauffeured the entourage, and the *bhishti*, the water-boy, who fetched the water from the school faucets to wash the children's faces and hands before and after the meals. There was often the odd child-servant who could run errands and carry the books into class for the children.

The concept of eating food prepared by an institution was a completely foreign one. A school cafeteria was not only unheard of, but it would be an impossibility to run. How could a school possibly provide for the individual dietary, religious and caste restrictions of each one of the students?

Rachel and I had to go home for lunch everyday. We would cross through the school parking lot and across the street, down the next lane to the third house on the left. Lakshmi would be waiting with hot rice and curry, spiced vegetables, and cool buttermilk. Lakshmi was Mummy's closest ally in putting just the right spin on events and things.

"Why don't we have our food at school like all the other children?" we would ask.

"Eat up your rice and don't ask stupid questions," Lakshmi would say. "You are lucky. Those poor children have to eat cold food and be exposed to the bugs and the tamarinds that fall off the tree on their heads and into their food."

I was often despondent about not being rich anymore like my other classmates. Since Papa had gone to Arabia and Mummy had moved us into the smaller house, our spending had been seriously diminished. I believed that it was highly unfair that we had to curtail our luxuries just because Mummy was unable to conjure up enough money on her teacher's salary to make us as wealthy as our classmates. I faulted my mother for her lack of skill and ingenuity. Consequently, my anger at the situation manifested itself in a decidedly rebellious attitude.

"You send us to a stupid school where there are only eight or twelve students to the class," I would complain to Mummy. "We have to listen to silly white women who insist we speak only English. Why can't we go to the Holy Rosary Convent? There are a thousand students in every class there."

"Yours is a better school," my mother repeated for the umpteenth time.

"How can it be? There are more students going to the Holy Rosary Convent or to All Saints than there are to our school. They wear pretty green and white uniforms whereas we don't wear uniforms at all. They can buy food from the street vendors; we have to eat 'certified' home food."

"Only special people to go to your school," Mummy tried to explain.

"Even in school we are outsiders. Our father and mother are not rich or important. You sent Papa away. And you," I said pointing an accusing finger at her, "you live in a small house without a husband."

My poor mother responded with a pained look on her face. Within our constrained financial circumstances, Mummy found it difficult to afford our school fees and she denied herself a great deal so that we could continue to go to St. George's. Of course, at that time we had no concept of the exclusivity of our education and therefore no concept of the measure of my mother's sacrifice and dedication.

I blamed my mother for everything that I decided had gone wrong in my life to that point: the fact that I had a scarred belly, my ugly appearance, her insistence on flawless academic performance from me, and her inability to provide us with lots of "pocket money" as allowances were called. I rebelled purely for the sake of rebelling. Knowing my fairly secure position in my mother's affections, I knew that I could get away with it.

Mummy had left her beloved stash of orchids behind in the garden at the old-house-with-the-garden. This was done at the insistence of the new owner – Mr. Sisodia. At the time of the sale of the property, Mummy assumed that she had a tacit understanding with the Sisodias which would allow her to buy back some of these orchids, particularly her favoured Phaelenopsis whenever she desired.

The Phaelenopsis orchids came into play at the end of the school year when our class put on a theatrical play. The event was called the "annual concert and prize-giving". Our class teacher decided on a performance which involved dancing butterflies.

Parents were always expected to extend funds for the costumes and stage sets, which we were hardly in a position to do now. In the interest of conserving money, Mummy reasoned that she would make my costume instead of paying to have it made through the school. All the other children in my class had tailors and dressmakers come to school to measure them for their costumes. I thought their results were splendid. I, on the other hand, had to make do with Mummy's amateur efforts. She cut up one of her favourite chiffon saris to make my wings and trimmed them with lace and silver ribbon. She made my body suit out of matching chartreuse twill. Mummy was hardly a seamstress and this must have been a very painful, albeit valiant, effort for her. Lakshmi joined in and fashioned antennae out of coat hanger wire, wrapped them in silver ribbon and fastened them to my green twill cap.

I took one look at the resulting costume that Mummy laid out on the bed and buried my head in the pillow, sobbing uncontrollably. I hated it and told her that I would rather die than wear it.

"I am sorry to disappoint you so much and so often. I try my best for you, you know," she said with great sorrow.

"You don't try hard enough," I retorted.

"Why don't you at least try the costume on?" Lakshmi asked.

After much cajoling, I finally did put it on, doing so with very little grace and even less gratitude. I looked at my reflection in Mummy's cheval mirror. Much to my surprise, the outfit was absolutely delightful. But in my defiance, I would neither concede that it was beautiful nor would I thank my mother for her effort.

The next morning I came down with a sore throat and a high fever. I was too sick to be in the performance. Mummy sat diligently by my bedside. As she held my fevered hand in her cool one she whispered, "I am so sorry that you could not go for the concert."

"Just as well," I replied flippantly. "I would have died of shame."

"Why would you?" she asked.

"Because of that costume," I said with a derisive gesture toward the butterfly wings of green chiffon.

My mother's head sank and her shoulders sagged. I could see her surreptitiously wipe small tears from her eyes. Lakshmi immediately came to her rescue.

"How can you be such a contradiction?" Lakshmi asked me in anger as she waved something colourful in front of my face. "You are smart and quick on the one hand, and completely dense on the other. You are kind and generous most times and then, to the one person who deserves the best of you, you are cruel."

I shut my eyes tightly, scrunching them closed so I would not have to look at what she was holding in front of me.

"You open those eyes up right now or I will pry them open," Lakshmi demanded.

There, held aloft for me to see was a breathtakingly lovely garland of pale green Phaelenopsis orchids intertwined with rosemary and spots of bright silver tinsel that Mummy had crafted during the night to complement my costume. The garland was absolutely perfect, just large enough to be fitted on my head and encircle the base of the butterfly antennae.

Lakshmi then told me the story behind the beautiful orchid lei. She had accompanied Mummy back to the house-with-the-garden to approach the new owner, Mr. Sisodia. When they arrived, Mummy asked him for his entire crop of Phaelenopsis orchid blooms in order to make the lei. Mr. Sisodia merely looked at her dismissively upon hearing Mummy's request. She soon realised that her chances of getting any orchids from this man were highly unlikely.

"They are *very, very* rare flowers and are worth a fortune," he said.

Sensing my mother's desperation, he eventually quoted her a price that was overly exorbitant. Although he was extremely wealthy and the sum was a paltry one to him, it was an exorbitant amount of money to Mummy. He seemed to be playing a vicious game with her, testing to see if she would actually deliver.

"I will be back," Mummy said to Mr. Sisodia as she got back into the rickshaw and returned home with Lakshmi. Mummy told Lakshmi to wait in the rickshaw as they pulled up to the gate. She then went into the house and returned with a paper sac which she put into her tote bag. Mummy then directed the rickshaw driver to go to a section of town not frequented by respectable people – it was a street where there were pawnshops.

When they got there, Mummy and Lakshmi darted into one of the shops. When Mummy withdrew the paper sac, silver cutlery and small silver cups came tumbling out on the counter.

"I need two hundred rupees," she told the man behind the counter at the pawn shop.

Turning to Lakshmi, Mummy bravely said, "I don't have any use for silver, anyway."

"Silver is a nuisance," Lakshmi agreed. "You have to keep it polished all the time."

"We never take it out anyway," went the reasoning.

"This will not get you two hundred rupees," the pawn shop man said with a bored indifference. He had seen this play re-enacted several times a day – women bringing in their pathetic little stashes of precious trinkets, deluding themselves into believing that they were worth much more.

With that, Mummy dug deeper into her tote bag and withdrew a small square packet. It comprised thick red paper folded to make an envelope and bound with a tasseled cord. Her hands shook as she undid the fastening. There inside was the Imperial jade bracelet that Yehuda Ching had given her upon his departure from her life.

"Are you sure you want to do this?" asked Lakshmi.

"No question," Mummy replied firmly, her eyes bright with unshed tears and newly unwrapped memories.

"That ought to do it," the pawnshop man said as he handed the money over to Mummy.

Mummy and Lakshmi then went back to Mr. Sisodia's house and bought the orchids.

That night, Mummy painstakingly strung them with rosemary and wrapped their cut edges with silver tinsel. I can still imagine her smiling with pride as she had made something unique for her daughter that no other student would have.

I refused to be moved by the story and Lakshmi's impassioned pleading for recognition of Mummy's efforts. My face remained set in stone. Lakshmi looked at me with unfeigned rage.

"How could you be so hateful after all that she did for you, you little baimaan (ingrate)?" she shrieked. "Your mother sacrificed the last reminder she had that a man would still pay her attention." With this, Lakshmi successfully crafted a scarring guilt in me about my mother that long defied absolution.

❖

After moving into the newer and smaller house and the house-with-the-garden receded into the recesses of our memory. In our new small home, we lived fairly close to the Bagh-e-Aam – the public garden, which also housed the zoo. From this house, the roaring of the lions and tigers could be heard very clearly, almost as if they were next door, or at most, only twenty yards away. In the quiet hush of twilight, we could hear the slamming of the doors of the metal cages that held the big felines captive and the clanging of the pails as the zookeepers brought the meat in to feed them. Then, the deep-throated growls would start, followed by roars which shattered the silence of the gathering dusk. As they grew sated, the tigers would emit rhythmic grunts, and finally the silence would reign again.

The first time I went to the Bagh-e-Aam was with Yehuda Ching, when we went to procure lotuses for Mummy's pond-in-a-pot. Subsequently, when visiting the Bagh-e-Aam, I would stand mesmerised at the railing outside the huge enclosures which housed the big cats and watch them with total absorption. This is where I laid eyes on one great male tiger who eventually became my favourite.

I named him Ali Pasha. He was the colour of tawny port. With muscles rippling under his skin, the port would change to garnet and gold. He would emerge from his cave and raise his massive head, letting the mid summer breeze ruffle his whiskers as he surveyed the surrounds. Once in a great while, Ali Pasha would come to the front of the enclosure, which was separated from the viewing public by two rows of forty foot high spiked fences. He would amble over to the foot of the inner fence and look straight at me. His mouth would open up and he would bare his fangs in a wide grin. Ali Pasha knew me personally; I was engraved on his heart, as he was on mine.

After the sun had gone down, the men who cared for the enormous cats clambered up on the rooftops of the cages. There was a small adult female tigress – Rani, in the cage closest to Ali Pasha's enclosure. A heavy iron gate separated Rani from Ali Pasha's walled garden. The men raised the gate and Rani bounded out with all the friskiness of a kitten. The main zookeeper called out to Ali Pasha from the rooftop of Rani's cage.

"*Aa bete aa* – come son, come. *Teri rani ai hai* – your queen has arrived."

Ali Pasha emerged from his man-made cave and looked around to see what all the clamouring was about. Then, with one bound and no preamble, he mounted Rani. This elicited a great deal of clapping, joking, and laughter from the zookeepers. I was completely mystified, and thinking that he was going to devour her, I asked one of them if he would kill her.

He looked nonplused, not realising that there was a little girl who was audience not only to Ali Pasha's odd behaviour, but also to their bawdy jokes.

"It is cold in the tiger's garden and he thinks she is a rug, Bibi," he explained.

It was nineteen fifty-seven, the year after the death of my aunt Anna, the monsoons were finally over. The festival of lights had been celebrated. The cool winter season was in and the leaves of the peepul trees on the street outside the little house had started to shed. I sat in Papa's planter's chair reading a book about tigers and drifted off.

I found myself back in school. Neither Papa nor Mummy had come to fetch me home to the old-house-with-the-big-garden. Most of the children had gone home with their parents or their ayahs. I waited seated on the parapet that ran around the kindergarten. I found myself wearing the chartreuse butterfly costume with the Phaelenopsis orchid crown Mummy had made for me.

The sun was setting fast and the mynah birds and ravens were flying home to the tamarind trees to roost. Mrs. Alder, the diminutive principal of the Nursery school, was waiting impatiently for someone to come for me. After looking at her wristwatch for the hundredth time, she turned to me and said, "It is late; I have to go home now. Your mother should be here soon. If it grows cold, lock yourself inside the kindergarten class room and wait for her there."

It had begun to turn dark. Floating out on the chilling evening air like a scimitar came the muezzin's call to evening prayer issued to all the faithful just as the light fades enough to make red objects indistinguishable from black. After the "*Allah hu Akbar*" – "God is Great" had receded into the shadows and the deepening silence had descended over the schoolyard, I heard a familiar rhythmic cough.

I strained my eyes to look in the direction of the cough. There, coming through the entry gate of the school, I saw the familiar muscled form of Ali Pasha, the tiger. His tawny eyes glowed as he looked at me. He threw his head back almost in triumph and split the earth with a roar. It was only a matter of moments before he would be on the verandah.

I jumped off the parapet and ran to the kindergarten classroom door. Pushing it open, I let myself in. Then, I bolted the door and hurried to bar the windows. I then waited, terrified. Ali Pasha soon reached the verandah and was circling the classroom, padding around on the catwalk. It was evening, and he had not yet been fed. I could hear his full-throated growls signifying his growing hunger.

Presently, there was a tearing sound followed by a crash as Ali Pasha had broken down the flimsy door and was in. My hands were clammy and my mouth was drier than dead peepul leaves. I found miraculously that Mummy's crafted chiffon-sari-wings allowed me to fly. I flew up effortlessly toward the ceiling and rested down carefully on the blades of the ceiling fan that was suspended from the central beam. I looked down where I saw Ali Pasha; he was looking at me with longing. He growled several times, and miraculously, I was able to understand what he said:

"Please little *Patherni* - butterfly, I am so very hungry, do come down. It will be quick, you won't feel a thing, and there won't be a trace of you left behind. No muss, no fuss."

"I don't want to die; I am so young and so pretty now with my wings and all," I reasoned.

"I don't want to die either, but if I don't have something to eat, I will die," he replied.

Ali Pasha found that if he stood on his hind legs and reached out with his forepaw, he could touch me. He did just that. He kept jumping up while attempting to swat me off my perch. Finally, he succeeded in securing a strike. His monstrous claws raked my calf and I screamed as I watched the blood make pretty little rivulets and drip on Ali Pasha's face. He flicked the droplets off with his tongue. Now the fan with me perched on it was swinging crazily back and forth. Ali Pasha stood below, moving his massive head in unison to the pendulum movement of the fan.

Just then, I heard the door open and there was my mother, standing silhouetted in the doorway.

"Be gone," she commanded, and Ali Pasha obediently slunk away.

She reached her arms out to me and I flew down to her embrace. "Wake up, child, you are having a nightmare."

Brushing the cobwebs from my sleepy brain, I said, "Oh Mummy, thank you for the magical butterfly dress. I always meant to thank you for it, really I did." I finally understood the significance of her efforts in crafting that costume for me and realised that she would always love and protect me with ferocity no matter what – even from tigers.

❖

Serious contests raged in our psyche from an early age – a fight between being little British subjects going to the perfect school, acquiring flawless diction and precise syntax on the one hand, and on the other, being little Indian girls with an alarming propensity for opulence and indolence.

As a salute to the aristocracy who sent their children to St. George's School, we were allowed to wear *mufti* – our own civilian clothes instead of the uniforms sported by the other parochial schools. We fretted over the fact that we had to wear "ordinary" clothes, while the students of St. Anne's or the Holy Rosary convent wore smart jumpers, starched white blouses and school ties. Once our circumstances had become constrained and straitened, it was soon to become obvious to Rachel and me that we had a limited supply of "school clothes". Compared to our classmates who rarely repeated an outfit in six months, Rachel started wearing my hand-me-downs and I had to contend with far fewer changes than my classmates. The school, of course, insisted that our clothes be freshly laundered and pressed which added to Lakshmi's burden of washing and pressing our clothes everyday. Mummy was kept busy with darning and letting out seams to accommodate our becoming taller.

Our teachers, those guardians of virtue and Christian modesty, would not allow us as small Indian schoolgirls adornment of any kind – no jewellery and no makeup. Since we had only to rely on pretty clothes and natural good looks, I was at a loss. My now sparse wardrobe and the injunctions not to use jewellery or clever makeup to counteract my homeliness only added to my suffering. I railed against this edict endlessly, adding to Lakshmi's annoyance and Mummy's irritation.

The only features I considered worthy of notice in my otherwise sad little body were my eyes and my hands. My eyes have always been large, luminous and brown reflecting every emotion I felt – some sorrow, but mostly anger and rage at my impotence and helplessness. I knew it would have bolstered my confidence greatly had I been allowed to wear kohl and add sparkle to my eyes. My mouth was unimpressive and my chin was so prominent that my cousins teased me unmercifully about it. The chin was a family trait, but in all the others who inherited it, the chin was balanced off with a high arched nose with flaring nostrils whereas my nose was small and insignificant. I had to rely on my eyes to distract from my non-existent nose. My hands were small and soft and I knew that if only I could wear bangles, I could set my hands off to advantage.

I was sure that I was trapped for eternity in the pincer grip of plainness and poverty. By the time I was ten I had had enough of it – my lack of good looks, my mother's frugality and the ridiculous mandates of the school. The summer before I turned eleven, I decided to break all the rules of "deportment and dress" at the school.

We had just come home from school and Lakshmi had finished all the cooking and cleaning for the day. There were certain times when we could get Lakshmi to join our world instead of the world of the adults. This was one of those special moments. I moved in to secure turf.

"Will you make something for me, Lakshmi, please?" I asked.

"What would you like?"

"Will you make *kaajal* for us?"

The interchange came in a mad rush, tumbling and fast.

"Mummy will be angry. What will you do about that?" she asked.

"Mummy is working late today. She will never find out."

"You are not allowed to use it at school. What will they say?"

"Don't worry about it. I have special permission to look Indian," I lied.

Lakshmi set to work while we followed her around in utter fascination. She peeled four pods of garlic and then roasted them on a flat griddle, crushing them as they turned soft and dark. We watched them char to a black congealed mass. She then transferred this into an earthenware pot. In another small vessel with a spout, she melted clarified butter. Carefully and deliberately, she added the clarified butter to the charred garlic, stirring it all the while. By this time we lost interest and left to play our favourite game of hopscotch. Presently we heard her call from the kitchen telling us she was done. Lakshmi held out a small silver receptacle and in it was a glistening black cream – the magical kohl which was designed to make me beautiful and unleash the goddess in me. I danced around her wild with joy, hugging her all the while.

"You will have to let it age for a few days, Bibi," she said. "If you use it too soon, your eyes will burn." Of course, this warning fell on uncaring ears.

The next step to my transformation was the bangle seller who came by with his wares in the summer time. His major talent was that he could coax rows and rows of small, tight, coloured glass bangles onto my wrists. The result of his artistry never ceased to delight me – after half an hour of squeezing, cajoling and massaging my hands into subjugation, I was rewarded with a cuff of perfect circles of brilliant colour at my wrist. The bangles jangled musically when I moved my wrists or waved my hands. They glinted invitingly in the sunlight and I was certain they added beauty to a form that needed beauty like the parched earth needed the monsoon. Paying the bangle seller was a hurdle I had not anticipated. I came up with the brilliant idea of giving him a gold bangle from my trousseaux in exchange for the two dozen glass ones. He looked at me in disbelief and hurriedly put the gold one away in the folds of his turban.

All I had to do now was to dye my palms with henna and the change would be complete.

It was claimed that henna had medicinal value – cooling one's blood and protecting it from the summer heat. This was as good an excuse as any for me.

It always seemed that the Muslim girls at school had the deepest stains and the most intricate patterns. They claimed to have sat immobile for ten hours. They also had servants who were far more skilled in the application of henna. The designs sported by our Muslim classmates were far superior to any that the others, either Hindu or Christian, could produce. They were reminiscent of the delicate tracery of arabesques, leaves and flowers embellishing the walls of the Taj Mahal.

In the corner at the end of the garden at the new house, we had planted a henna bush. We were under strict orders not to apply any henna to our palms until the summer vacation started because the school would not have countenanced this form of adornment.

Rachel and I plucked all the leaves that we could reach on the henna bush, gathering them into our little garden baskets. We then spent hours grinding them with a pestle in a large mortar until we had a fine dark paste. I sat patiently while Rachel applied the paste on my palms in the most intricate patterns of flowers and leaves, arabesques and curlicues. I had to sit almost immobile for two to three hours before the paste could be removed. In the end, I was rewarded for my patience with a deep orange stain on my palms, which reflected the designs traced with the paste. The next morning at school I would show off my hennaed hands to my friends who had not dared to flout the school's rules.

Mummy came back late from work that evening. I was careful to hide my hands from view. She left early for work the next day, totally unaware of what I had been up to.

After she left, I went to work on my eyes. Using my little finger dipped in the creamy kohl, I applied it to the rim of my eyelids. For a fleeting moment, before my eyes started to water, I caught a glimpse of my face in the mirror. My eyes were enormous and my face radiant. Finally, I had found the key to instant beauty.

I concealed my stash of glass bangles fitted snugly around my wrist from view by my long sleeved *kurta*. Since the summer days were very hot, I was uncomfortable in the long sleeves but this discomfort was a minor sacrifice to the altar of outward beauty.

I left for school with bangles cuffing my forearm, kohl adorning my eyes and henna tracery on my palms.

On the way to school, my eyes began to burn, but this was a small price to pay for looking gorgeous. Rivulets of black ran down my cheeks, but doggedly and bravely, I forged on. Rachel held my hand while we walked to school. I could not have walked without her assistance being almost blinded from my burning and watering eyes.

As I entered the school grounds, I realised that this was Tuesday and it was my turn to play the piano at assembly. I could neither see nor read the music from the hymnal. It was fortunate that we were to sing John Cardinal Newman's hymn "Lead Kindly Light" which I knew by heart. I muddled through the initial introductory until Rachel guided my fingers to the right keys and after that it was plain sailing. The rest of the morning prayer was uneventful, until Miss Greg – our piano teacher, came to put away the hymnal and lock the lid on the keyboard. There was a gasp as she spied my glass bangles, my hennaed hands and my black stained eyes.

"Why are you all painted up?"

In a trice I was on the carpet with no explanation in hand.

"You will have to get your bangles off instantly," she commanded. "You look like one of the natives."

"I *am* one of the natives," I bellowed with anger and defiance giving me a courage which I did not otherwise possess.

"Take those offensive things off *now!!*"

I was handed over to one of the *ayahs* in school. She could not coax the bangles off my arm. Rachel came out of her class to give me sustenance. We decided to try soap and water – the trick worked. I watched with sorrow as circle after circle of bright shiny glass bangles came off and were thrown into the trash basket. The last one was a deep blue with silver wire wrapped around it. The wire caught on my skin and in my hurry, the bangle broke. There was a lovely tinkling sound as it shattered, gashing my hand as it slipped away into the wash basin. I watched the blue of the glass and the curly silver wire festooned with bright red blood trace a kaleidoscope pattern on the white vitreous basin.

The rest of the day was a blur. Of course, I was sent home with a note to Mummy.

She looked at my hands and my stained face with wordless sorrow.

"I want to be beautiful, Mummy."

With a deep sigh she gathered me in her arms, "You are beautiful, you are beautiful indeed."

As I changed into my summer chemise, I stopped to look in the mirror at my face that had resumed its old familiar plainness. I caught Mummy's reflection in the mirror. As she reached out to place something on the dresser, a glint of gold caught my eye. Back on my dresser was the bangle I had given the bangle seller.

"The bangle seller brought it back," she said. "He knew taking your gold bangle for two dozen glass bangles might not have been quite an even exchange."

"Oh Mummy, I am so sorry."

"You provided the poor man a great opportunity to exercise his honesty. The gold bangle would have been more than he would ever make in a month, or even a year."

I loved her so very much at that moment for her deep level of understanding and not punishing me anymore that I was already punishing myself.

❖

As we grew older, Lakshmi became the guardian of our souls and lives continually dispensing homespun wisdom, love and constancy. She was always there to shield us from the minor sorrows and troubles that plagued us and she constantly succeeded in giving us the ability to see a different perspective on our constrained circumstances. It may have been with forethought and deliberation, or it may have been completely inadvertent, but Lakshmi anchored my future dreams; she anchored my dreams in America.

Lakshmi taught me how to play hopscotch beside the new little-house-without-much-of-a-garden on a small strip of land barely ten feet wide where we planted a few bushes. Lakshmi took it upon herself to make privation into an elaborate game.

She added a new twist to the game, which made the stakes higher and more desirable. She drew the series of rectangles in the dirt and topped it off with the traditional semicircle where you were to kick the flat stone home.

"You have to name your home," she said. "It is only then that you will get there."

"What shall I name it?" I asked.

"Why, America of course!"

This was the first time that I could remember America being presented in a positive light. Lakshmi's suggestions and praises of America didn't stop there.

In 1958, the year of the great influenza epidemic in India and we had all been laid low for several weeks – it seemed like an age. Lakshmi, and Mummy were the first to get well. Mummy was fiercely competitive when it came to our prowess at school or our standing in class. For the eight weeks we were out of school, she decided to teach us at home so that we would not lose any momentum. It worked out well since she was a teacher by profession anyway.

English was the most delightful part of our home study and my favourite subject. I vividly recall Mummy reading story after story to us from my textbook, but there was one special story that stuck with me:

There once was a little English boy who had lived in India all his life. There, he contracted tuberculosis. When it was clear that he was dying, his parents decided to send him back to England. As he embarked on his long journey home, the crew of the ship, particularly the captain, took a deep interest in him, keeping his spirits up with stories of England. They told him that the streets of this far away country were paved with gold; milk and honey flowed there in abundance; the sun never set; and the king and all his subjects were forever blissfully happy. The ship's crew watched with sorrow as they saw the boy's end draw near. Their stories of this golden land became more fanciful and utopian in the hopes of keeping him alive. As the ship came into sight of the White Cliffs of Dover, the little boy asked to be taken up to the deck to see the great kingdom come into view. Then, as his eyes closed in death, he was transported into the great Kingdom in the sky, where the streets were indeed paved with gold.

It was an undeniably foolish, sentimental story, but we loved it and would have Mummy read it to us over and over again. Lakshmi sat by the foot of the bed and heard the story almost as often as we did. Her knowledge of English was meager and this often resulted in our having to translate for her.

"You will not find streets paved with gold in England and you don't have to wait until you get to the Kingdom of Heaven either," Lakshmi would tell us. "The streets are paved with gold in America – you will find them there."

America was a completely foreign land to us. Due to the long presence of the British in India, we were much more familiar with England as a country. The legacy of the British Empire stayed with us for several years, well into our adulthood. It insinuated itself into the crevices and crannies of our psyche, only to come up into plain view as if laid open by the seismic changes of our lives. The British had brought much to India – their language, the English system of education, the Great Indian Railway, PAX Britannica, English flowers and gardens.

Lakshmi, although unschooled, possessed uncanny insight and had her own unique views on the subject of the British. I once asked her, "Why did the Rajahs and Nawabs invite the British to come into India? Was it to safeguard their interests?"

"Don't you understand anything?" she retorted.

"No, I don't," I said, hoping that this would lead into a story. She looked at me sadly – sad that I had not yet gained the wisdom to see things as she did. Then she sighed heavily and I knew that a story was forthcoming. And sure enough, it came:

"Many, many years ago, down deep in a well near Osman Saagar, lived a colony of frogs. They had everything they could ask for – lily pads on the lake, a plentiful supply of flies, great weather and so on. There was an occasional snake that disrupted their lifestyle, but all in all, they enjoyed a great life.

However, the frogs were not completely satisfied. The leadership council of frogs in that colony felt that something was lacking in their lives. 'Aha,' said one of them. 'We do not have a king.' They then went in one body to God and asked Him to give them a king. God then selected the brightest and best of the leadership council and with a great expansive gesture said, 'Here is your king.'

The frog leaders were angry with God. 'How could you come up with a king who looks likes us, croaks like us, and is barely distinguishable from the rest of us?' In a fit of rage, they fell on the poor hapless newly appointed king frog and killed him. Then they went back in a body to God and demanded a better performance. 'After all, you are God; you ought to select a king for us who is sufficiently different from us.'

So, God sighed and went about the business of selection again, and he chose a fish to be the king. The frog leaders looked at God in pained silence and then finally one of them spoke up, 'How could you select something that cannot walk on the land, gawps all the time, and cannot make a sound?' They fell on the poor fish and killed him too.

They again went back to God and with barely concealed impatience they explained, 'We want a king who can swim in the water like us, walk on land like us, is bigger than us so others will know we have a powerful king. He must look different from us so we can recognise him and make louder noises than us so he can scare away the other colonies.'

After much thinking, God took their specifications into consideration and selected them a king who was much larger than the entire colony put together and made enough noise to frighten the raven roosting in the gulmohar tree near the banks of Osman Saagar. He could not only swim and walk, but he could also fly. God had selected a stork for them.

The frogs looked at this wondrous creature with its white plumage and long sharp beak. He squawked loud enough for the ravens to fall from their roosts. They took him back and with great pomp and circumstance and they installed him as king of the frogs.

By nightfall, the leadership council of frogs had made a huge feast of flies for their new king – flying termites, ants, and dragonflies with blue and green wings. The stork looked at the bugs on the plate with great distaste. He looked down at the frog who had served him the meal. He was hungry after the long coronation ceremony and an unusually busy day. With no preamble at all, the stork then proceeded to swallow up one frog leader after another. In short order, the whole group of ringleader frogs was gone. The colony comprised only commoner frogs that subsequently rose up in a single body and drove the stork away, deciding that having rulers was unnecessary."

I had heard a different version of this story before. Lakshmi's version of storytelling was often novel and refreshing. She saw things differently and would spin a story to suit the circumstance. "Don't you see child? We do not need kings and rulers, and we definitely do not need a ruler who is unlike us," Lakshmi concluded.

"What about the jewels and precious artifacts that the British took from India when they left?" I asked.

"Oh, they took a few baubles along the way. You have to pay the *mazdoor* for his *mazdoori*," she responded, which translated roughly into the Biblical 'every labourer is worthy of his hire'.

"If we let them take it, it must not have meant much to us anyway," she added.

"So you think we got the best deal?"

"Of course we did," she told us. "Those poor *Angrez*, came to a strange country, had to learn our languages, deal with our customs, and live with a different set of diseases than their own. Most of them are now buried in a foreign land. How enviable is that? We allowed them to come into our country to teach us their language and ways of government and education; they even brought their railways. Once we had taken the best that they had to offer and after one hundred and fifty years, we told them that they must leave. We did not even have to take on their religion unless we chose to. We just used their services to get what we needed."

The English language in fact did unify India. We spoke various forms of English at school which reflected the pecking order and origins of the teachers along the way. There was the singsong Anglo-Indian English in kindergarten and preparatory school where teachers of mixed parentage cared for us. Then, as we moved into middle school, we spoke a nasal Australian English. Finally, we evolved to speaking perfect Cantabrigian English by the time we reached the final three standards (as grades were called) of high school.

Our Muslim friends and servants spoke Urdu, so when at home, we too spoke Urdu. We dreamed, breathed and quarrelled in Urdu. And most significantly, we could swear at and berate our opponents in fluent Urdu with words we did not know existed in other languages. Urdu is a heart-achingly beautiful language with a script composed of lovely sinuous arabesques and nuances subtler than a whisper.

After India became a republic, we had to learn Hindi. To my ears, Hindi lacked the refinement of Urdu with its script looking like endless rows of clothes hung on washing lines, its speech dissonant and discordant, and idiom contrived and dull.

Much against our natural inclination, we were required to learn Malayalam, the language of Travancore. This would insure that we would not become objects of scorn in our own community. In turn, the task of finding husbands for us would be made easier.

In the 1950s, a widespread linguistic agitation had India in a viselike stranglehold. In response, states came to be realigned along linguistic boundaries. This meant that we had to learn yet another language – Telugu, with an entirely different script and sound.

"I don't want to learn one more language, Mummy," I protested defiantly.

"Is that because you are not smart enough or because you don't want to get ahead in life?" Mummy asked.

"Of course I want to get ahead, but not by learning another @#+! language!"

Lakshmi and Mummy were a very effective tag team. Mummy was adept at getting me to do something by merely forbidding that I do it. When that tactic did not work, Lakshmi would sweep in with mastery.

"Well, you had better learn to cook and clean, wash dishes and scrub pots," Lakshmi would say. "I will start looking for employment for you as a maidservant in the houses of the neighbourhood. It seems that the heat has softened your brain. You are not as sharp as I assumed you would be."

This strategy invariably resulted in the success they were trying to achieve. That settled it; I would learn one more language. However, that didn't stop me from grumbling about it.

Lakshmi was putting my books away one day when she looked at me and asked, "If it is that bad, why don't you go away to a country where there is only one language?"

"Such as where?" I asked.

"America of course."

"Why not England?"

"Oh them," she said dismissively, "they are finished – don't forget the story of the stork and the frogs. America is the place to go. The roads are paved with gold and you can be anything you want to be."

So it was that all through our formative years Lakshmi tacitly and overtly instilled in us that we were destined to go to America – that land where streets were paved with gold and flowing with milk and honey, where there would be boundless opportunity, no suffering and no sorrow. It was there that we could shed our disappointments, break out of our constrained circumstances and come to realise our dreams.

7

Coming of Age

THE YEAR I WAS ELEVEN YEARS OLD, MARCH HIT THE CITY WITH an uncommon vengeance. The air turned hot and still; the occasional breeze stirring in the trees was like the breath of St. George's dragon. Then, the unthinkable happened.

It was lunchtime. Rachel and I were walking across the schoolyard and through the parking lot on our way home for lunch. The parking lot was full as usual – the Dusenbergs, the Rolls-Royces, the Daimlers, and the odd Cadillac or two. Parked past these cars were the military convoys. These vehicles brought the children of the colonels, the squadron leaders, the wing commanders and the brigadiers from the cantonments and the airbases to school in the city. They were manned by the sipahis and the jawans, young soldiers who for all intents and purposes served the same functions as the more conventional servants of our more conventional schoolmates.

These men looked very different from the men we usually saw around us as they were from the north. People from the south were small in stature, dark skinned, and had grizzled hair and flat features. The northerners were tall, lighter skinned and a generally more handsome lot. While we southerners had the higher incidence of literacy and provided the country with doctors, engineers, lawyers and administrative officers for the government, when it came to the real business of defending the country, the northerners supplied the brawn and repeatedly protected its borders over the years. Papa even went so far as to call them "barbarians" on occasion.

The men in the parking lot were made up of three different groups. The Gurkhas from the Himalayas were slight, taciturn and bandy-legged. The Garhwalis from the northeast provinces were long-limbed, sloe-eyed and divinely handsome. The Sikhs from the Punjab were turbaned, tall, mustachioed and very fierce looking. They spoke to each other in languages that we did not understand. In their working uniforms with their bandoliers and rifles, they looked like creatures from another planet, exotic and exciting and decidedly different.

One soldier from the group seemed much older than the rest. He was a Gurkha, shorter than the others, much quieter and wrinkled like a pickled mango. He had many more stripes on his epaulets. We had no idea what that meant except that the rest of the sipahis were deferential to him. I had seen him before.

"He looks like one of the gargoyles outside the church belfry," I would say to Rachel.

In the typical mean-spiritedness of children, I would look at him, pass close to him and whisper tauntingly, "*Pishaju-Shaitaan –* Devil". He never said anything back although it was clear that he understood what I had said. He would simply look at me evenly and silently and resume cleaning his rifle as if he had not heard.

On that day as we were walking home, I heard a resounding hoot of derisive laughter from the uniformed group which grew louder as we walked past. I turned around to look at the howling soldiers. There were three or four of them pointing at my clothes and laughing. I looked down and there, down the inseam of my salwar and along the back of my kameez was a rapidly spreading bloodstain. I had reached menarche at that moment. I was not prepared for this and had no idea that such things happened to normal people. My belly hurt, my legs ached and those funny bumps on my chest, my sprouting breasts, felt painfully sore.

"This blood," I wondered somewhat dispassionately, "what is this about?"

Eight-year-old Rachel, who knew even less than I did, put her arm around me. "You must be dying. Let's go home so you can die in comfort."

"My belly aches," I said, "but it doesn't feel like I am dying."

"Can you see Jesus now?" Rachel wanted to know.

"No, but I feel hot."

"Oh God, do you think you might be feeling the fires of hell?" Rachel asked ominously. "Let us recite the *Our Father* quickly so that it is finished by the time you die, then Jesus cannot refuse your entry to Heaven. *Our Father who art in heaven, hallowed be Thy Name...* Oh, save me a place in Heaven, I want to be sitting next to you when I come there."

"Stop! Stop! I am not dying, Rachel," I cried. "Maybe it is some form of stigmata like the Catholics have. I must be becoming a saint."

"Not from between your legs, you silly goose. ...*Thy Kingdom come, Thy will be done on Earth...*"

"'Saint Anna' sounds awful," I protested. "I wish that Mummy would have named me something else like 'Josephine' or 'Miranda'."

"Those are Anglo-Indian names. Nice people don't have Anglo-Indian names. ...*As it is in Heaven*... How about a pretty Indian name like 'Seeta' or 'Rukmini'? ...*Give us this day our Daily Bread*... But there are no Hindu saints in Christian Heaven. ...*Forgive us our trespasses as we forgive those that trespass against us ...*"

The laughing and the mocking from the soldiers grew progressively louder. Suddenly, there was a blood-curdling primal scream: "**Gurkhali Aayo**", followed by silence. This was the famous battle cry of the Gurkhas: "**the Gurkhas are coming**". Gurkhas are known to be intrepid and brave fighters having saved Britannia's royal "arse" on many an occasion. The little Gurkha, the one I called "Shaitaan", had jumped off the back of one of the trucks with his kukri, dagger, drawn.

"*Khamosh* – silence!!" he roared. "*Khabardaar* – beware!! *Chale Jao Ek dam* – leave immediately."

I wondered where so huge a voice came from in so diminutive of a man. The younger soldiers tittered a little nervously and then dispersed.

"Don't you have mothers and sisters, you sons of pigs and donkeys?" he continued at the soldiers in a quieter and more menacing voice.

He walked over to where we were standing and watching all of this uncomprehendingly.

Rachel was wide-eyed and hurrying to complete reciting the rest of the Lord's Prayer, "*Deliver us from evil...*"

"I am becoming a saint," I told the Gurkha.

"She might be dying," Rachel added. "We are going to finish the prayer so she goes to Heaven and makes a place for me. ...*For Thine is the kingdom, the power and the glory...*"

"...*Forever and ever. Amen*," he had joined us in our recitation.

"You are not dying," he informed me. "And the way you behave is a far cry from sainthood, although God can perform miracles. You are becoming a woman. Let me take you home."

So there we were, two children each holding a soldier's hand and trudging home in the noonday sun.

Lakshmi opened the door. She looked at the Gurkha, then at us, and finally at my salwar.

"Oh," she said a little breathlessly, "I was expecting this," leading me off into the bathroom to bathe me and clean me up.

She proceeded to lay out the voile pads for me to wear in order to absorb the blood.

"This will happen every month," she told me. "You are a woman now."

Rachel had pushed the bathroom door open. Looking in she asked, "Why isn't she dying? I thought for sure we would have secured two seats in Heaven by now."

"I am a woman now," I exclaimed.

"Is that better than becoming a saint?"

"Saints sing 'Holy, holy, holy' all day and all night long for eternity. What can be more boring than that? Being a woman is far more exciting."

"How would you know?" Rachel asked.

"I can feel it."

"Where?"

"Everywhere. Here, especially here," I said poking at my breast bumps. "You wouldn't understand, you are only a *chhoti bacchi*, a little girl," I added dismissively, rapidly forgetting that she was the one who had stood by me in my time of need.

"Go away and leave us alone for now," Lakshmi told Rachel while trying to towel down my squirming body. "Go talk to the soldier and keep him entertained until I come out."

We soon emerged from the bathroom; I was all clean and dressed. The Gurkha was still there. I felt terribly repentant for having been mean to him.

"What is your name?" I asked.

"Tikka Bahadur. Lance Corporal Tikka Bahadur. It means Mark of Bravery," he replied.

"That is a nice name," I said.

"Yes, better than 'Shaitaan'," he said grinning and showing his even white teeth which transformed his face from that of a wrinkled, pickled mango to one of a gentle, even handsome, man.

"I am sorry for ever calling you 'Shaitaan'," I told him.

"For the next few days, take the back route to school," he said. Then, seeing the puzzlement on my face, he continued, "until the rest of the soldiers get over their bad behaviour."

I went back to school the next day feeling as if I was a cut higher than everyone else, after all, I was now a woman. This pride only lasted for a few minutes until I found out that more than half of my class had already become women too and that the other half was far less ignorant than I was on the subject.

❖

As my father's natal star waned in power, my mother's rose meteorically. By the time we had moved into the smaller house and Papa was spending most of the year in Arabia, his contribution to my dowry or my dower chest had grown insignificant. Mummy and her connections had taken over the task. Mummy had ascended the ranks and become an influential official in the government's Department of Education. In this position, she had a *munshi*, a clerk-cum-secretary, a Muslim by the name of Mohammad Inayath Ali.

The Muslims I grew up with were an extremely refined, generous and beautiful people. They possessed a distinct inner beauty as well as an outer one. The universities where we studied, the hospitals where we were healed, the museums, parks and libraries of our city that we enjoyed all were built from the munificence of the Muslims of India. Neither the Hindus nor Christians ever contributed as much to the public, beyond building edifices to promulgate their religion or promote their own wealth. Even those Muslims who were poor had a spirit of generosity which transcended all social strata.

There were strict protocols and rules of behaviour one observed when dealing with Muslim friends. For instance, it was an unpardonable breach of etiquette not to attend a Muslim feast when invited. If the invitation were declined, the hosts would be constrained to pack up a large portion of the food and send it to your home. An even more unforgivable act was to openly admire anything that a Muslim owned or they would immediately give it to you, insisting all the while that the object was looking for a permanent home. I was to learn these lessons rather painfully.

Inayath was deeply loyal to our family and we reciprocated this sense of loyalty in return. We referred to him as Inayath Ali Sahib as a form of respect in consideration for his position as my mother's secretary. He was tall, dark, handsome, and endlessly entertaining. He came from a very large family and likewise bred a sizeable family of his own. I can remember that each time I saw his wife she was pregnant.

One of Inayath's greatest passions was to frequent the *Haraajkhana*, the auction houses in the city, every Sunday. He would bring incredible finds of furniture, artwork and porcelain back to his spotlessly clean and modest little home in one of the poorer Muslim sections of the city. Inayath's home was very tastefully furnished as a result of his successes at the auction houses.

At the time of the great Muslim feast, the Eid-ul-Fitr, our family was consistently invited to Inayath's house and we would always attend. He was a superb cook and would spend the entire preceding day preparing the lamb biryani, aubergines baked in a thousand spices, figs with walnuts, and other delicacies. As we entered the front door, we would be assailed by the aroma of the succulent lamb dishes steeped in spices and the rice thrice-baked with mint, saffron and cream. My favorite of all was the dessert Qurbani, apricots stewed with sugar for hours on end until they became a rich golden brown. Apricots were frightfully expensive, having to come south all the way from Kashmir. When it came time for the desert to be served, I would watch with impatience as the apricots were spooned into fine cups. Inayath's wife, Sajida, would then layer thick custard over them and garnish them with the finest almonds money could buy. The cost of this desert must have seemed like a king's ransom to a man who had a meager income with which to support a very large family, but this was yet one example of this Muslim family's enormous generosity.

Before our arrival, Mummy had forewarned me that I was not to comment admiringly about any effects in Inayath's house. However, one year I was so taken by the exquisite grace of their modest home that I quickly forgot the admonition. I readily admired the tasteful hall tree which Inayath had acquired at auction the previous Sunday. I gently fingered the brocade tablecloth and sighed longingly over the fine Royal Doulton tea service. I went on and on about the table linens and other similar items.

Mummy was ominously silent over dinner, Lakshmi was visibly mortified, and I was sublimely oblivious. It was a marvellous dinner and soon it was time to go home. When we stepped outside to leave, there was a small lorry parked in the front of the house with the hall tree loaded on, the tablecloth neatly folded, and the tea service carefully packed within. The lorry followed us back home with everything I had admired at Inayath's house.

"How is it that you are so lacking in grace?" Mummy scolded me.

I thought that I was being complementary to Inayath with my praises. I was remorseful of the consequences, but was soon to forget about his fabled Muslim generosity once again.

Sundays were always a great treat for us. There was church followed by breakfast and marvellous times with our favorite uncle John who would leave us by mid-day. We would then wait by the front door for Inayath who would come by to offer his newly purchased treasures from the auction houses to our family before taking them home. Much to my delight, he sometimes had jewellery.

Inayath would arrive in on his bicycle with saddlebags on either side which were always bulging with a multitude of acquired purchases. He would make a great production of dismounting his cycle while easing his long legs across the seat and saddlebags. His legs just seemed to go on forever. He always wore a sherwaani and loose white trousers. The sherwaani, which was mid-calf in length, made him look even taller than he probably was.

With infinite care, he would unhook his saddlebags and grasp one in each hand before approaching the house. He was so tall that he had to stoop to enter the side door with his bags of treasure. In deference to us, on special occasions such as Muslim festivals or Christian holidays, he always wore his finest clothes and his special red fez. On the occasions when he wore his fez, he invariably knocked it off when entering through the door.

The saddlebags on his bicycle were made of calf's leather and were as soft as butter; the years of use they had seen only made them more supple. They were equipped with fascinating little devices – multiple locks and buckles to help keep the contents in place. When he undid the straps and the locks and buckles, the whole contraption would open up like a sheet revealing the precious contents – silver goblets, bone china plates packed carefully in wads of newsprint, fine stemware, *repousse* pitchers, finely rendered miniatures and so on. The finest pleasure of all was when he would bring exquisite old jewellery that had been auctioned off to provide money for aging and unemployable nobility.

Mummy would make an elaborate charade of admiring and taking the least precious piece from his cache. Not to take anything would have been an insult to his effort and his taste. To take something that was valuable would have been unthinkable because he often resold the items to supplement his meager income as a government munshi.

One memorable Sunday after a jewellery auction, Inayath brought a package as large as the palm of my hand. It was wrapped in a square of bright green-blue *charmeuse* (silk) tied with red cord and tassels, which he took forever to untie. We waited, unable to exhale, with eyes as wide as saucers. Finally he held out his cupped palm. Nestled in the folds of the turquoise coloured silk was a *sarpech*, a headpiece worn on a turban. It was similar to the aigrettes worn by western women in the 1920s and '30s. In place of the egret plumes, there were fine sprays of Basra pearls interspersed with mine cut diamonds and cabochon sapphires. In the center of the piece, there was an enormous emerald the size of a robin's egg. It was a deep blue green with rutillated inclusions. It winked wickedly in the sun as he held it up for us to see.

"It belonged to the Avadh Nawabs and was given to a nautch girl in payment for an evening of ecstasy," Inayath explained.

"What is an evening of ecstasy?" I asked

The adults looked at each other and remained silent.

"So where is the girl?" I continued.

"She died in childbirth, they say. The girl's parents needed the money to take care of the baby."

I reached out to touch the sarpech. The emerald felt warm while the diamonds were cold. Inayath always encouraged us to handle the objects in sharp contrast to Mummy who expressly forbade us from touching these fragile pieces.

"If they don't get to touch these things, how will they learn of the right heft, texture, and sheer beauty of the workmanship?" Inayath would ask her.

"May I please have this piece for myself?" I pleaded to him.

Without hesitation, he placed it in my hands, folding one palm over the other to cup the Sarpech. "I will have it made into a pendant for your wedding," he added.

Since I was only thirteen at the time, it seemed that I would have to wait forever.

Noticing the pained look on my face and likely detecting that I didn't really believe he would give it to me, he went on to say, "I will have the goldsmith make it into a pendant for you. I will put it in my safe until the month of your wedding." He took it back and wrapped it up.

Mummy was clearly pained at my forward behaviour. She insisted on paying for the artifact immediately. Smiling conspiratorially at me, Inayath said, "This will be my gift for her wedding. She deserves something more valuable, but I am only a munshi and can ill-afford anything else." It was settled.

After Inayath left, Mummy and Lakshmi pounced on me like vultures on carrion.

"How could you be so greedy?"

"Didn't you learn your lesson the last time you were at his house for the Eid-ul-Fitr?"

"That poor man could have sold it to the new museum or to a jeweller and paid for his daughter's dowry!"

I was immediately overcome with shame and sorrow. My eyes filled with tears and my ears hurt from the boxing they had just received. I could hardly discern the figure standing in the doorway, it was Inayath.

"Leave her alone," he said. "The sarpech is my contribution to her dowry. After all, I am part of this household now, am I not?"

Turning on his heel, he left.

❖

Despite my lack of participation in Mummy's programme of grooming me for my future, she persevered in her efforts. She was determined that I would acquire sufficient accomplishments to satisfy even the most demanding of prospective bridegrooms. Consequently, I was forced to learn to play the piano and the violin, as well as to sing. To further complete the package, she also arranged for me to learn Indian classical music and play the sitar. That way, in the event that I did not make the grade, I would at least have enough accomplishments to keep myself amused in aging spinsterhood.

Another of the many accomplishments that Mummy thought important for a well rounded daughter was proficiency at sports.

My mother had always excelled at sports, as did Rachel. I, on the other hand, being athletically challenged, preferred to busy myself with reading and painting. Athletic pursuits had always been anathema to me. My mother concluded that one half of my brain was going to remain permanently stunted due to a lack of athletic activity, so I was encouraged to partake.

The British, who ran our schools, also emphasised athletics in addition to the academic. Several trophies were awarded for students who showed equal promise in the classroom and on the playing fields. I was considered a very good student throughout my school years, however, my performance in the gymnasium or in the sports arenas was a subject of considerable amusement to everyone.

It was mandatory for all students to attend physical education classes three times a week. I considered these classes to be a ridiculous imposition. The only incentives for me to strive at such activities was that I aspired to satisfy my mother and to win the trophies awarded to "All-Rounders", the appellation given to students who were good at both studies and sports.

Girls were encouraged to play some team sport such as basketball or volleyball. Badminton, tenniquoit and tennis were other games that we were also encouraged to play. Then there were the individual sporting events such as track and field, short putts, long jumps, and so on. I was completely hopeless at any and all of these and constantly mortified in my attempts to participate.

In an effort to help, Mummy arranged for me, with Rachel in tow, to have private lessons at a nearby tennis club. This, coupled with Mummy's total faith in my ability to master any challenge that I was to undertake, a sure formula for disaster. I hated the tennis courts – they were a silent and baleful reminder of my failure to make the grade.

There was always a goodly crowd of wealthy, clubby people who came around the courts to play. The club maali would water the courts down in the evening to cool them off and then sweep them clean for play in the morning. The club servants would set up small tables at the far end of the courts; some of them piled high with freshly laundered towels and some of them covered with tall pitchers of icy cold mango *phool*. This was a favourite cold drink of tennis players and tennis watchers alike. The court attendants made the mango phool every day. They would pluck semi-ripe mangoes in the early afternoon and bake them in hot ashes left over from the charcoal broilers. When their green skins turned ashen and soft, they were washed off and peeled to reveal the soft green pulp inside. The pulp was pureed and mixed with sugarcane juice and water. The large pitchers of juice were packed in ice for well over three hours. When it was time for the games to start, frosted glasses were set out and filled to the brim with the pale green drink. Just before the drink was served, bruised mint leaves were added for additional flavour.

A famous tennis player recently turned coach had just arrived in town. He belonged to the aristocratic class and sported the grand name of Badr-ud-din Hyder. His family had fallen on rough times and he had started coaching to supplement his greatly reduced income. It was claimed that he had once played at Wimbledon. He was well past his prime now, but what he lacked in agility, he made up for with his ineffable good nature and limitless patience. Mr. Hyder would coach young hopefuls and humour the mothers of not-so hopefuls, such as me.

When Rachel and I first arrived in our smart little white tennis outfits with our Spaulding rackets, Mr. Hyder sat us down to explain the routine. We would learn to practice serving without a ball. This was supposed to be done like the slow motion movement of a mime. There was this "pretend" ball, which we tossed high in the air. We were to follow this imaginary ball up and then thump it onto the court while pirouetting half a turn on the left foot. Rachel mastered the activity with predictable ease. In less than a fortnight, she had graduated to using real tennis balls.

I could not seem to grasp the maneuver, however. I kept getting the steps all wrong and out of sequence. There was many a time that I would pirouette before serving the ball and nearly fall flat on my face. Poor Mr. Hyder spent countless long hours with me trying to explain the simple mechanics of the serve. Both he and I grew more desperate because we knew that the day of reckoning would soon be at hand, the day when Mummy would ask to see us perform. I finally struck upon the solution.

"I get all mixed up without a real ball, Mr. Hyder," I explained. "Now if I were to serve an actual ball, I'm sure I'm sure that the rest would follow fairly easily."

I must have sounded fairly convincing, or else Mr. Hyder must have felt just as desperately reckless as I did for he agreed to let me have my way. As it turned out, the balls that Mr. Hyder gave me were clearly different from the balls everyone else were using. They had a life and an attitude all their own. Most of them thudded despondently to the ground instead of winging the graceful arc over the net that the others' did. Those that weren't leaden seemed somehow to be possessed – they went everywhere except for where they were supposed to. Rachel and the other hopefuls around the club watched in dumbfounded amazement at my performance.

Mr. Hyder seemed completely numb as he lowered himself onto the low wall at the side of the courts to watch me. He sat with his head buried in his hands. His shoulders were shaking silently and when he looked up, tears were streaming down his face. I couldn't tell if he was convulsed with mirth or whether he was crying due to potential loss of income after my performance was reviewed.

The day of reckoning had finally come after a month's worth of lessons and Mummy accompanied us to the tennis courts. Mr. Hyder loped towards us as we approached with his characteristic tennis stride. He took Mummy aside and they sat in deep, quiet conversation for what seemed to be an eternity. She appeared earnest and furious at the same time. He looked cowed and beaten, almost supplicant. I could see the set of my mother's jaw, and I feared for what was to come.

She finally walked over to me and proclaimed, "Wimbledon is not destined to see your brand of genius."

I never played tennis again. Badminton, however, was another story.

In the seventh grade, a magical thing happened which at least partly redeemed my athletic performance on the tennis courts. The monsoons had just exited with their final gasp. The stormy rains and flash floods had wiped out the summer's dust and the badminton courts were now fresh and manicured, ready for the school tournaments. It was with great pomp and circumstance that lots were drawn in a lottery to pair us up for the badminton matches which were to begin.

At school, there were three sisters who were extremely good at badminton. They represented the state in the national games. The oldest of the three sisters was named Nafees who was in the tenth grade. She was quite tall and wiry. She was also a girl of few words and fierce intensity. She was an average student, but was extremely competitive when it came to playing tennis or badminton.

For the lottery, the names of the tenth grade students would be written in a logbook and then read aloud. As each name was read out, the class teacher would draw slips of paper out of a goldfish bowl which contained the names of the students in the seventh, eighth and ninth grades to determine the partnering. Nafees' name was called. Miss de Sequiera then reached in and pulled out a folded slip of paper. With no show of emotion on her face she read the name aloud – it was mine.

There was a collective gasp from the assembled students. Everyone knew that my ability to even return a serve was completely nonexistent and I would have been anyone's last choice as a partner. Like Miss de Sequiera, Nafees showed no emotion either. She ambled over to me slowly.

"We must talk," she said.

Mind you, this was a senior class student; we underclassmen barely spoke to these divine creatures unless spoken to. My mouth was dry from sheer nervousness. I swallowed a couple of times while she looked at me curiously.

"What is it? What is wrong with you?" she asked.

"I could fall sick on that day and you would not have to be disgraced," I assured her. "On the other hand, you never know, I might die before we have to play."

"The match is in two days," she said. "You don't look sick, and I don't think you are going to die."

We sat down on the low parapet wall that separated the basketball from the badminton courts.

"Would you recognise a shuttlecock if you saw one?" she asked me, holding the feathered ball used in badminton. "Do you even know which end to hit when you serve?"

"Yes, yes I do," I replied, not wanting to disappoint her.

"Do you know how to serve?"

"I do," I said, still anxious to please.

"Good. After you have served, stay in one corner of the court and I will do the rest."

"I understand. Thank you, Nafees."

She started to walk away when something else occurred to her. She stopped, turned on her heel and looked at me. With her eyes squinting in the bright October sunlight, she called out loudly, "Anna!"

"Yes?" I squeaked.

"If you don't do precisely as I tell you, death might come to you sooner than expected."

Much too soon, the day of the badminton matches arrived. The entire school gathered around the courts to watch the matches. Here was the great Nafees, paired with a pipsqueak from the seventh grade, who had all the grace and agility of a performing circus elephant. This had to be thoroughly enjoyable for all the spectators, even if it only provided laughs.

Nafees came to me with her racquet swinging by her side. She looked down at me from her great height.

"Remember what I told you," she said.

Mercifully and quickly, the match was soon over. I had done exactly as I was told. I might as well have thrown down the racquet and sat on the bench with the referee for all the playing I did. Nafees was all over the court like a darting lizard, not missing a single shot. We won all three games and became the champion pair for the school.

Nafees looked at me and smiled."You did well," she commended.

One of my classmates, Sayeeda, along with her older sister, Sorayya, heard the comment and let out simultaneous guffaws.

"You didn't even play! She did all the playing," remarked my classmate.

I was mortified. I could feel the tears gathering in my eyes, but I was loathe to let them see me cry. Nafees, who had started to walk away, turned as she heard the comment.

"What did you say?" she demanded.

"Nothing but the truth," said the older of my tormentors.

Nafees transfixed the ninth grader with the coldest stare that I had ever seen. With her right eyebrow cocked up, she looked down at the offenders and said, "I meant it when I told her that she played well."

Not to be silenced, Sayeeda piped up again. "I am good at badminton and if we had been partners we would have trounced the whole group."

"The fact is that you would not have followed my strategy if you had been my partner," Nafees told her. "You think you are good, but you would have defeated any saves I might have made. Those who know their strengths and how to use them, teamed with those that keep their weaknesses from killing them, win games. Anna's strength was to follow my instructions to the letter. Her weaknesses never came into play at all. We are a winning team, where you and I would not have been."

Having said that, she looked at me kindly. "Thank you, partner," she added. And then she walked away.

That year, I not only won many prizes for academic performance, but I also won the much coveted "All-Rounder Award". I proudly came home to my mother with a trophy that I had no chance of ever winning, all because of the kindness and decency of a divine senior.

❖

Mementoes of the summer holiday always found their way back home with us from our journeys. In a vain attempt to rekindle Mummy's interest in gardening, we would always bring back some plant or the other from Travancore. With unfailing tenacity and optimism, we would arrive home with carefully wrapped cuttings of gardenias and tubers of tuberoses every summer. However, these plants resolutely refused to grow in the garden because of the dry heat of the Deccan Plateau. They had grown beautifully in the south where the rains were constant, the water brackish, and the weather extremely humid, but they remained stubborn in Hyderabad. The gardenias and tuberoses temporarily managed to elicit an evanescent, flickering interest in Mummy.

"They have finally taken root," Rachel exclaimed joyfully one summer after having tried unsuccessfully to coax them to grow in Hyderabad several years in succession. We dragged Mummy out into the garden to see the final real success of our perseverance. Mummy was impressed with our persistence and the hardiness of our latest offerings of gardenia saplings and tuberose tubers.

While they did "take", the gardenia and tuberose plants were grudging in their floral output, except for one eventful fall. It was as if they had forgotten their stubborn refusal to acclimate and they suddenly went wild, putting on quite a show in the tiny garden at the small house. The gardenias and tuberoses bloomed as if they could not stop, resulting in their heavy scent filling the garden and its adjacent rooms.

Mummy floated the gardenias in bowls of water in the dining room. There were tall stalks of tuberoses in vases gracing the drawing room. She braided them into our hair everyday and we took them to school for our teachers and friends. She stored those that she did not use in the refrigerator so that every dish – the butter, the yogurt, the lamb, the saffron rice – everything eventually smelled of the wretched flowers. This went on for over a month until everyone was heartily sick of them and their cloying scent. There were only two in our family who did not tire of the flowers – my mother and my aunt Anna. Sadly, there were not too many other things they agreed upon.

Anna's husband's sudden death from a heart attack had just released her from the gulag of a physically and psychologically abusive relationship. She became a widow at the age of thirty-eight, and the day that she became widowed was a memorable one.

Anna and her husband were attending a party at a friend's home. We had been invited as well – possibly as a concession to Anna. Most of the people at the party were high society folk at a fancy dinner, with fine food and plenty of prize alcohol. Women did not usually imbibe, but the men certainly did. By the end of the evening, Anna's husband and his friends were roisterously drunk.

"Let's go home and get a good game of cards going," he said to some of his gin-rummy friends. They were all known to gamble quite heavily and as of late, Anna's husband had been having a run of bad luck, losing large sums of her money.

Turning to look at her, he beckoned her to come home with him.

"I would like to stay longer with my friends, if you please," she entreated.

His alcohol had gotten the better of him. His face thickened with rage, his eyes became more bloodshot than usual and the veins in his neck stood out like thick cords. He raised his hand and viciously struck her across the face. Blood seeped out of one nostril and dripped on to her butter and caramel coloured, creamy silk sari. She raised her hand to wipe the blood away and he struck her again. As she cowered against the onslaught and backed away, he rained blows on her back and her shoulders. There was absolute silence as all the partygoers watched the drama unfold. He then reached behind her neck and yanking her chignon loose, he proceeded to drag her to the door.

While all of us had suspected that he was physically abusive to her in their home, he had never actually done such a thing in public. Her eyes filled up with tears of humiliation and pain. Everything was quiet and in a split second a realisation dawned on Anna. She suddenly realised that she was the mainstay of the family, the breadwinner and the true source of his affluence and bravado. With her hair in disarray she extricated herself from his grasp and drew herself up to her full height. She said calmly to him, "I will join you later."

He read the look on her face and must have decided that it was wiser to avoid public confrontation. He turned back to his friends and said sneeringly, " She will come crawling back to me tonight and I will then teach her a lesson or two."

The group of men were gone and Anna stayed for an hour longer. The party became more subdued – at least for a while. There were long awkward silences until the strident ringing of the telephone interrupted the strained quiet. Someone asked for Anna.

She went over to the phone, nodded a couple of times and said, " I will be home right away."

Then, turning to the rest of the party, she announced, " He had a heart attack. They say he is dead." As she walked out of the house, I saw a very small smile of triumph on her lips as her chauffer let her into the back seat of her car. But she was now a widow.

Widowhood in India for both Hindus and Christians was like living in limbo. By contrast, among Muslims, marrying a widow was considered a worthy act which would deserve accolades in a virgin-infested Heaven In years past, Hindu widows even practiced sati. Its purpose was to expiate the sins of both husband and wife and to ensure the couple's reunion in the afterlife. The practice was facilitated by the low regard in which widows were held. In spite of being abolished by British Indian law in the early 1800s, isolated cases of sati still occur.

Hindu and Christian widows were considered accursed creatures who had caused the death of their husbands and brought misfortune to their household. Those who were not employed would now put added financial burden on their families. Hindu and Christian widows never remarried – they were supposed to be models of rectitude and propriety. As such, they were forbidden from wearing colour or much in the way of adornment. They were limited to white cloth and gold jewellery with an occasional diamond – which of course had to be white. "The colour is gone from their lives with the demise of their lord," was the explanation. The brightly coloured silks and satins were forbidden forevermore. The lovely tinkling luminous glass bangles were to be replaced with the dull sound of gold bracelets. Among Hindus, the breaking of glass bangles on the recently widowed woman's wrist is a specially orchestrated event at the husband's funeral. Further, they could never again adorn their hair with the fragrant flowers that most Indian women prized.

Men of course had no such restrictions. Their lives returned back to normal as soon as logistically possible. Men who had been widowed did remarry, often before their wives' bodies could turn cold in their graves. "Men can paint colour right back into their lives," was the refrain.

Anna was still young and attractive when her husband passed away, and fortunately for her, very wealthy. Although we were Christian, after her husband's death, Anna adopted the garb of the traditional widow. She started to wear crisp cotton saris, dazzling white and starched to perfection. Every fold and pleat in the sari was ironed to knife-edge crispness. She had the dhobi dust them with a liberal sprinkling of mica so that the material would glisten in the sun.

She wore no adornment except for a pair of diamond earrings which must have cost a king's ransom. There was a cluster of seven diamonds in each ear lobe, sparkling like a million tiny suns with her every move.

Then we noticed that about a month after her husband's death, she seemed to bloom like a gardenia. Her step became lighter, her face which was ordinarily always somber was now wreathed in smiles, and her eyes seemed to dance with an inexplicable joy and mirth.

"It must be the release from physical abuse," Lakshmi opined.

That year, my father's brother Joey who was studying to be a chartered accountant, came to help Anna with her books. He was much younger than she was. It became obvious to the servants that they shared more than an interest in keeping her accounts in order. The usual underground wireless among the servants transmitted the gossip to Lakshmi who subsequently revealed it to us. Of course, since there was no proof of this entanglement, there could be no remonstrations. It was difficult for Mummy to contain her accusations and finger pointing; she would have loved to gain the upper hand in this sibling duel of theirs. Ammachy, who had the uncanny ability of ignoring people and their circumstances into oblivion, blithely pretended that there was nothing happening between her daughter and her daughter's lover.

Late one evening, on her way back from her work, Mummy stopped to visit her sister. Anna's sons were away at a Boy Scout camp. The servants must have been in the back of the house when Mummy walked into Anna's living room unannounced. It took her some time to accommodate to the darkness. When she did, she saw her oldest sister and her youngest brother-in-law locked in a naked embrace on the living room sofa.

"How can you be so shameless?" Mummy exclaimed. "You have sons to bring up and a standard to uphold."

Her anger at Anna was not really a righteous indignation although it was posed as such. It was actually a combination of envy and regret. After Papa's departure to Arabia, Mummy lived a rigidly virtuous life. She did not allow herself to deviate at all from the straight and narrow. There were men who came knocking at her door, but Mummy prided herself on her probity. We never really knew whether or not she chafed against this self-imposed sacrifice. Heavily endowed with an unfortunate sense of righteousness and propriety, she had grown more rigid and unbending as she grew older.

Mummy stalked out of the house in a tremendous show of moral outrage and refused to speak to Anna for several months thereafter. It was probably a triumph of sorts for Mummy to be able to lord her own faultlessness and rectitude over Anna.

Anna ultimately gave up her accountant and her "sordid affair". Joey found himself a suitable young woman whom he married shortly thereafter. Anna threw herself heavily into working with the newly established Family Planning Association of India – travelling far and wide in an attempt to help the nation stem the rising tide of humanity which was soon to engulf India. There was a rumour, not quite unfounded, that Linus Loncraine, an English big game hunter she met in the north, had fallen in love with her. It must have been short lived though for all we saw was that Anna's life had become progressively desolate and joyless. She had always been a quiet woman by nature but now she became more withdrawn, uncommunicative and almost reclusive, except with her patients. With them she was known to be compassionate and caring and they adored her in return.

Finally, Anna healed the breach with Mummy by admitting that her actions had been selfish and immoral. The sisters resumed their relationship and began speaking to one another again. As children we welcomed this rapprochement – we could go back to playing cricket and flying kites with our cousins, and we could once again eat at Ammachy's table. Most importantly, I could observe Anna and store lessons about her deportment and general demeanour for my future.

One Thursday evening after reuniting, Mummy invited Anna for supper. She came with her sons – my cousins, Thomas and Samuel. Mummy and Anna went into the garden to admire the gardenias and tuberoses. My aunt stood looking at the flowers thoughtfully for a very long time. Turning around deliberately she said to Mummy, "Weave a garland of these for me on Sunday, Mary."

"What is so special about Sunday?" Mummy asked. Anna did not answer. We went in for the marvellous supper Mummy had prepared. Anna seemed oddly euphoric that evening causing Mummy to question her on it. "I have found the Path to Heaven," she replied cryptically in response to Mummy's probing.

The next morning, there was a loud honking of a car horn at the gate. We ran out to see who it was. It was the older of my cousins, Thomas. My mother looked up from what she was doing as he came running toward the house.

"I cannot wake my Mummy up," he said.

My mother became as pale as a sheet. She dressed quickly and drove with him to my aunt's house. There my aunt Anna lay on her large ebony bed, all decked out in her wedding sari. She had draped her bed with the length of silk brocade given to her by her late husband at her wedding.

This is the common manner in which married Syrian Orthodox women are dressed for burial. Her arms were neatly folded across her chest. Yehuda Chang's black robe with the embroidered crysanthemums was folded neatly into a rectangle and placed under her head. Mummy noticed a purple bruise in the crook of her left elbow. We were told later that she had injected herself intravenously with enough morphine to kill five horses. She was taken to the hospital where they worked for three whole days to try and keep her alive. Sadly, it was all to no avail.

Practically all of Hyderabad and the neighbouring city of Secunderabad turned out for her funeral. Her coffin was placed in a beautiful white hearse and drawn by two massive white stallions. The crush of the people at the funeral was so great that it was difficult for the family to get to the cemetery.

The Syrian Orthodox priests, who had benefited greatly from her largesse while she was alive, now took an unforgiving and unbending stance in her death.

"One who has committed suicide cannot be buried on consecrated ground," they said.

"That did not prevent you from taking her money while she was alive," raved my mother furiously.

"Her donations earned her forgiveness only while she was alive," came the rejoinder. "Not for this act; she threw God's gift of life in His face."

It was the Anglican clergy that agreed to officiate at her funeral. Her remains were interred on the Anglican side of the cemetery.

Her coffin was covered with an avalanche of flowers sent by her adoring clientele. The flowers were cleared off to allow the coffin to be lowered into the grave. A solitary garland of gardenias and tuberoses that Mummy had provided remained, draping the coffin.

The gardenias and tuberoses in our garden instinctively went back to their grudging, niggardly few flowers every spring thereafter.

8

Love, Lust, and Abandonment

AMMACHY CONTINUED TO RULE ANNA'S HOUSEHOLD AFTER Anna's death. The main house where Ammachy lived, stood at a higher elevation than the rest of the structures in the compound. The kitchen and the servants' quarters were separated from the main house by a large verandah and a dozen odd stone steps. Ammachy ruled over it all much like the Queen empress issuing orders to the kitchen staff from the elevated sanctity of her bedroom verandah. Managing the servants and the finances, she ran it like a smoothly oiled machine. Among the large retinue of servants who populated Ammachy's house, Krishnan-kutti was the most important. Krishnan-kutti was Ammachy's chief cook. He had been brought up from Travancore by the family as a young boy to help in the kitchen and ultimately graduated to the level of chief cook.

My cousins Thomas and Samuel continued to live in the grand house with Ammachy until Thomas' own emerging manhood and Krishnan-kutti's death rained curses and bad fortune down on my cousin Thomas. Krishnan-kutti died a rather tragic death. However, in their typical fashion, the servants converted his death into a romantic event.

My initial recollections of Krishnan-kutti were when he was in his early thirties. Rachel and I, along with our cousins Samuel and Thomas, were still young children. My cousin Thomas was the oldest among us and the apple of Krishnan-kutti's eye. The rest of us were inconsequential satellites around this sun.

Krishnan-kutti could conjure up the most amazing delicacies in a trice. His most special favours were always reserved for Thomas. All Thomas had to do was ask and Krishnan-kutti would fly away like a little whirling dervish disappearing into the bowels of the kitchen only to reemerge with trays of goodies for his young master. Krishnan-kutti's devotion was returned with the tolerant and amused indulgence of a master for his favourite pet. Thomas would tousle Krishnan-kutti's hair and tease him unmercifully. The rest of us would never have presumed to be this familiar with anyone so much older, especially a servant. Krishnan-kutti was a morose, cadaverous looking little fellow, frequently given to muttering under his breath. He had an unhealthily protuberant belly and a faint yellow tinge to his skin from his frequent drinking. Thomas towered over him, even when he was just a boy.

In her usual imperious manner, Ammachy decreed that since it had become stylish to have a drive bordered with bricks, they should have one as well. In accordance with her fiats, her maali placed red bricks, positioning them on their side to make a brick gadroon along the driveway. He embellished the border with a purple fern called the wandering Jew. The wandering Jew bore strange little white flowers which appeared to spring out of a deep purple bicuspid bract. These little cup-shaped things were home to an odd assortment of bugs and insects. It provided us with endless hours of fascination to pour water into the bracts and watch the insects scurry out.

Krishnan-kutti, who always harboured more superstitions than the rest of the household, maintained that bivalve bract of the wandering Jew housed evil spirits manifesting themselves as bugs and insects.

"When the wandering Jew blooms, it presages bad luck — someone will die," He warned the imperturbable maali.

"You will die of drink before anyone else, so it should not affect you," the maali retorted in exasperation.

The wandering Jew bloomed year after year, and no one died. Since Krishnan-kutti was almost always drunk, off as well as on the job, his dire predictions were ascribed to his affection for the bottle. No one ever paid any particular attention to his rantings.

Krishnan-kutti was sufficiently important in my grandmother's hierarchy that he was given his own garden. This was his very own private preserve. No one, not even the maali was allowed anywhere near it. He guarded it with a strong fierceness. The produce from the garden found its way into the food that was served in the great house. Whether it was the perversity of plants, or the devilry of one of the younger servants, one spring the wandering Jew from the driveway border found its way into Krishnan-kutti's private kitchen garden.

His ravings now grew intolerable. To appease him, the maali agreed to plant an expensive tree of his choice in his kitchen garden. For propitiation Krishnan-kutti chose a fig tree which was selected from the Nizam's nurseries. It was planted in the quadrangle in front of the kitchen. The tree bore figs which were deemed singularly unpalatable by everyone except Krishnan-kutti. They were plucked just before they ripened and stored in an earthenware jar filled with brown sugar, cloves and saffron. How old the figs were, and whether they were fermented, we would never know.

Krishnan-kutti proceeded to age a hundred years over what was merely just a few. He had taken to drinking the rotgut moonshine available to the poor folk in the city. When he was thoroughly inebriated, he would go into a cooking frenzy and make the most wondrous dishes we ever tasted. His prized creation to emerge from his drunken state was his roasted squab stuffed with figs from his special tree. It was one of Thomas' favourite dishes. Most of the making of this dish was done in secrecy. He claimed that he had learned to make it from the Iranians who lived next door.

The Iranians owned many of the restaurants in our city. These were the favourite haunts of all the Muslim lorry drivers who passed through carrying cloves, cinnamon and coffee to the north, and saffron and tea to the south. I had eaten squab cooked in their kitchens, but Krishnan-kutti's version with figs was far superior to anything they ever served up. This lead to all kinds of speculation about Krishnan-kutti by the other servants who claimed that he practiced black magic and that there was more to the stuffing than one would care to know.

When the spirit moved him to make his squab dish, the earthenware jar with the figs would come down off the shelf. He would dip his capacious ladle into its dark recesses and withdraw an unspeakably evil appearing mixture. Water chestnuts, sweet snap peas and walnuts were sautéed in butter, along with the figs and a concoction of mace, nutmeg and other spices. By this time, the stuffing had been transformed into a splendidly aromatic, buttery and luscious mixture. The cleaned and gutted squab was then dressed by one of the lesser servants. Krishnan-kutti bolted the kitchen door from the inside when he roasted the squab. Only one other person was allowed in the kitchen during the process – this was Mariam.

Mariam was another of Ammachy's acquisitions along the way. She had been hired from some obscure little village in Travancore to assist with various household tasks. Krishnan-kutti became very much enamoured with Mariam who was only nineteen or twenty years old at the time. Mariam was an incorrigible coquette and knew that half the world was in love with her. She was a lovely, small-boned woman with finely chiselled features. Her skin was like the unblemished, highly polished rosewood of Ammachy's armoires. Her exquisite almond eyes were set above impossibly high cheekbones . Her perfectly shaped eyebrows soared upward at their outer ends like a pair of outstretched raven's wings. She had a husky voice and an irrepressible giggle which would bubble into a lovely tinkling laugh. What she had not bargained for, however, was that my cousin Thomas, caught in the toils of his burgeoning stormy adolescent hormones, would also fall victim to her charms.

Unlike me, my cousin Thomas was tall, perpetually bronzed and extraordinarily handsome. Where Ammachy constantly berated me for my shortcomings, she pointed out to all and sundry that Thomas' noble brow and patrician nose epitomised a noble visage. He walked with an easy, lazy lope. He had a slow, winsome smile which was slightly lopsided, just enough to make it heartbreakingly endearing. His eyes were a deep, deep amber. His only passions in life were flying kites and cricket – these were the only activities that ever fuelled his fire. He always looked debonair and suave in the togs he wore for his cricket game on Saturday afternoons. All else he played at was done with a slow, luxurious pace.

It is easy to imagine what must have happened. He must have come home early one Saturday afternoon, claiming that the summer sun had made playing cricket unbearable. No one must have been home other than Mariam. Ammachy and Samuel had probably gone out shopping. The other servants were probably off on errands or just asleep in the back of the house. He must have taken off his shirt and V-necked cotton pullover. Standing at the verandah of the main house, he must have called to the dhobi to take his clothes to be laundered. Mariam must have come out from the servants' quarters to pick up the clothes since the dhobi had gone home. As she climbed the dozen or so stairs up to the main house, he must have come into full view. There he must have stood, the young Lord and master of the house, in all his bronzed beauty, quite unaware of the effect that he had on her. It was only just a year prior that his voice had changed and gone from a warbled soprano, through an unbearable falsetto, to a deep baritone. And in just that year he had grown tall, very tall, to just under six feet.

"What are you staring at?" he must have asked.

"You," she must have said in that honeyed-voice of hers. "You've grown."

"Yes, I've outgrown my shoes several times this year," he said somewhat self-deprecatingly, smiling in embarrassment with his sweet lopsided smile.

What happened after Mariam reached out to touch him, none of us will ever really know, but can well imagine. However, in the weeks following that fateful Saturday we noticed that Thomas, who was usually always jovial and convivial had become silent and preoccupied given more to growling than smiling. Mariam, on the other hand, became more radiant. Her body somehow seemed to have blossomed. Her breasts, which had been quite small, had become larger and her gait sported a more provocative sway. She laughed more freely and seemed far more ready to accommodate everyone's demands of her culinary artistry. Krishnan-kutti was more in love with her now than ever. She appeared to derive an extraordinary sadistic pleasure in spurning his advances, which had once been welcomed.

It was a particularly hot July that year and the monsoons were late in starting. We were all at Ammachy's house for our weekly visit. Thomas was noticeably absent for the afternoon tea and by the time dinner came, I wondered aloud where he was. A strange silence fell over the table. Mummy kept her eyes steadily riveted to her plate. After what seemed to be an eternity, Ammachy looked up from her food and with a tone of exasperation in her voice she said, "I have sent him south to fetch the monsoons."

Suddenly there was a sharp gasp of breath and a loud clatter as Mariam dropped the tureen with the curried chicken, spilling it all over the polished granite floor. She ran out of the dining room towards the servants' quarters. Rachel and I ran after her and waited outside her door. We could hear a great deal of loud wailing from within. This was punctuated with entreaties from Krishnan-kutti. He kept saying over and over again, "I will marry you and no one will ever need to know."

The door suddenly opened and Mariam came rushing out. She walked quickly up the steps to the main house. When she reached the dining room, she stood with her arms akimbo looking at my grandmother with a rebellious glare in her normally soft brown eyes.

"What are you going to do with your great-grandson?" she demanded, sticking her belly out defiantly.

I had witnessed Ammachy in difficult situations several times before and knew that she possessed the ability to look regal and dismissive in even the worst of circumstances. This was one of those times.

"You will be gone from this house before sundown," Ammachy said evenly as if she might have been choosing the luncheon menu. Looking at Mariam with one-arched eyebrow, she continued, "My great-grandsons will be sired of my own choosing."

Mariam seemed to shrink before her gaze. She retreated back and down the steps. Krishnan-kutti was standing at the bottom of the stairs. Mariam stumbled on the last step and fell backwards into his receiving arms. His face was transformed as he caught her, breaking her fall, as if he had been privileged to receive the Holy Grail.

"Let's go away together," he whispered into her hair.

A look of disdain swept over her face. "I would rather kill myself," she replied, spitting venom at him.

We do not know what transpired later that day except that Mariam was dispatched that evening by train back to her parents. Jamal-ud-din, my grandmother's Chokra boy, took her to the train station.

Almost a month later, the monsoons finally arrived; so did my cousin Thomas. Mariam came back after the monsoon season was over, childless. She had changed from the Mariam we knew.

She seemed much more chastened, quieter, and no longer beautiful. Her eyes did not dance anymore. We were never to hear her gay, infectious laughter again and the dishes she cooked became insipid and uninspired. Her face was the same delicate face, but her breasts, which had been small and pert, were now saggy and lifeless. It was as if her breasts had been punctured and her life's force had been drained slowly out of them.

After that, Krishnan-kutti's drinking became much worse. That winter, we ate a lot of roasted squab at Ammachy's as he was drunk most of the time. One Saturday when he was more silent and far more intoxicated than usual, he served up the squab again in the evening. It far surpassed anything that he had ever made before. The meat was tender and succulent, the figs and the water chestnuts were unbelievably flavourful and sweet, and the spices more aromatic than they had ever been.

I went to the kitchen to tell him that the dinner was spectacular. He was lying on the floor in a pool of blood and quite dead. The servants, as usual, romanticising death and every adverse circumstance, maintained that his soul had bled out for the two people he loved most in the world – Mariam and my cousin Thomas – both of whom had, in a manner of speaking, betrayed him.

◇

Out the gates and down the road from our little house was the old Kaale Nawab's summer home – a place I often used to pass on my way to school. It was a huge rambling bungalow which had been rented by the government from the aging nobleman until the usual multi-storied government buildings could be constructed somewhere. The home now housed the Weights and Measures Office. There were wide banyan trees in its ample courtyard and in between the roots of the banyans grew the *neelambaram* plants. These were nondescript little things which did not grow much beyond a foot. When they bloomed, however, they were very prolific, putting out an abundance of violet-blue flowers.

Most government offices were guarded by the chowkidaar, the gatekeeper. This one was no different. They had hired a man from one of the villages south of the city for the job. He had left his young wife and child in the village, he said, and had come into town to find work. He lived in one of the servants' quarters behind the main bungalow.

"They call me Mukkundam," he said when he first introduced himself to me. It was the most sonorous sounding name I had ever heard. Mukkundam was tall, very tall, and extremely dark. He had the whitest teeth and the most languorous smile you ever saw. His eyes were bold and probing and his heavy eyelids crinkled upwards when he beamed his lazy smile. His dark hair curled around his forehead. He always wore a white cotton tunic and a length of white muslin to cover his lower torso.

In the evenings when it was not raining, he would sit cross-legged on the verandah playing a simple stringed instrument, singing simple village songs to the blue-skinned god, Krishna. On occasion, he would play the drum while he sang. His drums were cylindrical with taut skins stretched at both ends. It was mesmerising to watch his fingers stroke the drum skins with an ever-increasing frenzy. Finally, the tempo would slow to a sluggish hypnotic thrumming as his song came to an end.

When I was younger I would sit on the steps with Mukkundam and listen to him tell stories about his village or sing some of his songs. He would cook his evening meal on a simple little charcoal stove. The meal usually consisted of flat pan-fried wheat bread and spiced lentils. On special occasions, he would cook the most delicious dish of potatoes laced with green chili peppers and dill. I always managed to find my way into his kitchen when he cooked the special potatoes. He would look up from his cooking and smile at seeing me. Without a word, he would fetch two battered tin plates – speckle ware as we call them now, and serve us both. I relished these meals with Mukkundam.

Mummy would have been appalled had she known of my daring escapades and Papa would have been furious had he known that I was spending time supping with a lowly chowkidaar. Lakshmi didn't even need to ask; it seemed that she had eyes in the back of her head. She always knew instinctively where I was going or where I had been. I had a sneaking suspicion she frequently lied to cover my absences.

After entering my early teens, I forgot all about Mukkundam. I would see him occasionally on my way to school and acknowledge his greeting with no more than a wave and a smile.

The year I turned fifteen the southwest monsoons were unusually torrential. It rained and rained for days on end without remitting. Rivers of muddy water flowed fast and furious past our house and in the gutters of the street. The mynah birds, normally noisy and raucous in the summer, huddled silent, drenched and miserable in the trees during the monsoons. The only sounds to be heard were the kettledrums of thunder and the castanet-like beating of the rain on the tin roof above the shed behind the house.

Lakshmi had planted a border of neelambaram plants in our small garden and they flowered profusely. The monsoon didn't seem to faze them and they thrived in spite of the torrents. Every evening she would weave them into garlands to decorate the little statue of Krishna she had placed in the kitchen. The statue of her blue-skinned god bore an uncanny resemblance to Mukkundam, or so I thought.

Late one afternoon the rains ceased and the heavy blue gray clouds parted to let out a teary-eyed sun. The trees shrugged the water off their green mantles, the birds hurried out to dry off, and the muddy tumescent streams became inconsequential little rivulets. The street urchins came out to play hopscotch and wade in the receding waters. At dusk, a slight drizzle started once again, sending the urchins home. Lakshmi had left a neelambaram garland on the steps. I picked it up cupping it gently in my hands and found myself walking out of the gate.

My feet seemed to find their way unbidden to the old Nawab's house. The main gate was closed and barred for the evening. However, I could hear a familiar, haunting melody coming from beyond the walls. It was Mukkundam singing with the voice of an angel.

I opened the small side gate letting myself in and then closed it securely behind me. The singing stopped as I walked up the drive towards the verandah. The house was dark save for a distant light in the servants' quarters.

Mukkundam stood up and leaned against one of the pillars watching silently as I walked up the steps. He looked leaner now than I had remembered him. I had forgotten how beautiful he was. Actually, I had not forgotten, I had just never seen his beauty before, truly seen it.

By the time I reached the verandah the rain had started in earnest again. I stood there wordlessly becoming drenched. He stretched his hand out to lead me up and under the shelter of the verandah, out of the rain.

"I brought this for you," I said, hesitantly handing him the garland. He took both of my hands and helped me drape it around his neck.

"You've grown," he said wonderingly, with a smile in his voice. "You must dry off. I have a towel for you here in the *charpoy*, the guard house."

As I dried myself off, he had fetched his drum. He then sat cross-legged on the floor.

"Would you like to hear me sing?" he asked.

I nodded.

He sang in a soft, plaintive and low voice. I could feel my eyelids grow heavy. My body felt as if it had been thrown into a flaming cauldron.

Then he led me back out into the courtyard and the rain towards his small quarters behind the main house. I followed him wordlessly and willingly. I was as completely drenched when we got there, as was he. It seemed to matter little to me that it was getting colder and darker, and I was unconcerned that I would be missed at home. I was almost in a trance like state while in his room where he unbuttoned my blouse and patiently unwound my sari. It seemed like an aching eternity until he finished. I simply stood there waiting in my long underskirt as my clothes fell in a heap onto the floor. He took a towel from a clothesline in the room and proceeded to dry my shoulders and back. He turned me around to face him and cupped my breasts in his hands. Then he bent down to kiss them. He then gently forced me down onto his bed. He tugged impatiently at the drawstring which fastened my underskirt and managed to loosen it. His long fingers stroked me gently at first and then expertly and insistently until I started to shiver. As he continued the stroking I hoped I would never stop this delicious shivering.

"Oh God! Stop, stop!" I moaned, not really wanting him to.

All of a sudden I realised that the rain had stopped and that I had gotten what I had come for. I pushed him away with more strength than I thought I possessed. Picking up my clothes, I ran out of the door and down the driveway. I looked over my shoulder expecting to see him on my heels in hot pursuit. He was merely standing in the doorway, immobile like Lakshmi's statue of the blue-skinned Krishna. I dressed as hurriedly as I could while on the run. After unlocking the gate, I flew for the safety of home. I must have been quite a sight – looking all drenched and dishevelled as I dragged myself in.

"And where have you been?" Lakshmi demanded, looking up from her seat outside my bedroom.

"Nowhere," I lied.

"Pretty drenched and disarrayed for being nowhere."

I must have looked wretchedly guilty, but I volunteered nothing, absolutely nothing.

"Get changed before your mother sees you," she said while bustling around, picking up my wet clothes.

Later that evening, Lakshmi settled down to brush my hair.

"When men don't get their usual release they go mad and then they go blind," she informed me. "That fellow Mukkundam, the chowkidaar – he is mad now they say. He will be going blind soon."

"What is their usual release?" I asked.

"You are not a man; you don't have to worry about that until the time comes. "

"Until when is that?"

"Until you get married," she said with the kind of finality that would brook no more questions. "You must stay clear of men until you are given away to one in marriage."

Even after my father had lost his wealth, his ancestral home in Travancore was never sold. Had our constrained circumstances forced the sale of this property, our family would have suffered an ignominy from which we could never have recovered. This would have been the *coup de grace* to our tenuous hold on respectability in our homeland. No decent Travancore family would have entertained a continuing alliance with a household that was forced to leave their home. So, false appearances of prosperity were maintained in Travancore despite a serious inability to do so.

One summer, when I was about sixteen, we embarked on our usual journey south to the ancestral homestead. By this time, railway lines had been laid into the towns and it was no longer necessary to travel part of the way by boat.

The servants would always fetch us from the train station and escort us home. George, the property's major-domo, orchestrated the Travancore end of the journey. He was in his thirties when I first became aware of him. He was of medium height and built like the jackfruit tree in the front yard – taut, stocky and muscled. His arms were powerful and he had rough, calloused hands with spatulate fingers. He walked with a swagger that grated on me; it was as if he owned everything in sight. He had a thick mop of curly dark hair and a full black moustache which was peppered slightly with gray. His face was unremarkable except for a slow grin which spread lasciviously to his eyes.

George maintained my father's home and plantations in Travancore while we were in Hyderabad throughout the remainder of the year. He harvested the pepper, the tea, the coffee and the coconuts. He arranged for their sale and turned the profits over to my father. He supervised the kitchens where the cook – usually his wife fixed our meals. He kept the rest of the servants and field hands in check. They viewed him as a tyrant and were afraid of his quick temper and powerful arms which could deal a swift and punishing blow. We addressed him respectfully as *Chetan*, "Older Brother", as a mark of recognition for his position on my father's estate and because he was older than any of us children. Above all, George worshipped my father and would do anything to win his approval. As much as my father loved him, I found him revolting and yet secretly fascinating at the same time.

The home in Travancore was the ideal country home for the adults providing them with a holiday from the year's strivings. But for us children, the fascination and diversion was evanescent. There was precious little for us to do throughout the summer but read and play in the courtyard which had a very low and scalloped wall with wide masonry posts at regular intervals. The courtyard separated the compound from the cultivated area.

Rachel and I would frequently amuse ourselves by walking along the top of the masonry wall which skirted the perimeter of the courtyard. It was quite a balancing act to be able to walk the uneven wall without tumbling off of it. As I did it more often, I grew more complacent and careless with my steps. It wasn't long before I fell off and twisted my ankle as I went down. I sat there in a daze for a while, watching in anxious horror as my ankle swelled.

"Oh no, school will be starting in the next two weeks and I cannot afford to be laid up with a sprained ankle," I thought.

I felt gingerly around my swollen ankle to determine if any of the bones might be broken. There was a sound behind me and I looked up to see George standing there over me. The *lungi* he wore clung to his solidly muscular thighs. It was too hot to wear a shirt so he was often bare-chested as he was now. His chest was broad and smooth.

"Let me look at your ankle," he said as he poked and prodded it with a look of great concern. I could sense his fear that he would be blamed for having let harm come to the eldest daughter of the house.

"Nothing is broken," he said reassuringly. "It is just a bad sprain. I know these things." I was skeptical.

He bent down and lifted me in his powerful arms with great ease, cradling my head in the crook of his shoulder. He carried me across the compound with giant strides and when he reached the verandah, he set me down on my father's planter chair. He left me sitting there with my foot elevated on a small stool.

In a short time, he returned with a basket filled with an assortment of bark, fruits and leaves from plants that grew outside the perimeter wall. He called imperiously to one of the servants in the kitchen and ordered her to bring him a small mortar and pestle. He fed the contents of the basket into the mortar and had the servant grind it into a fine paste with the pestle. I remembered then that he was an herbalist of sorts and was often called upon to administer remedies for whatever ailed the servants in my father's employ. With swift and delft strokes he applied the paste to my swollen ankle and then proceeded to massage it. The pain from his manipulations was intense, but mercifully shortlived. He then wrapped it with a soft splint.

It was late in the evening by now. My father and mother had gone visiting relatives and were not expected home until quite late. George fed me my supper and carried me to my bed. He covered me with a light blanket and dropped the mosquito curtains around me. He stood up to leave and blew out the lamp on his way out of my bedroom.

"Please leave the lamp burning, Chetan. I am afraid," I whispered.

"What are you afraid of?" he asked gently.

"Of snakes, of ghosts, of not waking up in the morning," I replied.

"I will stay right here until your parents come back," he reassured me.

When I woke up the next morning, I found him asleep at the foot of my bed on a makeshift pallet made up of a reed mat and an old quilt. He stirred when he heard me awaken.

"Your parents will not be back for two more days," he said. "They have gone to negotiate a marriage proposal for one of your cousins. Your little sister left this morning to join them."

"She left me alone!" I exclaimed.

"She was convinced that she would be bored, with you laid up with your swollen ankle," he replied.

One of the maids then brought in a basin of lukewarm water. George proceeded to rinse my face with a small soft towel. While I sat there seething at the idea of being left alone and incapacitated, he left me with the maid who was to help me with my ablutions. I then stood up to put weight on my ankle fully expecting it to hurt. To my great surprise, I felt only a mild ache.

When George returned, I saw that he had bathed and changed into a fresh shirt and lungi. He had brought me a warm cup of coffee and a plateful of steamed plantains with fresh coconut and brown sugar. He then knelt down and unwrapped my ankle. It had shrunk back to its normal size and there was only a faint bruise visible. I noticed a satisfied smug look on his face as if to say that he was better than any doctor, and most certainly better than the doctor I was to become. Any gratitude I felt was instantly forgotten as I felt an overwhelming urge to slap him at that moment. He must have read my thoughts for he reached out and intercepted my hand. He held it for what seemed to be an eternity and set it down gently on the arm of the chair looking into my face with an amused grin. Then, as if nothing had happened, he proceeded to wash my ankle. He sat down, cross-legged in front of me with my foot in his lap, and gently massaged my ankle with some medicinal oil he had poured into his broad and calloused palms.

"That feels good, doesn't it?" he said.

I nodded.

"Would you like me to massage the other foot?" he asked.

"Yes," I replied. "Oh yes."

It was a soothing and comforting motion. Before long, I had leaned back into the chair and drifted off to sleep. He must have shifted and scraped the chair accidentally as I came awake and found that he was kneading my calves.

He was looking at me strangely. "Do you want me to go on?" he asked in a hoarse and husky voice. His face flushed and coarsened visibly as he spoke.

"I don't know," I replied.

"Do you want me to stop?"

"I don't know," I repeated, totally mesmerised while watching his powerful fingers work up beyond my knees to my thighs. I felt a strange pounding in my head and an intriguing warmth in my groin.

"Stop," I said sharply. "Stop right now."

The strident note in my voice had broken the spell. He stood up to readjust his clothes, trying to hide the sudden new tumescent growth in his garment.

"My God," I thought in instant recognition. *"That is an enormous erection!"* Embarrassed, he retreated into the far reaches of the house.

My parents returned home after unsuccessful negotiations and much haggling over unreasonable dowries. I avoided George for the rest of the summer, partly frightened of my ready response to his immense sexuality, and greatly afraid of my parents' reaction to my unseemly behaviour.

By the time the summer was drawing to an end, we soured on what we had initially enjoyed in Travancore and were ready to return home to Hyderabad and the delicately fragrant rice and refined piquant sauces of the Mughal cuisine there. We missed the succulent fowl dishes cooked with almonds and cream and dozens of spices. Our palates craved the exotic deserts and sweetmeats that followed the sumptuous Muslim dinners at home. By summer's end, we were heartily tired of the simpler fare, the intellectual snobbery, and the Christian superiority of Travancore.

When it came time to leave for Hyderabad, the usual retinue of servants accompanied us to the railway station. I was comfortably ensconced in my seat by the open window with my arm draped across the sill flipping through a book when I noticed a somewhat forlorn figure standing on the platform. I pretended not to notice him. The whistle blew and the train started to chug slowly out of the station. I felt a light touch on my arm and I looked up. There was George with a beseeching look on his face as he was running to keep up with the moving train. I stood up to watch him.

"What?" I called impatiently. "What do you want?"

"I don't want you to forget me," he said with his eyes welling up. "Here," he said reaching out to give me a parcel wrapped in burlap. "Make a paste out of the leaves for a poultice the next time you sprain your ankle."

I took the parcel from him wordlessly, watching his face as the train began to gather speed. I watched as he retreated into the distance, became a small speck behind and then disappeared altogether.

I sat down to unwrap the parcel and found two little saplings well packed in wet loamy soil inside. One of them was a Margosa sapling and the other was a small amaranthus plant.

"What is that?" Mummy asked.

As I showed her the saplings, I could see her eyes go dull with the pain of memories of the house-with-the-garden.

"Oh yes," she said. "George uses those for poultices. He had given us some saplings once when we had the old house. I planted them by the chicken coop; they are probably still there."

We reached Hyderabad three days later. I planted the saplings near the kitchen in the little garden of our smaller house where they struggled to grow and were soon mercilessly snuffed out by others plantings that competed for space.

❖

One day during our last years in high school, Rachel sought me out to talk. I could detect the urgency in her voice and sensed that she was quite distressed.

"Papa has a mistress," she blurted out.

"What? Who, where?" I asked.

"Down south in Travancore."

"How do you know? He didn't tell you, did he?" I asked sarcastically to cover my dismay.

"No, I read his diaries and opened his mail," she replied.

I could not believe my ears. My sister who was normally so prissy and good had done something so unthinkable – she had pried into someone else's life without their permission.

"What is her name?" I asked.

"I think it is Sosha. He calls her his beloved Champak bud."

"So what did you do when you found out?"

"Nothing, I came to talk to you." I could feel her desperation. "We have to save our parents' marriage."

"There is nothing left to save," I replied. "They will not get a divorce, at least not until we are married. He is entitled to some happiness too. Let's leave well enough alone." This, however, was not to be the case. Rachel adamantly insisted that we confront Papa with what she had discovered.

Papa was in Hyderabad nearly as often as he was in Arabia by this time. We challenged him with what we knew about Sosha one evening in his study. He sat at his rosewood desk with his head in his hands, weeping. It was then that I noticed his shoulders were starting to stoop. He looked up at us and wiped the tears from his eyes.

"I will send her away," he promised apologetically. "I will never see her again."

"You cannot do that," I replied. "You are going to have to provide for her."

"I will do no such thing."

"Oh yes you will, Papa!" I was surprised at my own temerity. "You will give her the house at the edge of the paddy fields on the old estate in Travancore. You will also deed some of the plantation fields to her."

"Now why would I do that?" he asked.

"Because if you don't, we will tell Mummy," I answered. We did not have to lay out the holocaust that would follow if we carried out on that particular threat.

"I'll think about it," he replied.

"No you won't, Papa," said Rachel in a brave but squeaky little voice following my lead. "Your secret is out now and you will do what is responsible."

He looked at us in stark disbelief, as if he could hardly believe his ears. His darling obedient little daughters had become blackmailing monsters overnight.

Rachel and I were later appalled at what we had done. In one fell swoop we had not only destroyed any chance Papa had for happiness, we had also completely disrupted the life of his mistress.

Sosha had originally come from an Orthodox Christian household. She had then invited social ostracism upon herself by consorting with a married man. Her family had cast her out; leaving her to the whims of the man she had chosen to follow. If he sent her away, she would have no sustenance, physical or otherwise. No man would ever marry her. She might as well have had an "A" for "adulteress" branded across her forehead.

My father, of course, would be forgiven and all would be fine with the exception of the wrath and ire he would surely suffer at the hand of my mother. His behaviour would invite my mother's criticism, who by all social dictums would appear to have clearly fallen short of the ideal. The impression lent would be that she had failed to be the perfect wife thereby causing her husband to find solace elsewhere.

The whole situation would also prove to be a problem for us as we approached marriageable age. We would be the daughters of a woman who had proven herself to be an inadequate wife. However, there was some salvation in this predicament for us. This major defect in my mother's character, which would more than likely be inherited by her daughters, could almost certainly be rectified with very large dowries.

Papa never saw Sosha again in that way, but she was well provided for.

Rachel and I went to visit her in Travancore one summer. She still lived in the house on the edge of the paddy field that Papa had provided for her. We knocked on the door which was ajar and let ourselves in. She came out from the kitchen as if she had been expecting us. I was surprised to find that she was only half a dozen or so years older than I was. She was as dark as night with deep velvet-like skin which showed no blemish at all. Her straight, thick hair fell like a curtain below her knees. She was unusually tall and slender, and wore white as is customary for our women. Her voice was deep and mellow, like a conch shell summoning devotees to worship. Every move was a paean of grace. We just stood there, gawking, and completely dumbstruck by her beauty.

"You look just like him," she said looking at me. "And you, you are as beautiful as your mother," she said to Rachel.

She offered us coffee and homemade fruitcake. As she extended the coffee cup to me, I saw her long and graceful fingers. I understood then why Papa had called her his beloved "Champa kali." Her fingers resembled the long and graceful petals of his beloved flowering champak tree from the old garden – there was the significance that the plant had for him, the one that Mummy resented him so for spending so much time with.

Rachel and I remained silent wending our way back to the summer house. In our shared silence, we knew that in our self-righteous adolescence, when we had confronted our father about Sosha, we had destroyed something as beautiful as it was defenseless. It was then that I also remembered the Puukenikeni vine that Mummy had planted in the garden long ago – the one that Mrs. Cotter had warned could bring a mistress into her marriage.

On the Sunday that followed our confrontation with Papa, other beautiful things were destroyed as well. We were at the last part of our beloved Enfield ritual with Uncle John when he looked at both of us with sorrowful eyes. He reached out and laid his hand on my head as if in benediction. His eyes filled rapidly with unshed tears.

"I will read you my favourite poem which I want you to remember as long as you live. It is my gift to you," he said trying to smile at us as he withdrew an old book with hand-tooled leather covers from his worn saddlebag.

The poem "*Pied Beauty*" was written by the Jesuit convert Gerard Manley Hopkins.

"Why is it your favourite?" we asked.

"It will teach you that God makes all things, even many of them flawed. In His sight, however, they are always beautiful.

This will help you to learn that there is less beauty in perfection than there is in the flawed things of this world. You will learn to love and forgive."

"Glory be to God for dappled things –
... ...Landscape plotted and pieced – fold, fallow and plough;
... ...All things counter, original, spare, strange;
Whatever is fickle, freckled (who knows how?)
With swift, slow; sweet, sour; adazzle, dim;
He fathers-forth whose beauty is past change:
Praise Him."

"When the time is ripe, God will reveal its significance to you," he said.

Then Uncle John dropped the bombshell on us. We were not going to have the ritual together with him anymore.

There was a sharp intake of breath.

"Why not?" I asked, almost afraid to hear the answer.

There had been a falling out between Uncle John and Papa. No one ever actually articulated the reason for the rift to us, but occasionally we would hear whispers and snippets dropped by others in the family about the matter. John had apparently also discovered the existence of Sosha. While he condoned most of my Father's foibles and loved him in spite of them, this inexcusable abrogation of responsibility was one he could not forgive.

"I have to work out my own salvation. I have to improve my willingness to forgive. I will tell you about it some other time," was all he ever told us. From then on, uncle John came to visit us far less often and usually did so only when Papa was not around.

9

A Fine Doctor

*T*HERE WAS ALWAYS A PART OF ME FOR WHICH MUMMY HAD NO patience. I had inherited it from my father – the ability to dream. I could sit for hours on end and do nothing but dream. Even as a child, I would daydream. There were dreams of being the brightest and the best, dreams of bringing riches home to my father so he would never want for anything, dreams of becoming so important that my mother would always be proud of me, dreams of taking Rachel on my adventures to new and foreign lands, and dreams of building a home for Lakshmi.

"You have to get started by dreaming," Lakshmi informed me. "Most men dream. Great men fight for their dreams; that's what makes great men great."

"It is much better to have your own dreams, isn't it, Lakshmi?" I would ask.

"Yes, you can then decide who can or cannot gain admission to your dream," she added.

Ever since I had been a young child and fashioned my self-image after that of my aunt Anna, one of my dreams was to become a doctor, and by the time I was in college I was even more determined to do so. There was a significant factor that featured prominently in my decision to apply for admission to medical school. My late aunt Anna had been far wealthier than most of the people I ever knew. It was the affluence surrounding her household that convinced me very early in life that becoming a doctor would provide deliverance from the privations that now surrounded our home. The large retinue of servants, the fine china, the unlimited supply of fine linens, the endless variety of sweets, and most of all, the insouciance of my cousins about acquiring things which would have given me grave concern persuaded me that becoming a doctor was my passport to comfort.

I was to secure admission to medical college much over the objections of my mother who believed that I was better suited for the study of mathematics and physics. Nothing I could say would convince her that I found those subjects not only boring, but extremely daunting. Finally, in a fit of desperation I told her, "Mummy, the only reason I even bother going to college now is to stare at the physics professor and the Muslim boys." I knew that this would elicit the response I wanted.

The physics professor belonged to one of the more prominent aristocratic Muslim families of Hyderabad. He was so handsome that he could have been the model for Michelangelo's David. As such, my friends and I would spend hours scribbling his name all over our physics textbooks. Although he taught thermodynamics, there was nothing dynamic about his teaching. Scribbling his name in our books was far more interesting than listening to him drone on about the physical laws of the universe.

While it was true that the Muslim boys were all supremely handsome and one could easily stare at them all day, I was not as interested in them as I was in gaining acceptance to medical college. I could see myself like my aunt – wearing a white coat, wandering importantly through the hospital wards followed by a gaggle of junior staff hanging on my every word and being asked for my opinion on some monumental diagnosis or the other.

My mother finally gave up her protests. Applying to medical college was a highly competitive process as several thousands of students sought admission. The list of successful entrants would be posted in the newspapers and on the bulletin boards of the college at the end of May, as medical college would commence in July.

One of my neighbours and good friends who was already a medical student – Shuja-ud-din, Shuja for short came to knock on our door at the end of May with the newspaper in his hand.

"You are in!" has said, grinning like a Cheshire cat. I had gained admission to that holy of holies – medical college when I was sixteen. I had realised one of my greatest dreams. The following year, my sister Rachel followed suit.

After securing admission, medical students were required to spend a year in pre-medicine where subjects other than medicine were taught. This year of pre-medical education for the female students was done in what had come to be known as the Women's College. The first year of pre-medicine and the six years of medical college that followed were fruitful and fulfilling, just as they were poignant and painful. I was to learn much more than just medicine.

Our favourite pre-medicine professor was one who taught us Botany – Dr. Wahaab. She was a pretty young thing who was scarcely ten years older than most of her students. She had an infectious, diminutive giggle and a smile that suggested she was the repository of an enormously divine secret – some unbelievable cosmic joke. The mirth in her would come bubbling through at the strangest of times. Most people would have called her fat, but to our eyes she was like a delicious round rice dumpling with pale olive skin, dancing brown eyes, and fetching dimples. She constantly entertained us with gossipy little stories that were laced with interesting bits of the college's history.

In the distant past, the college campus and buildings had been the palace of the British Resident who had served as an emissary of the British Crown in the Nizam's kingdom. The college had a main set of buildings which had been the Resident's office and living quarters. The buildings were built in the classic British style – large and rectangular with typical restraint, barely hinting at the grandeur and splendour inside. The many marble steps at the front of the palace were guarded by the requisite carved British lions. The buildings sat in large, lovely gardens which spread over eighty acres in the middle of the city.

I had my favourite haunts in the old palace, of which there were three. The first was the principal's reception room which had once been the gentlemen's smoking chamber. Dr. Wahaab allowed me access to the bookshelves in the room. I spent hours poring over the old books that were piled high and pell-mell on the shelves.

"Look," she once said directing my wondering gaze to a delicate portrait that hung there. It was rendered in the usual two-dimensional Mughal style. I thought I could feel a faint fluttering in my heart; there was something special about the man in the painting.

"Who is he?" I asked.

"That is Faqhr-ud-Doulah Bahadur, Hushmuth Jung," she replied. Dr. Wahaab was sitting beside me; she seemed breathless with excitement.

Pointing to the portrait she said, "Notice that his hand rests on the jewelled hilt of a Saracen *talwaar*, sabre. Look there on his index finger, there is a large *zammarud*, emerald ring. It is actually a poison box made into a ring. Rumour has it that it can hold a secret stash which allows one to surreptitiously open it and drop poison into someone's drink without running the risk of being observed. As the story goes, the sabre and the emerald ring belonged to the Resident's wife, the begum," whispered Dr. Wahaab. I was puzzled that the Resident would have a begum, which implied that his wife was Muslim.

"She observed the strictest *purdah* tradition of Muslim women not to show themselves in public, even after she married him,"

Dr. Wahaab further explained. This meant that she never showed herself in public.

"Who is he?" I asked.

"That is Faqhr-ud-Doulah Bahadur, Hushmuth Jung."

There was something wonderful and resonant about the titles awarded to the nobility of Muslims in Hyderabad. I could feel stirrings in my soul – possibly from a previous life.

"*Hushmuth Jung* – Glorious in Battle," I translated. "What battles did he fight?"

"Ah!" she exclaimed, "the battle of Muslim India against the British Empire."

"There was no such battle."

"Ah but there was – it was a battle he fought in his soul."

She opened up a large book in the chamber and pointed to a picture of a man in it.

"Here is an earlier portrait of him as Colonel James Achilles Kirkpatrick," she pointed out.

I could barely see any resemblance between the two. In this picture he was very British – tall, imposing, mustachioed and looking resplendent in his uniform. He had a gentle sad face which was quite different from the contented one in the Mughal portrait.

"You see," Dr. Wahaab explained, "he was the British Resident who married a begum –Muslim aristocrat."

"British did not marry Indians and Indians did not consort with the *gore log* – white people," I said.

"Oh, but they sometimes did indeed. That was before one of the viceroys in the early 1800s decided it was unseemly to mix with Indians, forcing men like Hushmuth Jung to give up their Indian wives and their children of mixed ancestry."

The second of my favourite haunts at the college was the main library. It was vast and had well-lit little nooks and crannies where one could settle down comfortably with a book of choice. The librarian was probably as old as the library, a tall martinet who could transfix you with a stare in an instant. Behind her ancient crusty exterior hid the soul of a true connoisseur. She took an instant liking to me and it was because of her that I could stay in the library long past closing time. I gained access to books which were not meant for the prying prurience of most of the callow young women who came to study at the college.

The collection of books in the library was old and had that wonderful smell that only old books possess. The ink in the books was ancient and had faded to a dull sepia. Many of the writings were in Urdu – which I was unable to read. The sinuous script still fascinated me endlessly with its ever-changing calibre as it glided across the page from right to left with dots atop the alphabets like diamond ink drops. I sat there endlessly looking at them, making up stories in my mind about the good Colonel James Achilles Kirkpatrick and his beloved begum – Khair-un-nissa.

The Botany department at the college occupied what was once the *zenana* – the women's section of the palace – the third of my favourite haunts. Our classrooms were Indo-Saracen in design with marvellous and exquisite tile work on the floors. There were cool verandahs flanked with balustrades along the perimeter of the zenana. These looked out over the begum's gardens. Long colonnaded walkways led into the gardens and the walkways were separated from the gardens by trellises.

During summer, the enormous curtains that flanked the verandahs would be let down. These were no ordinary curtains. They were woven from sheaves of *khus*, vetiver, and then encased in muslin. They served to muffle the crazed calling of the brain fever bird, which punctuated the torpor of summer afternoons in the zenana. In the heat, the gardeners who scurried around the grounds like ants tending the plants would spend the entire afternoon wetting the curtains down with water. The hot summer breezes that wafted across the arid Deccan Plateau would then come whistling through the curtains to turn cool by the moisture and become perfumed by the vetiver as they blew into our classrooms.

If we finished our botany labs ahead of schedule, Dr. Wahaab would take us out on field trips to gather botanical specimens of medicinal value since we were all headed for medical college the following year. She first took us to the begum's gardens.

The begum had ordered the planting of a wide assortment of medicinal plants in her garden that would have been an apothecary's delight: *digitalis purpurea, datura stramonium, cannabis sativa, papaver somniferum,* and *nerium oleander.* All along the cobbled garden path and around the fountains there grew mushrooms of every colour and shape.

"Some of these are intensely hallucinogenic," warned Dr. Wahaab. She went on to entertain us with some of the more popular and most romantic rumors of the Resident and his begum which went something like this:

The British Resident was a young man fresh out of England. Soon after he had settled into his position as the emissary of the British crown in the kingdom of Nizam, he would go around to the provinces making himself seen and heard as the living symbol of *Pax Britannica.* In the late 1700s the British were much more accepting of all things Indian. They learned the many languages of India and its previous invaders – Hindi, Persian, Arabic and Urdu. James Achilles Kirkpatrick was an avid student not only of the languages, but also of the culture and the practices of the court of the Nizam. This made him invaluable as a liaison between the British crown and the kingdom of the Nizam.

The Nizam's court was full of factions warring against each other and jockeying for positions of power. Adding to this incendiary mixture was the presence of the British. The story goes that the British Resident James Kirkpatrick became the unwitting pawn of the courtiers surrounding the Nizam. He had been invited to a celebration of the marriage of one of the noblemen he did business with. It was there that the Resident looked beyond a curtained doorway and found himself lost in the eyes of the nobleman's daughter – Khair-unissa Begum.

When she saw him, the Begum quickly drew the curtains together and withdrew from the stare of the intrigued foreigner. Her body was veiled and all he caught a glimpse of, besides her lustrous face, were her hands and her feet. Her hands were small, perfectly formed with delicate wrists and sinuous fingers. Her feet were adorned with long, graceful toes and a high arched instep. As was customary for Muslim women, her palms and soles were adorned with henna. She wore fine silver filigree bracelets around her slender ankles. Strangely enough, her hands were devoid of ornament except for a large emerald ring.

The Resident was unable to keep his attention focused on the task at hand as he had become so smitten with the delicate creature which he had spotted beyond the curtained doorway. He had fallen instantly in love with her face, hands and feet, since he could not have seen much of anything else.

It is entirely likely that the young woman found her way into his quarters later that evening. There probably was also the tacit collusion of her mother and grandmother. The Resident was allowed access to the young woman on several occasions thereafter. In any event, Khair-unissa Begum fell just as much in love with James Kirkpatrick as he did with her.

After she became pregnant, he married her. This union was only agreed to by her guardians on the solemn promise that she would be his legal and only wife, and not a mere plaything to be discarded after he had indulged himself. The alliance was made under a cloak of secrecy, and not revealed to his British masters until much, much later.

James Kirkpatrick brought his prize back to the city and had her ensconced in the palace, which was to later become our college. She never ventured out in public again, staying for the rest of her life behind the trellised walkways and curtained halls. She was a devoted and faithful wife. More importantly, she was an able political advisor and confidant. She kept abreast with the intrigues outside of the palace with her own network of servants and spies. It was rumoured that she helped her husband by swiftly dispensing his enemies with many poisons concocted from her extensive garden from her large emerald poison box ring.

The Indians say she survived Kirkpatrick – widowed at the young age of twenty. She was subsequently abandoned by the British and the Hyderabadi nobility. She was stripped of her wealth and position and eventually died a lonely death in exile.

Dr. Wahaab, forever the romantic, maintained that one could still see them walking the gardens on moonlit nights.

"If you are very quiet," she said, "you can hear them."

I knew that I could – at least in my dreams and in my heart – I could hear a faint laughter, the tinkling of glass bangles, and the rustling sibilance of silks beyond the walkways in the begum's garden. If I was quieter still, I knew I could hear the heavier and firmer booted footfall of a man walking beside his woman. And if I was absolutely and perfectly still, I could even hear the raspy scraping of the Saracen sabre along the balustrades of the verandah.

✧

The Anatomy Dissection Hall was our abrupt introduction to medical college after the relatively easy year of pre-medical studies at the Women's College. It was located on the top floor of the south wing of the medical college building. We entered it with trepidation, not knowing what to expect. The class of two hundred-odd students was divided into multiple groups of four that stood in frightened little huddles as the chairman of the Anatomy Department, accompanied by his staff of professors and associates, explained the mechanics and logistics of the study of human anatomy.

The dissection hall was enormous and stretched for what seemed to be miles. There were two rows of steel tables on either side of the hall which had holes in their centers that drained into large pails placed below. Surrounding each table were steel stools which looked like bar stools. Along the sides of the Anatomy Hall were large windows looking out into the courtyard of the college on one side and the warehouse and delivery section on the other. Under the windows were open shelves for dissection instruments and manuals. A long enclosed verandah ran along the inside of the hall where there even were more steel tables. At the far end of the hall were the formidable "tanks". These were huge steel and masonry vessels filled with formaldehyde where bodies awaiting dissection floated in the thick brown solution.

On the first Thursday of every month, a fresh supply of cadavers would promptly arrive at the college. We could watch them being unloaded from the windows and verandah of the Anatomy Hall which overlooked the delivery area. There was never a shortage of bodies as the indigent of the city and the neighbouring villages kept the Anatomy Hall generously supplied. These were the legions of poor in India who had no one to bury or cremate them. If they had not been ravaged by disease and were still reasonably intact, they would be sent to the medical college for dissection. The staff in the dissection hall termed them the "inconvenients". It was inconvenient to care for them when they were alive and inconvenient to bury them when they were dead. As such, they would wind up on our dissection tables.

The bodies were sent up by special elevators to the storage facility from the delivery and warehouse section. The dissection hall staff comprised mainly Muslims or untouchables, since the higher caste Hindu would never touch inconvenient bodies. These men prepared the cadavers by cleaning the guts, shaving the heads, and injecting the blood vessels with formaldehyde. When they had finished the preparation, they would punch a hole in the left ear of the cadaver and attach a metallic tab which was numbered. The groups of medical students would be given a number which signified which one of the cadavers was assigned to them for dissection.

Early in the morning, the staff would arrive and hose down the hall for the dissection sessions. When the students paraded in after their morning lecture they would make their way to their assigned tables and wait by them. The doors to the tanks would then noisily clang open.

I never quite got used to the manner in which the bodies were retrieved from the formaldehyde tanks. The staff would cast long poles with meat hook like implements at one end into the tanks and fish out cadavers one by one. Cadaver after cadaver was then piled onto steel gurneys and wheeled into the hall for dissection. The steel gurneys would rumble down the central aisle with three or four cadavers piled on each of them. Then a pair of the dissection staff would heave a cadaver onto the assigned table for the awaiting students.

One cadaver each was assigned to a team of seven students – four first years and three from the second year class. There was always a senior second year student who was considered to be academically superior and who served as the head of the team. They directed the process and helped the first year teams with their dissection. The first year students would disarticulate and remove the arms and the legs of the cadaver. They would then move the limbs out onto the verandahs where they completed their dissection on the tables waiting there. At the same time, one of the seniors would start working on the head and neck, the second on the abdomen and pelvis, and the third on the thorax or chest.

We had fully expected to be assaulted with the stench of putrefying flesh and varying degrees of decomposition and decay. Instead, the hall was surprisingly clean and the only smell present was the strong odor of formaldehyde. Initially our eyes stung and our noses watered from the formaldehyde, but we soon became acclimated to it. We had fully expected to use gloves while working, however, we did not because fine dissection was better achieved without them. We diligently scrubbed our hands thoroughly after each dissection to try and rid them of the permeating smell of the formaldehyde. Ordinarily, the repeated washing and constant contact with the formaldehyde would have dried out our skin. Instead, it was curious to note that our hands became extraordinarily smooth and soft. The dissection hall staff explained that it was the human fat that rendered our hands so smooth and our skin so pliant.

Walking down the many aisles of steel tables, one would see bodies in various stages of dissection. Most of the bodies were whole at the beginning of the academic year, but then as the months progressed and the first year students disarticulated the limbs, there were strange looking forms left behind – heads attached to torsos with limbs missing. Sometime the first years were slower at dissection, which meant that there might be a limb or two still attached to the body.

After the students had finished their morning dissection sessions, the dismembered bodies were thrown back into the tanks for the night. The limbs were tagged and similarly stored. It was like a scene out of an intense horror movie.

The first three months were nightmarish, almost ghoulish for most of us. I was too frightened to sleep alone and would insist on sleeping with Mummy in her bed. But after the initial shock of working with the cadavers wore off, anatomy actually became enjoyable for me. We eventually became immune to the gruesome site of the parade of body parts on the long rows of the dissection tables. Four mornings a week, for two years straight, the first and second year students mastered anatomy by dissecting these cadavers.

By the time we were in our second year and had completely overcome our revulsion of the corpses and the Anatomy Hall, we would often come back after hours and continue to dissect late into the night. The obliging staff in the dissection hall would stay around to accommodate us for extra money and free meals. They would dutifully retrieve our cadavers for us and put them back in the tanks when we had finished with them.

Anatomy Hall was initially one of the most disquieting experiences of my life. Then, as I continued with my studies, I found anatomy to be an utterly fascinating subject. It was awe-inspiring for me to discover how totally complicated the human body actually is. I found the dissection of the head and neck especially intriguing. After disarticulating the jaw and removing the tongue from the floor of the mouth, we had to carefully delineate the complicated paths taken by the cranial nerves. It was wonderfully satisfying to locate them as they exited the skull through narrow little crevices and foramina, tracing circuitous paths to their ultimate destinations. By the time I finished my second year, my fear and revulsion of Anatomy Hall was replaced by awe and reverence for the forces that design our bodies and shape our destinies.

It was equally fascinating to me to try and fathom how all this could have developed from a single fertilised ovum. There were so many things that could possibly go wrong, but in the majority of instances it did not. Most people have two eyes, two ears, a heart with four chambers, a liver on the right side, and a spleen on the left. Occasionally things did go awry and in those instances the defects could make life problematic.

This feeling of awe was cemented during the study of Embryology, the study of how the body develops in the uterus. It encompasses the study of internal biological clocks that order and ordain the development of various complicated organ systems, some in tandem and others in unison. If one portion of the sequence were to fall out of rhythm and cadence, the whole parade could be affected. It was even more fascinating for me because of the birth defect I was born with – the omphalocele. As a result of this developmental abnormality, I was to require multiple abdominal surgeries well into my adulthood.

As a student of anatomy, my professors noted that I showed great promise in the field. I loved to study the subject and as a consequence my dissections were pristine. On the first day of my second year, the chairman of the department sent for me.

"You are one of the finest students I have ever had," he said. "You show true respect for the study of anatomy. I expect that you will top the class and receive the University's Gold Medal for Anatomy." I loved the subject enough that studying it was hardly an effort for me and I did succeed in being awarded the Gold Medal for Anatomy. However, at the beginning of the second year, I had to overcome a psychological setback.

My sister Rachel had succeeded in gaining admission to the same college following the year behind me. As a first year student, she was assigned to the same dissection table that I was at the beginning of my second year. On our first day in Anatomy Hall of that year, I waited for the familiar roll of the cadaver-stacked gurneys to come steadily down the aisle. As expected, a gurney stopped at the side of our table. The body slated for us was lying face down on top of the other cadavers on the gurney. The men lifted our cadaver onto our table, still face down. One of the students helped them turn the corpse over.

"Hey, what have we here?" commented one of the men.

"This is a castrato," said the second man.

I knew that this would pose a problem for the senior student who would be doing the pelvic dissection. I was the team leader and casting a cursory glance at the cadaver I said, "This one is useless to us. Get us a replacement," speaking dismissively of the cadaver.

The cadaver's arms then flopped listlessly in front of its pelvis, almost as if to cover its castrated state.

"Ha, ha," one of the men laughed mirthlessly, "covering her shame."

I heard a sharp intake of breath and strangled cry. I turned around to look towards the source of the gasp – it was Rachel.

"You'll get over the queasiness soon," I assured her.

"No, no," she said with a strange look in her eyes, "look at the left hand."

There it was, that familiar calligraphic tattoo from years ago in the web between the thumb and index finger of the left hand.

It was Narsa, our servant, the eunuch who had left our service years ago when Mummy distrusted her and discovered her secret. Her head had been shaved, but the same beautiful face remained except that her eyes were shrunken in death and her lips stretched over her teeth in the final rictus of rigor mortis.

I just stood there, transfixed with shock. The chairman of the Department came over to see what was happening.

"Is there something I should know about?" he asked.

"We could remove the pelvis and still use the body," volunteered one of the second year students.

The chairman looked at me and asked, "Do you want to tell me about this, Anna?"

"Sir, this person was our servant long ago; it would be difficult for me to dissect this body."

He was a rotund little man with a sweet smile and perfectly chiselled features. He looked at me with infinite compassion.

"We will bury her with proper ceremony then." Turning to one of the staff and handing him a large roll of rupee notes, he said, "Raheem, make the arrangements for the burial."

Narsa's body was removed. She received a proper Muslim burial, this Hindu hijra.

Rachel and I paused in momentary reverence for this being who had once been our servant. We then began our dissection on another one of the Inconvenients.

❖

Medical College exposed me to endless daily lessons in the various faces of human suffering, pathos and privation. As students, we were to learn first hand that benevolence was not a natural accompaniment to the white coat of the physician – Hippocrates notwithstanding. My family, my parents, my uncle John and Lakshmi served as guides along the way.

"Benevolence and goodness are difficult challenges," Mummy said. "The choice and the willingness to stay the course despite temptation can be daunting undertakings."

"Evil is necessary in life because it forces you to make choices," my father once told me. "In the making of those choices, in the fires of Hell, God forges you into fine gold."

"I remember reading somewhere that Gautama, the Buddha, had said that a man could not effectively eschew what he had never experienced. If you were only to encounter goodness, how would you then recognise evil or know what to do when you encounter it?" Mummy said.

"Wealth and power are not evil," Papa added. "It is how you use them that defines the role good or evil will play in your life."

All these things they spoke of were abstractions and had no real meaning for me whatsoever. until I came face to face with the Enemy and his invitation to join forces with him.

Our Medical College and hospitals were built by the Nizams of Hyderabad. It was in these haloed halls of learning and mercy that I brushed elbows with the enormous power of avarice and Evil and learnt of the temptations that besieged the wealthy and the powerful.

These rulers of Hyderabad were stalwarts – militarily, spiritually, and as governors. Their reigns were characterised by profound compassion, tolerance and rectitude. Before Indian Independence, Hindus and Muslims lived in amity and harmony. The Nizams were potentates and their word was absolute. It was their powerful influence which made the Nizam's dominions a confluence of cultures that coexisted without bloodshed.

The Muslims I knew during my childhood were a gentle and generous people. They were patrons of the arts and provided the impetus for many of the things we recognize as Indian – the Indo-Saracen architecture, the art, the cuisine, and so on. The last Nizam of Hyderabad built universities, hospitals, colleges, parliamentary buildings, and public works projects which even today are still considered architectural marvels.

The city of Hyderabad was divided by the River Musa – named for the prophet Moses into an old city and a new one. The old city, the Purana Shehr, which occupied the south, was built in the 1500s. It is still the center of commerce with its jewellers, confectioners, *boulangers* (bakers), cloth merchants, flower-sellers, and so on. Sizeable portions of the Muslim population live in the old city.

My mother's Muslim secretary – Inayath lived there. In order to come to work in the new city, he had to cross one of the many bridges that spanned the Musa River which he did on his principal mode of transportation, his bicycle. He had made this commute routinely every morning for the entire time that he had been in government service as a clerk.

One morning before the hot weather set in, Inayath was crossing the bridge on his bicycle when a car being driven by a prominent barrister ran into him. He was thrown off his bicycle and knocked onto the footpath of the bridge. Many of the passersby stopped to assist him. The lawyer who had struck poor Inayath took him in his car to the Osmania General Hospital, which was close by. He was attended to immediately in the Emergency Room. When it was discovered that he had shattered his hip, he was admitted to one of the public orthopedic wards of the hospital.

The Osmania General Hospital, even to this day, is an extraordinarily tasteful example of Indo-Saracen architecture. The last Nizam, Osman Ali Khan, built this hospital on the banks of the Musa River. At the time I was in Medical College, the hospital had at least three thousand beds, and at any given time at least twice as many inpatients. This was a government-run hospital where the doctors were primarily government employees. Patients who were admitted to the public wards were provided free care subsidised by the Government of India. The doctors were, however, permitted to run private outpatient clinics in the evenings out of their own homes and these patients could be admitted to private rooms in the hospital. These private patients paid substantially for their care and were a source of legitimate revenue both for the government and for the doctors.

Inayath had been placed on one of the public wards under the care of the chairman of the Department of Orthopedic Surgery, Mr. Ganesh Roy, FRCS,. According to British tradition, all surgeons are addressed as "Mister" rather than "Doctor".

I was in my fourth year of Medical College at the time and had just started my clinical rotations. From my exposure to the wards and the clinics, I knew that Mr. Roy was a gifted surgeon. He was a short little man, who like his namesake the Elephant God Ganesha, was extremely homely and sported as large a potbelly. To complete the picture, he was wall-eyed with large protuberant eyes, which made him look like a bug-eyed goldfish. One could never tell if he was looking at you or someone else. He was also well-known for his explosive temper and lack of patience. Most of his entourage walked on eggshells around him in fear of a fierce tongue-lashing at any moment. Another of his distinguishing traits was that he was an extremely devout Hindu. As such, he would arrive for morning rounds with marigold garlands in hand and his forehead smeared with sandalwood paste and *kumkum*, a red powder used for anointing the altar of his private deity.

Inayath's family was told that he would need a surgical repair of his fractured hip. The surgery was scheduled for the next morning. Clerks like Inayath in the service of the government are paid meager wages and as one could easily imagine, a mishap or unplanned illness befalling the breadwinner could often throw the entire family into desperately penurious circumstances. Inayath's children were very young and all under the age of twelve. His wife was unschooled and had probably rarely ventured outside of her house. Inayath's accident presented a significant blow to the economic health of his family.

Doctors in India are held in great reverence and accorded due respect. As such, one did not go to see a doctor dressed in anything other than their Sunday best.

On the day of Inayath's surgery, Mummy and I went to the hospital and waited in the corridors outside the operating theatre. I was waiting for Inayath's family on one of the large verandahs which encircled each floor of the hospital. Inayath's wife, Sajida, arrived breathless and worried but she was well dressed with her only set of gold bracelets. I knew well that this was the only gold she possessed and was probably acquired as a result of several long years of saving. The bracelets would have been used as part of their daughters' trousseaux unless their circumstances were to improve significantly.

"Do I look alright?" she asked. She did not want to appear dishevelled and unkempt when the great doctor arrived. "The doctor is a good man isn't he? I will pray for his family and their good fortune," she added. Her nervousness made her babble on and on until Mummy reached out and touched her reassuringly.

Sajida had brought some beautifully woven marigold garlands and a box of traditional Indian sweets to be given to the surgical team who were going to be working to make her husband well. Marigold garlands are generally used for weddings, decorating altars, and placing on funeral biers. Most importantly, they are also used to pay one's respects to a person of high standing.

The flower shops of the old city were renowned for their skilful weaving of garlands and clever use of additional fragrant herbs like rosemary and lavender. These shops are small stalls where the vendor sits cross-legged, surrounded by mounds of freshly picked flowers which are arranged in piles – pink musk roses, unscented red roses, jasmine, and of course the marigolds. While haggling with customers over the price of a garland or two, the flower seller keeps his hands busy, continuously stringing the flowers into fanciful garlands. They were significantly more expensive than the ones you could purchase from the street vendors who frequented the courtyards of the hospitals.

"Do you think these are okay?" she asked showing them to me. "I stopped to purchase them at a flower shop in the old city which is why I was late," she said apologetically.

I had told Inayath's wife of the orthopedic surgeon's partiality to marigolds.

I looked in amazement at the flowers.

"Omigosh, these were expensive," I said fingering them carefully. I knew that this must have been a significant expense for her.

She smiled self-deprecatingly and said, "They are not good enough for this great doctor who will make Azmath's father well." It is common practice, especially among Muslims, not to address a husband by name or refer to him in any fashion other than as the father of the oldest child.

Inayath had been taken into the operating theatre at seven in the morning and was expected to return to the recovery area at around noon. It was around eight in the morning when a young man came to the corridor announcing Inayath's name and asked his family to come forward.

Mummy and Inayath's wife went forward, expecting the worst.

"He has probably had a bad reaction to the anesthesia," we thought.

"Is he alright?" Mummy asked anxiously.

"Yes madam, he is fine," the young man replied.

Inayath's wife looked at the young man and proffered him one of the exquisite marigold garlands. He impatiently pushed it away.

"No, no, no! What do you expect me to do with these?" he asked with great disdain, throwing the garland on the floor. "There is a small complication."

"What kind of complication?" I asked.

"Mr. Roy has made the incision to start the repair on the hip. He is unable to proceed unless a payment of two thousand rupees is made immediately."

The enormity of what had just transpired left us dumbfounded. The patient had been anesthetised and had been filleted open, but the surgeon would not operate unless he was prepaid for his services. The fee that had been demanded exceeded the amount that Inayath earned in wages for an entire year.

I then pointed out the fact that Inayath was a public patient and was entitled to free care. This only served to rouse the young man's ire and we saw his eyes flash in anger.

"You do not understand," he said. "Mr. Roy will not proceed with the surgery unless he is paid."

We looked at him in amazement and horror.

"Where are we to get the money now?" Inayath's wife asked. "Can we possibly pay him tomorrow?"

"No indeed, madam, we will have to close up the wound and by tomorrow it will be impossible to operate." He delivered this message with an iciness that I had never experienced before.

Instantly Inayath's wife slipped off the gold bracelets she wore and offered them to the young man.

"These will barely pay for the fee needed," he lied.

She became frantic and began babbling in her desperation. She attempted to tell him that she would have to go home and make other arrangements. He looked at her with a cold gaze.

"You can hand them over to this person," he said gesturing to yet another young man who had miraculously appeared from inside the operating theatre.

It became clear to me that this was a set up that was played out every day, even several times a day. The poor of India did not have a prayer against this particular brand of greed where the promise of health is held up against a lifetime of work. It is my belief that in the days of Osman Ali Khan, or any of the Nizams, this would not have been tolerated and there would have been swift retribution and punishment.

Inayath made it through the surgery and was discharged in record time.

Mr. Ganesh Roy was a good surgeon, but an extremely corrupt one. He could not have been a solitary figure in this racket. The other personnel who ran the operating rooms – the anesthesia team, the nurses and the orderlies had to have been aware of this practice, either as silent bystanders or as participants. What made it doubly tragic was that there was no one to appeal to other than God.

Inayath at least had a small amount of money, but the majority of India's billion people are far poorer than a government Upper Division Clerk. If there was in fact someone in their corner, it was not readily obvious to me. The amount of money demanded from Inayath and his family would have bought only a bauble or two for Mr. Roy's very lovely wife. But in the end, it mercilessly decimated the financial state of Inayath's family.

Later in the year, one of my clinical rotations was on the orthopedic ward with none other than Mr. Roy. In addition to being a talented surgeon, he was an outstanding teacher. The opportunity of doing a rotation with him was one that students clamoured for and rarely secured. I was extremely fortunate to have succeeded in getting this rotation for having scored the highest grades on all my exams thus far.

Mr. Roy would arrive at morning rounds accompanied by his retinue of staff orthopedic surgeons, postgraduate trainees in orthopedics, nurses, orderlies, and medical students. He was always garbed in his white coat which comically was longer than he was. He would, as was his usual practice, attend *puja* before rounds and emerge from the temple with the customary sandalwood paste mark on his forehead and a marigold garland in his hand.

During rounds one morning, Mr. Roy waxed on eloquently about the qualities of compassion and caring which he said were essential to the making of a fine doctor. I must have laughed audibly as Mr. Roy turned to look at the source of the annoying sound.

"What do you do about doctors who are guilty of graft and corruption, sir?" I bravely asked.

"Fine question," he commented expansively. "This must be routed out. These forms of vile behaviour should no longer be tolerated. Mother India has no place for it." His hypocrisy sickened me.

Being a lowly medical student, I could say no more, I had already overstepped my bounds.

I was weary and heartsick that evening as I found my way home. Much to my delight, I saw the familiar but less frequent sight of the Royal Enfield parked outside our gate. I knew my cherished uncle had come to see me in my hour of need. My heart was too leaden to greet him with my customary joy and enthusiasm. We ate dinner in silence.

After dinner he came to me and while holding my hands in his, he lovingly asked, "What can I do to make it better?"

"How do I know that I will not become like him – like Mr. Roy?" I asked after I had told him the whole story.

"You do not. The path to salvation is like a walk on the seashore. With every tide, your footsteps are wiped out and have to be traced again and again. Salvation is a birthright that has to be claimed every day."

We sat in companionable silence for a long while. My uncle stayed for evening prayer and after the blessing he rose to leave. I walked him to the gate.

As he pushed the kickstand out from under his motorcycle, he looked at me with his sad brown eyes and said, "You should consider yourself specially blessed because this doctor has held a mirror up to you. You know that you do not want to be like him and you have the knowledge to make a choice. Not many people are as fortunate as you are on this day. "

He reached into his saddlebag and withdrew a sheet of paper on which he had typed out a poem for me on his ancient Smith-Corona typewriter.

On crisp gray Basildon-Bond onionskin it read:

Screaming loudly the orphan blood flowed on.
No one had the time or sense.
None bothered to listen.
No witness, no defense;
The case is closed.
The blood of the downtrodden
seeped mutely into the dust.

"This is from Faiz Ahmad Faiz's – '*Nowhere, No Trace Can I Discover*'. I found myself a Penguin Book of Modern Urdu Poetry."

As he turned to leave, he gave me a kiss on my forehead.

"If you keep your conscience aware and awake," he said, "no blood will seep mutely into the dust on your watch."

I watched as he rode away enveloped in a roar of dust.

❖

Despite my many successes in medical college, Mummy still remained vaguely displeased that I had chosen to pursue a career in medicine. However, my vindication came on graduation day in 1968.

Before a crowd of several hundred people, the chancellor of the University called me up to the podium to receive awards in Anatomy, Physiology, Biochemistry, Pathology, Pharmacology, Surgery, Medicine, and Mid-Wifery. I was also awarded the President of India's Medal for Academic Achievement. This was one of the highest national awards given to a graduating medical student who had stood first in their class in all subjects. There was no person on earth prouder than my mother was on that day.

As a reward for my achievements, Mummy offered to buy me a piece of jewellery of my very own choosing. By the time I graduated from medical college, my father had paid off his debts and had once again amassed a fair amount of wealth from working in Arabia. Mummy had been promoted to a fairly high level position in the government, with corresponding increases in salary. I had received several scholarships from the government in recognition of what was fatuously labelled "great academic prowess" thereby lightening the burden of the cost of education. All of these circumstances improved our economic position significantly. Purchasing jewellery now was less of an extravagance than it would have been just a few years earlier.

We set out for the old city to the section where jewellers sell gold and precious stones. It was there that goldsmiths fashioned ornaments of incredible beauty. Three of us set out on this adventure: Mummy and I and of course Inayath, who accompanied us mainly because he was a master at haggling and the old city was his turf.

When we got there, we entered the shop of a highly acclaimed gem merchant. The shop was known for its large selection of rubies, diamonds, emeralds and sapphires. Like most of the gem merchants in the city, the shop owners were Marwaris from the state of Marwar in northern India. Their families had been involved in the trade of jewels and gold for several centuries.

The shop was large and capacious. A traditional jewellery shop in the old city is quite unlike what one might see in America. There are minimal items on display. At the entrance, there are a few vitrines and display cases which contain a series of small scales and balances, a panoply of delicate brass weights for weighing the merchandise, an assortment of tweezers, and finally there are the bright red and black seeds of the *Manjaadi* tree. These seeds are so uniform in weight that they are used to counterbalance very small amounts of gold or miniature precious stones.

One or two of the younger brothers of the gem merchant's family sat at the entrance to the shop. As we disembarked from the car to enter, they stood up to greet us and welcome us in. We shed our footwear at the doorway as was customary before entering.

"Can we offer you something cool to drink, or maybe you would like some chai?" Without waiting for an answer, one of the brothers clapped his hands to summon a young servant.

"*Arre bacche – chai-vai, cola lao jaldi.*" It fell to the youngest of the servants to fetch the tea and cool drinks for the customers. While the young boy ran off to do their bidding, we sat down on the large and comfortable floor cushions which covered the floor of the shop. After the blinding heat of the June summer day, the cool cave-like interior was a much welcomed reprieve.

By this time the oldest brother who was the head of the household had been informed of our arrival. He came out of the office from the back of the shop to greet us. His name was Punamchand and his acquisition of high quality gems was legendary throughout the city. In the service of the Nizam and his nobles, the ability to apprise and acquire gems of the finest quality was a highly desirable talent. Punamchand had honed his talent to a finer pitch than most of the others in the city.

"Aha," he said, recognising me from a picture in the city's newspaper chronicling the graduation ceremonies for the Medical College. "This is the young doctor. You must be very proud of her, Madam," he said, beaming at Mummy.

This was followed by a torrent of complimentary comments from the younger brothers who came forward to assess me as if I were some unusual creature from another exotic land.

"Are we buying some small trifle for the graduation or is there to be a wedding on the horizon?" he asked.

"I am interested in a rubies necklace," I said attempting to stem the uncomfortable questions about impending weddings.

The next person to be summoned was the jeweller.

"I want to look at cabochon rubies the size of my thumbnail," I said holding out my hands to him.

The jeweller was a handsome man of slight build looking for all the world like a secretary bird. With a slight stoop and receding hairline he seemed older than he probably was. He adjusted his rimless spectacles on the tip of his nose. With long delicate fingers, he gathered my hands into his and turned them over to look at my thumbnails. Then he turned them over again and examined my palms with great concentration and smiled.

"Good choice," he exclaimed. "Diamonds are not appropriate for you yet." When parents bring their daughters to select jewellery for their weddings, jewellers frequently will advise them on the precious stones best suited for the occasion.

More servants were then sent scurrying to retrieve the rubies. They came in large vats and were of every size and shade of red imaginable. The men then strained the rubies through a sieve to eliminate the smaller ones, retaining only those large enough to accommodate my choice. We poured over the mounds of stones picking up only gems of the desired size and clarity. With a loupe and fine tweezers, the jeweller examined every single chosen stone, rejecting and selecting, rejecting and selecting again, until he had finally collected about fifty rubies the size of my thumbnail. With a satisfied smile, he sat back against the cushions and said something in Marwari to one of the younger brothers. I surmise this was to signify the next step of the process. He then gathered the rubies into a small neat pile. There they lay glistening like freshly gathered pomegranate seeds – deep scarlet and translucent.

By this time, the young servant boy had arrived with ice-cold freshly squeezed limejuice and the wonderful cardamom flavoured tea that Hyderabad is known for. We took a break from the selection process and sat back to savour our refreshments.

The next person to come in this whole process was the goldsmith. He arrived with several dog-eared pieces of paper that bore pencil renderings of designs for necklaces and I selected one of them. He then sat down crosslegged in front of the small pile of rubies that we had selected and smoothed out the paper with the design I had chosen. Then, picking up the rubies with a fine pair of tweezers, he arranged them on the paper with infinite precision to form a schematic of the necklace that was to be made.

Just at that moment there was a commotion outside. A woman was standing at the steps leading up to the shop. She was wearing a *burqa,* but the piece of material which ordinarily covered the face had been thrown back to reveal a sweet young face lined by sorrow rather than age. She was fine-featured with eyes the colour of clear tea and she had thick eyebrows like raven's wings. She held out a small cloth bundle in her hands.

"Could you please tell me how much you could pay me for this?" she asked.

One of the younger brothers picked up the bundle with a fleeting hint of distaste that showed across his rotund face. He opened it and withdrew a gold choker. The choker appeared to be in need of cleaning and had obviously seen years of use.

"How old is this?" the brother asked.

"It belonged to my great-grandmother's aunt," the woman replied.

"The design is not modern and has no value. I can only pay you for the gold."

"How much can you give me?

"Not more than fifty rupees."

She was crestfallen. "I need at least a hundred and fifty."

"I cannot help you," he said with finality.

I noticed that her eyes started to fill with tears as she began to pack the bundle away.

"Wait," I said to her. "I would like to see it."

Mummy and Inayath were mortified. A well-bred person would not behave in such a manner.

The woman hesitated. Her eyes looked up at me, daring to hope.

She handed me the bundle and I opened it to examine the necklace. It was easily more than a hundred and fifty years old. It was an absolutely exquisite piece of jewellry. The choker was made up of a series of intricately carved beads of the richest and finest gold. These beads were in the shape of trefoils and were separated by deep coloured rubies, each the size of my thumbnail. It was a very old traditional design called a *Paan ka Laccha*, named after betel leaves.

"I will give you the hundred and fifty rupees," I said as I opened my purse to pay her.

Inayath was horrified. "You don't know how much gold there is in that thing," he said.

"It may be worth nothing," Mummy added.

"You should leave these transactions to people like us," said the youngest of the gem merchants.

"I want that choker." I said it so firmly that I even surprised myself. Ordinarily, one did not argue with people who were older and wiser.

I took the bundle from her and handed her the money. She counted it and thanking me with a shy smile, she left the shop.

Punamchand looked at me contemplatively for a minute and then said, "Doctor *Sahiba*, that was a fine purchase." To be addressed as Doctor and with the honorific of "Sahiba" took me by surprise; I adored the sound of it. I smiled inwardly; my dream was beginning to take shape.

"That woman is a daughter of one of the noble houses," Punamchand said. "They have fallen on bad times and she often comes here to sell her jewellery."

Punamchand sent for the goldsmith and gave him some rapid-fire instructions. They took the bundle from me.

We went back to arranging the other rubies. Sometime later, the goldsmith returned with the cleaned and now gleaming restrung choker. Punamchand carefully set it in a new case of black velvet and handed it to me.

"If you are truly as perceptive and as decisive as you just demonstrated," he said, "you will make a fine doctor. That choker is worth a hundred times what you paid for it."

It was then that I understood one of my dreams had come

true. I had graduated from medical college and would in fact make a fine doctor.

❖

After Krishnan-kutti died, Ammachy engaged a Muslim woman to do the cooking in her household. She was the wife of the chauffeur – Imtiaz Ali. Her name was Meherunnissa – Meher for short.

Meher was far more generous with her largesse and less territorial of her position than Krishnan-kutti had been. All the servants now shared a marvellous little patch of the garden by the kitchen where they grew all sorts of herbs and vegetables. They planted cilantro, oregano, rosemary, mint and dill. There was an odd assortment of vegetables with an abundance of squash, aubergines, okra, tomato and serrano peppers. We loved it when the mint and cilantro took off and overran the patch. This meant that Meher would use these particular herbs to jazz up her dishes.

This overgrowth of mint and cilantro occurred during the forty holy days of Ramzan when Imtiaz Ali fasted during the day and required special meals to be fixed for him at sundown. There was one dish prepared at this time that I particularly loved: haleem – a concoction of wheat, lamb, and lentils cooked for several hours with cream, yogurt, and a large number of spices. It was served up sizzling hot, garnished with onions which were fried to a crisp, and then covered with copious amounts of cilantro and mint.

It was years before on the last day of Ramzan when Meher gave birth to their sixth son who was named Ramzan Ali in honour of the occasion. He was a precocious and beautiful little child with a bright smile and tender touch. When he was barely three, he could converse far better than children who were much older. He would visit us often, follow us around the house and sit cross-legged on the floor beside us in our study while we poured over our books. He was prouder than any parent ever could have been when I gained admission to medical college. He would wait at the gate every evening to help me carry my books in. If he saw me nod off while studying at my books he would tug at my sleeve to wake me up.

"Doctors are *farishtey*, angels. They can't fall asleep, Bibi," he would say.

It was in the mid nineteen sixties that hostilities had begun between India and China that the Muslims and the Hindus of India forgot their ancient animosities toward each other and there prevailed an unusual sense of unity and brotherhood amongst them. During that time, all the country's finest resources were required for use by the Armed Forces of India. All the best medicines and other consumables were corralled in order to supply the Army hospitals.

That was the same time, seven years after Ramzan Ali was born, that a pall descended over the chauffeur's household. We knew all was not well in Imtiaz Ali's house. Nothing was ever said or suggested, it was just that every one appeared dour and sullen. Meher had a frown permanently etched between her eyebrows and she wandered about her daily tasks with an unaccustomed listlessness. Imtiaz Ali, who was never given too much to conversation, was even more silent than usual. No amount of cajoling or wheedling would elicit any information as to what was ailing the family.

We looked forward to Ramzan that year, hoping that a month of fasting might purge them of whatever it was that afflicted them. On the day following Ramzan, there was the customary celebration and feasting. However, the meal Meher prepared was lackluster and bland. Imtiaz Ali was not even around for the festivities. He was not to be found for several days after. It wasn't until later in the year that I was to find out what had happened with Imtiaz Ali and his family.

This was also the year that I finished medical college and started my internship in one of the many hospitals in the city.

The poor, the infirm, and the hungry streamed in from the surrounding villages to crowd the city's hospitals. The hospital wards were large and always clogged, overflowing with patients. Each ward had three sections separated by half walls. Each section had two rows of beds which were lined up with the heads of the beds against the walls. Those who needed intravenous fluids or medications got to occupy beds while the others spread their own bedding out on the floor. There were never enough nursing personnel on the wards, so families of patients who were willing to stay with them and perform the functions that a practical nurse or a nursing assistant would ordinarily perform did so. So it was that the patients were frequently fed, bathed and cared for by family members.

It was also fortunate for these patients that the abominable hospital cuisine was supplemented by food that their family members usually brought in. It was only the extremely destitute who truly suffered here since there was no one to augment their meager rations.

The food served in the hospitals was incredibly poor by our standards. The Government of India provided enough funds to feed the denizens in the hospitals reasonably well. However, the invariable take occurred at every step of the way along the veritable Indian food chain. At every conceivable station, there was the outstretched hand for the *baksheesh*, the bribe.

Every hospital had a physician who lived on the premises and managed its operations. This was the Resident Medical Officer, or the RMO. By the time the RMO, the hospital stewards, the cooks in the hospital kitchens, the scullery staff, and sundry others had their share of the take, what was left for buying provisions for the meals was meager at best. This showed in the dreadful quality of the rice, the occasional piece of meat that one found in the meat stews, and the watery lentil and vegetable soups. The milk was so diluted that there was barely any difference between the watery milk that was served up on the wards and the milky water that drained from the faucets of the city.

Unfortunately, the same food was served to the house staff when we stayed in the hospital on call. Those of us came from fairly affluent families would have their servants bring food in for them from their homes. Some of the less wealthy and louder interns in our group complained bitterly about the quality of the hospital food to our superiors – all to no avail. It was then that I decided to try a novel approach.

I was on the General Surgery rotation of my internship at the time. Depending on one's academic ranking in class, we were assigned to one of the seven professors in General Surgery. I had graduated at the top of my class and was part of the surgical team working for the chairman of the Department of Surgery, Mr. Rai.

Mr. Rai was an extraordinarily brilliant man who had taken most of his education in England and Scotland. He was very tall, very light skinned and a very devout Brahmin. Being Brahmin, he was a strict vegetarian. His was an imposing presence on our teaching rounds and in his clinics. Medical students and those training to be surgeons would flock to his clinic to listen to him as he was a splendid teacher and a very talented surgeon. He could turn a mundane disease into a completely fascinating entity. His discourses were erudite and informative and he would leave an entire audience spellbound as he wove his lecture around a subject he had chosen at random from the droves of patients who came to his doorstep. He was known to take on cases that a less courageous surgeon might have turned down. Indeed, he was the Pied Piper of the Medical College.

Mr. Rai was afraid of no one, except for his wife – the indomitable Mrs. Rai. She was a diminutive woman but a veritable virago. She could reduce even the most intrepid to a pile of dust with her strident voice and her sharp tongue.

Mr. Rai was also the chief of staff of the hospital and therefore, as I saw it, ultimately responsible for the quality of the food served within its walls. My plan was to invite him and some of the other stars in his constellation, including the RMO, to dinner in the house staff dining room to make my point. Since this gesture had never been made before by any of the house staff, our invitation was accepted with an air of delighted surprise from the unsuspecting Mr. Rai and his entourage.

The fateful evening arrived. As usual, the meals were delivered to the house staff dining room from the hospital kitchens. We went to work arranging the spread as tastefully as was possible using the motley assortment of cutlery and crockery available to us. It was with much fanfare that Mr. Rai and his retinues were announced. After they were seated, we served them the same meal that the entire rest of the hospital would be dining on that evening.

"They were out of vegetable stew," I stammered nervously as I leaned over to serve him. "I wouldn't worry, though," I reassured him, cognizant of the fact that he was a vegetarian, "there is rarely any meat in the lamb stew anyway." The rice served was lackluster in taste and had the consistency of sawdust.

I watched with growing satisfaction as Mr. Rai found the food progressively and positively unpalatable.

The dessert was the *piece de resistance* of the meal. It was an unnamed concoction of lumpy flour flavoured with the odd cardamom and sweetened with jaggery. It all floated in a translucent liquid which was attempting to be passed off as milk.

By the time the bearers had served him the dessert, Mr. Rai was almost speechless, but not quite.

"Was there some deep meaning to all of this, Anna?" he asked, spluttering over the dessert.

"Yes, sir," I replied. "This is representative of the food that is served in the hospital every day; day in, day out. We thought you would like to know."

The rest of the meal was finished in silence. I knew that I had scored a victory. The RMO was sweating visibly, the stewards appeared unable to finish their meal, and Mr. Rai kept moving his dessert around in his mouth as if he could barely swallow it. He made a few inane statements about the plight of the poor in the country. Some pleasantries were exchanged, Mr. Rai thanked us and, almost as one body, he and his entourage left.

It was to be a short and pyrrhic victory for me.

Subsequently, it came to light that the largest portion of the take of the hospital food budget was delivered to the redoubtable Mrs. Rai. Mr. Rai's complicity in the whole sordid business was driven by his fear of her. But almost immediately, things were at least partially remedied. From that day on, the house staff came to be served fine meals. The patients, however, continued to eat the same unpalatable fodder.

The subsequent ramifications to my career were to become obvious in less than a month. It was decided by some unnamed God in the Department of Surgery, likely encouraged by Mrs. Rai, that my surgical education would benefit greatly by my working on the burn wards.

Making rounds on the burn wards was to prove to be the most daunting and most unpleasant task of my entire internship. It was my duty as the intern to change the dressings on the burn patients. That year, almost all medicines including morphine and all other narcotics usually available in India were diverted exclusively for use by the military due to the skirmishes on the Chinese border. Peeling dressings from the burned bodies of the patients without the benefit of morphine to dull the edge of the pain proved to be a torturous process. It was torture for both the patient and for the intern.

Self-immolation, was and still is, a common form of suicide. Several of these women will set their children on fire as well. Frequently, and most unfortunately however, these efforts at suicide were crude and unsuccessful. These women and children would be brought in to the burn wards to suffer through long and arduous stays in the hospital. When they barely recovered, they were soon put out on the streets, charred beyond recognition – pathetic scraps of humanity who now had to beg for survival. They were too unsightly to be taken back by their spouse and too much of a disgrace to be welcomed back by their families.

It was on one of my morning rounds that I saw that I had two new patients – a woman and a child. Sitting by the child was a man that seemed vaguely familiar to me. As I got closer, I recognised him to be Imtiaz Ali's father-in-law. When he saw me, he came running toward me with tears streaming down his face.

It was disclosed that Imtiaz Ali had left his wife Meher for a younger woman. Meher had proceeded to douse Ramzan Ali and herself with kerosene and set fire to themselves. She was not too badly burned, but Ramzan Ali's face and body were burned beyond recognition. His eyes and lips were swollen completely shut. He heard my voice and tried to move his hands to touch me.

"You will be alright," I said to him, trying valiantly not to cry. "You'll see; you will be well in no time."

It was much less difficult to make rounds and change dressings for patients whom I did not know personally. I would talk to them while changing their dressings, hoping to divert their attention from the pain. With Ramzan Ali, however, it took all the courage I could inwardly summon.

I learned that I could sing to him and this seemed helped to assuage his pain, or maybe it actually just kept me preoccupied so that I was less aware of my own pain. I learned in time to transcend my pain and to concentrate solely on him. About a week later, overwhelming infection set in as the antibiotics we had prescribed for him seemed to fail in their effect.

One night after a particularly trying day, I retired to the house staff quarters to assume my on-call duties. The phones had quit working as usual and the nurses had to send the ward orderlies to fetch us for any emergencies that might arise during the night. It was past midnight when the ward orderly came to wake me up.

I trudged sleepily back over to the ward. The only lights shining seemed to be those at the nursing station. It was very quiet in the ward, all one could hear were the low breathing sounds of twenty-odd patients.

Then I noticed one other light on at the far end of the ward; it was at Ramzan Ali's bed. There was the tall familiar turbaned figure of the technician from the morgue bending over him, the man from the North, "the Ghoul" as we called him. Ramzan Ali's intravenous lines had been disconnected as had his oxygen. I had been summoned to pronounce gentle Ramzan Ali dead. I watched in numb misery as they wrapped his little body in white sheets and placed it on to a waiting gurney. The bed was stripped in record time. The efficient young student nurses had swarmed in to prepare it for the next burn victim.

The next morning I went back to see the great Mr. Rai. I had genuinely experienced all I could take of this torment.

I was truly contrite as I requested, "Could I please go back to the surgical wards and the humdrum world of hernias and hydroceles?"

He looked at me over the half glasses perched on the tip of his long nose. It seemed an eternity before he spoke.

"I hope you have learned, Anna, that meddling with fate and your superiors is not a wholesome occupation," he pronounced.

By afternoon, I was mercifully transferred to the Pediatric Hospital to do a surgery rotation there which came with its own particular brand of heartaches and joys.

❖

I was twenty-one before I learned to appreciate the sunrise. Sunrise rarely appeared as spectacular as sundown.

At sunset, everything turned to gold and orange. The lengthening shadows became soft purple and then deepened into dark indigo. By the time the birdcalls became sleepy little chirrups, the fleeting dusk would be filled with the sound of temple bells.

As the first evening star appeared, the bells would fade into a soft silence. The mogra and chameli would then start to bloom – perfuming the night air. It was only after the nightjar had started to call that the night-blooming jasmine would slowly open.

Indian sunrises had always seemed pedestrian in comparison.

"But it is in the stillness of dawn that God roams the earth," Lakshmi used to say to me when she brushed my hair in preparation for school. As she coiled my hair up high on my head, she would put one single flower in the coils of the braid, often a *madanmusth* flower.

I learned rather painfully to love the quiet joys of sunrise at the Pediatric Hospital with my first patient there. He was a twelve-year-old boy named Yaadgiri.

Yaadgiri had been named after a place of pilgrimage where his desperate parents had journeyed to pray for his health. He was stunted in his growth because of a condition known as Tetralogy of Fallot, more commonly known as "blue babies with holes in their hearts".

I carefully recorded all of Yaadgiri's symptoms and after a fairly thorough physical examination accurately diagnosed his condition. The surgery professor was proud of me as I presented the "splendid case" to the entire entourage that followed the great man. I was his star pupil for that short month. He gave me the distinct honour of taking care of young Yaadgiri until he was to have his surgery, which was to be "sometime soon".

Yaadgiri was unable to walk for long distances without having to squat to catch his breath. He carried a crude little staff to lean on and help him ambulate. He had long spidery fingers with clubbed ends which was a characteristic of his disease. His eyes were enormous and outsized his wizened little face. He looked for all the world like a little blue tree frog when he squatted or leaned on his staff to rest from his exertions.

Yaadgiri's parents were poor people from a village quite far from the city. They had other children to look after, so they left for home just after his admission to the hospital. After my rounds each day, I would sit by Yaadgiri's bedside and feed him his supper. He would always insist that I tell him a story at bedtime.

"Tell me another story, Little Mother," he would plead endearingly. When I had run through my repertoire of stories, I took to bringing in books for him to look at. He loved looking at the pictures as he was illiterate. I would read to him in English, translating into his language as I went along. He would finger the pages with great care and look at the myriads of colours with awe and amazement.

Those were the days before cardiopulmonary (more commonly known as "heart-lung") bypass equipment had become common. This equipment takes over the function of oxygenating the body's blood during the operation, allowing the cardiac surgeon to perform his magic. In the mercifully distant past, when such equipment was unavailable, such a patient undergoing cardiac surgery had to have their heart slowed down by immersing their body in ice. This immersion was performed after the patient had been anesthetised. It was my unenviable task to explain this process to Yaadgiri. He just smiled at me trustingly, assuring me that all would go well.

He was to have his surgery during the last week of my rotation on the cardio-thoracic service. However, for a whole host of reasons, it was postponed for another month. As I had become so attached to him, I continued to visit Yaadgiri as often as possible in the month that followed even though I was no longer his doctor. His care had been taken over from me by another of my classmates, an irreverent young man who kept Yaadgiri and me in stitches with his impersonations of the Gods and demi-Gods that populated the cardio-thoracic surgery faculty. It was almost three months after his admission when the day of Yaadgiri's surgery finally arrived.

I went to visit him on the evening before the operation. He had blossomed since the time of his admission with all the attention and regular meals that he had received in the hospital. He informed me that his parents would be coming to be with him the next day and help to nurse him back to health after the surgery.

It was evening as I sat by Yaadgiri's bedside. The giant tamarind trees outside the hospital wards were home to hundreds of crows, ravens, doves and mynah birds. At sunset, they would come home to roost setting up a raucous din which by nightfall would fade into soft cooing and murmurings.

Yaadgiri was excited and happy in anticipation of being cured with his surgery.

"I will learn my father's trade and I will make you the finest pair of sandals you have ever seen," he promised.

I remained with him as he dozed off. The nurses lit the lamps on the wards. As I rose to leave he opened his eyes and tugged at my white coat.

"Do you pray, Little Mother?" he asked.

I nodded affirmatively.

"Then will you pray that my sunrise is beautiful?" he requested. He leaned across his bed and picking up his crude little staff, he passed it to me. It was from a madan-musth bush.

"I won't be needing this anymore," he said as he handed it to me. "You can plant it in the earth and it will bloom."

I went by his bed the next morning. The sheets had been changed and the covers were turned down in anticipation of his return from the operating theatre.

"These surgeries are very long," one of the nurses said to me. "He should be back from the recovery ward by tomorrow morning."

I returned to the ward the following morning. There he was, my bright-eyed young friend sitting up in bed. I approached him with a smile, amazed by his speedy recovery.

"Yaadgiri, I almost didn't recognise you," I said.

"My name is not Yaadgiri, Little Mother," the child replied.

"Yaadgiri died on the operating table yesterday," said the nurse that I had spoken with the day before. "This is our new Tetralogy patient."

There was an insistent tug at my white coat.

"Look! It is a bright new sunrise, Little Mother," the child chirped.

I looked out the window and saw the beginnings of the sun creep over the horizon. The early morning light shone down on the delicate little blossoms on the tamarind tree outside. I knew that in a few hours they would open toward the light and the warmth of the sun. The sunrise was beautiful – it was just not Yaadgiri's.

I planted Yaadgiri's madan-musth staff in the warm wet earth near the rose bushes in the small garden at home that evening – little knowing what would become of it. It sent out several branches and abundant leaves shortly thereafter.

The madan-musth belongs to the same family as the passion flower. The flowers are rare and used only for the most special of occasions. They have five thick bright green petals which curve protectively around a myriad of purple stamens and a single pale green pistil. The flower's perfume is its most extraordinary feature – heavy, musky and seductive. It is the perfume that gives the flower its name, madan-musth, which means "heavy intoxicant". At dawn, when the morning star pales into the lightening sky as the sun rises, the madan-musth bush puts out its strange little yellow-green flowers.

Almost four years after Yaadgiri had given his madan-musth staff to me, it bloomed at sunrise for the very first time, bearing flowers just in time for my wedding.

10

To the Altar and Beyond

THE ACRIMONY AND THE FINGER POINTING BETWEEN MY mother and father had been sharpened over the years into incredibly fine and lethal weapons. The silence between them had become deafening. It was as if they had moved into separate orbits, barely acknowledging each other's existence. However, as Rachel and I came of marriageable age they resumed the pretense of sharing their lives again as they had to make cooperative and concerted attempts to arrange suitable marital alliances for us. They dared not dissolve their own marriage, for who would marry a girl whose parents had severed the sacred bonds that God and the Church had joined together.

> "And here we offer and present unto Thee O Lord, our selves, our souls and our bodies, to be a reasonable holy and living sacrifice unto Thee...
>
> ...And although we are unworthy, through our manifold sins, to offer unto Thee any sacrifice, yet we beseech Thee to accept this, our bounden duty and service, not weighing our merits, but pardoning our offences..."

This passage from the Rite of the Eucharist was standard fare during evening prayer in our family. The implied duty of Syrian Christian parents was to raise their daughters as exemplars of chastity and rectitude. My parents accepted this duty with the requisite solemnity and the gravitas it merited. The countless relatives who hovered around also made sure that we would be delivered blameless at the marriage altar. In marriage, a daughter was offered up as an oblation of sorts.

The Church's injunction was that husbands should love their wives even as Christ loved the church. It followed that as good Christian women, we would spend a lifetime preparing ourselves as an oblation to this Christ–like being who would love and cherish us. Between prayer, exhortation and substantial dowries, we were expected to make the final climb up the Holy Mountain to Christian bride-hood.

We knew that the issue of finding fitting partners to marry was most definitely not our responsibility. It fell on the shoulders of our parents to find for us men of suitable education, status and character. Our role in this process was simply to stay chaste and virginal, do well in school and college, and hope for the best.

I, however, inadvertently interfered in this traditional process at one point.

Toward the end of my medical college days, the extracurricular activity that I enjoyed most was singing in the church choir. On Friday evenings, I found myself in choir practice where I sat behind the sopranos and sang contralto. The tenors sat opposite us on the other side of the aisle. Most of the tenors, baritones and basses were young men from the adjoining school, while few of them were faculty. The music was enthralling and wholly captured my attention until it was supplanted by something, or someone else.

There had been a new arrival in town from England – Jock Stewart, the Reverend Jock Stewart. He sat opposite me in the tenor section of the choir. He did not sing very much, but stared and smiled at me a lot instead. This was fine by me since, with his emerald green eyes and thick red hair, I found him handsome in a rugged sort of way. Again, it was the green eyes that got to me. It excited me to be smiled at by a perfect stranger. But, given the repressive environment in which we were raised, I knew that this burgeoning lust would not amount to much other than surreptitious looks across the narthex of the Church.

One evening I was summoned to my father's study. Papa swivelled his chair around and looked sternly over his horn-rimmed glasses at me.

"What have you been doing to encourage the Reverend Stewart?" he demanded to know.

"Why, nothing Papa, nothing at all," I replied.

"Then why would he be asking for permission to marry you?"

"I haven't the faintest idea, Papa. I hope you said yes," I exclaimed breathlessly.

"Have you lost your mind, child? Do you know what happens when Indian people marry English people?"

"They live happily ever after?" I volunteered quizzically.

"No!" he thundered. "They have strange looking children."

"What kind of strange looking children, Papa?"

"Children who are striped or stippled like zebras and leopards."

"Oh, Papa, that is absolutely not true. I've never seen such people."

"Precisely, my dear, they keep them hidden from view. Besides," he said with great finality, "the English don't bathe, they have yellow teeth and fat ankles. What's worse, you would have to endure all of this embarrassment in poverty. The clergy make no money at all. You would have to live on the salary of a vicar which would not pay for anything, not even for stippled children." There was no further argument. Jock Stewart was summarily dismissed from my life and any further marriage prospects were to come only at the suggestion of my parents.

It was indeed a formidable task to arrange a marriage in our community. The selection of a spouse had to be made from a small band of Christians – specifically the Syrian Orthodox Christians who were concentrated in the southwestern coast of the Indian peninsula.

It was said that the Syrian Orthodox Christians were descended from ancient Jews who came to India over two thousand years ago and settled in the south where they traded actively in spices. During this time, Thomai C'naan, Thomas of Canaan or Thomas, "the doubting disciple," came to India accompanied by a band of fifty other Jews who followed the teachings of a renegade from Nazareth whom they believed to be the Messiah – Jesus the Christ, or *Yesu Kristu* as they called him. They became known as the Nazarenes after the man from Nazareth and formed a group distinct from the other Jews who were fairly insular. Unlike the traditional Jews, these Nazarenes proselytised those people in India with whom they conducted trade. Fifteen hundred years later they came to be called the Syrian Orthodox Christians by other Christian denominations introduced into India by the Portuguese and the English. So it was that there developed in the states of Travancore and Cochin a very strong Christian church with Jewish underpinnings that thrives today – two thousand years later.

"We were Christian when you fellows were still running around in blue paint and skins," I used to hear my father say to some of his English friends.

Reflecting on the Legend of the Kiss Curls, I often chafed at the fact that there were no princes, no rajahs, and no nawabs in the galleries of Syrian Orthodox Christians that we could aspire to be joined with. There were rich men, brilliant men, accomplished men, and even handsome men – but alas no royalty. There were occasional Christian royals in north India where some princes had converted to Christianity because of a personal interest taken in them by Queen Victoria herself. These kinds of princes simply would not do. After all, they were from the north, they were converted by the British, and they could not lay claim to a genuine Judaeo-Christian lineage spanning hundreds of years. They were "New Christians" to be distinguished from us – the Syrian Orthodox, Christians of antiquity.

My great grandmother was married at the age of eleven and my grandmother, Ammachy, at fifteen. For my mother's generation, getting married at the age twenty would have been ideal, but Mummy was married at the ripe old age of twenty-four as her father had no dowry to offer the intended husband. In my generation it was accepted that parents would find appropriate alliances for us after we finished college.

So when I finally reached the age of twenty-one it came time for my father and mother to find me an appropriate husband. There was also the ever-present question of the dowry. My parents had worked feverishly most of their lives to accumulate dowries for both Rachel and me. In addition, they also had to provide for an extensive trousseaux, gold jewellery and precious stones. Further, there would have to be promises of real property and inheritance.

A man with only daughters could face the prospect of a life of servitude dedicated totally to establishing dowries for them. Our community also insisted on educating their daughters. While this further made the financial burden egregious, it allowed women to maintain their independence in the event that the alliance was less than optimal, or even worse, was dissolved.

The search for a bridegroom was a long and laborious process – lasting almost four years in my case. It was as unpleasant as it was nerve racking with far more haggling involved than that which took place in a local fish market. It was not uncommon for one party to parade skeletons out from the other one's closet. Long forgotten feuds were dredged up and family black sheep were resurrected. The purpose of this exercise was merely to renegotiate the dowry – up if it was the bridegroom's party and down if it was in the bride's. My aunts, cousins, and distant relatives all joined in the expedition with great gusto. We irreverently referred to them as our "Fishing Fleet".

The photographer to the Nizam was pressed into facilitating this effort. It was his task to take hundreds of photographs of me – formal and informal – in the garden, at my books, playing the piano, all smiling a perfect Mona Lisa smile into the camera. I had to change from outfit to outfit until he was satisfied with one. He was a patient man and amazingly put up with my frazzled disgruntledness.

"If you don't stop being difficult with the poor man," warned Lakshmi, "he will cast a spell on your photographs while he is hiding behind that black cloth."

"I don't care. I will go away to America and get married there," I threatened, which brought shocked disapproval from all around. Allowing an unmarried daughter to go to the modern day Sodom and Gomorrah of America was sure to invite social ostracism on my family.

"They have slaves in America," said the photographer who had finally reached the limit of his tolerance. "A dark-skinned girl like you will not fare too well there."

The photographs had to show me in the best possible light – overexposed enough so that there would no hint of my dark complexion. It was highly desirable in India for women to be fair-skinned and men to be dark-skinned. Fair skin in a woman, in addition to being considered beautiful, was a sign of docility. However, one could not be too pale, for then the virtue and chastity of the women in the family would naturally be questioned. Dark skin in a man was a sign of strength and virility. While it was a favourable characteristic in a man, it was an unseemly one in a woman. Consequently, I hated my dark skin.

The photographs also had to subtly show just enough evidence of wealth in the background to entice the groom's family. I had to wear just the right amount of jewellery so as to suggest that there was much more of it than there actually was. Women of our community were not supposed to indulge like the Muslims or Hindus and show off their acquisitions. I rebelled against this edict, however, wanting to wear some of the exquisite pieces of Mughal jewellery I had personally selected for my trousseaux.

Looking at the finished product with utter distaste, Ammachy pronounced, "You look like you could be the lead caparisoned elephant in the Mysore maharaja's parade." We finally compromised on the jewellery and the photographer commenced his assigned job.

The proofs were finally ready. Selections were made from the hundreds of pictures that were taken. They were finally pronounced satisfactory by all the relatives, the servants, and the other hangers-on involved. Scores of copies of the photographs were sent out to the far comers of the earth, or so it seemed to me. The entire process seemed to me like casting bait and reeling in a catch. Finally, they started to arrive: many photographs of prospective bridegrooms with accompanying letters describing their many achievements. As the prospective bride, at least I was given the right of refusal.

My mother's second sister Lizzie wrote to us enclosing photographs and a description of a young man who was studying law in England. I was enamoured with him instantly. There was a colour photograph taken outside ivy-covered walls of some ancient college in England that captured my heart. He was a tall, handsome fellow with brown eyes and a cheerful smile. He asked for permission to write to me, which was granted, and we exchanged letters every week. He said he was anxious that we get to know each other. About four weeks into the romance, one of the Fishing Fleet raised a serious question: "He looks very thin."

This was a rallying cry. Instantly an expedition party was formed consisting of my father, several uncles, and other well-wishers. They set out on a long three-day train trip to the thin man's ancestral village in Travancore. The purpose of this excursion was to investigate if the rest of the family "looked as malnourished" as he did. Two weeks dragged by and the party finally returned.

"Well, what did you find?" I asked.

"This kind of anxiety is unseemly, my dear," said one of my great aunts.

"The whole family has congenital tuberculosis." This statement was from a distant cousin who looked like a bereaved bloodhound.

"There is no such thing as congenital tuberculosis," I argued.

"You young doctors think you know everything," said Cousin Blood Hound. "His grandparents are all dead."

"So are three of my four," I interjected.

My arguments and entreaties all seemed to fall on deaf ears. So I wrote to my soon-to-be-ex-fiancé to inform him that I could not correspond with him anymore since he was "too thin". I never heard from him again.

Another prospective marital alliance considered for me was a Ph.D. who had recently returned from England named Babu. He was from an extraordinarily wealthy family and came from ancient Syrian Christian roots, thereby having a suitable resume. I remember seeing him for the first time and thinking that my life would be unendurable if I were to be married to a man that looked like a clean-shaven Jehovah. What made it even more ominous was the fact that he had older brothers, all of whom looked like older versions of that awesome Semitic deity. In this case, I exercised my right of refusal. When I did, his eager family asked if they could have my younger sister. So it came to be that my sister Rachel eventually married Babu.

After several subsequent months of searching there still did not appear to be a suitable bridegroom on my horizon.

"I know you don't need my opinion, Mary," Ammachy would tell my mother, "but with that poor child you are going to have to spend handsomely on a large dowry." In some of her rare and more charitable moments Ammachy might let out a deep concerned sigh and relent, "Perhaps they will overlook everything else, she is a doctor after all."

Finally, to everyone's immense relief including mine, one of my father's associates located a husband for me. He had told my father about a young man named James who was of marriageable age and came from a very good family – which translates into extremely wealthy, not given to drink, and without any traces of congenital tuberculosis. He was of the same Christian community as ours which of course was essential. I had been sent a photograph of him that had been handled so often it was dog-eared and ragged by the time it reached me. He appeared to be handsome enough in the photograph. The only downside was that his family was settled in the Federated States of Malaya, which later became Malaysia and Singapore. Despite this, everyone, including me, was in agreement that a match was found.

At last, the dowry was settled and the date for the wedding was chosen. We were to be married in the first week of June on the anniversary of my uncle Benjamin's death. I was not to meet my intended husband until the day before the wedding.

❖

My wedding was drawing near and there was still much to do as well as much to learn.

Despite the sexual encounters in my childhood and adolescence and the fact that I had completed medical college and graduated at the top of the class, my knowledge of sexual intercourse was sparse at best. For me, the actual process of intercourse was shrouded in superstition, old wives' tales, and much speculation.

A few days before my wedding I had asked Mummy what was to be expected.

"You will find out soon enough," she delivered in a bland and uninspired tone. She might as well have been discussing the chopping of tomatoes for all the significance it seemed to carry for her.

I then opened up my anatomy and physiology textbooks and pored over them with Rachel; however, the books and my sister were of little help. The texts described in great detail how the autonomic nervous system controlled things such as erections and ejaculations, the process of fertilization of the ovum and how it became embedded into the wall of the uterus, and so on. There was nothing written about what was to be expected of me or what I would actually have to do.

My friends and classmates, Devayani and Aruna, had been married to suitable husbands in our fourth year of medical college. They were "old hands" at this business and I knew that I could ask them direct questions. While we sat at lunch in the gardens outside the hospital, my questions elicited great mirth and gales of laughter. When they had stopped giggling, they put their arms around me and spoke in conspiratorial whispers.

"It is your duty to submit to your husband," said Devayani. "He is your Lord."

"That is Hindu palaver," I responded. "Will you please just tell me what actually happens?"

"It is painful sometimes and messy all the time," said Devayani. "You just have to endure it."

"For how long?" I asked.

"You should pray that he is quick."

By this time I was thoroughly confused and intimidated. Hoping to get more satisfying information, I redirected my questioning. "Aruna, what do you think?"

"It is a great deal of fun; the oftener, the better," Aruna offered.

"Don't listen to her, Aruna is a nymphomaniac. Enjoyment is not what it is about. It is about submission and obedience, the rest will fall into place," Devayani said. "It is also your duty to have children, unless of course you are barren."

"Or your Lord is shooting blanks," this irreverent comment came from Aruna which elicited some more giggling. "Forget her nonsense," she continued. "We are not performing monkeys or dogs. Sex is for your enjoyment as well as your husband's."

Although I had thought that their very different views would have covered what I might have experienced on my honeymoon, I was soon to realise otherwise.

It wasn't until two days before my wedding amidst the last minute preparations that I decided the Church should be decorated with bouquets of *laburnum* for the ceremony. Adding one more task to my already beleaguered parents was unthinkable, so I went to Lakshmi for help.

"It is inauspicious to use laburnum in a wedding," Lakshmi warned. According to her, "The cascading sprays of the flowers symbolise showers of tears." Since she knew laburnum portended disaster, she refused to have anything to do with the venture. I was quick to dismiss her superstitious nonsense.

Brushing her remonstrations aside, I enlisted Rachel and assembled a group of my closest companions from College which included Shuja, my Muslim neighbour who lived next door and was a year ahead of me in school, my classmates Aruna and Devayani, and the last of our gang – an enigmatic Hindu fellow named Vasu from Secunderabad. Vasu was mouthwateringly handsome and had the sweetest nature of us all, always volunteering for even the toughest and most odious of tasks.

It was my plan that we would descend upon the-old-house-with-the-garden in search of laburnum. There had been a laburnum tree there; it was called the Indian laburnum. Every June in the years of my childhood, the tree was completely covered with flowers, leaving very little greenery left to be seen. Every bough was laden with multiple cascades of the golden yellow flowers. The tree constantly shed its flowers creating a thick carpet of gold at its roots. If the maali could have had his way, he would have dug the tree up and disposed of it. He was a practical fellow, more so than I realised at the time. He could not see the carpet of gold; he could only see "the rubbish which had to be swept away every morning." I remembered these glorious flowers with nostalgia and wanted them to be a part of my wedding.

When we arrived at the-old-house-with-the-garden, Rachel and I found it in significant disrepair. Mr. Sisodia had subsequently sold the property to newer owners and it was rumoured that they were going to subdivide it to build apartment houses in its place. The wall that once separated the house from the stream had been replaced by one with an unimaginative cinder block construction. The chicken coop was now serving as a storage shed which held lumber and bricks, presumably for the apartment houses to come. The main house had lost all of its grandeur – its creamy pink walls had been replaced with a garish fuchsia now framed by a copper-sulfate blue molding. There were red and gold *Fu-dogs* sitting atop the posts at the gateway as a definitive acknowledgment of the Hong Kong source of the new owner's wealth.

Weeds had taken over my father's section of the garden and there was unattended pavement over my mother's. There was no longer any vegetation of note in that enormous courtyard other than the weeds. The moringa-moringas were gone, as were the mango, the champak and the jasmines. Sadly, there was no laburnum tree.

In the pallid silence, we stood immobile as memories came flooding back. On the eve of my wedding, I was overwhelmed by the passing of such a significant time in our lives in such a significant place. I gave an involuntary shudder; this was not the time for regret nor repining. We had much to accomplish before the great day dawned with all of its promises. We walked away as the gate creaked shut behind us. I turned to take in one final look and as I did, I saw a small Rangoon creeper struggling up behind the wall – a small promise of beauty amidst the dankness all around.

We walked towards Vasu's car where he was patiently waiting for us. He was engaged in conversation with one of the people who lived on the street. Vasu learned from him that there was a nobleman's garden outside the city which was rumoured to have several laburnum trees.

In order to maximise our time and the amount of laburnum gathered, I dispatched Shuja and Rachel to pick laburnum from the churchyard. Devayani and Aruna were sent to the Bagh-e-Aam nurseries in search of more. Vasu and I drove to the nobleman's garden outside the city.

We rode for several miles out of the city and finally reached the nobleman's garden. Vasu parked the car at the gate and helped me out. The garden was in a walled enclosure. We called to the gatekeeper who presently arrived at the gate and let us in. Vasu and I headed straight for the laburnum grove.

It was pleasantly warm and we picked bough after bough of laburnum until we had filled four very large baskets. Vasu carried the baskets back to the car and returned with a small picnic basket containing fruits, savouries and lassi bottles packed in ice. He spread out a little dhurrie for me to sit on and I made myself comfortable. I was sweating from all the effort and from the sun which had now climbed high in the sky. I squinted into the sun and closed my eyes. I could visualise the church with its flood of golden yellow sprays. There I was in the midst of it all, resplendent in my gold wedding sari walking down on the aisle on my father's arm.

It was a cold wetness on my forehead that broke my reverie. As I opened my eyes, I saw Vasu bending down to wipe my forehead with a wet washcloth. I noticed for the first time in all the years that I had known him that Vasu had the thickest eyelashes I had ever seen on anyone. His eyes seemed moist.

"What is it Vasu?" I asked. "Are you crying?"

"I am sad," he replied.

"About what?"

"You will be gone from my life."

"No, I won't. You can come and visit with us. I am sure that my husband would love to have you come."

"You don't understand. I can't bear the thought of you leaving my life."

"You are being somewhat melodramatic," I said now beginning to get alarmed. Then with a dawning realisation I asked, "Are you in love with me? Is that it?"

"You never even noticed me. I might as well have not been there."

"Oh Vasu, you are one of my best friends."

"That doesn't matter. It is not me that you are going to spend your life with."

"Vasu, please stop. I could not spend my life with you even if I wanted to. You are a Hindu and I am Christian. That kind of alliance is unholy; it is unheard of."

"The point is that you never even wanted to."

I leaned forward and closed my eyes. Vasu bent and kissed me lightly on my lips. I had never been kissed on the lips before. It was the most delicious sensation I had ever experienced. I lowered myself down on the carpet and felt Vasu's body envelope mine, his legs entwined around my body, my head resting in the crook of his elbow. My fingers traced the lone tear running down his cheek. I tasted the tear; it was salty and somehow sweet. I touched his lips gently. With a great moan, he buried his face in my hair. I moved slowly against him and then caught a glimpse of the watch face on his wrist. It was almost half past two – four more hours to my wedding.

"Oh my God, what are we doing?" we then cried in unison. Hurriedly, we stashed our food in the basket and ran pell-mell out of the garden and into the car. We drove all the way back into the city in complete silence.

The rest of the gang was impatiently waiting for us with hordes of laburnum.

"Where were you guys? What took you so long?"

"You'd have thought you had gone to the Garden of Eden."

Vasu and I looked at each other and hoped that our guilt wouldn't show.

We worked feverishly late into the night ????fastening bouquets of laburnum to every pew. By evening ????we had lashed enough of the flowers to the pews to bury the aisle and its walkers in an avalanche of laburnum. The church resembled a bower in a fairy tale.

✧

I met my intended husband James for the first time just briefly on the day before our wedding. This was not an unusual occurrence in our tradition of arranged marriages.

I was told that he was seven years older than I was. This was deemed to be a perfect separation in ages by the fishing fleet who were all milling about waiting to make a formal presentation of me to him. Height was another measure they used to evaluate him.

"He is five foot ten," someone said.

"And, you are…?" someone else asked me.

"Five two," I replied.

"Perfect! Eight inches – a seemly difference."

"Auspicious," echoed another.

"Auspicious for what?" I asked, looking up from my preparations for the meeting. "What would eight inches portend?"

"Long, happy, married life."

"Many, many sons."

"May you be the mother of a hundred sons."

"What about daughters?" I asked.

"Unimportant, merely by-products of a liaison."

The entire day was a buzz of activity for the family and a blur for me. Three o'clock finally came – the time set for the meeting. I sat in the parlour trying to quell the butterflies in my stomach. Thoughts were racing around and around in my head, chasing each other like kittens chasing their tails.

"Will I pass muster? What will he actually look like? What will we say to each other?"

Rachel and Lakshmi sat on either side of me, each holding one of my hands attempting to calm me.

Finally, Mummy came into the parlour, a little out of breath and announced, "They are here." She then retreated to greet the entourage.

I peered out of the window and saw a bevy of people disembarking from a motorcade of cars. From the worn photograph, I recognised who I thought was James – he appeared tall and handsome. He stumbled a little as he got out one of the cars.

Mummy returned presently, accompanied by my new mother-in-law-to-be. Brief introductions were made. They then led me to the reception room to meet my husband-to-be while the fishing fleet remained behind.

James stood in the room assuming a rather shy posture. He was indeed handsome – tall, dark and with kind eyes. His most outstanding feature was a twenty-thousand watt smile that lit up his entire face. Our parents then left us alone to make our acquaintance. In the awkwardness of the moment, we sat there looking down at our feet without saying much for awhile.

After brief introductions and minor small talk, he told me that he had just completed medical college in the north of India and that his many brothers and sisters-in-law were also doctors. I learned of his home in Malaysia and how his whole family lived there together. After a short time together, we said our good-byes and did not see each other again until the wedding ceremony the next day.

It was gnawingly unclear to me as to why James, who was in his early thirties and so much older than I, had only just completed his medical studies. When I attempted to learn more about the whys and wherefores of James' long stretch in medical college from the fishing fleet on the morning of the wedding, Ammachy warned me off with an admonition.

"He is a doctor, probing into things that don't concern you might lead his family to discover that you are defective goods," she said in reference to my birth defect. According to her, it was a miracle that there was even going to be a wedding at all.

I became determined that this was to be *my* day and that not even she would spoil it with her venom. *I* would be the most important and the most beautiful woman in the crowd. All eyes would be trained on me – not on my grandmother, not on my aunts, neither on my mother nor my sister, although they all remained far more lovely than I could ever hope to be. On my wedding day, I would be dressed finer than anyone else, my hair would be coiffed more elaborately than any of them, my makeup would be flawless and all the jewellery that my father and mother had worked so hard to acquire all my life would finally be on display.

My wedding was to be the culmination of all the energy and efforts my parents had expended over the years, raising me up to be chaste and virginal, providing a dowry to compensate for my flaws and giving me an education which would allow self-reliance and command respect.

Extensive preparations were being made for the momentous event. A thousand people were invited to join us for an enormous feast after the ceremony in our Church. My father and his brothers had worked themselves into a constant state of frenzy before the wedding – scurrying around buying the rice, the milk, the lamb and the spices for the wedding feast. My mother and the other women relatives scampered around in an equal state – ensuring that nobody was left out from the list of invitees.

Mummy had made arrangements for us – the bridal pair – to spend a week following the ceremony in a guest suite at the Falaknuma Palace, one of the many palaces belonging to the Nizam. She had used all the influence at her disposal and several political connections to pull off this magical feat. I was allowed to see the suite before the wedding and I knew that this would be a dream come true – a prince and princess in a fairytale castle. I fell in love with tall vaulted ceilings, the lovely heavy damask curtains, great vases filled with every rose known to man, and a bed as large as the Karbala Maidan, a very large field situated between Hyderabad and Secunderabad. I knew that our honeymoon would be memorable and inexplicably grand.

"How many people had the opportunity to spend their wedding night in a real palace?" I asked myself.

On the morning of the wedding, I was happily caught up in thoughts of the palace while applying the last of my make-up. The hairdresser had come to the house to style my hair and the darzi arrived to put the tassels on my gold brocade sari. Lakshmi hovered tending to every other need.

Suddenly and unexpectedly, my father came into my room. I could see that he was weeping. My mother was right behind him looking sorrowful as well. It took me a little while to realise that their grief was out of proportion to the notion that they were losing their daughter to a stranger from a far away land. More commonly, the overwhelming sentiment over the loss of a daughter to a son-in-law is one of enormous relief. The burden would lifted – there would be no threat of a frustrated spinster at home, barbs would no longer be leveled on their unsuitability as parents or on mine as marriageable material, there would be no more having to save for the dowry.

However, my parents appeared panic-stricken.

All sorts of irrational thoughts came scrambling through my mind. "*The bridegroom's party had discovered my birth defect and were calling off the wedding. They had probably learned of the tryst that I had with Vasu in the laburnum grove. One of them was psychic with the ability to read my mind and discovered that I knew nothing of how to please a man.*" I found myself becoming hysterical with an endless thought stream of possible scenarios.

The panic must have shown on my face. Lakshmi hurried over to my side.

"Everything will be fine," she reassured me while cupping my face in her hands. "By evening you will be a wife and the mistress of a wealthy household. Your parents' sorrow is due to something else entirely."

There had been a great deal of communal unrest in the city in the past weeks. It was not between the Muslims and the Hindus as usual, but between two different groups of Hindus based on an imperceptible difference in their dialects. The government stepped in that morning and declared a curfew. Special permission was needed from either the chief of police, or some other similar authority, to allow more than ten people to congregate in one place. One of my uncles was dispatched to secure such permission and he came back with approval for a mere fifty people. This would be barely sufficient for my family and the relatives of my husband-to-be, who had come all the way from Malaysia and Singapore. That was the first of my wedding dreams to go up in smoke.

A cousin had been dispatched to retrieve my jewellery out of the vault. He came back empty-handed. The bank was barricaded and there was nothing he could do to get past the police who guarded the entrance. That was the second great disappointment of the day. I would be the first bride in the history of India to wear no jewellery.

"Stop weeping," Ammachy commanded. "Your eyes will swell up and your makeup will run. You will look even more of a mess than usual."

Then there was another knock on the door and there was Inayath – his tall frame silhouetted in the doorway with his fabled saddlebags in hand. Like Mandrake the magician, he opened them up. There, dazzling in the afternoon sun was the beautiful bejewelled emerald sarpech that he had promised me several years ago for my wedding day. It was strung with nine long strands of exquisite baroque pearls. He placed it around my neck and lovingly fastened the drawstring closed. Cascading down the front my dressing gown was the most magnificent necklace I was ever to possess.

Over the next hour I was transformed from a very ordinary looking young woman into a radiant creature. My hair was coaxed into an elaborate coiffure garlanded with jasmine and small roses. My palms were elaborately hennaed, my eyes were lined with kohl, and my lips were reddened with fresh lipstick. Lakshmi helped me with my sari – an extraordinarily heavy gold brocade with a form-fitting silk blouse to match. But above all, driving the radiance home, there was the incandescence of expectation that lit me up from inside. I finally saw my own beauty as I looked in the mirror.

"You have to be awakened by a god," Radha had said so many years ago. "The Dance of Awakening is important. When a god touches you into wakefulness, you can never be ordinary or ugly ever again, no matter what the mirror tells you."

My Gods were all around me and my true awakening into beauty had finally come at the age of twenty-five.

At that moment, there was yet a third knock on the door – it was Vasu. How he braved to pass the police barricades from Secunderabad to Hyderabad was nothing short of a miracle. He stood there hesitantly, looking handsome in his navy blue suit, crisp white shirt and scarlet tie.

"You look so beautiful," he said shyly. "I brought something for you."

Everyone else in the room must have known that I wanted a moment alone with Vasu and they left us. I held out my hand to him, but he did not take it. Instead, he knelt down at my feet and delved into his coat withdrawing a small package. When he opened the package, I saw that it contained heavy toe rings made of gold. In India, among the Hindus, only married women wear toe rings. He gently nudged the rings on to the first toe of each my feet. This is a function performed by the Hindu bridegroom in their tradition.

"I hope you don't mind that I do this," he said as he placed the rings.

I was speechless. I looked at him, his eyes were full of unshed tears.

"Why didn't you say something all these years?" I asked.

"Would it have made a difference?"

"We will never know now. Thank you, Vasu."

When I emerged from the dressing room adorned with the toe rings, their significance was lost on most of my Christian relatives – at least those who even noticed.

Lakshmi, of course, did notice.

"Romance is for the story books and the movies," she said. "You have a destiny that you must not squander away with unseemly alliances."

"Why would it be an unseemly alliance?" I asked her.

"He is a Hindu Brahmin and you are a Syrian Christian. He is not suitable for you."

"Lakshmi," I said looking at her in stupefaction, "you are a Hindu. Why would marrying a Hindu be unsuitable?"

"Would your children go to church? Would you teach them all the songs your uncle taught you on Sundays? Or, would they go to temple? Would you sit out the days of menses in the outer house? Would you do all the things required of a good Hindu wife? Above all, would you give up your name and your God? Would you break your father's heart?"

"It would be difficult," I finally acquiesced.

"Let us stop all this nonsense and get on with what is important," she concluded. "There is a wedding to take place."

I started to remove the gold toe rings and she gently stopped me.

"They will remain as food for daydreaming about things that might have been, but could never be," she quietly added.

Just before I left for the Church and the ceremony, Lakshmi wove a small madan-musth flower into my hair from Yaadgiri's plant, complementing the jasmine and small roses.

Finally, after all the confusion of the earlier part of the day, I entered the church on my father's arm and processed down the laburnum-framed aisle. The church had very few people in it and the laburnum was beginning to wilt. My immediate family, my uncles, Inayath and Lakshmi were nearly the only ones there seated on the bride's side of the aisle to witness my marriage. Neither Ammachy, my cousins Thomas and Sam, nor most of my family's friends or my own friends could attend since permits were not granted for more than just a handful of people to congregate on the day of the curfew. The thousand-guest feast had quickly deteriorated to a paltry handful of people. Not even the choir was able to come and it was only by a small mercy that the priests could even be present.

The third and most significant of the disappointments on that memorable day was that my reckless bridegroom had neglected to procure the wedding ring. It was not as if he had simply misplaced it, as unbelievable as it may seem, he had actually overlooked purchasing it.

I could sense Mummy's gathering anger in the middle of the ceremony as this oversight came to light. I detected some movement and rustling of silks behind me as I stood at the head of the aisle with my soon-to-be-husband. I turned to see her struggling with the ring on her finger which she had specially made to wear for the festivities. She removed the ring and handed it to the priest with scant grace, who dutifully blessed it and assisted James with the task of sliding it on my finger. I looked up just long enough to catch the coy and sheepish look on my husband's face.

Then, disappointedly witnessed by only a few and with a borrowed wedding ring on my finger, I was pronounced to be the wife of a man I had only met the day before.

We then left the church for the dinner reception which was uneventful save for the small number of guests in attendance. Most of the tables remained conspicuously empty. The usual conviviality of weddings – the songs, the loud celebration, the bustle and the joy were all sparsely absent. Indeed, I had witnessed funerals with more life to them.

I remember little else of the event except for the image of my father sitting on the verandah after the dinner supervising the servants while they poured gallons of milk and perishables down the storm drains. As I left with my new husband I turned for one last look, and floating away on a tidal wave of milk and cream, was my wilting laburnum. Lakshmi's prediction about the laburnum suddenly flashed across my consciousness.

✧

After the fiasco of the wedding and the untimely curfew that surrounded it, James' family decided to take matters into their own hands. They unilaterally decided to cancel the accommodations Mummy had made for us at the Nizam's palace and declared that we would go to Madras on our honeymoon instead. Much to my disappointment, my parents who were benumbed from the wedding disaster, silently acquiesced. Since no alternative arrangements had been made for our wedding night, I stayed the night with my parents and joined James the following morning at breakfast with my suitcase packed, ready to begin my new life.

After many long goodbyes and well-wishes, James and I left for Madras on our honeymoon. Among other things, James' father had given him a car as a wedding gift. We drove from Hyderabad to Madras, stopping along the way in many little picturesque sea-side towns. We sang songs along the way and ate at quaint little stalls that dotted the coastline.

James was an amusing and interesting companion in those few harmonious days. I was deliriously happy at my tremendous good fortune of having landed a fine husband and the prospect of a happily married life ahead – unlike that of my parents. Vasu was forgotten, memories of my family retreated into the haze of Hyderabad left behind, and the disappointing wedding had become a paltry part of history. The drive to Madras was a happy time.

When we set out from Hyderabad, the monsoons were imminent but had not yet arrived.

The summer heat stayed outside the air-conditioned comfort of the car, presenting itself in the dancing and shimmering of the air hovering over the asphalt. When we opened the car doors to stop for a short respite here and there, the blast furnace of the unmerciful season would assault us with its full force. Summer in India declares itself with a frenzied rising of the temperatures and an increasing brilliance of the noonday sun until the southwest monsoon arrives, announcing a merciful reprieve with gigantic cymbal-like claps of thunder, followed by torrential rain. The monsoons would be coming soon in full force.

As we drove in the southeasterly direction off the Deccan Plateau, over the spine of the Eastern Ghats to the supposedly cooler coastal plains of the Madras Presidency, the terrain and the climate changed.

Madras was uncomfortably sticky as well as unbearably hot. The ocean was brackish and smelled quite foul. The people looked very different from those more familiar in Hyderabad. Here they were shorter, squatter and darker. They spoke Tamil, a language which I did not understand. Mercifully, James spoke several languages fluently, Tamil among them.

I was determined not to let such minor setbacks spoil my newfound happiness – nothing was going to interfere with my marriage. I was going to make everything as smooth as glass.

Our honeymoon destination was a small *dak bungalow* – a pension on the outskirts of the city of Madras. The bungalow was a lovely little cottage by the sea. The honeymoon suite was unassuming but deliciously private – a bedroom and a parlour both opening out onto a verandah which overlooked the ocean. Our first night spent together was memorable. We left the doors open, sleepily watching the waves as the curtains swayed in the summer breeze. We slept sporadically through the night, waking to the sounds of the surf and the night birds.

My husband James was an artful and obviously experienced lover. Surprisingly, I was not fazed by the fact that he was not virginal. Fumbling and clumsiness might have added to my distress after the disastrous events of the wedding. Mercifully, I was spared that obstacle and delightedly discovered that all Aruna had told me about sex was true. I learned that there were secrets to my body which I had never even dreamed of and responses for which I had no language.

According to Lakshmi's instructions, I rose early the next morning intending to bathe and change into yet another of the many lovely outfits Mummy had packed for me. I had been told over and over again that the early morning baths were all-important in the lives of married women in India. They cleansed one after intercourse and guaranteed a propitious start to the day. To break this tradition was to invite disaster. True to form, I decided to alter the proscribed routine and chose instead to savour the only part of the day that was cool before taking that all-important bath.

I sat myself down in the wicker chair on the verandah by the sea wall while James continued to sleep. The air was warm and the morning star had not yet set. I felt a languorous fatigue in my body and watched the terns as they wheeled above the wave line. The fishermen were already out and had started pulling in their nets. Their women congregated on the beach to pick through the catch and dump it in the large baskets that would be taken to the market later in the day. The pale grey dawn and the sound of the surf enveloped me as I sat there in my cotton shift – lost in happy thoughts.

A light rustle at the door interrupted my delicious reverie which caused me to look up. The curtains swayed softly in the morning breeze and parted to reveal the *khansama* – butler. He had come in on silent feet to bring me "coffee-by-the-yard, madam," – freshly ground Madras coffee brewed with creamy buffalo milk and coarse granulated sugar. Breakfast was Madras coffee accompanied with rice dumplings and cumin-flavored lentil soup. I was ravenously hungry from the exertions of the night before and polished off the dumplings to the khansama's approving smile.

The sun rose quickly as it always does in India. In one instant, the silver and blue of the ebbing night was replaced by a golden morning, followed by a harsh daylight which arrived with unseemly haste. The khansama removed the plates and the cups and set a fresh table.

The curtains parted again and there stood James in the doorway. He had pulled the sheets off the bed and changed from his nightclothes. The khansama came forward to retrieve the clothes and linens from him. As he picked up the rumpled and soiled sheets, something caught the khansama's eye. He looked up at James and a smile came across his wizened face. He spread the sheets for James' scrutiny and there it was – the telltale bloodstain, the proof of my virginity.

"Everything fine sir," he said. "Madam – good lady."

"Yes, she is," my husband answered. James then turned away from him almost dismissively, as if my virginity was to have been expected and not something to occasion comment.

I watched them and speculated fleetingly how much of an issue my virginity might have been had it not been there. For a fleeting moment, I wondered why James had not been a virgin as well. The thought then passed through my mind as softly and silently as it had arrived.

On the third day of our honeymoon, we were sitting on the verandah. The monsoons were looming in the distance with a darkening sky and an increase in the swell of the ocean.

The telephone rang and James answered it. He looked preoccupied after he hung up and started dressing as if to leave.

"What is it, James?" I asked.

"I have to go to the airport," he said abruptly. He was gone before I could even ask why.

Hours passed. I was alone in a strange city. I knew no one and did not even know the language. The only person I knew was my husband.

As I sat there wondering what to do, or how long I should wait before calling my parents, James walked in. Behind him was a lissome young woman who looked as if she had travelled a long distance by train. Her clothes were disheveled and soiled with soot from the train journey. Her eyes were swollen; it appeared that she had been crying.

"He said he would marry me, and look what he has gone and done," she wailed.

I was quite taken aback.

"What do I do with the baby?" she went on.

"What baby?" I asked.

"The one that I am pregnant with."

I rose from my seat and looking past her directly at James I said, "I am going for a walk. By the time I return, you will have cleaned up this mess." Without even a glance behind me, I walked out into what was left of the midday sun.

My only recollection was that I had walked on the beach for hours on end – my mind completely blank and my soul entirely numb. I returned to the hotel as the sun was going down and the monsoons were coming in from far offshore.

I knew for certain that there would be no hysterics. There was nothing to discuss. Words would only be superfluous. Foolishly, I had hoped that there might be some romance between a husband and his wife.

Lakshmi's advice was to guide me now as it would throughout my life. I could hear her voice in the back of my thoughts, "Romance is for the story books, you have a tryst with destiny."

I found no traces of the girl, only a contrite James sitting on the verandah waiting for me. I said nothing and neither did he for a very long time.

Finally, breaking the silence I said, "We are going home now, James."

We moved around the room like a silent dance troupe, handing our clothes to the khansama. James' silence was that of a temporary repentance. Mine was the silence of prematurely shattered dreams being replaced with the certitude of taking charge of my own life.

The khansama packed our suitcases with efficient haste. Before mid-morning, our car was loaded down with our belongings and we were ready to depart. The khansama held the door open for James as he eased himself in behind the steering wheel.

"I need fifteen minutes to myself," I said as I turned and walked back to the suite. This was my time, just me and my God. I needed to come to terms with the hand that had just been dealt me.

I heard a loud peal followed by a crash of thunder as the skies finally and completely darkened. A hundred or so yards from our verandah the ocean had gone from a strong swell to a menacing and roiling boil.

I strode out past the verandah, leaving James and the khansama in wonderment as to what I was going to do. I walked out on to the beach, my feet bare except for the gold toe rings Vasu had placed on them. The rains came pelting down – the threatening southwest monsoons had finally begun.

Unbidden in my soul rose the psalmist's lamentation:

"Out of the deep have I called unto Thee,
O Lord. Lord hear my voice.
Let Thine ears consider well,
the voice of my complaint."

Did He hear my complaint? – I wondered. What was there to actually complain about? I had been delivered safe, chaste and educated to my marriage bed, my dowry had been paid and my parents were relieved. Hopefully one day there would be sons to brighten my old age and wealth to cushion the storms ahead.

I had met James only once before the wedding. It was foolish of me to hang romantic dreams on a perfect stranger. James' indiscretion was but a small ripple on the placid face of the life that my parents had slaved for and designed for me. I decided that I was not going to do anything to change this destined future – not just then.

◇

Except for his time in medical college in India, James had lived all of his life in Penang, a lovely little island off the west coast of the Malay Peninsula. After our disastrous wedding and aborted honeymoon, we moved to Penang to join and live with his very large and extremely wealthy family.

The family lived in a massive compound with James' father and stepmother, as well as his many brothers and their wives, all as a joint family. The house was enormous – larger than any I had ever lived in and made the-old-house-with-the-garden actually seem diminutive. Each of the sons had their own private suites but they gathered together in the common drawing room, had food prepared for them in the common kitchen, and ate together in the common dining areas.

This household formed a wonderful cocoon for a new bride to enter. I had just come from a different country and landed into a family that was exceptionally wealthy and far more cohesive than my own had ever been. The occurrences of our wedding and honeymoon paled into insignificance once I was enveloped in the affluence of the family and the camaraderie of my sisters-in-law.

As soon as I set foot on Penang soil, the most important item on my agenda was to prove that I was capable of bringing healthy sons into the family. I discovered that I was pregnant just three months after the wedding. For the first two months when my period still appeared with regularity, I had started to wonder if I was barren or if James was "shooting blanks" as Aruna had once mentioned. Then mercifully, my period did not appear in the third month.

"I have done it! Alleluia, praise God! I have done it!" I delighted.

It was extraordinary that I thought that this pregnancy was all of my own doing. In my mind, while my husband had provided the social sanction for my getting pregnant, he actually had little to do with this tiny child growing inside of me. I barely conceded that James had provided half the genes for the child or his efforts to get me pregnant in the first place. This baby was mine, and mine alone.

In my pregnancy, I became large like a seagoing vessel in full sail with its spinnaker billowing out in the wind. I actually enjoyed waddling around with my spine in a high-arc and my gravid belly in everyone's face. All the while I continued to wordlessly proclaim, "I did it, I did it!" All I really had to do now was pray that this would be a male child.

By summer's end, James was assigned as an obstetrician and gynecologist to the General Hospital in Alor Star which was in another state, the state of Keddah on the western mainland of the Malaysian Peninsula. We moved out of the Penang cocoon into a house of our own in Alor Star. It was a day's worth of travel by boat and car from the motherhouse in Penang, but it might as well have been a year's.

There, I felt alone. I was away from not only my mother, my sister Rachel, my trusted Lakshmi and my former classmates; but now also away from my new family of sisters-in-law and their many children. James preferred that I not "work for a living," so I was not even able to benefit from the companionship of newfound colleagues. I attempted to settle into this unfamiliar life of a newly wedded and pregnant wife. We had enough servants so that I did not have to do much more than "supervise" the household. As a result, I started to become somewhat unsettled in my boredom.

I decided to take up gardening – this was a worthy and genteel enough occupation. I could combine this with some of the "wifely" things that the spouses of important men such as the ruler of the state, the high state officials and the local princes did to entertain themselves. A favourite weekly diversion for other bored wives was to visit the club and learn meaningful things such as Ikebana. One of the wives of the local princes decided to fly in an Ikebana expert from Hong Kong every Wednesday to provide us instruction. We would bring an assortment of flowers from our respective gardens to the club. This provided me with the added incentive to plant a garden at our home.

James hired a gardener for me. I never knew his real name. I called him "*Abang*" which meant "brother" in Malay. He was a diminutive, sinewy old man who rarely spoke. Anything he did say was delivered through a mouthful of tobacco or betel nut which made it even more unintelligible. Furthermore, my knowledge of Malay was severely limited. In Abang's case, I would simply point to one of the plants that I wanted placed in the garden and say "*Boleh*" with an upward inflection, which roughly translated in my mind to "would you?", "could you?" or "is it possible?" He would return with "Boleh" if he agreed or "*Taboleh*" if he disagreed. It was almost as if we were engaged in some sort of duet around garden issues.

On one of my forays to the local nursery I found a Puukenikeni sapling. I decided to bring it home – yearning for a familiar planting and something from India. I ignored the warning that Mrs. Cotter had issued so many years ago and the fact that Papa had taken a mistress after Mummy had planted the vine in her garden.

I turned to Abang and asked, "Boleh?" while pointing to the vine.

He looked at me through his ancient mariner's eyes and started on a long diatribe in Malay, little of which I understood except that it began with "*Jangan*" which meant, "do not".

It was more the tone in which he delivered the message that actually got to me.

With that I dug my heels in and ordered, "You will plant it right there by the kitchen window. There will be no more nonsense."

Abang dutifully planted the Puukenikeni vine by the kitchen window and the incident was soon forgotten. He left our household shortly thereafter – never to return. The vine subsequently thrived and delivered many flowers in abundance.

After Abang's departure, I decided that I would do my own gardening to help occupy my time. It was not the soul-sustaining experience that my parents had found or the fulfilling one that I had hoped for. The air was torpid which added to my ever-growing lethargy as my pregnancy progressed. There were unfamiliar snakes at the edge of the property along with centipedes and scorpions. The entire experience was different and unfamiliar compared with that of gardening in India. I soon became tired of forced gardening and turned my attention to other things.

With all the servants in our employ, there was little I could think of to do to engage myself. One day in a fit of wifeliness, I decided that I would personally launder James' white doctor's coat while the rest of the family and household laundry would still be taken care of by the dhobi. It seemed to me to be a meaningful gesture of support for my husband's profession.

I devised a little routine for myself. James would throw his clothes in the hamper and I would subsequently fish out his white coat. I would carefully turn the pockets inside out in the event that he might have left money or something else in his pockets by mistake. There was often money left behind and I would take the odd coin or ringgit note and give it to the boy who hung the white coats out to dry before I pressed them.

One fateful day I found a crumpled piece of paper in one of James' pockets.

It had been hot and muggy that day, more so than usual. I stood by the sink in the kitchen. I was sweating profusely from the heat of Alor Star combined with the unaccustomed exertion of doing laundry by hand late in my pregnancy. The baby was now moving around inside of me quite a bit, more so than it had in the last few weeks. My back ached from being on my feet with the baby jostling for space.

Standing by the window with the Puukenikeni vine, I filled the sink up with hot water and soap flakes, idly swirling my fingers through the mixture. I arched my back to ease the ache emanating from deep within. The baby had pushed its little rear end up below my rib cage to form a shelf on the top of my belly. By this stage I could rest several small objects there.

I placed the crumpled paper I had found in James' pocket on my belly-shelf. With my pudgy fingers – fat and swollen from pregnancy and heat, I smoothed the paper out. My hands were still wet from the washing and sweat ran down my forehead and dripped onto the piece of paper. The ink started to smear and smudge. As I began to read what was written on the paper, I realised that it was a letter.

"*Dear Dr. James,*" it started. The contents, though smeared, were discernibly fairly steamy. I was appalled that someone would actually write my husband a letter filled with such open lust.

Finally, there was no mistaking the last line: "*Always and forever, yours with all my love and kisses, Pauline.*"

My mind began to race.

"Who was Pauline?"

"Oh God! What do I do now?"

"I mustn't panic. I have the baby to think of."

If I went to my father he would more than likely welcome me home, but there would always be the unasked question, "Could you have tried to be a better wife?"

"*What would a 'better wife' have done?*" I hadn't the faintest idea.

I began to hyperventilate. While my insides had turned an icy cold, heat enveloped me outside and sweat poured off me as if a faucet had been opened. Then I knew that there was only one issue at stake – I had to take care of my baby and myself.

This was a singular defining moment for me. Almost as if in agreement, the baby kicked me hard in the rib cage. "Get with the program, mother," it seemed to be saying. At this very moment, I knew that the baby was a boy. I also knew that this baby and I would have a bond that would transcend all else.

Like the women before me – my grandmother, my mother and Lakshmi, I knew then that I had to take destiny by the horns and shape it. I realised that whoever Pauline was, she was neither important nor material. There would be other Paulines; they were destined to come back again and again. I had to develop a strategy which would make me stronger, and in the process, make them pale into insignificance.

I moved from the kitchen and sat myself down in the coolness of the bedroom where I reached for the phone. It was almost as if by instinct that I called Juliet, the chief nurse in the hospital where James was working. She was a pretty and petite woman of Sri Lankan origin with skin the color of caramel, laughing honey-brown eyes, and a cap of curly black hair. Her buxomness transformed her loveliness into something extraordinary. She was the quintessential Earth Mother, yet in a flash, she could transform from nurturer to one who took charge. Most importantly, she was a good friend, one that I trusted implicitly.

"Is James having an affair?" I asked her. My voice was quavering hysterically.

There was an ominous silence on the other end of the phone.

"Juliet!" now I was panicking. "Juliet, are you there?"

"Yes, yes," she replied in answer to both questions.

"Oh God, what will I do?"

"Nothing, it will pass as all affairs do. Leave well enough alone."

"Juliet, I have to see her."

"What are you going to do?"

"I don't know yet. But I must see her. Who is she?"

"She is his obstetrics nurse. Her name is Pauline."

"Yes, I know her name. It is imperative that I meet her. Would you please set it up?"

"I can arrange for her to meet with you," she said cautiously. "You are not planning anything rash are you?" She was probably thinking that I might kill Pauline or myself, or both.

"Of course not," I responded reassuringly.

With Juliet's assistance, the meeting was set.

Thankfully it was a cooler day than most when I arranged for Pachi – our driver to bring Pauline to the club where we learned Ikebana. Pachi was an avuncular older man, probably of Eurasian descent, hired by James to drive me about town. His real name was Mahbub Ali but we called him "Pachi" which translated to "Uncle" in Malay out of respect for his advanced age of fifty-five. He spoke pristine English and wore impeccable clothes which always included his sartorial signature – a silk cravat of which he seemed to have an endless assortment. A cravat was an incongruity in steamy Malaysia, but he wore them nevertheless. He had the inimitable knack of combining deference with concern. I loved him dearly as one would a favourite uncle and he returned this love in double measure.

I sank into one of the overstuffed armchairs at the club and waited for Pauline. My feet were propped up on a low coffee table swollen and out of shape in the late stages of my pregnancy. If I had any left ankles at all, they had become as stout as those of the British and characterless as the rest of my now misshapen body.

The ceiling fans overhead stirred the air listlessly and there was the constant hum of the cicadas beyond the verandah. I must have dozed off when I was awakened with a start. It was the bearer, the uniformed young man who guarded the entrance to the *sanctum sanctorum*.

"Your driver is here Madam," he informed me.

I gazed up to see Pachi standing there in front of me. He looked at me with a sadness in his eyes and said, "Madam, the young lady is in the car."

"What does she look like, Pachi?" I asked.

"She looks fine enough, Madam." He must have seen the hesitation in my face and probably surmised that I would soon lose my nerve. "You are the mistress of the household, Madam," he reminded me. "These are mere annoyances."

"Yes, yes, of course, Pachi. Please show her in."

Presently, he came back accompanied by one of the most beautiful creatures I had ever seen in Malaysia. She was taller than most Chinese and the faint peachy tone of her skin betrayed her mixed ancestry. To say that she walked across the teak floor of the verandah would have been an understatement of the worst order. She floated across it, almost as if she were a feather wafted on a breeze.

My heart was in my mouth. *"I will never be able to compete with her,"* I thought. *"Not with that grace and loveliness."*

"Please sit down," I said to her, not rising from my chair. Any attempt to stand would have been clumsy at best and with my self-confidence now at the level of my swollen ankles, I decided not to chance an undignified fall or a stumble.

She sat on the edge of a chair close to me poised like an exotic bird on a perch. Sweat was beading up on her upper lip revealing her discomfiture. Her hands were folded politely in her lap. She wore a pale yellow chiffon frock which would have looked dreadful on me with my brown skin and likewise just as bad on a pure Chinese person. But on her, with her peach-coloured skin and blue-black hair, yellow fly away chiffon only served to enhance the ethereal quality she exuded.

"What is your name?" I asked.

"Pauline. My mother calls me Yuk Laan – precious jade."

"How old are you?"

"Nineteen."

She is just a child, I thought compared to my advanced age of twenty-three.

"Are you having an affair with my husband?"

Her nostrils flared defiantly in anger. She looked at me with a hint of rebelliousness in those sloe eyes of hers.

"Oh God, he could lose himself in those eyes," I conceded inwardly. *"The bastard certainly does have taste."*

"I love him very much," she said defensively.

"My husband will never marry you. You were not chosen for him. Besides," I said, patting my belly, "I will soon have his son."

"You know," she continued with the bravado and optimism of youth, "Dr. James will choose me every time."

"Well, in that case, you have nothing to lose and nothing to fear," I said.

I could see her spirits flag visibly. I pressed home with my advantage, moving in for the kill. "The only attraction with you is the fact that an affair is clandestine and forbidden. Once it is out in the open, he will lose interest in you and you will join the ranks of the many that have gone before you."

"He loves me. He promised he would – forever." With this, she began to cry.

I knew that I had succeeded in slipping my knife into her flesh. With a final plunge and twist I added, "Don't be stupid. He promised before God that he would cherish me and me alone – forever."

Her face became thickened with her crying and her eyes which had been clear and wide, were now reddened and dull.

"Men's promises are written with spit on the wind. They are dried up and gone before the words are complete." My wisdom surprised me, and her as well.

"What will I do now?" she asked.

"What do you want to do?"

"I want to be Dr James' wife."

"That will never happen. I do not intend to give up my position."

"I cannot think of anything else I want to become."

"Yes, you can," I said with great conviction and finality. "What was it you dreamed of becoming before James came into your life?"

"I wanted to complete my nursing education in England."

"Excellent! We can make that dream come true as long as you do what I tell you. Now, dry your tears, you look dreadful when you cry."

"Yes, my mother always says I look like boiled bok choy when I cry," she said, laughing through rapidly retreating tears.

I settled down beside her to unfold my plan.

❖

Christmas was always a grand occasion in James' household and this being the first one since my arrival, there was to be a huge party in our home where I would be shown off to family and friends like a worthy brood mare. James was determined, even adamant, that I be dressed to the nines for the occasion.

"Why don't you go to Singapore and buy yourself some jewellery and silks for the party?" he said, writing me out a cheque for a princely sum of money.

"That is not enough," I told him. "I will need at least three times as much."

"Why that much?"

"I am pregnant now and need more cloth to drape around me." This was a patent lie since Indian saris are the same length irrespective of one's girth or gravidity, but he had no idea.

He sighed deeply and wrote out yet another cheque for a small ransom.

My plan then began to unfold. Unbeknownst to James, Pauline and I flew the next morning to Singapore and then on to Hong Kong on a buying spree.

On the day before the Christmas party, I again called my good friend Juliet.

"I need your help again," I told her.

"Ye-e-es?" she responded tentatively.

"Could you schedule one of James' elective surgeries to be finished around the time that the party begins here?"

"Why?"

"I am not going to tell you. Plausible deniability – don't ask – what you don't know can't possibly hurt you."

The day of the Christmas party dawned. The household was all in a flutter – abuzz with scores of hired help. The kitchen was a beehive of activity. All the rooms had been aired out and the furniture had been spit polished to shine to a high gloss. The verandahs were cleaned and huge vases of fresh flowers were strategically positioned everywhere.

By mid-afternoon, the guests began arriving. I looked out the window to see Pachi coming up the drive with James in the back of the car. I then strategically positioned myself on one side of the grand double spiral stairway which ascended from the entrance hall. The front door opened and James walked in. He seemed pleased with my acquisitions and appearance as he looked me up and down.

"Nice," he said approvingly, "not bad at all."

And then, as he turned around to hand his briefcase to one of the hovering servants, his eyes widened in disbelief.

"Ww-w-hat is she doing here?" James stuttered in his discomfort as he looked toward the other side of the double staircase. There stood Pauline – Yuk Laan – Precious Jade, dressed exactly as I was, same sari, same jewellery, same hairstyle and same makeup. Pauline mirrored me on the other side of the stair with the exception that she was tall, gorgeous, Eurasian and very nervous. I was small, pregnant, Indian and very triumphant.

"Well James, if she is going to share your bed with me, then she is going to share all my other duties as well. Her duties as hostess begin here and now."

"Mm-m-my father will be here shortly. Ww-w-hat do you think he will say?"

"He might applaud your choice of mistresses," I purred reassuringly, knowing full well that his father and the entire puritanical group that made up his family would probably disown him.

"Dr. James," Pauline pleaded pathetically. "We love each other – until the end of time – you said." James scarcely cast a glance at her.

"I was your key to the joys of Heaven – you said – how could you forget?" she went on rapidly becoming despondent.

James then turned full face to me.

"I want her out of this house before my father gets here," he demanded.

"Not so fast; I will give the orders here," I replied. "You will write her a cheque for her trip to England and all expenses for her studies there."

Pauline looked at him with mute appeal in those lovely obsidian eyes. She fell to her knees sobbing, "You promised that we would make a future for ourselves."

He cast a dismissive glance at her. "Get her out of here," he said to the servants who were watching the exchange in disbelief.

"Please, please, Dr. James," she begged as the servants unceremoniously started to bundle her out of the house.

"Get those clothes and jewellery off of her now," he added imperiously.

"Don't you dare," I screamed at the servants who were homing in on her. "They are hers, she has earned them."

The servants moved away quickly. Pachi came forward and took her into one of the reception rooms off the foyer.

Later, as we sat at James' desk, he looked at me with an ill-concealed rage. "That was blackmail," he said.

I rose from my seat with Pauline's cheque in my hand. "That was not blackmail, dear," I said softly. "That was a small lesson for you, and insurance for me and my children. The next time you choose to do something that is likely to bring dishonour to me and my children, you will be completely circumspect, you will not compromise my children's inheritance, and you will not bring any diseases home." I turned on my heel with as much brio as I could summon in my pregnant state and triumphantly left the room.

Pauline left for England shortly thereafter.

James inevitably continued his philandering, but did so with far more discretion. I had to focus on protecting myself and my child.

11

Fragrant Tree Country

JAMES AND I EVENTUALLY MADE SOME SEMBLANCE OF PEACE WITH each other and both of us learned to come to terms with the other's peculiarities.

In Malaysia, all male doctors were required to serve for three years in the armed forces. Accordingly, James was scheduled for assignment to a military base in the suburbs of Kuala Lumpur. We packed our home and moved once again.

It was during this period that a letter of significance arrived in our mailbox. Apparently the letter had arrived in India shortly after my departure. Then, after being forwarded, it had travelled the world over to finally come to rest in our mailbox in Kinrara on the outskirts of Kuala Lumpur. The letter contained an offer from foundations recruiting doctors for medical residencies in America; it was an invitation to do postgraduate residency training in the United States – the land of milk and honey.

I consulted James on the opportunity and, much to my surprise, he encouraged me to go.

"I am soon to be deployed to East Malaysia as part of counterinsurgency maneuvers," he said. "You would be bored remaining here all by yourself. You have wanted to work as a doctor. There really does not seem to be any harm in your going to America."

"Should you choose not to avail yourself of this opportunity," the letter stated, "kindly notify us so that we might offer the position to the next person selected by our board." I was past the suspense date posted on the letter, but decided to chance it anyway and responded in the affirmative. This brought an immediate answer from the foundation offering me a position. I was going to continue my medical training in America!

I was conflicted – both frightened and excited at the same time. Was America everything that I heard it was? Were the streets there paved in gold? Or was it the modern day Sodom and Gomorrah where dark skinned women such as myself were enslaved?

James and I arrived at the US Consulate to work out the particulars of the expedition with the proper authorities. We were ushered in to meet with a man who seemed to be in charge. He was an extremely handsome black man with a ready smile who was taller than anyone we had ever met. The fact that he was of African descent took us by surprise; we had thought all Americans were white. Our surprise must have been an occurrence he encountered often and he just responded with a lazy and knowing smile.

"And Doctor, where would you like to go in America?" he pointedly asked me as he made a steeple with his long black fingers.

"Well, all I know is that I don't want to go to Chicago," I said in response.

"And, why is that?" he questioned me with his smile now fading as he looked up from his desk.

I had been reading authentic American magazines in preparation for my meeting with the Americans – "True Police Story" or "True Detective" or something of that ilk. It had discussed in gory detail the life and times of one Alfonse Capone.

"Because Alfonse Capone lives there," I replied.

The man began to roar with laughter until tears came rolling down his dark face.

"I assure you Doctor, Al Capone is dead and has been so for a very long time," he sputtered, after he could bring himself to stop laughing.

"Who did you say is dead?" I asked.

"Our buddy, Al."

"Same as Alfonse?"

"The very same," he answered, laughing some more.

"Well, in any case, I don't want to go to Chicago," I insisted.

He rose to his full height still gushing with laughter and gestured expansively to a map of the United States on the wall behind me.

"You can have your choice of cities and hospitals. How about 'Mass General'?" he asked, pointing to Boston in reference to "Massachusetts General Hospital".

"Sounds like Mass murder," said James. "Why don't you go further west?"

"Don't you have any thing farther west of Chicago?" I asked him.

"There is UCLA or UCSF," he replied, jabbing at points along the west coast of North America.

"Don't you fellows have any colonies?" I asked.

"No, I'm sorry. We are not a colonial power." He was starting to laugh again.

I looked even farther west on the map than the borders of continental North America when it dawned on me.

"Hawaii!" I shouted with the triumph of discovery.

Hawaii it was, "Fragrant Tree Country," as the Chinese émigrés named it after the sandalwood which was harvested there in the last century. I was soon to begin my postgraduate medical training there at St. Francis Hospital in Honolulu.

I stayed in Malaysia until shortly after the birth of my son. James named him Jacob after his paternal grandfather as all first-born Syrian Christian sons are named. I gave him the name of Andrew. He was a squally little red-faced baby at birth who grew into a pleasingly fat little fellow with a smile that could melt my heart and tears that could just as easily break it.

Beside my fat little son and the unalloyed pleasure of being a mother, I had the excitement of America to look forward to. The only thing that added a wistful sadness to the exhilaration was that Andrew and I were to be parted for a year. I would be unable to care for him in America with the rigorous schedule of being a physician in training. I decided that Andrew would be best cared for with Mummy and Lakshmi. If it happened that America was all we had dreamed of, Lakshmi and I, there would be a new life for me there. I would then craft grand things for my son and soon be reunited with him.

❖

I stopped off in India to leave Andrew with Mummy and Lakshmi before going on to Hawaii. They were delighted to welcome a grandson into the fold.

"I will prepare a wonderful place for you, my son," I said through my tears as I kissed him goodbye, releasing him into Mummy's arms.

As I set foot off the plane into the balmy softness of Hawaii's arms, I instantly knew that I was in love. I fell in love with this land – America.

For all my life thus far, someone else had taken care of the milieu around me – my parents, followed by my husband. Now I was truly alone at the age of twenty-six.

I had retained my Indian citizenship despite having moved to Malaysia with James. The Government of India did not allow its citizens take more than eight dollars out of the country with them at a time. So when I left India, I set out with only eight dollars in my wallet. I could have asked James or his family to send money, but out of some misplaced sense of pride, I opted not to do so.

When my father had left for Persia many years before, his employers – the British Petroleum Company had provided him with a year's salary in advance. I was certain that a similar arrangement could be made with the Sisters who ran St. Francis Hospital where I was presently to begin my internship and residency. As I counted out the three dollars for the cab ride from the airport to Liliha Street, I was uncomfortably aware that I had only five dollars left in my precious stash.

I found my way into the lobby of the hospital. It seemed curious that there was no one there to meet me. I stood in the lobby reading a bulletin board, dressed in my strange Indian outfit and with my large suitcases, looking quite forlorn and lost. A handsome woman with a lovely lilting voice and dimpled smile came out from behind a glass partition to ask if she could help me.

"I am one of the new interns," I told her.

"I am Ramona," she said, "one of the telephone operators. Let me find out where you are to go."

With great dispatch and efficiency, she deposited my suitcases behind her desk and led me to Sister Maureen Kelleher's office. After showing me in the door, she turned and left.

Sister Maureen Kelleher was an imposing and regal figure. Although she was quite plain, her great height and creamy white habit imbued her with a daunting air of authority. She was looking out the window to the left of her great desk as if something in the parking lot below seemed to have captured her attention.

I stood for a while in front of her desk while she continued to gaze out the window. I coughed hesitantly in the hopes of securing her attention, but this did not seem to have any effect at all. I waited awhile longer, shifting from one foot to the other.

"I am one of the new interns," I finally announced. It then occurred to me that this was the only thing I had uttered since my arrival at St. Francis.

"You are a day too early," she said in a displeased and accusatory manner. When she finally spoke, her voice seemed to come booming from somewhere else in the room. As she wheeled around to face me, her great white robes swirled around her large frame. Her beak-like nose supported a glinty pair of spectacles. She looked me up and down as if I were some prize rodent and she a great white eagle.

"This was the only flight I could take or I would have arrived too late," I explained. "I thought it might have been better to be early rather than late."

"Hmmph!" she sounded disbelievingly.

I bristled inwardly. She must have sensed my resentment.

"I will have to house you somewhere before the others arrive," she said in a tone that conveyed a mixture of impatience and reproach. She spoke into a box on her desk and summoned whoever was on the other end to come into her office.

A beautiful and petite Japanese nun – Sister Mary Petra, presently came bustling through the door. Her wimple was black as opposed to Sister Maureen's white. It framed her delicate oval face accentuating her appearance of an elegant porcelain doll.

"I am one of the new interns," I said for the third time that hour, just in case she thought I was a refugee from one of the far-flung outreaches of the Catholic empire. She smiled in acknowledgement as she bent down to pick up my small bag and lead me out of the office.

There remained the issue of the advance on my salary to deal with. I realised that I had not won a friend with Sister Maureen and decided that I had nothing to lose.

"I was only allowed to bring eight dollars with me, three of which I had to spend on a cab ride from the airport. Do you think I might have an advance on my pay cheque?"

"Our charities are only for the indigent," she responded. "You will have to be resourceful and find your own way to make do." She turned back to survey the parking lot. Clearly, I had been dismissed and there was nothing further to say.

I was hustled out of the office by Sister Mary Petra and I accompanied her back to Ramona's station to pick up my suitcases. We walked down the front steps of the hospital and turned right towards the convent.

"Sister Maureen really has a heart of gold underneath all of that," Sister Mary Petra offered apologetically. Reaching into the voluminous pockets of her habit, she withdrew a five-dollar bill and pressed it into my hand.

"You can return it to me later," she said. "Unfortunately, that is all I have."

We collectively struggled up the stairs to the convent with the now battered and unwieldy suitcases.

"What do you have in here, the gold of India?" she asked in an attempt at humour to lighten my darkening gloom. Shuffling down a long dark corridor with me in tow, she stopped and opened a door which led into a postage stamp sized room.

"Since you have no family with you, this will be your home."

"Omigosh" I said in disbelief. There was barely enough space to turn around in the room. Along the wall opposite the door was a single bed that could slide under a low square table which was adjacent to it. The bedspread and carpet were both shaggy, one avocado and the other the yellow of mildewed mustard. Teetering drunkenly on the table was an incredibly hideous and overly large lamp. There was an old GE clock radio on the table as well; the buttons which set the alarms had long since disappeared. At the foot end of the bed sat a tiny little refrigerator topped with a tabletop cooking range. The walls were bare except for a crucifix above the bed. An impossibly Aryan tortured Christ hung suspended from the cross. The silence of the room was punctuated by an utilitarian alarm clock which ticked loudly beside the bed.

Noticing the look of disbelief on my face, Sister Mary Petra said, "You can dress the bed up with some of those **delightful** cushions from India." She stopped as she realised it was unlikely that I had lugged any delightful cushions from India. Now with only ten dollars in my pocket, there would be other far more important priorities to claim my attention. She turned the radio on to KUMU – a Hawaiian radio station. The soft strains of a slack key guitar played over the obnoxious ticking of the alarm clock.

"Have faith," she said reassuringly. "Oh, by the way, idols are not allowed."

"Idols?"

"You know, the heathen – er – Indian ones."

My pent up anger and disappointment finally came bursting through.

"I suppose Catholic idols are okay then," I remarked snidely, glancing at the Aryan Christ.

She glanced at me for a second and then burst into peals of laughter.

"That was a good zinger," she replied.

"Zinger," I repeated after her – I was delighted to have learned an American colloquialism.

She then showed me the bathrooms which were across the corridor. I noticed a massive door at the end of the corridor. I looked at it inquiringly.

Following my gaze, Sister Mary Petra explained, "That is the convent. Only the nuns, the kitchen and housekeeping staff are allowed in."

"Where will I eat my meals?" I asked her.

"When it is supper time, you can go to the hospital cafeteria and buy your dinner."

"How much does a dinner typically cost?"

"About a dollar or two depending on how hungry you are." Her face turned a bright shade of red as we both realised that at that rate my stash of ten dollars would not feed me through to my first pay cheque.

With that, my introduction to my new living quarters was complete. Sister Mary Petra left shortly thereafter.

I then proceeded to unpack my lovely saris and hang them up in the closet. When I had finished, luminous silks and soft voiles in every hue and shade hung neatly in the closet as a reminder of the life I had left behind. From one of the side pockets of the suitcase I withdrew two framed photographs – one of James and me exiting the church after our wedding, and the other of my chubby baby Andrew against the backdrop of our garden in Malaysia. The glass on the wedding picture was shattered, an ominous sign. I carefully removed the shards of glass and arranged the pictures on the small table by the bed so that they would be the first things I would see when I awoke from my sleep.

It had become twilight by the time I finished putting my few worldly possessions away. I then heard a curious rumbling outside of my door. I opened it a crack to peer out and see what was responsible for the noise. A very long cart was being wheeled in front of the large door to the convent by a short little Filipino man. The cart was laden with food of all kinds – fruits, breads, meats and desserts. There was a stack of plates and an assortment of cutlery on the lower shelf of the cart. I watched him as he rang the doorbell to the convent and left. I waited to see if anyone would come to the door – no one appeared.

My concern for managing my ten dollars until the first pay cheque continued to plague me. I had to be creative and resourceful about it; even Sister Maureen had said so. It suddenly occurred to me that God had just provided me with an avenue by which I could accomplish this.

With lightning speed, I darted out into the hall and heaped a plate full with food. Before anyone could see me, I darted back into my room. I had committed unthinkable act – I had stolen food from the brides of Christ. While I was certain that Christ would forgive me, I was far less confident that one certain bride in particular would.

After I finally received my first meager pay cheque, I discovered several great American bargain institutions with great fascination – fast food restaurants, laundromats, and the greatest of them all: flea markets. I had never encountered flea markets in India or Malaysia. Even the concept of such a practice was alien. "Respectable people" would never consider buying other people's discarded belongings.

On weekends that I was not on call, I eagerly took public transportation to flea markets around the island. I found my forays to these places endlessly fascinating – I was learning and assimilating how Americans lived.

On one such trip, I purchased a rather lovely print of Edouard Manet's painting – *Dejeuner sur L'Herbe*. The picture was of a picnic in a park showing several fully clothed men surrounding a completely nude woman. In Manet's day, it had caused quite a scandal. Apart from the considerable talent in the execution of the painting, what I most admired about it was the courage Manet showed in painting it. It took extraordinary valour to flout the morality of the time with his choice of such a racy subject.

I purchased some of those delightful Indian cushions Sister Mary Petra had spoken of. They were a little worse for the wear, but would provide a splash of colour to an otherwise dreary room.

I brought my finds home with the pride of a huntress. I arranged the cushions on my bed over the mustard-coloured corduroy cover. I then proceeded to affix the Manet print to the wall under the crucifix with thumbtacks. I looked around my little room and was pleased with the few changes I had made. It was beginning to look a bit more personal.

The following day when I returned from a shift at the hospital I found a large garbage bag sitting outside my door. Cautiously, I opened the door to my room to find that my Manet poster had been removed and in its place was a note.

"The content of the picture is not in keeping with the moral code of this establishment." It was signed by Sister Eileen, Sister Maureen's right-hand and enforcer.

The cushions were gone as well. Another note on the bed said, *"The décor must conform."*

I began shaking with rage as I stormed over to Sister Maureen's office. She and Sister Eileen were poring over ledgers when I burst into their office.

"How dare you!" I raged. "How dare you enter my room without my permission."

"What makes you think that we entered you room?" replied Sister Eileen. "Your door was ajar when we discovered the picture and those perfectly dreadful pillows."

"The picture was on the same wall as the door into the room. It could not have been visible to anyone unless they actually entered the room."

I had caught the brides of Christ in a lie. Their retreat was a masterpiece of adroitness and skill.

"There will be no further discussion on this topic," said Sister Maureen. They turned back to their ledgers. I was no longer visible to them and had been effectively dismissed. I slunk away with my tail between my legs, having been outfoxed by the brides of Christ.

I embarked on a mission, determined to teach them a lesson. The closet in my room had two plain wooden sliding doors which were painted white. With the help of my band of fellow interns, I procured two very large cans of paint – one was a bright yellow and the other a high gloss black.

I spent all weekend painting. I first painted the backgrounds of one closet door yellow and the other black. Then, on the yellow closet door in the style of Miro, I painted the outline of a large nude well-muscled male figure in black. On the black closet door, I painted the outline of a Raphael-like nude female figure in yellow. Her hand was stretched out proffering a partially eaten apple to the man. Where the closet doors met in the center, I painted the large trunk of an apple tree. Along the upper edge of the doors I filled in the elaborate foliage of the tree. Finishing it all off, wound around the trunk of the tree, I painted the serpent. When completed, the entire scene was quite lovely. I surveyed my handiwork, and like God, I was pleased.

"Now let's see what you will do!" I said to myself triumphantly.

I left for my shift at the hospital as usual on Monday morning. That evening when I returned, the painting was gone and the closet doors had mysteriously transformed back to their old white painted state.

I strode deliberately back to Sister Maureen's office.

"What did you do with my painting?" I demanded, seething with anger. "It was of a religious subject so your excuse for painting over it will have to a be legitimate one. You are a horrid creature with fixed ideas about what is right and what is wrong." I ran on, frothing at the mouth. "You may be a bride of Christ, but you are not Christ. No one has made you an arbiter of morals."

Surprisingly, she listened to my tirade and said nothing. When I had finished, she rose to her full height, swished past me to her door.

"Come with me," she beckoned.

I followed her out of her office, down the hall, and out of the hospital to the convent. We went through the hallway past my room to the door to the convent. She drew a series of keys on a ring from the folds of her habit and unlocked the door. The world inside was far different from that of our seedy dormitory. While the rooms were not ostentatious, they were well appointed and cheerful. Beautiful paintings hung on the walls and objects of art were tastefully displayed all around.

She led the way deeper into her suite. There on the wall displayed to full advantage with focused lighting were my closet doors with the Adam and Eve painting. She then reached into a drawer of an antique credenza along the opposite wall and withdrew an envelope which she handed to me.

The envelope had my name on it written in Sister Eileen's tight little hand.

"Open it," Sister Maureen ordered.

I did so mutely. There was a cheque for three thousand dollars in my name from her account.

"As you can see," she said, "we make it a point to acquire meaningful art."

There was a rustle of robes behind me. I turned to find Sister Eileen standing in the alcove nearby. "We felt that your art was important."

"Although I admit it was high-handed to have removed it without your permission," Sister Maureen said, "we hope that you will not ask us to return it."

My mission to teach the brides of Christ a lesson had unfolded differently than I had planned. This was to form the foundation of my own nest-egg and financial freedom.

❖

It wasn't long before I settled into a familiar routine at the hospital and came to enjoy my new colleagues – the other interns. It was shortly after I landed on Sister Maureen's doorstep that the other interns trickled in from all over the world – Ricardo from Mexico, Linda from Mindanao, Azucena from Manila, Margaret from Toronto, Atherton from Boston, Ludwig from Austria, Dreyer from Los Angeles, Ching from Macao, Djon from Borneo and Deppe from Deutschland.

The Filipinos instantly huddled together and found a great support structure among their own kind in the local community. This left the rest of us to find solace and camaraderie with each other. We formed a motley band of comrades – some of us more friendly than others, some less sensitive and yet others trying hard to just fit in.

Shepherding us all was the unenviable task of our chief resident, Nadine. She had the appearance of a younger clone of Sister Maureen except that she dressed in civilian attire and was a kinder and gentler person.

Atherton – the Brahmin from Boston was the most preppy of the lot. He sported a moustache and beard that gave him a vague resemblance to George V of England. He claimed to be related to the missionaries who had come from Boston and ultimately taken over Hawaii. He was known for playing practical jokes on his colleagues, but had very little tolerance if the favour was ever returned. One could always count on Atherton to make comments that were exquisitely designed to elicit pain.

Deppe-from-Deutschland was a tow-headed, sun-tanned, sinewy, handsome god-like creature with a serious problem. Although we never talked about it, most of us tried our best to escape partnering with him during surgery. This stemmed from the fact that Deppe-from-Deutschland was loath to use deodorant which resulted in standing next to him in the warm operating room, even for a short stint, to be quite taxing.

"You ought to try 'Right Guard' on your left side as well some time, old boy," Atherton would quip in a phony British accent. No one really believed that Atherton deliberately meant to be hurtful. We learned to ignore him and ascribed his behaviour to a quirky sense of humour – perhaps peculiar to Boston.

"It's all the tea in the harbour polluting the water supply," he would explain.

Deppe-from-Deutschland was a sweet-natured fellow who either ignored Atherton's barbs or simply acted as if he did not understand them. He would just half-close his eyes and smile lazily at the world as if he were about to go to sleep. He was having fun providing women around St. Francis with an object of desire, learning a great deal (including some surgery and medicine) and he was not about to let others spoil his time in the sun.

Dreyer was Jewish although he hesitated to admit to it. His name apparently had been changed from Yankelowicz. He was very quiet and quite bright with an encyclopedic knowledge on every topic under the sun. The most extraordinary thing about Dreyer was that he was so unassuming, one never suspected that he knew very much.

Ludwig from Austria said his real name was Ludwig George Hohenhammer, although that was not the name by which he had come into the program. He often claimed to be related to mad King Ludwig of Bavaria. On other days he would expound on how he was of Jewish origin and had to be smuggled out of Dachau or Belsen as a baby. He was tall and spider-like – the spider appearance enhanced by tight blond curls and baby blue eyes, which he often kept hidden behind dense black sunglasses. There were wild mood swings and he could go from being morose and withdrawn to gregarious and ebullient.

On his dark days, it became routine for us to tap him playfully on his forehead and sing, "Will Georgie-Peorgie come out to play?" Conversely, on his rowdy and rambunctious days, "Will the real Ludwig please go back home."

"Say there old chap, are you sure you are a *Yid?*" Atherton would opine periodically, looking pointedly at Dreyer. "You certainly don't look like any of them."

This invariably sent Ludwig spiraling into a maniacal rage. There would be long unintelligible sentences in German or Polish and imprecations about the Krauts with daggers directed at poor Deppe-from-Deutschland.

"We are surrounded by *Yids, Chinks, Flips and Wogs,*" Atherton would warn the world at large, and Ludwig in particular. "We have to preserve the turf for ourselves you know. Otherwise, we will be overrun if we are not careful."

It was a complex relationship between all of us, but a special bond forms between those who experience an internship together and these people became my comrades on the frontlines of the wards.

Over the year that was my internship, there were several little events that appealed to my sense of adventure – imbrications in a fabric whose purpose I did not know yet, but would become part of the material that makes up my life.

I found myself on call on Halloween. After most of the daytime staff had gone home, those of us that were left behind sat around the house staff lounge entertaining each other with ghost stories and watching horror movies on the little black and white television. One of the ward clerks, who had been there longer than most, recounted some of the stories peculiar to St. Francis.

"Did you know that the on-call sleeping rooms for the house staff is where the old convent used to be?" she said.

"No. Is there some significance to that?" I asked.

"There are lots of ghosts in the old convent," she replied. "There is a headless nun there who roams the corridors and hallways accompanied by a black cat."

"Oh come on now, that can't possibly be true," I said, trying to sound brave despite my fears.

"You will know if you encounter her," she went on, "she always announces her arrival."

"And just how does she do that?"

"The windows will begin to bang and clatter and objects in the room will rattle and shake."

Having had enough of such nonsense, I made my way to the on-call room with my "scrubs" and toiletry bag. It had been a tiring day and I found myself readily falling asleep, despite being frightened by thoughts of a headless apparition materialising in my room. I had taken the added precaution of carrying a Bible and Rosary borrowed from Sister Mary Petra to the room with me.

It was around one o'clock in the morning when I drifted off to sleep. Sometime later I was awakened when the room started to shake and there was a clattering and banging emanating from the wall by my bed. I had bolted the windows shut in some misguided belief that it would keep the headless nun and the cat at bay. At least I could see that the windows were not adding to the pandemonium. I could hear groans and then finally a low moan, accompanied by a shriek. *That must have been the cat,"* I thought.

I looked at the clock which read a quarter past three. I quickly gathered my things and clutching the Bible and Rosary, I ran out of the room as if the hounds of Hell were perched on my back. I spent the rest of the night at the nurse's station in the intensive care units.

Fearful that I would be labelled a coward, I said nothing about the incident to anyone.

The following week when I was on call the entire occurrence repeated itself with great regularity.

The following month when Nadine was drafting the call schedule for us I went to speak to her.

"I want to be allowed to spend the night in my own room in the dormitory," I pleaded with her. "Since it is on the hospital premises, I can be reached there without difficulty."

"You know I cannot allow that, Anna. All the others will soon be asking for similar favours."

"I absolutely cannot sleep in that room, Nadine," I said with great finality.

"Is this a religious thing or something of that nature?"

"No, the headless nun haunts the room next door to mine."

"What are you talking about," she asked. "What headless nun?'

I then recounted the story of the old convent, the headless nun and her cat.

"I will make you a deal," she said. "The next time you are on call, I will come in and spend the night with you in your room so we can tackle the headless nun together."

"Fair enough," I said.

The following week it was my turn to be on call again. True to her word, Nadine packed her overnight bag and moved a cot into my room. After completing my nightly rounds, I returned to my room and we chatted for a bit before going to sleep.

At a quarter past three on the nose, the room once again began to shake. I sat bolt upright in my bed and looked over at Nadine in her cot. She was still fast asleep. I reached over and shook her by the shoulder – she woke up. It took her a moment to become oriented and when she did, she sat up paying rapt attention to all the noises and goings-on. Just as I had told her, there was the banging and the clattering that I had heard before with the low-pitched tortured moans and a final high shriek.

"Well, what do you make of that?" I asked her. "I was right, wasn't I?"

By this time Nadine, was convulsing with laughter. She got up and ran out of the room to the bathroom. Clearly, she could not contain herself. When she returned, she was still laughing.

"What is so funny?" I demanded.

"Come with me," she said, "I will show you."

We walked out into the hallway and quietly into the room next door which had been the source of the commotion. It was the call room for the surgery intern – Deppe from Deutschland. There he was, fast asleep in a high state of undress with Ione, the night shift telephone operator, wrapped around him.

"The night staff gets off at three," Nadine explained. "It could be Mary Lou or Lovey or Ione or Chuchi, or any one of a host of young women who come up here to the call room to find satisfaction and relief. The banging and clattering is just Deppe providing a little late night comfort to the weary. If their husbands ever found out, someone would soon be headless, but it won't be the nun."

My next rotation was on the surgery service. I thoroughly disliked the lack of intellectual stimulation that it provided and did not have much of a stomach for the blood and guts involved. Most of the functions we performed as interns were labeled "scut" work – low skilled but nevertheless necessary functions. We performed the pre-operative physical exams on the patients when they were admitted, made sure that the laboratory results were in before their surgery, and on the following day in the operating room, held the wound retractors while those great men, the surgeons, executed their miracles. None of this required much in the way of mental exertion. The knotty conundrums that provided fancy intellectual footwork and were grist for the mill in Internal Medicine were lacking in surgery. However, a surgical rotation was a necessary evil and there was nothing to do but tolerate three months of physical fatigue and mental torpor.

◇

My social life was also beginning to expand. I came to love and cherish my friends, Ramona and her husband Swede, and my Nunny-Bunny friend, Mary Petra. I was often invited to the homes of some of the people who worked at the hospital and there were the occasional picnics with fellow interns.

To be invited to dinner by yourself seemed to mean that you were very special and had finally arrived. This phenomenon called a "date" was a completely foreign concept to me.

"Why don't I take you out to dinner?" Atherton said to me one day. "We will go someplace fancy so that you can see how the cultured side of America lives." I was thrilled to be asked, so I accepted the invitation and we set the date. Although rare, there were days when Atherton could be charming and gallant enough that one almost forgot that there was an underlying streak of malice in search of humour at someone else's expense.

"What kind of place will we be going to?" I asked in anticipation. "Will it be fancy? Should I dress up?"

"Of course, we will be going to a fancy place," he replied. "Do dress up in one of your Indian costumes."

I was very excited and spent a great deal of care in selecting my outfit – a deep royal blue silk sari with a scarlet paisley design woven all across the material. I wore one of my favourite ruby necklaces to match the scarlet of the paisley.

I was to meet Atherton in the parking lot of the hospital. He was waiting there for me, punctual as expected. He was in a bright new red MG convertible with the top down which suited his uppity preppy Boston background.

"Birthday present from my folks," he said proudly, in reference to the car. As I hovered over the open top to peer in, I noticed that it had that wonderful new car smell. I fingered the burled walnut console and the luscious leather seats. Since leaving home, I had almost forgotten what affluence smelled and felt like.

Atherton was extraordinarily polite. Hopping out of the car, he held the door open on the passenger's side to let me in.

"You look wonderful," he said approvingly. I was flattered.

"Where are we going?" I asked.

"A delightful and exclusive little place that I think you would find charming," he said with a smile, "worthy of your sartorial splendour."

I observed that he, on the other hand, was dressed rather casually.

"What is it called?" I asked.

"*Les Arc d'or*," was his reply.

"Is it French?"

"No, not really. It's actually quite American. The chefs are Vietnamese ex-pats." I was now even more intrigued.

We drove down Liliha Street towards School Street and about two blocks away, Atherton maneuvered the MG into a parking lot. I wondered what he was doing at a McDonald's. He got out of the car and opened my car door to let me out. He raced to the 'restaurant' door and with an exaggerated courtesy, he bowed low and opened it. "Madame, allow me."

"You said this was a French restaurant."

"Actually, I distinctly told you that it was American. I merely translated 'The Golden Arches' into French. And as you can see for yourself, the chefs are Vietnamese," he said pointing to the short order cooks behind the stainless steel counters. He could barely contain his mirth with having carried off such an enormous joke on me.

There I was in all my sartorial splendour standing in a McDonald's fuming inwardly.

Seeing the anger rising to my face, he laughed and said, "Lighten up, it was just a joke."

Obviously the Vietnamese 'chefs' behind the counter were also in on the joke as they joined Atherton in uproarious laughter.

"Got you to dress up for dinner at McDonald's" he continued to tease. "That was pretty funny, you must admit."

I remained silent and with as much composure as I could muster, I went to the counter and ordered a cheeseburger with two large orders of punch, Coke and a milk shake for myself. While I was politely eating the cheeseburger, Atherton excused himself to go the Men's Room. I walked out to the parking lot with my drinks.

The convertible top was still down and I poured the punch, the Coke and the milk shake on both the car seats. I then proceeded to walk back to St. Francis in my sartorial splendour.

Atherton never spoke to me for the rest of the year.

❖

It was a lovely October afternoon. The miserable Kona weather had been replaced by the normal trade winds. Hawaii was once again back to being Paradise.

I had just finished my shift on-call and was waiting for Ludwig to take over for me. However, there was no sign of him. After waiting for about an hour, I called Nadine.

"Ludwig is not here yet and I need to go home," I told her.

"Have you tried calling him?"

"Yes, without any luck."

"I'll be over in an hour," Nadine said.

An hour passed by and then two. I settled down in the arm chair in the house staff lounge and fell asleep. I was very tired from having been up most of the night.

"Hey, wake up." I felt someone shake me gently. I opened my eyes to find Nadine bending over me.

"Where's Ludwig?" I asked.

"We are still trying to locate him."

"Have you checked his house?"

"He moved to another house since he is expecting his wife to come in from Europe. I don't know where it is."

"I do," I said. "I helped him to decorate it in anticipation of her arrival."

Leaving one of the other interns behind, Nadine and I took off down the street behind the hospital to Ludwig's new house. It was in a section of housing that belonged to the hospital – tiny little ramshackle homes on a small derelict street.

As we walked up the steps to the house, we could hear that there was loud and raucous music emanating from within. Nadine knocked loudly on the door. After getting no answer, she pushed the door open and walked in. I followed right behind her.

We walked through the diminutive living room calling out to Ludwig – still no answer. We continued on to the bathroom which seemed to be where the music was coming from. There, lying in the bathtub and shot through her head was Ludwig's new bride – quite dead. Huddled in the corner, between the toilet and the vanity and splattered with blood, we found an incoherent Ludwig.

Ludwig was gone and out of the programme a few days later. We never really learned what happened to him and who actually shot his bride.

Crazy Ludwig's departure created a vacancy in the internship programme and wonderfully, my sister Rachel soon came from India to fill the position. I was thrilled to be reunited with her after our separation which began with my marriage. From then on, Rachel and I remained together off and on for many years, further strengthening the bond between us.

12

Collisions

AFTER COMPLETING OUR RESPECTIVE INTERNSHIPS, RACHEL AND I decided to take a year off before continuing our medical training. Rachel returned to her husband Babu in India. After stopping in India to pick Andrew up from my parents, I returned home to Malaysia and James. I was delighted to be reunited with Andrew who had grown so much in my absence.

I decided to make another attempt for success with my marriage. I was older now and had matured. I had seen more of the world and felt confident that I could stand on my own. And we had a son. This would all serve to make me less needy and less anxious when dealing with James' foibles. With my new found confidence and resolve, our marriage started to acquire stability. We grew out of our dissensions and began to mold ourselves into a more cohesive unit.

Once I was back in the fold with James, every care of mine which might have been an issue in America disappeared into a deep and comforting bank account, never to surface. I lived in a lovely home and was surrounded by many servants; I wanted for nothing – well, almost nothing.

James was still serving in the Malaysian Army and was frequently away on exercises. Since he was gone a great deal, I found that I was lonely. I did have the company of my beloved son Andrew and delighted in the joys of motherhood, but I was starved for the company of my peers. Deep in my heart I knew something was amiss.

Much to my delight, Mummy came to visit from India for a short holiday. She was great company for me since James had been deployed to Sarawak on the island of Borneo at the time.

One day after attending a Sunday service with Mummy, the dean at the Anglican Church in Kuala Lumpur mentioned to me that there was to be an ecumenical council held locally whereby several priests and ministers would be coming from all over the world.

"There is a priest coming from Hyderabad," he said. "Isn't that where you were brought up?" He pored over a list of the attendees.

"Let me see, here it is," he continued, finding Hyderabad on the list. His stubby finger traced a path across the much-folded page.

"Jock Stewart," he read. "Jock Stewart will be attending. Do you know him?"

Despite my renewed commitment to James, my heart began to race. It was my green eyed Jock Stewart from the choir in Hyderabad, the one who wanted to marry me.

"Yes, yes, I know him," I answered, somewhat breathlessly. "Would you ask him if he can come over for supper?" The dean looked up at me with curiosity. I quickly rearranged my face in an attempt to project the appearance of innocence.

"Oh yes, doctor, I am sure that can be arranged," he replied.

On the prearranged evening, I sent our car and driver to Jock Stewart's hotel to pick him up. I felt like a school girl in anticipation of a prom date. I was waiting at the door when the car returned and ambled up the drive. Jock stepped out of the car. He was even more handsome than I had remembered. His face was now fuller and slight wisps of gray at his temples had turned his red hair to sable. His eyes were still that heart-stopping green, bold and probing just as in the old days. I felt a familiar rush in the pit of my stomach. Right away I noticed that he had a gold band on his finger.

Jock and I kept glancing at each other, making eye contact throughout the supper. This of course did not go unnoticed by my disapproving mother. She detected that I was holding my breath.

"You can exhale now," she whispered sarcastically, just quiet enough for Jock not to hear.

We made polite conversation through the supper and at the end of the meal, we rose and retired to the parlour. Jock had brought a gift with him for me which he then presented.

"It is one of my favourite books," he said as I tore the package open unceremoniously.

It read *The Mountain Is Young* on the cover.

"By Han-Suyin, who also wrote *A Many-Splendored Thing*," he said.

I opened the book to the fly-leaf. Jock had inscribed it there, quoting from the book:

Dear Anna,
"Today is nearly gone, but other todays stir fecund in the word tomorrow, many other todays when this one has lapsed from existence."
I hope that your todays are filled with pleasure and your tomorrows with promise.
Ever, Jock.

Mummy, watching my visceral reaction to Jock and the events of the entire evening, was obviously in a state of disapproval. She made the usual obligatory polite remarks and then excused herself to retire to her suite of rooms.

I asked Jock if he would like to see my son, Andrew. We went to the nursery together. There was Andrew – fat and happy, all curled up in his cradle, fast asleep.

"Isn't he lovely?" I asked, half turning my head.

Jock was right behind me. He laid his hands on my shoulders and buried his face in my hair with a sigh.

"So are you," he whispered.

He peeled the straps of my chemisette down from my shoulders. I drew his hands down around my waist and turned my body into his embrace.

Something made me look over Jock's shoulder. There was my mother's full-frame in the doorway. I disentangled myself from his embrace, hurriedly and without dignity as I was reminded of James and the promise that I had made to myself to make our marriage work.

"You must go back to your hotel now, Jock," I said.

"Yes, I suppose I should," he agreed. "It would be the wise thing to do."

Mummy did not say anything about the incident that evening.

The following morning at breakfast I said to her, "I am entitled to some happiness too, you know, Mother. Besides, I am old enough to know what I am doing." The defiance and belligerence expressed caused my voice to grow louder and more shrill by the word.

Mummy resolutely sat and said nothing. She looked up from her plate and gazed at me for a fraction of a second in absolute silence. Then, she resumed her eating.

"It was the green eyes, Mother, it was the green eyes that made me do it."

James came home the following week and Mummy returned to India.

I soon came to realise that if I did not occupy myself with meaningful work, I would find myself in a state of despair. I had tried to immerse myself in my role of wife, mother and socialite at home, but the unfamiliarity of Malaysia and the pointlessness of my existence disturbed me. My sleep became fitful, I was distracted during the day and in the evenings I was heart-sore. I was discovering, somewhat to my dismay that the adrenaline high I craved came from the freedom that America had provided.

"I find the household stifling," I said to James. "Everything I do has to meet social dictates."

"There are many women who would kill to be in your place with all the comforts of a wealthy household," James countered. When I was with James, there was little room for entrepreneurship, breaking the mold or thinking out of the box.

"I need to feel useful," I told him. "I have to work as a doctor. I am tired of learning how to arrange flowers, plan menus, and learn to walk in a dignified manner down a flight of stairs. I feel like a zombie just going through the motions of living."

James finally acquiesced and allowed me to go back to work. However, this change in my life was not the unqualified success I hoped it would be. What I had not planned for was that I had acclimated to America far more than I had realised.

I began working as a general medicine officer at a small government hospital in Klang – a town outside of Kuala Lumpur. Every morning, Ramasami, the chauffeur, would drive me to the hospital, remain there for the entire day and drive me home in the evening after work. Kuala Lumpur had not yet started its sprawl across the Malaysian countryside. My ride to Klang took me through the densely cultivated countryside – palm oil and rubber plantations stretched for miles around. The roads were lovely, wide and smooth. Ramasami entertained me with a constant patter of stories and his version of world news and current events.

The hospital was small but served a variety of clientele. As a general medical officer, I served a large spectrum of patients. I delivered babies, attended to children who were extremely ill, took care of young men who had been injured on their jobs on the surrounding plantations, and performed autopsies on prisoners who had died at the hospital. There were many wards for different medical specialties and patient age groups, sprawled over a wide complex and connected by covered walkways. It was a lovely facility, but austere by American standards.

The people I worked with were knowledgeable and helpful, tolerant of my youth and inexperience. But in the back of my mind there played a constant refrain – I wanted to be back in America. It was a tugging at my heartstrings; America had become a part of the fabric of my everyday life, like a mild and constant toothache which would not be assuaged.

My initial introduction to the hospital was an interesting one – I was to find that medicine in Malaysia was quite different than that in America. The nursing superintendent and the chief medical officer (CMO) lead me over to the ward that I would be working on. It was a large and open ward with two rows of white hospital beds against the walls. Unlike in India, the wards were not at all crowded. There were no patients on the floors. The verandahs and walkways were spotlessly clean. The nurses and orderlies were outfitted in clean starched uniforms. Huddling outside on the verandahs were families of the sick patients who would return to attend at the bedside just as soon as doctors rounds had been completed. The patients and their families were made up of a gaggle of Indian, Chinese and Malay. The cacophony of the languages and dialects was deafening.

As soon as we entered the ward, all the voices died down except those emanating from a bed in the corner. An oxygen tank was being wheeled in and set up at the side of the bed. There were screens surrounding the bed, over the top of which I could see intravenous poles with glass bottles of saline and glucose.

"This patient is dying," explained the nursing superintendent. "We can come back later."

"Shouldn't we at least see the patient?" I asked.

"He is past help. He is old and is dying of cancer."

"Let's have a look anyway," I said. The CMO and the nursing superintendent exchanged glances.

"Unlike in America, we let our patients die gracefully," said the CMO.

As we reached the screens, I could hear some excited conversation coming from the other side. I peered past the screens where I saw a huddle of four or five hospital personnel gathered around the head of the bed. I watched in fascination as one of the orderlies tossed bits of folded paper around the patient's mouth and nose. He repeated this process each time the patient let out a breath. The breathing had become laboured and agonal. With the patient's last breath there was an exclamation as another orderly scrambled to retrieve the bits of paper that had fallen off the patient' s face. There was a great deal of excitement as they all gathered together to unfold the bits of paper.

"Ayya, great good luck for me," said the orderly who had picked up the pieces of paper that had fallen the farthest.

"Is that some sort of religious practice?" I asked in a puzzled tone.

"No, it is a superstitious one, I am afraid," responded the red-faced CMO. "When a patient is dying, people who gamble on the lottery will write numbers on small pieces of paper and then place them around the patient's nose and mouth. As the patient exhales his final breath, the pieces that fall the farthest from him are used as betting numbers."

"It works," said one of the orderlies looking up from his preoccupation.

They then aroused themselves to unhook the oxygen and the intravenous lines from the patient. Just as they prepared to drape the sheet over the patient's face, he raised his head and took in a loud final and rasping breath. He then exhaled slowly in a prolonged hisssss and fell back dead on the pillow.

"Those numbers won't work now," the orderlies cried in unison.

"Wasted effort," added the nursing superintendent.

"I would not let this colour your judgement," the CMO said, turning to me. "It is just one of those cross-cultural things."

I still had a lot to learn about medicine in Malaysia.

Not long after my introduction to the hospital I found myself reporting for on call duty one evening. As soon as I reached the hospital I was told that I was needed immediately in the Labour and Delivery Ward. Labour and Delivery caused me great anxiety – there were two lives at stake instead of one.

I walked onto the ward trying to project a confidence that I did not have. The Labour and Delivery rooms were utilitarian. They were narrow rooms containing an obstetric table which was draped with a primitive tarp-like material. Archaic looking leather stirrups poked up through the foot of the tables and steel buckets sat the foot of the tables to catch the after-birth.

My focus of attention was on a sixteen year-old Chinese girl on the table hooked up to an intravenous drip which was flowing at a furious clip. An aide stood by her side monitoring her blood pressure and pulse. She had just given birth and was lying pallid and almost lifeless on the table with her arms flopping listlessly on either side of her. Her husband was outside the door gesticulating wildly and speaking raucously in a Chinese dialect to the nurse. The angry and squally little baby was in the arms of the man's mother who was busily cooing over it.

"What's the problem?" I asked, not comprehending the language or understanding the commotion in front of me.

"We have given her oxytocin but she will not stop bleeding," the aide said. "She probably needs a hysterectomy, but they won't take her in without any blood available."

"Her husband will not give any blood, Doctor," said Zaitoon, the outraged little Malay nurse.

The Red Cross insisted on receiving an equal amount of blood to replenish their supply before they would release any for the patient. Most Chinese felt that their vitality would be diminished if they gave blood so they never did so. They would generally pay Indian labourers to donate their blood instead.

"This man will not pay for blood either," Zaitoon explained to me.

"Why not?" I asked.

She turned to him and they argued for a long time with a great deal of yelling and screaming on both sides. By this time the girl was bleeding copiously from the vagina and I realised that she did not have much time left.

"Why can't you give your blood?" I asked desperately hoping to appeal to his sense of rectitude. "She will die without it, you know."

Zaitoon translated for him what I said. The husband looked at me with dumb incomprehension. Hustling his mother out of the room, he called down the hall to summon some other young men from his family. They arrived with a stretcher and with great dispatch, removed the girl's intravenous line, laid her on the stretcher, and started to leave the room with her.

He turned around and crisply said something else to Zaitoon.

"He says that it is her fate to die," Zaitoon explained to me. "She has given him a son and has served her function. It would be unwise for him to give up his vitality since he needs to raise his son and other sons after him. He can always have another wife."

In a fit of uncontrollable rage, I pounced on the man and pummelled him with my fists – all to no avail. One of the orderlies pulled me off of him. I then watched helplessly as they made their way to the parking lot and piled into an awaiting van, unceremoniously lifting the girl who was now dead on top of their luggage. They then drove off.

The next day I found myself in the chief medical officer's office awaiting a reprimand.

"There are certain cultural ways that will take a very long time to change," he said, not unkindly. "Doctors here do not assault patients or their families. See that this does not happen again."

While I was relieved that no further action was taken, I found myself longing to practice medicine in the civility of America.

Several weeks passed and I settled into the rhythm of work and practice. One day a young Indian patient on one of the wards, where they housed prisoners, had passed away and I was summoned to pronounce him dead. He was about thirty years old and had worked as a labourer in one of the *kampongs* near the hospital. I arrived at the ward to find the usual hospital screens surrounding his bed. The ward nurse was unhooking his intravenous line and the orderlies were releasing the shackles around his ankles. I placed my stethoscope across his smooth burnished brown chest to listen for his heartbeat while I placed my finger on his neck to feel for a pulse. He looked so peaceful that one might have thought he was merely asleep. The only thing that indicated otherwise was the bluish pallor on the inside of his lips – he was quite dead.

His young widow and four little children stood at the foot of the bed. She was crying silently while the children watched with mute wide brown eyes. I then heard a sound off to my side. I looked up from my task to find another Indian man in a police uniform standing beside me.

"Is he dead?" he inquired quite unemotionally.

"Yes he is," I responded.

"An autopsy will have to be performed in the morning," the police officer informed me. "He was in jail for petty theft at the time he fell ill. The autopsy will be necessary to determine whether or not he was mistreated while in jail."

It was my unenviable task the next morning to oversee the autopsy. I set off for the morgue at the far reaches of the hospital. There was a man there waiting for me; he was the technician who would perform the autopsy while I supervised. He wore a large plastic apron looking for all the world like a worker in an abattoir. There was a brace of uniformed men positioned outside the morgue. The young widow had also come to receive her husband's remains for cremation after the autopsy.

The technician handed me an apron and clipboard as we went in. The nude body of the man was lying on a steel table inside. Before beginning, I noted that there were no obvious discolorations, wounds or swelling of the skin to indicate any external injury. It was difficult to see much in the poorly lit morgue. His dark skin and the dim lighting in the morgue might have disguised any bruising. The technician then expertly made a long elliptical incision from the breast bone to the pubis. As the fat underlying the skin came into view, I noticed the splotchy colours of haemorrhage underneath. As we proceeded with the autopsy, I discovered that he had been severely, but expertly beaten – resulting in laceration of his bowel and pulverisation of his liver.

Upon completion, I shed my apron and stepped outside the morgue to finish my paperwork.

"What are you planning to record as the cause of death?" demanded one of the uniformed men who were waiting for me.

"Multiple internal injuries," I said matter-of-factly.

"I wouldn't do that if I were you. He was nothing but a common thief."

"I suppose that changes the cause of death," I replied.

"Doctor, the inspector would be very upset if something like this were to spoil his record."

"Record for what?"

"Humane treatment of prisoners."

"Go to hell," I said as I walked away after having recorded the cause of death on the form.

The following day I was again called into the CMO's office. He was not there. In his chair instead was a uniformed police officer. His uniform was different from those of the officers that I had spoken to the day before. He introduced himself as the police inspector.

"Oh!" I said. "You are the one who is worried about the autopsy report destroying your record."

"The man was a thief," he said to me as if he were speaking to a small child.

"What did he steal?" I asked him.

"Bread from the Catholic bakery. He was caught in the act."

I could feel the bile rise up in my throat.

Before I could say anything more, he continued, "One cannot steal from people of the cloth without suffering the consequences."

"Maybe he was just trying to feed his family," I said.

"The circumstances of his personal life do not excuse his stealing."

"You are a regular Inspector Javert, aren't you?" I said in reference to the inspector in Victor Hugo's *Les Misérables*.

His face darkened with anger as he rose and stalked out of the room. The CMO then entered.

"I would change the autopsy report if I were you," he said with a worried and concerned look on his face. "You drive quite a distance to get to the hospital. Your drive takes you through some long stretches of deserted plantation where there is no one around."

I was unmoved.

When I returned to my car later, Ramasami was not his usual garrullous self. When we arrived home, he handed me his chauffeur cap.

"I will not be back to work any longer, Madam," he said with a great finality. Sensing the puzzled look on my face he continued, "I cannot work for an employer who has so little regard for safety – her own and mine."

During my year in America I had learned to become less tolerant of general societal indifference. In Malaysia, as in India, the attitude was far more fatalistic. They were oblivious to individual misery and placed minimal importance on individual joy.

After a night of soul-searching and prayer, I went back to the hospital the next day, walked in to the administrative offices, changed the autopsy report and submitted my resignation.

It was approaching the time that James was due to complete his service with the Malaysian Army. We now had to decide what we were going to do with the rest of our lives.

We could always return to Penang and join James' oldest brother and his wife in their medical practice there. This option, however, would place James back under family shackles which he chafed against.

It seems that during his years in medical college in India, they had supported him financially. James had not always been particularly responsible or very grateful for the financial support which was provided to him. He had wasted his time in extra-curricular activities, being far more interested in making romantic conquests than in studying. Where it had puzzled me so at the time of our marriage, I now realised that this was the reason James had taken so long to complete his medical studies. He left a string of broken hearts and pregnant women in his wake. His brother and sister-in-law had to repeatedly bail him out of unsavoury situations with large donations to the medical college, which left them feeling that James had squandered their money. Of course, these skeletons had stayed firmly in the closet at the time that my parents had arranged the marriage. Any hint of dishonour and disgrace would have driven down the value of the dowry.

It was understandable that James was reluctant to return to Penang.

There was also a political and social storm gathering in Malaysia that further warned us off. The three races – Malay, Chinese and Indian present in Malaysia made for an interesting cauldron. While there was an uneasy truce between the Malays and Chinese after the Malay uprisings and massacre of the Chinese, the Indians remained on the sidelines and were not valued for much. Poor Indians would never rise above their positions of servitude as labourers. Wealthy and educated Indians such as us never really severed their ties to India – they studied in India, went back there often, and stayed fairly insular.

The Chinese, on the other hand, had little to go back to. They were industrious and focused, survivors of countless displacements who adapted well to changing situations. Despite the recent history of animosity between them, when the Malaysian government decreed that Muslims or Malays would enjoy special privileges, several Chinese converted and took Malay wives.

Malays were a gentle people thrust unwittingly into the twentieth century. With the British vacating their position as rulers, a vacuum was created into which the Malay stepped. They were ill-equipped to govern a country so rich in resources and diverse in culture. They were mostly generous and kind, occasionally quixotic, and sometimes unpredictable in their rages.

Malaysia was wallowing in racial turmoil and remaining there was not a viable alternative. Singapore might have been a valid option for James and me, however, the proximity to incendiary Malaysia and its even more unsettled neighbor Indonesia ruled it out for us.

My year in America had sensitised me to all that was wrong with Malaysia and India. I wanted to escape Malaysia with its simmering cauldron and forced silences. I wanted to avoid India with its exploding population and primitive caste system. I was not only thinking of myself, but also of Andrew. America became my choice of where I wanted to live and raise my children.

"I want out, James," I said. "I propose we go to Honolulu where I can start my residency in Internal Medicine and you can pursue a career in Obstetrics and Gynecology. We will bring Andrew with us."

Much to my delight, James agreed – we would begin a new life with our son in America. It likely would not be as grand a life as we were used to, but it would be one of our own.

"But," he said, "we have to have an escape clause. If it does not work out, we will return to Asia – Malaysia, Singapore or India."

I agreed to the escape clause. James was later to refer this as "The Rumpelstiltskin Agreement". In the fairy tale, the princess does not feel the day will ever come that she has to pay for her bail out. Similarly, I never paid heed to the consequences of our choices.

◊

Before leaving for America, James and I decided to try and enjoy our few remaining weeks in Malaysia. In our newly contrived rapprochement, James organised what was to be a romantic week for us at Port Swettenham on the west coast of the Malaysian Peninsula. He selected an idyllic spot which belonged to a friend of his – an accomplished eye surgeon named Leila.

The West Coast of Malaysia is one of the loveliest places on earth. The roads leading to our destination were spectacular – clean "rubberised" blacktop snaking across small stretches of jungle and vast expanses of plantation. Tall rubber trees dominated the landscape like gothic flying buttresses arching over the chancel of an endless green cathedral. Pristine deserted beaches glinted like carpets of diamonds in the warm Malay sun while the turquoise and indigo oceans were framed by frothy white spume. By the time we arrived at Leila's home, I was drunk with this surfeit of beauty and anticipated a lovely time.

Leila was a much-married and well-known socialite. She was a woman of independent means from her ophthalmology practice as well as legacies of her several departed or divorced husbands. I had never met her before, but had heard all about her from James and the social crowd that surrounded us. It was said that she was the daughter of a Ceylonese surgeon and an English woman. There were yet others who claimed that she was the illegitimate daughter of a local royal and that the Ceylonese surgeon had provided cover for the liaison. The questions of her pedigree only served to add to her mystique which was enhanced by her fabled wealth.

We arrived at Leila's late on a Friday afternoon with Andrew and some of our servants in tow. It was a lovely home on the coast overlooking the straits of Malacca that seemed to stretch on for miles as we approached. The gardens were vast but unobtrusive, immaculately manicured, and tended by an army of equally inconspicuous gardeners.

As we alighted, Leila met us at the door.

I was quite unprepared for the vision that greeted us. She was very tall and as thin as a rail. She had a long unruly mane of brown curly hair which looked oddly out of place against her very tanned face – the color of caramel and cream. She had enormously large eyes that were fringed with thick dark lashes. Her mouth was set in a permanent pout that was framed by lips painted in a garish neon pink. Her neck was wrapped in multiple strands of gold wire, giving her the appearance of one of those Burmese tribals who elongated their necks with brass rings. She wore a fuchsia spaghetti-strap dress with straps that appeared lost and lonely on her bony brown shoulders as they dropped off to barely contain her large watermelon-like breasts. Her waist was improbably thin, her bony hips jutted out, and she sported "the sweetest arse this side of Trenggannu" according to one of our mutual friends. Her long legs which seemed to go on for an eternity were encased in violet leggings. They reminded me of a newly calved foal – all spindly and springy as she pranced down the steps toward the car to greet us.

Despite the fact that we had never met, she gave me an effusive welcome and a vigorous hug. She then turned her bright headlight smile on James. In that split second, I caught the look that passed between them. A feeling of nameless fear roiled in my belly for a fleeting moment but I immediately quelled it, ascribing it to my weariness from the long journey.

Leila's home was impeccably outfitted and furnished with refined European furniture, courtesy of her last late husband – "dear Hans, mein Liebkuchen". She had set aside a large suite of rooms to accommodate the three of us and our servants.

That evening we were treated to a splendid repast on her verandah which jutted out over the soothing waters of the ocean. She had invited several of her other friends to join us and had even hired a small band of Malay minstrels to entertain us.

Being exhausted from our long journey, we excused ourselves shortly after supper to retire to our rooms. The rest of the crowd kept dancing and supping into the wee hours of the morning.

At around half past three in the morning, Andrew's cries and clamouring for a diaper change awakened me. I walked sleepily through a doorway to his crib in the next room, stumbling on furniture while finding my way around the unfamiliar rooms. When I returned to bed, I eased myself in and reached over to touch James. He was not there; the bed was empty. I looked towards the bathroom door assuming that he might have been there but there was no expected pencil-thin light coming from under the closed door.

With my curiosity now raised, I tip-toed to the bedroom door and slipped out. I traversed the length of the verandah with the feet of a cat. All the guests had left. The house was dark and fairly quiet except for the lapping of the waves just below the promontory.

As I neared Leila's master suite, I noticed that the door was ajar and I peered in. There was James, in the room with a naked Leila. It was clear that they had been making love. He was naked, seated on a capacious planter's chair. She was on the floor resting her head in his lap. Her hair formed a glorious dark nimbus around her caramel-colored face and her profile was faintly outlined in silver by the pale glow of starlight. Their clothes were thrown pell-mell in a heap on the floor.

For a moment, I was stunned. As I recovered, I felt a nausea hit me like a punch in my solar plexus. I stumbled back slightly; my footfall must have alerted them.

"Who's there?" Leila asked into the darkness.

I held my breath.

I could hear satiation and renewed lust thicken James' voice, "It's just the sea breeze, darling. Let's get back to where we left off."

I quietly tip-toed back to my room. Sitting on the edge of the bed, I tried to clear my head of the rage rushing through my body and pounding at my temples, finally leaving me cold and murderously resolute.

"Calmly now, there is not much you can do," I thought to myself.

In my head I could hear Mummy and Lakshmi soothing me.

"Your children should be your only concern. Everything else is incidental," was Mummy's imagined counsel.

Lakshmi's ever-ready advice was, "A lame horse will always remain lame. You can't use it for racing. You have to find other uses for it." The sound of her voice in my angry brain was strangely comforting.

I then knew instantly what needed to be done for myself and for my child. I had to get to America and find a way to stay there – permanently. Having a child born on American soil would make it that much easier for me to obtain American citizenship.

I proceeded to lie down on the bed facing away from the door and pretended to be asleep. About an hour later, the door squeaked open and James quietly let himself in. He came back to bed and sat there for a minute, likely checking to see if I was asleep. Detecting my even breathing, he headed for the shower. After what seemed to be an eternity, he came back to bed and lay down softly beside me. I turned over sleepily and moved into his back – curling up against him like a couple of spoons in a cutlery drawer.

"James, this place is so romantic, we should take advantage it," I whispered in his ear.

"Now?" he said in disbelief. Then, with a remarkable recovery he added, "I thought you were asleep."

"You smell wonderful, like you just took a shower."

"Yeah," he lied facilely, "I took one last evening."

Then there was the familiar fumbling and hurried mindless coupling that I had come to know from James, after which he fell exhausted and into a sound sleep.

"Pretty good for a lame horse, several times in one night," I mused silently.

The only thought in my mind through the entire act had been that I should become pregnant. *"If there is a God in Heaven, I will become pregnant. That will be my reward for my forbearance. I will have my baby in America which will secure US citizenship for Andrew and I as the new baby's immediate family."*

We returned to our home in Kuala Lumpur at the end of the week. By the end of April, I had missed my period. I knew then that my future was assured.

I elected to leave for America earlier so that I could accommodate a visit with Mummy, Papa, Rachel and Lakshmi in India. James and Andrew were to join me later in Hawaii. My brief visit to Hyderabad was wonderful; all were thrilled by the news of my second pregnancy.

During a stopover in London, I toured the museums to my heart's content and I shopped at Harrods until I could shop no more. It was on one of my forays into Harrods pastry shop that I ran into a voice that stirred memories from my no-so-distant past.

"Anna, how are you?" came the voice.

I was startled as I found myself bumped by an ample Eurasian woman, spilling my coffee and pastries all over the checkered marble floor. I gasped with a sharp intake of breath as she enveloped me in an expansive embrace. It was clear that she knew me while I had no inkling of who she was.

"You look well," she said. "Pregnant again, I see. Me too."
My puzzlement must have been obvious.

"Don't you remember me? I am Pauline, Pauline from
Malaysia." Laughingly she added, "You remember, one of Dr.
James' many conquests."

I looked at the woman who was speaking to me in disbelief.
Before me stood a harried looking matronly woman with three
children in tow and an obvious fourth on the way. That delectable
young Eurasian creature who was such a threat to me in my youth
had disappeared.

"Yes, of course, Pauline – Yuk Laan – Precious Jade. You
are as pretty as ever."

"Yeah right," she said, laughing disbelievingly.

After a brief exchange of small-talk, she gave me another big
hug and then walked out into the gray drizzle and fog of London
with her children trailing behind her like a mother duck with her
little ducklings in tow.

Later, at Heathrow Airport – the crossroads of the world,
on my final leg of the journey to America, my distant past caught
up with me again. I was very pregnant and quite tired from all
the museum outings and shopping. I had propped my swollen feet
up in an undignified manner on my suitcases and dozed on and
off. I felt faintly uneasy in my stupour, as if someone were
watching me. I then noticed a handsome man sitting across from
me, staring at me. He looked vaguely familiar. I stared back and
amused myself with the thought that he was certainly not awestruck
by my loveliness. I felt the stirrings of recognition again.

"*Where have I seen that face?*" I wondered. Then it dawned
on me – there were those fine chiselled features and that beautiful
scimitar nose. It was my uncle Benjamin's friend, Major Mustapha.

"*But wait,*" I said to myself, "*he appears too young. And,
'Uncle' Mustapha's nose had been irreparably broken and his
face badly scarred in the Hindu-Muslim conflicts of my childhood,*"
I recalled.

The man rose from his seat and approached me. While smiling, he extended his hand.

"I am Farrookh," he said. It was Uncle Mustapha's son!

"Omigosh!" I exclaimed. "Your pimples have all gone away and you have Uncle Mustapha's nose!"

His face was in fact as smooth as the Baynishaan mango that Major Mustapha had given us many, many years ago. We laughed and laughed until tears streamed down our faces while drawing stares from all the passersby — this strange duo: a very pregnant Indian woman and a very handsome Pakistani man — laughing as if they would never stop.

❖

Now that I was pregnant again and returning to St. Francis with my family, Sister Maureen allowed me to live in a "regular" house as opposed to the dormitory. I had my choice of two fairly decrepit houses tucked away behind the hospital. My sister Rachel would also be returning with her family so I took both houses for us, so that we could live next to each other.

One of my first tasks now that I was back on American soil was to begin to immerse myself in becoming American. I took driving lessons and proudly posed for my Hawaiian driver's license. After much debate with my friends Mary Petra, Ramona and Swede, I selected a very large and lovely American car for purchase — a two-tone Plymouth Satellite Sebring.

"James is accustomed to Mercedes and Daimlers. I have to pick something that won't be too much of a shock for him," I had said.

Having never purchased a car before, I was totally unfamiliar with the process. Mary Petra accompanied me to provide her guidance. I found it fascinating that haggling for a car was similar to the bargaining one did in India over such items as vegetables or eggs. It was settled that I would pay twenty-seven hundred dollars for the car. Having never embarked on transactions so large in America, I never thought to take out a Cashier's cheque for the car. Instead, I asked for the money in cash from the credit union.

When it was time to complete the final transaction for the new car and assume its delivery, I stuffed my pregnant self with an overnight bag into Mary Petra's convent car.

"What's in there?" she asked, looking at my overnighter.

"Money," I said as I opened it up for her to look in.

"Oh God, someone will think we stole the cash and are wearing getaway costumes," giggled Mary Petra, looking at her own habit and my sari.

When we arrived at the car-dealership, I walked directly in and plunked the cash in evenly spaced piles on the salesman's desk. He had never seen anything like it before.

"Hey guys," he yelled, "Come here and look at what we've got." Presently, we were surrounded by a group of salesmen who were laughing wildly.

I signed the papers and drove proudly out of the showroom in my brand new Plymouth Satellite Sebring.

Shortly after Labor Day James and Andrew joined me in Honolulu.

I met them at the gate and waddled proudly to the parking lot to show James my new car. The look on his face could only be described as politely pained.

"Very nice," he said charitably.

We drove back to the hospital housing in silence.

I pulled into the driveway and led the way up the steps to the little ramshackle house. I had fixed it up with delightful Indian cushions, second-hand throw rugs, and flea-market acquired prints in an attempt to liven the place up. When I led them in, I realised how tawdry it must have actually appeared to them.

"Are the servants off today?" James asked.

"Not exactly," I replied evasively.

"These servant's quarters are really quite cramped and pretty sparse, aren't they."

"James, we don't have any servants and this is our house," I said.

I watched with trepidation and sorrow as his face and shoulders sagged in anticipatory defeat.

"Tell me again why exactly we gave up the comforts and luxuries of home to rough it out here?'

I had nothing to say other than, "It will grow on you, you'll see."

Over the ensuing weeks, he grew more depressed and sullen. All the enthusiasm with which we had discussed developing a life in America had·ebbed away from him. However, I knew that James was mercurial and I relied on this transience to assure myself that his feelings would change. I was sure that after the baby's birth everything would improve.

Meanwhile, our silences became strained and longer. When we were not silent, we quarrelled loudly and frequently about the most trivial of things. Living in the modest house and constantly scrimping to get by seemed to be a matter of shame for James. He could have sent home for money, but to do so was unmanly and an admission of defeat. We mutually agreed to wait to make any major decisions until after he started his Obstetrics and Gynecology residency.

I resumed my life at St. Francis leaving James home to study for the exams that would allow him to begin practicing medicine in America. He would drive Andrew to a little Episcopal pre-school everyday in the Plymouth, drop him off and return home to study, or so I thought.

I elected to cover the hospital during the usual lunch break so that my fellow residents, Linda and Margaret, could spend some time with their boyfriends. It was difficult for me to walk far in my advanced sate of pregnancy anyway. Most of my lunch hour was spent with the nurses in the intensive care units seeing to the patients who were most seriously ill. The head nurse, Mayu, had become a good friend. We would laugh and giggle about a hundred different things and often share confidences over a bite to eat. This was a pleasant part of my day.

"Why do you cover every lunch hour for the others?" Mayu asked.

"Oh, because it is so difficult for me to move around in my pregnant state. I would have to waddle all the way home and waddle back just to have lunch. Besides, I don't want to interrupt James' studying."

"Come with me," she said as she led me to the window of the nurse's lounge. "I want you to see something." She pointed in the direction of the hospital housing.

From the window I could see the driveway to our house. There were two cars parked in the driveway besides ours. I instantly recognised them as Linda and Margaret's.

"That's funny, Linda and Margaret must not have been able to find parking in the hospital lot," I said.

"The patients are fairly stable," said Mayu. "Why don't you wander over there and see what is happening."

Obligingly, I left for home. As I opened the front door to the house, I could hear giggling coming from the bedroom. I walked in and there was James in bed with my two friends, Linda and Margaret.

"It isn't what it seems," spluttered one of them.

I could feel my heart turn leaden.

"Had I known you were that good in bed, James, I would have put you out for stud fees."

My second son Josef was born in early December. While Andrew's birth had been an easy one, Josef's was difficult and complicated. There was a prolonged period of recovery and this seemed to bring James and me together to some degree.

Shortly thereafter, Rachel arrived with her son. My mother accompanied her to look after our children while we worked in the hospital. Rachel's husband Babu was to join her later. With Rachel and Mummy's arrival, James again began to feel estranged and more distanced from me. His sullenness returned.

Even with Mummy's help, I felt harried and overburdened with all the cooking and cleaning, the chores with the baby, and my work at the hospital. Where James had helped occasionally with the housework before Mummy's arrival, he now firmly dug his heels in and refused me any assistance. His routine was to deposit Josef with my mother at Rachel's house, take Andrew to school and then disappear all day until was time to fetch Andrew in the afternoon.

I found that managing my schedule became more and more difficult. Determined to streamline and make more efficient use of my time, I decided to cut my hair short. It was long, curly and difficult to manage – consuming too much precious time caring for it.

"James, can I cut my hair short?" I asked, still influenced by my subservient role as an Indian wife. "It is getting more and more difficult to manage."

"Absolutely not," he said with great finality. "I like it long and spread out." What remained left unsaid was that he liked it long spread out on the pillow.

"You know, I don't care for your moustache," I reasoned. "But you will not shave it off for me. Why should I keep my hair long for you?"

"You are the wife," he said with finality, and that was that.

The following weekend I took myself to the hairdresser and had my hair cut in a fashionably short style. I loved the new look, as did my friends. I arrived home thinking that James would love it once he saw it. He just glared at me in silence.

Then, after a long while he said, "I will never speak to you again."

For the three months or so that followed, we only communicated through Andrew.

"Andrew, tell your Daddy that his dinner is ready."

"Andrew, tell your mother that my shirts need to be ironed."

Finally, after three months he said, "I have decided to forgive you and will speak to you again, as long as you grow your hair out."

My only response was, "I haven't missed your conversation and what is more, I will not grow my hair again, least of all, for you."

Seeing him constantly crestfallen, my guilt got the better of me and I relented. I attempted to resume a relationship of sorts with him. Although I was determined that I would never grow my hair again, in all other things, I made a concerted effort to please him. He reciprocated by agreeing to apply himself to carving out a joint future for us.

We agreed that it would be unwise to burden ourselves with a third child at the time and opted to wait on expanding our family. I went to the obstetrician-gynaecologist and had an intrauterine device, an IUD placed as a method of birth control. This had unexpected and untoward consequences. The IUD lodged itself in my uterine wall setting up a chronic infection and inflammation which resulted in moderate pain and frequent courses of antibiotics. This all put a great damper on our newly carved out conjugal bliss which James saw as my rescinding on an unspoken contract.

James soon completely quit studying and gave up all pretenses of doing so. Gone were all the dreams of his passing the exams and our great life together as practicing physicians in America. I had paid the registration fees for his exams more than once, only to find that they were returned sans the cancellation charge. On one occasion, he claimed that he had forgotten the date of the exam. On another, he maintained that he was not feeling well. The third time was the final straw and I accosted James with the third cheque from the Educational Council for Foreign Medical Graduates.

"What is the meaning of this?" I demanded.

"I am not ready to settle in America. I find it ludicrous to have to prove myself as a doctor in this country. I resent having to take exams again."

"It is not a personal affront to you. Every physician coming into the country has to take these exams," I said in desperation. "What about all our plans?"

"They were your plans, not mine," he said angrily. "I only went along with you. But you have changed. I am no longer part of your future. You can do just fine without me. You have your mother and your sister to look after you."

"They participate in my life more than you do. You are no longer a part of my life," I said while dashing away tears of anger and frustration.

"Fine, I will return home to Malaysia next week. You can join me when you are ready to resume being a good and obedient wife."

I realised that I had in fact taken him from his familiar environment. I felt as if I had been party to imposing a new life on a reluctant participant, thereby destroying his confidence. He needed to go off and rediscover himself. And he needed to accomplish it without me. The following week he packed his bags and was gone; gone from the country and out of the proximity of our lives.

❖

James and I wrote to each other often, but perfunctorily – exchanging news of our sons and family. The boys were growing like weeds and I was enjoying my new-found liberty. I naively thought that he would ultimately return and we would be a family again. Despite all the fits and false starts, I actually looked forward to the day when we could be mature and stable – more committed to our children and to each other. In James' absence, I had developed a new circle of close friends and a greater sense of purpose and commitment to my family.

In the meanwhile, something ominous was happening with my body. The IUD penetrated my uterine wall and had worked its way out into my abdominal cavity. About six months after

James' precipitate departure, I found myself wracked with severe pain and difficulty in breathing. My panic-stricken family rushed me to the hospital where it was believed that I had thrown a blood clot to my lungs.

The doctor who examined me suggested that the source of the blood clot was my now-infected and irreparably damaged uterus. My gynecologist was invited in to consult and he subsequently recommended that the best option would be to remove the offending organ – a hysterectomy.

"The sooner the better," he cautioned.

I called James several times in Malaysia to tell him what was happening only to learn that he was away on a short vacation and unreachable. Without his acquiescence, I agreed to have my uterus removed. In my typical hell-and-be-damned fashion I also said, "You might as well remove my ovaries while you are in there."

"You are very young to have your ovaries removed," my gynecologist countered.

"I will take hormones," I sad dismissively.

I had the surgery immediately thereafter. I woke up in the recovery room hooked up to intravenous lines and had a tube which passed through my nose and headed south to my stomach.

"I have to call my husband," I said to the nurse.

She wheeled a phone into the room and I placed the call. After many unsuccessful tries, I finally reached James.

"James," I said, "I have been trying to get through to you."

"I was in Chieng-mai." I knew Chieng-mai was the garden spot of Thailand.

"What's in Chieng-mai?" I asked.

"Beautiful women," was his quick and thoughtless reply. "Are the boys okay? Why were you calling me?"

"The boys are fine. I had to have a hysterectomy and bilateral salpingo-oopheorectomy."

"You what....?" he sputtered.

"I had a hysterectomy and bilateral salpingo-oopheorectomy," I repeated. "I tried calling you, but you were not available. I left word with your manservant. Didn't he tell you?"

I could hear him crying over the crackly static on the line to Malaysia. I could feel my heart melt – James was actually concerned about me. Things were looking up for this marriage.

"Oh James," I said. "There's no need to cry. I will be fine."

I heard more crying and sobbing on the other end of the phone line.

"James, James dear, please don't cry. I will be fit as a fiddle in no time. You will be back soon and we will have a great future together."

Then came the thunder bolt.

In a strangely angry voice which I knew from times before he said, "I have no future with you! What good is a wife who is not a woman any more! You are an IT! No uterus, no ovaries, you are an IT!"

"Please, come now, James, be reasonable," I pleaded. "Not having a uterus or ovaries does not make me any less of a woman."

"Yes it does," he said with a great finality. "In my eyes, it most certainly does."

As I hung up the phone I rose from the bed and asked the nurse to hook up my intravenous lines and stomach tube to a mobile IV pole.

"What are you doing? Where are you going?" she asked with a puzzled look on her face.

"I am going to try to move around so that I can get better sooner," I lied.

"You are a doctor and you know that it is a little early to be ambulatory," she said, pleasantly enough. I dismissed the advice and refused any further assistance after the pole had been positioned and I was adequately covered in a hospital gown.

I shuffled slowly and painfully to the elevator where I boarded and hit the button down to the basement to the Pathology

Department. I found my way to the office of the chief resident in Pathology, Beverly, who was a friend of mine. Beverly was a handsome black woman with a great sense of humour and wisdom beyond her years. She was seated at her desk.

"What are you doing here?" she said surprised, as she looked up from her work and saw me in the door.

"Do you have my uterus and ovaries from my surgery?" I asked. My eyes were filling with tears of anger which she mistook for tears of sorrow. "Beverly, I have to have them."

"What? What do you want to do with them, put them back inside?" she asked in alarm.

"I will not gain salvation if they are not properly interred in India by the banks of the Ganges River," I lied. "They are my uterus and ovaries and I would like them prepared, packed and ready for interment."

"That is going to be quite a feat. We will have to get all kinds of releases from the Public Health folks here and the like," she countered.

"Oh Beverly, come on, specimens get lost in Pathology all the time."

"I will get into all kinds of trouble if anyone were to ever find out."

"No one ever will. After you are done examining them, please just get them ready for me. I don't want to have a set of organs stand between me and my salvation."

About a week later when I was getting ready to be discharged, Beverly came up to my hospital room to see me. She had a rather heavy package in her hand.

"Everything is all ready for you and for your salvation," she said as she handed the package over to me. She continued with amazing prescience, "Funny though, I almost feel like this is going to procure a different kind of release."

I smiled and readily accepted the package while giving her a big hug and kiss.

Mummy and Rachel soon arrived to bring me home from the hospital.

"I have to stop by the post office," I told them.

"Today?" they asked in disbelieving unison.

"Yes, today, absolutely."

We stopped off at the post office. I went inside alone and wrote a short note to James. I sealed it up with the package and addressed the bundle to him in Malaysia. I then stepped up to the counter to mail it.

When the postal clerk asked me what the value of the package was I said, "It is worth the price of my freedom."

"We have to have an actual value, Ma'am. An abstract concept will not do," he said, looking at me with typical bureaucratic disapproval.

I mentally converted the dowry my father had paid from rupees into US dollars and wrote the figure down. The clerk whistled in astonishment.

"Do you want to insure it?" he asked me.

"No, the only value it has is for the recipient," I said as I walked out into the Honolulu sunshine to my awaiting family.

I was to hear from one of my Malaysian sisters-in-law a month later.

She was spluttering with laughter when she called.

"You should have seen what happened when your package arrived."

"Tell me," I said breathlessly, "tell me everything."

It seems that the entire family had been sitting at the dinner table with James' father at the head. Prayers had just been said when the servants brought in the mail and there was the large package from me addressed to James.

"Who is it from?" my father-in-law asked.

"It is from America, Father," James responded.

"Well then, open it," he ordered.

One of the servants then ran forward and opened it, removing all the brown paper and plastic wrappings. There, bobbing in a vitrine filled with formaldehyde, were my uterus and ovaries suspended like an angel poised with outstretched wings.

"What is that?" the old man demanded. All the others at the table were physicians who instantly recognised the pathology specimen.

A shocked silence descended on the table. Spying the accompanying note, my father-in-law demanded to see it. He read it aloud to the table with a gathering anger:

"Dear James,
Fuck this.
Your Loving Wife – now an IT."

He then rose from the table and casting a murderous glance toward his son, he stormed off.

My uterus and ovaries were sent to one of the local hospitals for incineration.

James and I were divorced some months later. I was finally free of the last of my shackles; I was now free to live in America unfettered.

I went on to complete my residency training in Internal Medicine at St. Francis with Andrew, Josef, Rachel and Mummy ever present for support. I then furthered my medical training with the study of Nuclear Medicine at the University of Rochester in Rochester, New York, taking my nuclear clan with me.

13

Freedom's Refrain

SO FAR, NEITHER MY MARRIAGE NOR RACHEL'S HAD BEEN A SUCCESS. It seemed though, that I had the better fortune to have my marriage falter earlier and be done with it. Of course my mother blamed my father for making such poor alliances for her daughters, and my father in his usual manner, dutifully accepted the blame. In return, he charged my mother with raising non-compliant daughters who were defiant in not pleasing their husbands. It was like a long tennis match with no end in sight: serve – return – serve – return, and serve again. It was a match with no winners and no losers, only survivors and victims.

When we came to live in Rochester to pursue further medical training, Rachel and I had our children and Mummy with us. All three women, Mummy, Rachel and I, had shed our husbands, leaving them behind in a variety of different places – Papa now in Travancore, James in Malaysia and Babu in California, continued to float in and out of our lives. While we were in Rochester, Babu had gone back to India to live with his brothers.

Rachel and I were determined to eventually return to Hawaii, although it was still unclear exactly how this was going to be accomplished. The possibility of returning to India seemed quite out of the question. Leaving India, the comforts and conveniences of having servants and a structured, safe life quickly faded to a series of sepia-tinted memories – nice to occasionally reflect upon, but quickly overshadowed by the seductive bright colours and the rotgut-liquour headiness of America. America's incandescent freedoms, while accompanied by their own brands of difficulties and pain, had become far too addictive to give up.

There were very few days in the bleak Rochester winters that were considered special, but Christmas was one of them. As to be expected, it was a snowy white Christmas morning in the university family-housing complex where we now lived with our clan.

The housing department would have been horrified if they had learned that there were so many of us living in such cramped quarters – three children, two sisters and a grandmother all in a two bedroom apartment. I thought that I had once heard my neighbours muttering something under their breath about "black holes of Calcutta" or "Indian ghettos". It wasn't as if Rachel and her son did not have their own apartment, we simply chose to all live together. It was far cozier that way and felt much safer.

The snow crackled on the windowsill and thick clumsy icicles hung off the window frames. The wind had picked up and was whistling through the quadrangles of the university yards blowing the powdery snow up in ghost-like spumes. It was warm and toasty inside the apartment, but I still shivered, partly from imagining how cold it was outside and partly from the prescience that something momentous was going to happen that day.

Rachel and I were in the second year of our fellowship training programmes and had the day off to celebrate Christmas with Mummy and the children. We were busily preparing for the day's events. Mummy was up at the crack of dawn as usual, bustling around the tiny kitchen making me a mug of fragrant chai. Rachel was sitting by the tiny artificial green Christmas tree filling stockings for the children who were still asleep in their beds. I stood by the tree rubbing the sleep from my eyes, rearranging the ornaments for the millionth time and adjusting Pooh Bear, who was perched precariously on top of the tree. The children had unanimously voted down the traditional angel or star topper in favour of Winnie the Pooh.

"Rochester is so different from Honolulu," I said, reflecting and musing to no one in particular.

"Now there's an understatement," replied Rachel sarcastically.

"Rochester is just a means to an end," Mummy said as she entered the living room from the kitchen with my chai. "You've got to keep your eye on the ball." Curiously, Mummy had begun watching American football on television. Football metaphors, which were quite alien to us, were now frequently peppering her speech.

We always received presents from Mummy at Christmas. Her gifts were practical, utilitarian and invariably stodgy. They were also a means by which she would issue unspoken and unwritten edicts. You received a hand-held vacuum cleaner when she wanted you to know that it was high time you vacuumed your bathroom floor daily instead of waiting for the weekly cleaning. Occasionally, she would stretch the envelope and give you a bundle of multicoloured clothespins instead of the plain wooden ones. This could be interpreted that she wanted the clothes sun-dried and not dried in the communal dryer at University Park. The bright colours and the plastic of the clothespins was her effort to be outlandish. One never really associated Mummy with much in the way of whimsy. Her gift-wrapping too, like all her other efforts, were of the highest quality – precise and highly disciplined. Mummy was the Rock of Gibraltar, unmoved by storms, providing us shelter from them, but without frills or frivolity.

Mummy handed me her present and I unwrapped it. It was an Osterizer for the dozen odd spices we had to grind each day to make our Indian food – totally utilitarian, absolutely necessary and completely practical. Of course there was an edict – she wanted the spices mixed, grated, pureed, chopped, blended, ground, whipped or liquefied. She was no longer going to tolerate the coarse haphazard results of a mortar and pestle.

Letters from Papa in Travancore had been arriving with clock-like regularity every week throughout the year. However, Christmas-time was different. Instead of Papa's standard pale blue aerogrammes, air mail letters, we received cards and presents from instead. His cards were gifts in and of themselves as he always carefully painted and decorated them by hand. His presents were invariably quite artfully wrapped, and while not expensive, they were whimsical and thought-provoking in contrast to Mummy's.

The night before, Rachel and I had wrapped all the presents in Sunday comics and brown paper from grocery bags. They were piled up around the base of the little Christmas tree all pell-mell and helter-skelter. But now, standing there amid the chaotic jumble, was one lone large square box that stood out. It was wrapped in shiny red paper and tied with a bright green ribbon. I had not spotted it the night before when I placed battered old Pooh bear on top of the tree. There was a card decorated with a gold foil doily leaning against the box. My name was written on it in my father's familiar scroll with gold ink. I immediately reached for it with excitement.

"Don't you want to wait for the children?' Mummy asked.

"No, Mummy, it's a present for me from Papa and I want to open it now," I said defensively.

Sensing I wanted to be alone, she and Rachel left the room.

The box was quite heavy and I almost dropped it on the blender Mummy had given me. I steadied my hands and carefully unwrapped it so as not tear the red paper. I finally succeeded in taking off the lid of the box and found it filled with the pale fuchsia tissue paper typical of India. I loved opening Papa's gifts; there was always a period of keen anticipation followed by surprise and delight. This sequence had never failed before and was being repeated this time.

I hurriedly pulled the tissue paper out of the box. It rustled and tore as it caught on the object contained within. As I continued impatiently, I caught my thumb on a sharp edge of the item in the box. With the rapid onset of excruciating pain and an exclamation of frustration, I reflexively withdrew my hand and sucked on my bleeding thumb. I watched for a few moments with fascination as the blood dripped onto the tissue paper forming strange Rorschach patterns. Anxiously pushing the remainder of the tissue paper away, I uncovered a glint of red gold metal and finally withdrew the heavy object from its encasing sarcophagus.

There he stood in semi-naked splendour – a bronze statue of Lord Shiva. Papa had remembered. I had always yearned for a statue of Shiva in his dancing form: *Nataraja* – Lord of the Dance, like the pendant that Mr. Ching had given me so many years before.

I gently set the statue down in front of me, my eyes filling with tears. I traced his beautiful form with my finger – his multiple arms, his powerful legs, his delicate face, his smiling full lips and the stylized circle of fire that surrounded him. I then turned to open the card. It read:

"*My dear daughter:*

I am sorry that I am unable to be there to spend Christmas with you and the family. You had always wanted a statue of Shiva in his dancing form. I found one that I thought was beautifully wrought. I send it to you with my love, my blessings and my prayers. The man who made it, besides being a skilled artisan, is also highly educated and well read. He shared a poem with me which I enclose for you. He tells me that a priest from Chicago composed it:

May the tunes of angels echo in your brain,
May heaven's rhythms tap your twitching feet,

May you sing along with Mary's sweet refrain,
And may you sway to the Lord's demanding beat.
Dance with all the lovers He has taught your song,
And, sure spin with Him at every chance,
Whenever He invites you all night long,
Never say, 'no' to the Lord of the Dance.

I know that at the end of the academic year you will be
returning to Honolulu. The New Year will hold promises
of many new opportunities for you. I hope and pray that
they and the chosen people in your destiny will uplift your
spirit and sustain your soul. Choose your path wisely,
choose your partners with gravity and forethought, and
you too will dance with the Lord.

> *Yours lovingly,*
> *Papa."*

❖

Rachel and I succeeded in returning to Hawaii with Mummy and our children. The way in which we accomplished this goal was to join the United States Army and start our careers as physicians in the Armed Services. Medical positions in Hawaii were much too coveted and competitive to obtain otherwise, particularly for two Indian women.

Overall, life was pleasant. While we were not wealthy, we were comfortable and raised our children together. Mummy, of course, was part of the continued fabric of our lives. Papa rejoined us months later, after we had settled in. There seemed to be a prolonged and uneasy truce between my parents during the time we were all together in Honolulu.

Papa would often sit on the lanai of our home and stare off into the distance for hours at a time. The playful grandchildren would tug at his shirtsleeve, asking him "What are you thinking of *Veliappacha* – grandfather?"

His response was always the same. "My end is near."

Turning so that we would hear of his final wishes, he would add "I want to be buried beside my mother in Travancore."

Papa and Mummy had been frozen in my mind, as if in a time warp spanning four decades. He remained thirty-six, and she stood still at thirty. And then suddenly, the time warp disintegrated releasing them both.

I now saw Papa as he had become – a frail seventy-six year old man who had grown more refined and handsome with age. Mummy went from being a very beautiful and resolute young woman of thirty to a curmudgeonly dowager in her seventies.

It was one trivial event that precipitated Papa's final departure from us. Although it seemed to be for the most insignificant of reasons, it was in actuality a gathering and culmination of all his sorrows and disappointments – a drum roll that was to announce his exit from our lives forever.

There was a small lime known as the Kalamanzi lime that had made its way into the culinary repertoire of some of the major chefs on the island. It was tiny and had a thin silky skin – "*peau d'Soie*," I called it. Cutting the lime required much maneuvering and skill. The skin was so soft and malleable that it would be bent away by even the sharpest of knives. One had to stab it with the knifepoint and then swivel it around the knife to cut it. The flesh was surprisingly juicy and the color a pale turmeric. It was mostly tart with a slow hint of sweetness, which came in as an afterthought and then lingered.

When Rachel and I found a Kalamanzi tree during one of our foraging expeditions in of the nurseries in the Hawaii Kai valley, we brought it home. We found a place for it by the crown flower tree that had been growing in the western corner of the garden. Planting it was going to be a joint effort for the two of us – Rachel would dig the hole for the tree and I would plant it.

As we lifted the tree out of the trunk of the car, Papa looked at it with a dawning recognition in his eyes.

"What tree is that?" he asked in a forceful manner.

"It is a Kalamanzi lime, Papa," I replied.

"I know this tree," he said, now even more agitated. "This tree makes widows of the women in the house. Get rid of it!"

Rachel and I looked up at him in amused disbelief as he struggled to snatch it away from us.

My mother, who had been listening from the verandah now chimed in, "You are like a little old woman with all your beliefs and superstitions. If there was even a modicum of truth to this, the Philippine islands would be completely inhabited by widows."

Rachel proceeded to turn over the soft and wet earth with her trowel creating a hole in the ground. I eased the Kalamanzi tree out of its temporary container and gently lowered it into the small pit; I then packed the earth around the base of the tree.

"One will be a widow if one is destined to be one," Mummy went on. "The Kalamanzi does not make widows, life does."

"It wouldn't bother you to be a widow now, would it?" said Papa in accusatory voice.

"Oh God, here it comes," I thought to myself, catching the gathering mischief in my mother's eyes. Then, sure enough, the response came.

"Not any more than it would bother me to be a wife," was the lightning-quick retort delivered in Mummy's customary biting fashion.

Bearing witness to such an absurd argument and unable to control ourselves, Rachel and I burst into peals of laughter. Mummy looked at us and began to giggle herself, like a naughty child.

Papa's countenance darkened. He clearly saw this exchange as a long-standing conspiracy of three women poised against him. He began his packing to leave us that afternoon. No amount of begging of pleading would sway his decision and determination to leave. He was on a plane headed back to India in less than a week. He returned to Travancore to live his final days in his ancestral home.

Rachel and I bought our final home in Honolulu in a splendid section of the suburbs overlooking the ocean and Maunalua Bay. We planned to raise our children there and have Mummy remain with us. Our careers in the military – Rachel's and mine, led us up in the ranks and to different locations over the ensuing months. For me it was San Francisco, for Rachel it was Seattle. While our locations may have changed, we were always drawn back to the center, to Hawaii, the nidus of our equilibrium in America.

❖

Once back in Travancore, in anticipation of his final days, Papa signed all his lands over to his youngest brother Joey. He then passed much of his time helping to supervise the building of a new home for Joey, his wife Kuttiamma, and their children.

Two years before his death, Rachel and I went to visit him in Travancore with hopes of persuading him to come back and live with us in Hawaii.

He was firm, even obdurate in his unwillingness, "I am not moving! And I am most definitely not moving back to live with your mother. I will never live in a household run by women again, and that is final. While very flattering, all your pleading is to no avail. My mind is resolutely made up, end of discussion." This was met with tearful remonstrance from Rachel and sullen silence from me.

A year later, I was assigned to the Presidio in San Francisco, while the rest of the nuclear family stayed on in Hawaii. I was living alone in a small studio apartment overlooking the marina and the St. Francis Yacht Club. I was in the throes of heaving pre-menopausal storms and going through boyfriends like I would overripe plantains – sampling them and discarding them.

My father continued to write to me as regularly as clockwork. While I did not always reply as diligently, his letters always came. Every Saturday morning without fail, a letter would arrive in my

Presidio mailbox, a fortnight after he had mailed it in India. They were always in the form of pale blue, onionskin aerogrammes. He addressed them with every title I had ever lay claim to – Colonel, Dr. and Mrs., with the "Mrs." in parentheses. He somehow chose to ignore the fact that I had been divorced for years. It took me some time to master the fine art of opening the aerogrammes without mangling them. His beautiful tight script written in fountain pen occupied every millimeter of available space on the inside. As he grew older, the tremors of aging found their way into his fingers which manifested themselves in fine undulations of the loops of his consonants.

The letters would contain news of neighbours I had long forgotten, news of the cows and water buffaloes calving, news of the Drosophila infestation of the *Muandan* mangoes in the garden, and on and on. There would always be a myriad of questions about relatives' sons or daughters in America – "You may have run into them?" or "Do you know them?" It didn't seem to matter that they were living three thousand miles away in New Jersey. The final paragraph of Papa's letters would invariably recant how he was praying for me every morning and night, commending me to the care of the Almighty.

Six months before his death, the tenor of his letters started to change. He began to hint that he wanted to return to America. I would normally have sensed the undercurrent of his desperation had I been less self-absorbed. He wrote repeatedly and more often, imploring me to let him come live with me in San Francisco. He frequently even telephoned with the same request. I somehow managed to dodge the issue as often as I was asked. I lied to him and told him that I had applied for military base housing on the Presidio and was on the waiting list, which was two years long. In actuality, I had never even made the request.

"When do you suppose they will find you housing?" he would ask on the phone. "You are a colonel after all, shouldn't that count for something?"

"Not to the civilians who run the housing office, Papa. A colonel is just another customer in a green uniform that they have to lodge until the other officers are transferred out."

"Why don't you report them?"

"Who would I report them to? The surgeon general? The president? No one has any authority over the civilians. They cannot be banished to outer Slobovia or be sent off to war; they can't even be fired."

"Well, why don't I come and stay with you in your apartment and we can both wait for housing together?" he would ask with his voice growing more quivery and tearful.

"My apartment is too small, Papa. Besides, I am too busy working to look after you or take you around San Francisco."

"I will make myself as small as a mouse, I promise. I don't have to see any of San Francisco as long as I can see you. I will look after you; you don't have to take care of me. After all, I am your father. I will prepare you hot and fresh meals everyday. Your uniforms will be laundered and pressed – ready for you every morning."

Although the prospect of my father preparing my meals and doing my laundry was a very tempting one, albeit unrealistic, the temptation to allow him to do so passed even before it had time to gain form in my mind.

The real reason for my not wanting him to come and live with me lay with the fact that it would be much too inconvenient for me to have him underfoot while I was dating. My father was far too refined a man to ever actually voice open disapproval of anyone I might bring home. But, one could always tell by the set of his jaw and the manner in which he pursed his lips that the gentleman caller was not the sort he would have chosen for me, not even in times of total desperation. Total desperation here translated to the fact that I was "left goods" or "discarded by a husband".

Papa's last letter arrived a fortnight after the news of his death did. Filled with remorse, guilt and grief over the way in which I had ignored his recent pleas, I could not bring myself to open it. Rather I stored it with the rest of his letters in my black leather family Bible that closed with a zipper.

A few nights later I dreamt of him and the dream seemed to be coming to me from the Heavens. In the dream he told me, "Child, I have something to say to you." I finally gave myself permission to open his last letter on orders from another world. The letter began with:

"You must be wondering what I have been doing these past six months. I finished working on my brother's house and then began to plant a garden. I wanted to reproduce your mother's garden from Hyderabad as a labor of love and atonement. I myself thought it was turning out quite lovely and it reminded me of a happier time in our lives......"

The letter went on. He explained that he had left for Hyderabad to retrieve some of the plants that are not indigenous to southern India in his efforts to reproduce the garden. When he returned, he found that Joey's wife Kuttiamma had ordered that the entire garden he was in the process of recreating be uprooted and a Japanese tea garden be planted instead. She had not even discussed it with him.

The letter concluded by relaying how heartbroken he was at the loss of his efforts and memories with the cruel destruction of the garden. Now, more than ever, he desperately wanted to come and live with me as a result.

The ink was smudged and smeared in several spots and at the corner of the letter, I noted his ink-stained fingerprints. *"He must have been shedding tears while he was writing,"* I imagined. *He must have wiped his eyes with those long and beautiful fingers of his. He must have inadvertently touched the aerogramme while they were still wet."*

Later we were to learn that when my father expressed his distress at having had his garden destroyed, Kuttiamma transfixed him with a cold gaze and pierced his soul by saying, "Now that our house is finished, we will be moving in and you will have to find lodging elsewhere. It is time for you to move on."

We were horrified to learn that Papa not only had relinquished his children's inheritance to his brother and his family, but he had also poured his soul into building them the finest house around only to have his gift thrown back in his face.

My father had packed his bags and told the servants that he was planning to return to his daughters in America. The boy who was his manservant was standing in the door as Papa left the house to embark on his journey.

Papa turned to him rather suddenly while clutching his chest in pain and said, "Fetch me some water, I am dying. Tell my daughters about the garden that I planted here – it was their mother's garden. Tell them that some things are about tradition, others are about convenience, but everything ought to be about love and forgiveness." This was Papa's final message.

Although he had mercifully died suddenly and rapidly, Papa died alone. He had been alone for the last four years of his life. Now he was gone. I was wracked with sorrow, regret and self reproach that I had not made the effort to have him come spend the end of his life with me.

Just as he had wished, he was buried beside his mother, high on a bluff that overlooked the verdant countryside of Travancore where he was raised.

❖

Since both Rachel and I were officers in the Army at the time of my father's death, we would be required to apply for permission to go abroad to attend the funeral. The red tape and bureaucratic hurdles made it impossible for us to leave the country in a timely fashion. Mummy had become fairly old and frail, so we felt it wiser for her to not make the long journey either. Rachel's estranged husband Babu was elected and sent as our representative and emissary. Mummy, Rachel and I convened at our home in Honolulu to mourn.

Rachel and I were seated on the lanai distracting ourselves by watching the mynah birds cavorting on the branches of the kukui tree in the front yard. We were anticipating Babu's return from India and our father's funeral. The car came up the driveway and we hurried down to meet him. He looked grim and sighed melodramatically as he set his suitcases down on the drive. Everything always seemed to be a melodrama for Babu.

"How did it go?" I asked.

After several more sighs and a cup of chai later, Babu began to dribble out a scanty description of how my father had met his end.

"He was intending to come back to America this week," he began.

"We already knew that." Babu's statements were frequently redundant and uninformative.

"Did he suffer?" I asked.

Babu also had the unerring habit of delivering every statement as if it were an accusation. He looked over his horn-rimmed reading glasses and down his long beak with scantily disguised disapproval.

"We all suffer; it is human to suffer," he said in response. "This is, after all, a vale of tears." There was an enduring sourness etched on his face that looked as if he had bitten permanently into an unripe green persimmon.

"Joey has claimed all the lands and the ancestral home for himself," he continued as he looked up expectantly in anticipation of an argument. He then embarked on a long and defensive diatribe on how the rights of the men in the family had been surrendered to the women, how Joey had finally won by acquiring the land, thereby winning for all the men in the family, in the country, in creation, and so on. Rachel and I remained silent.

Not having elicited any response, Babu continued, "Of course it is his right as your grandfather's youngest son of to have the house." He was hoping that this would finally raise a protest from us, a dissertation on unfairness, or at least some comment about the lines of inheritance.

We just continued to stare at him in total silence. Our mutual strategy was to practice "mental aikido" on him.. He had been outgunned and outmaneuvered as usual.

"Your father gave him the lands without thinking of either of you," he said in his final attempt to provoke a response from us.

Rachel lazily looked up from her quilting and asked "Did Joey give you Papa's pens and diaries?"

"Some diaries, but no pens."

Many years before, Papa had given each of us a Parker 91 – a scarlet and gold one with an eighteen karat gold nib and cap to me, and a similar one in navy blue to Rachel. There were open arrows on the heads of the pens, similar to the markings of a Hamadryad. We treasured these gifts as children but they were long since lost in our many odd moves from India, through Malaysia and finally to America. We had hoped to at least be able to regain some memories of Papa through his pen collection. Our hopes had been dashed.

We felt fortunate now at least to have some of his journals which Babu had brought back from India in a packet. I noticed one in particular that appeared less worn. I looked at its cover as I extricated it from the bundle. The date "1950" was inscribed in bright gold letters across its camel-colored leather front. My father had only written on the pages for the first month. The last of the entry read:

"I lost my son, my future and all my dreams. I will go to my grave with no one to whom I can pass my legacy."

It was just after the time that Mummy had her abortion that Papa stopped writing in his diary.

"That worthless bastard Joey," I thundered, "taking away Papa's pens and the remainder of his diaries is the last straw."

"What does that mean?" Babu asked looking at me quizzically.

"It is nothing I care to discuss right now," I said in the hopes of silencing him, which it did.

Babu then went into the house to unpack. Rachel and I continued to sit on the lanai in our sadness. We aimlessly tossed breadcrumbs out onto the lawn and watched the mynah birds feed, which were soon joined by a brace of brazen Brazilian cardinals. We then looked at each other almost as if by tacit consent.

"What, what? What does that look mean?" Rachel asked.

"Nothing! Nothing! Please, just leave me alone."

"There's more than just Papa's pens and diaries," Rachel probed. "There's something else, isn't there? Tell me! I am your sister."

I sat with my head buried in my hands.

"Yes Rachel, there is something else. That monster Joey molested me when I was just a child. He did it repeatedly, from when I was four until the age of eleven."

"You are not serious!" she exclaimed, now bursting into uncontrollable peals of laughter.

"Why on earth are you laughing?" I asked with puzzlement. "I just told you a secret so painful that I have not ever shared it with anyone."

"He did the same thing to me! He threatened me by saying that if I spoke about it to anyone, he would completely deny it and that no one would believe me."

"So what's to laugh about? It appears that we are the greatest victims of all time."

As the enormity of the deceit dawned on me, my response also became paradoxical. Rachel and I sat on the porch swing together and laughed and laughed until tears ran uncontrollably down our faces. It came as a sort of catharsis and relief.

Hearing the strange whooping laughter, Mummy came hurrying out of the kitchen onto the lanai. She had just fixed a huge meal for all of us and was sweating from the effort. She wiped her hands on her apron and smoothed her grizzled hair back.

"Are you okay?" she asked, now puzzled when she saw us. "Were you crying or laughing?."

"Yes, Mummy, we are fine. We were laughing, not crying."

"You were laughing?" she said in horror. "Just what is so amusing about your father's death?"

"Mummy, it's not that, we were talking about how Joey had sexually molested both of us when we were children," I said, not really expecting her to understand.

She sat down heavily on the chair by the swing. A look of disbelieving shock came over her face and she was absolutely speechless.

And then it came tumbling out, "Joey raped me repeatedly and said that if I told anyone, he would rape the two of you. So, I kept quiet and said nothing; I remained silent all those years. I thought that I was protecting you."

"You told no one? Not even Papa?"

"He would never have believed me, you know how he felt about Joey. And, I had to protect you – that was my main concern."

She looked defeated and beaten – my mother the most formidable, the most indomitable of us all, had been taken as well. All the time that she thought she had been protecting us, she had really not been able to protect us at all.

It then became our mission to get Papa's pens and the remainder of his diaries back. We strategised that the best tack for us to take would be to appeal to my uncle John who was now the *de facto* head of the household. We knew that he loved us and that he had always been scrupulously fair. I telephoned him in India right away.

"You must help us," I pleaded. "We are not asking for much. Joey has the house and land, which were rightfully ours. All we are asking for is Papa's pens and the remainder of his diaries."

"I will see what I can do," he agreed somewhat hesitantly. Some days later, we received a return call from uncle John.

"Joey says that your father left everything to him," he relayed. "He is not going to give you anything."

"Oh God, this can't be," I said in disbelief. Then, almost as if compelled by some inner urging I blurted it out, "Did you know that that monster raped Mummy and molested Rachel and me?"

"You really oughtn't be making such rash accusations just to get your father's property back. It is unbecoming of you."

"It is the truth!" I insisted.

"I don't understand," said my uncle John. "Why have none of you ever said anything before? Why are you just coming forward now?"

"Who would have believed us?"

"You are right, I am not convinced."

I graphically recounted for him every detail of what had happened to me. I went on to tell him what had happened to Rachel and to my mother. This was all received with a disappointing and complete silence.

"Are you there?" I asked into the telephone receiver.

"Yes, I am."

"Do you not believe me?"

"It remains difficult for me to understand your long silences. You remained quiet until now, now that you want something that was given to Joey by your father. Only now do you come forward with these wild accusations."

"You mean you still don't believe me?"

"I didn't say that," he responded.

"What *are* you saying then?"

"I don't know what to say. I will have to get back to you after I have spoken to Joey."

It was almost a fortnight before we heard back from my uncle John.

"Have you spoken to Joey?" I asked him.

"Yes, yes I have..." There was a long silence while we waited for him to say something. This did not portend well for us, I thought.

"Please Uncle John, don't you believe what we are telling you?" I implored. "Please, please tell me what you are thinking."

"Very well then, I will tell you. Your uncle Matthew and I believe Joey. He denies that he ever did what you are all accusing him of. He says that your mother probably put you up to making these false accusations. As you well know, your mother has never liked Joey."

"Uncle John, I swear to you on my sons' lives, we have not fabricated this." I went on to tell him how none of us knew what had happened to the other and how we had made the discovery serendipitously. He was unmoved by my pleas or any other arguments presented. I was defeated, unable to reach him – my long cherished uncle John.

I felt a white-hot rage envelope me.

As I hung up the phone I said to him, "I will never speak to you, ever again!"

This was the ultimate betrayal.

It was tragic that the fates obliged me. I did not speak to uncle John again – my beloved uncle John as I knew him. Bright, sweet, intelligent and loving uncle John soon developed Alzheimer's disease. It was a limbo for him and a purgatory for us. He lingered for several years, reduced to the intellectual capacity of a young child.

The uncle John I went to see in India some years later barely recognised me. His mind and spirit had fled his ravaged body. He stared at me vacantly and wonderingly, then reached out to touch my face.

"I love you, you know," I told him.

A sweet smile crossed his face for a brief moment, a smile like that of a very young child.

"Yes. Yes, I know," he said. And then, almost as if I wasn't there at all, he turned his face to the wall and nodded off to sleep.

It was only after my uncle John had lost his mind that Joey's predatory history was finally exposed. He was caught in an attempt to assault one of the neighbour's prepubescent daughters in Travancore who escaped from him and screamed bloody murder. The girl's father told all the elders in the village of the incident and they then turned on Joey. The remainder of Joey's family defended him and circled their wagons around him – none of the brother's wives or their sons acknowledged that such a thing would or could happen. As far as we were concerned, we were never vindicated in uncle John's eyes and this was our greatest tragedy.

My uncle John died last year. When his death finally arrived, it was a merciful release for him, his wife and his sons. Joey still lives. We know nothing of him or his family.

❖

I have shed my shackles and new horizons now beckon me in America – Fragrant Tree Country. I remember naming my home long ago as a child on the hopscotch template while playing hopscotch in the garden with Lakshmi.

"You have to name your home," Lakshmi said. "It is only then that you will get there."

"What shall I name it?" I asked.

"Why, America of course!"

Lakshmi, our guardian angel, remains in India. As I once dreamed of as a child, we built her a modest home in the old Gunfoundry section of Hyderabad between the old British cantonment and the New City where she lives and is surrounded by her children and grandchildren. I frequently still visit her on my trips back to Hyderabad, and although she doesn't say much, she regards me with a look of pride that is far more eloquent than words.

Relinquishing her self-imposed exile, my mother has planted a garden again in America. Rachel and I watch her from the verandah of our house in Hawaii as she busies herself with her plantings. She looks up to savour the liquid benediction of the golden Hawaiian sun and the balmy trade winds that blow through her grizzled hair. Her indomitable spirit shows a new resolve. She and God have come to a mutual understanding with one another. She has absolved Him, and forgiven my father, who has been dead now for over a decade. She too has finally shed her shackles.

She turns to me from the garden with the sunlight on her face and says, "You know, E.M. Forster said that America is like life – you find in it what you are looking for."

My mother and my sister have found their own freedoms in America.

My father and my uncle John have been released to theirs in death.

As for me, my needs no longer hold me in thrall – my need to be physically beautiful, and above all, my need to be a son.

The amaranthus and the antignon, the rangoon creeper and the jasmine, the artillery fern and the phaelenopsis orchids are all in bloom again in my mother's garden.

A Glossary

Most of the Indian words used in the book are in Urdu. Where words are used other than in Urdu, the source language is indicated in parentheses.

Abang (Malayalam)	brother
Accha	honorific for "Older Brother"
Allah	God
Angrez	Englishman
Attar	scent
Ayah	maid
Bagh-e-Aam	public garden
Bay-Imaan	ingrate
Begum	Muslim woman of rank
Bhang	marijuana
Bhishti	waterboy
Bibi	a respectful form of address for a young girl or woman
Buddhu	an idiot
Burqa	a veil worn to cover the face
Chai	hot tea
Chatta	a type of loose-fitting blouse
Chetan (Malayalam)	honorific for "Older Brother"
Chhoti Bacchi	little girl
Chokra boy (Anglo Indian)	errand boy

Choli	a type of tight-fitting blouse short enough to expose the midriff
Chowkidaar	gatekeeper
Coolie	porter
Cumbly boochie (Anglo Indian)	hairy caterpillar
Dakbungalow	houses serving as rest stops originally instituted by the British to provide housing for government officials en route to various districts in the Raj
Darzi	tailor
Dhobi	washer-man
Dhurry	flat-weave rug
Eid-ul-Fitr	a great Muslim feast
Farishtheh	angels
Ghurial	a small variety of Indian crocodile
Gore Log	white people
Gowli	cowherd
Guatama	Buddha
Gur-jaggery	a type of unrefined brown sugar
Halaal	the Muslim equivalent of "Kosher"
Haleem	a stew made of wheat, lamb, and lentils
Haldi	turmeric
Haraajkhana	auction houses
Hijra	eunuch
Hira	ruby
Jawan	soldier
Kaajal	kohl, eyeliner
Kaali	black
Kali	flower bud
Khansama	butler
Karbala Maidan	a very large field situated between Hyderabad and Secunderabad - often used for city fairs, circuses, etc.
Kavani (Malayalam)	a length of fine voile worn to cover the blouse and hence the breasts
Kewra	a fragrant type of grass leaf
Khus	vetiver, a type of fragrant grass
Korandi (Malayalam)	small wooden stool

Kumkum	a red powder used for adornment
Kurta	tunic
Lassi	buttermilk
Lingam (Telugu)	stylised phallus worshipped as a symbol of the Hindu God Siva
Loban	frankincense, resin from the olibanum tree
Log	people
Lungi	a short wrap of cloth draped around the lower torso
Maali	gardener
Mailedaan	clothes hamper
Maistri	mason
Malayalam	language of the Malayalee people
Malayalee	people originally from Travancore-Cochin and Malabaar (now called Kerala)
Mazdoor	labourer
Mehndi	henna
Mufti	civilian attire (as opposed to a uniform of any sort)
Mundu (Malayalam)	a sarong type of garment
Munshi	a clerk or secretary
Nawab	a Muslim aristocrat
Neelgai	a very large deer or moose
Nimbupani	cold fresh-squeezed limejuice
Nizam	king of Hyderabad
Nowkarani	an indentured female servant
Ood	myrrh
Pathalum (Malayalam)	fires of Hell
Patherni	butterfly
Phool	cold drink
Pishaju (Malayalam)	*Shaitaan* – the Devil
Pomfret-karimeen (Malayalam)	a type of flat fish
Ponnu Mon (Malayalam)	golden son
Puja	worship
Purana Sheher	old city

Purda	the tradition of Muslim women never showing themselves in public
Purdah	curtain
Pyari	beloved
Qameez	tunic
Qurbani	apricots
Rajah	a Hindu king
Ramzan	Muslim Holy holiday
Razai	a blanket-like comforter
Sahib, Sahiba	terms used to address someone in the honorific, male and female respectively
Sambraani (Malayalam)	a special blend of frankincense
Sang-e-murmur	marble
Sarpech	ornamental headpiece worn on a turban
Seer	a measure of weight
Shahzadi	a princess
Shalwar	pantaloons
Shendi	an alcoholic drink made from the areca palm
Sherwaani	close-buttoned long jacket with a high mandarin collar worn by Muslim men
Shikari	a big-game hunter
Sipahi	sepoy – soldier
Solar topi	a hat favoured by the British to shield oneself from the sun
Sunnar	goldsmith
Suraahi	a long-necked earthenware pot
Suttee	a widow's practice of cremating herself on her husband's funeral pyre
Talwaar	sabre
Tamasha	spectacle or show
Tawariq	also known as Tuaregs – nomadic tribes of Western and Saharan Africa
Tiffin carrier	luncheon carrier
Trisul	trident
Veliappacha	grandfather
WOGS	an acronym for Worthy Oriental Gentlemen referring to Indian and Chinese subjects of the British Empire.

Yesu Kristu (Malayalam)	Jesus Christ
Zabaan	tongue
Zammarud	emerald
Zenana	women of the royal court, or the place where they congregate